T0197003

BEAUTY IN THE BRIGHT LIGHT

BEAUTY IN THE BRIGHT LIGHT

DIANE EZIEKE ANYANSI

BEAUTY IN THE BRIGHT LIGHT

This is a work of fiction. All of the characters, names, incidents, organizations, and dialogue in this novel are either the products of the author's imagination or are used fictitiously.

iUniverse books may be ordered through booksellers or by contacting:

iUniverse
1663 Liberty Drive
Bloomington, IN 47403
www.iuniverse.com
1-800-Authors (1-800-288-4677)

ISBN: 978-1-5320-4750-3 (sc)
ISBN: 978-1-5320-4751-0 (e)

Library of Congress Control Number: 2018905242

Print information available on the last page.

iUniverse rev. date: 06/15/2018

DEDICATION

THIS BOOK IS dedicated to the divinity of Jesus Christ, to Leo Anyansi my husband, to the sweet memory of my beloved mother Late Mrs. Maureen Ezieke, to all youths and young couples worldwide, and to all lovers of creative writing.

ACKNOWLEDGEMENTS

I THANK THE almighty God for the inspiration He kept showering on me from above. My gratitude also goes to my husband Leo Anyansi for his unflinching support, love and care, and to my wonderful children Chimbusomma and Ikemsinachi for their love and giggles. Thanks to my dad Chief Chinechendo Emmanuel Ezieke and my most wonderful siblings: Nneka Ezieke Okeke, Uche Ezieke Okoye, Dr. Emeka Ezieke and I.K Ezieke for their encouragements; for making me feel so solidly there in my creative ability, for the togetherness, love and laughter and the stories we shared in the full moon.

Thanks to my editors Dr. Mbanefo Ogene and Dr. Friday Akporherhe, for taking their time to edit my manuscript.

I'll always remain grateful to Rev. Fr. Emmanuel Ikenga, Rev. Fr. Godwin Ukaegbu, Rev. Fr. Mike Ogboi, Rev. Fr. Anthony Chimekwene and Rev.Fr. Philip Mordi: catholic priests from Issele-Uku diocese of Delta state in Nigeria who made themselves available for my inquiries about the catholic faith in marriage. My thanks also go to Barrister Reuben Chukwura and Barrister John Oguejiofor for their useful information about the law.

These people inspired me so much in my journey as a writer: Chimamanda Ngozi Adichie, Akachi Adimora-Ezeigbo, Rev. Fr. Emmanuel Obimma (ebube muonso), Rev. Fr. Anthony Chimekwene, Rev. Fr. Christopher Unigwe, Rev. Fr. Leonard Onwugbonu, Mrs. Ifeoma Ojukwu, Mrs. Maryrose Nworah, Mr. Frank Egbuna, and Miss. Laggio Okoro. I am very grateful for their remarkable inspirations.

PROGNOSIS

IT ALL STARTED in their three bedroom apartment in Odoakpu Onitsha, right after their daughter Raaluchi was welcomed to the world, on the nineteenth day of December, in the year 1990. At first, Mummy understood it to be a father-daughter love but when Raaluchi became a full blown teenager still in her early teen, this love became overwhelmly excessive and it scared Mummy so much that she began to consider her daughter as her threatening rival. She did not understand why Chief Nnanyelugo Ezechikwelu her husband treated their daughter with so much love as though she was his wife. He would take her along for his outing and would leave her behind with her son. Nnanyelugo could never eat his food without Raaluchi their daughter eating with him. They no longer ate from the same plate as husband and wife. Raaluchi took that postion just because of her husband's flimsy reason of loving to watch her eat with him. She condoned it hoping that it would change with time, but it remained permanent and she had to get used to it.

Her husband spent almost all his time with their daughter, instead of with her. He never missed telling Raaluchi moonlight tales; tales that annoyed her and aroused her jealousy whenever she heard their singing voices and highpitched laughter that came from the veranda. Her husband loved to tell this tale whenever he discovered that she had entered the kitchen to cook dinner. As he told the story, he would blow his flute for Raaluchi to nod to the rhythm of the music.

Her husband could not make a decision without his precious

daughter approving. Mummy had discovered how much she had lost her sense of choice in her husband's life when one night after dinner, Nnanyelugo brought up a discussion about erecting a building. He was confused about building in the city first or in the village. Mummy suggested that he rather built in the city because they needed to move out of their three room apartment, on a third floor of a three storey building; a smouldering house in Odoakpu Onitsha: a place where they lived, a place surrounded by different sets of old storey buildings, a place where Mummy thought was already begging for mercy because of its obvious over- familiarity to the family.

Mummy knew that it was tiresome to their house seeing same faces everyday and hearing same voices for the past sixteen years. They needed a better house in G.R.A Onitsha, a cozy environment, a place that could show how rich her husband was, instead of giving his status an indelible mockery. But Nnanyelugo turned down her choice, and bought Raaluchi's idea of building in their village first, even when they already had an extended family mansion in their village. Raaluchi insisted that they needed privacy and Nnanyelugo approved.

Mummy did not like that she was so much like a maid in the family, instead of a wife. She did not like this bond between her husband and her daughter, and she couldn't doubt the crazy thoughts that trooped in her mind ever since she discovered within her that she was feeling very uncomfortable about this bond: "*Is my husband doing it with our daughter? Why does Raaluchi always have to come first in the heart of my husband? Something must have happened and I didn't know when and how it happened.*" It looked stupid to her, to even imagine herself wallowing in those thoughts, but she couldn't help it. She felt an urge to break that bond when she woke up early one Saturday morning and prepared to attend a Morning Mass. She was a slim woman, and so, after her bath, she didn't have any problem with finding what to wear, and wearing it with ease. She wore a green liccra gown her hand reached out to in the wardrope. She was a naturally beautiful woman; the shiniest chocolate skin, the pointed nose, the full and curvy eyebrows were impeccable. She sneered at the sound of her husband's snore in his sleep. She wished that her husband would agree to go to the church with her, but she already knew that he wouldn't, and so, she didn't bother to wake him. She knew full well that her husband detested Morning Masses, and if not for Raaluchi who had encouraged him to be attending Sunday Masses at least, he wouldn't have been attending Masses at all. She was going to book a Novena Mass after the Morning Mass, for Raaluchi and Nnanyelugo's separation.

But the bond still remained unbreakable even after she booked a private Novena Mass, praying that her husband should give her the attention she needed as a wife, and that God should destroy the bond he shared with any other woman. She had wanted to tell the Cathechist to write on the Mass book that it was really her daughter her husband shared this bond with, but changed her mind when she discovered how weird it sounded to the ear: "*an anonymous is praying that God should disconnect the bond her husband has with his daughter and connect it to her; his wife.*" She had said it in her mind before changing her mind. Nothing seemed to change between Raaluchi and Nnanyelugo, even after nine days of Novena Mass. This great bond between father and daughter was an Electra complex: that a father's love for her daughter was so great that it could not be destroyed, come what may.

Mummy's jealousy knew no bounds, especially when Nnanyelugo ignored her birthday, but spent hours in a traffic just to get a birthday present and shawarma for Raaluchi, and when she complained to her husband, Nnanyelugo acted vaguely by telling Mummy that she had outgrown birthday celebration and that she was always in his mind as his wife, but Mummy doubted that, and couldn't remember the last time her husband gave her a present.

In terms of medical treatment, Raaluchi her daughter would

be driven to the hospital by Nnanyelugo to see a doctor over any slightest sickness, Arinze her son would be given a transport fare if he really needed to see a doctor, while a Chemist would be employed for her or she would be given a transport fare to take care of her self in the hospital, if she needed a doctor. Whenever Arinze and Mummy needed a medical attention, Nnanyelugo would have no time to spare. Raaluchi would be given the attention she needed: a therapy for her healing, while Mummy would be neglected. When Mummy spoke out to her husband about this, he reminded her that Arinze was a boy and boys were much more independent than girls. Raaluchi was young, soft and dependable and so, she needed more attention. This attitude of her husband pissed Mummy, and it was as though he was indirectly calling her a 'faded woman' who did not need any attention, but simply had to take care of herself whenever she felt like it; as though she was too big for an attention.

When Mummy returned from the Catholic Women Organization meeting, on one of those graciously warm Saturday afternoon in June 2004, she ran up the stairs, hurrying to the house to get herself ready. The meeting was quite interesting to her, but she had to leave earlier because of her appointment. The C.W.O President, a woman that always wore the most glistening white uniform, had talked about 'wives becoming the reason their husbands cheat on them.' She had said that some women prefer to spend their money on Chinese weavons, manicures and pedicures, to buying white and attractive underwears that can attract their husbands in bed. She had said that some women are so stingy to their health that they prefer to use chewing sticks, to buying a good toothbrush and toothpaste for their teeth, and so, they drive their husbands away with their mouths' odour when they come close for a kiss. She had also said that some women still use cookery books to cook because they simply cannot cook, and lazily avoided their mothers' kitchen when they had the time to learn how to cook. And some women don't take their night bath; they wear a particular night gown for a week before washing, so, why wont men cheat?

This particular topic raised lots of arguments from the women present in the meeting; that Mummy didn't want to leave but had to leave. She was supposed to go to Abatete with her husband for a traditional marriage ceremony. She was sure that Nnanyelugo had told her the previous day that they were going to attend a traditional marriage ceremony and she had happily prepared for it, pleased to go somewhere with her husband once again. But when she got to the bedroom, Nnanyelugo was already dressed up, looking good on a cream colured embroidered caftan, his chieftancy red cap on his head, and he was holding his big chieftancy handfan that had his name CHIEF NNANYELUGO EZECHIKWELU boldly engraved on it.

Nnanyelugo her husband was an average height plumpy man in his early fiftees, light skinned and handsome. He had a good looking flat nose and a well shaped mustache. He had full eyebrows, a natural red lips and a smiling face; a demeanor that made him appear more womanly. He was a successful International Business Man, importing tailoring materials from China. He was ready to go with his light skinned pretty daughter, who was looking very gorgeous on a red silk long gown and a pair of silver high heel sandals. Her long brown hair hung down her shoulders, her face looked attractive in a light make up and there was a black birth mark on her forehead that looked like a dot. Her pointed nose was attractive enough for any finger to fiddle with, her curvy and full eyebrows were appealing and there was a gold necklace glistening around her neck. Her appearance made her look older than just a fourteen year old girl and as Mummy watched her with an air of disgust, her heart sank, her belly swiveled and feelings of jealousy churned in her again, knowing full well that her daughter was taking her place again.

"Nkem, you are all dressed up, are we no more travelling together?" Mummy asked her husband, although she already knew what his reply would be. She called him Nkem, even when she knew that he wasn't really hers.

"I was thinking that you should stay back and cook dinner. I don't want to feed on the *onugbu* soup you cooked yesterday and you know that I love eating fresh food. Let me go with Raaluchi. I don't want her to feel bored staying at home. I want her to enjoy the weekend with me. I want to explore Abatete with her because I'm sure she doesn't know her village well," Nnanyelugo said so easily, as though he expected Mummy to understand that it was a normal thing to do and that she ought to have gotten used to his frequent outing with Raaluchi alone.

"You should also take Arinze. He's also bored staying at home and I'm sure he doesn't know his village well."

"I hope you are not trying to force an argument on me, Obiageli. You should simply understand this."

"Nkem, you are spoiling our daughter. I mean, at her age, she cannot cook any meal, and I think she should stay back and cook the dinner with me while you take Arinze with you, *Raaluchi amasho esi nni,* Raaluchi cannot cook," Mummy spoke angrily to her husband with a mixed language of Igbo and English, her Igbo spoken in Abatete dialect. She was sweating profusely because she had walked anxiously from the church's hall to her house, to prepare for the occasion, only to find out that there was a change of plan. Her forehead wrinkled when she spoke in anger and her voice sounded as though she was on the verge of tears.

But Nnanyelugo did not care, he only took Raaluchi's right hand and left the room, and in no time, Mummy heard the start of the car outside. Nnanyelugo was ready to drive out with her darling Raaluchi sitting at the front seat of the car, expressionless and silent. Nnanyelugo's cell phone rang, and he answered it. It was his father, Nnabueze. He was demanding for money from his son, telling him that his snuff just finished last night, and he needed to replace it. Nnanyelugo promised to see him in Abatete and give him some money. His father laughed through the phone, and Nnanyelugo imagined his weak black and brown teeth, revealing through his opened mouth. He imagined him dancing in excitement with his shriveled body, and praising him. And just as he had imagined, Nnabueze began to praise his son, telling him that he was the only son that makes him happy.

"My happiness comes from Nnanyelugo my son. I'll never forget where my happiness lies. I have two sons, one gives me money for snuff; the other one gives me medicine. I keep telling him that my medicine is in my snuff, but he thinks I'm sick to be too in love with snuff, because to him, everything is about medicine." Nnabueze said to himself, without realizing that the telephone connection was still on, and that Nnanyelugo was hearing him, because he did not hang up as his father had thought. Nnanyelugo smiled, before he finally hung up and drove out.

Mummy was drained in anger and jealousy. She opened the door of Arinze's room and saw him snoring in his sleep. Arinze was a twelve year old boy who was very much independent, probably because that was the way Nnanyelugo had made him to be; because he was denied a fatherly attention. He looked so much like Nnanyelugo in his demanour and inherited Mummy's complexion and oval face. He was fond of his room as his only companion. He would stay there and play his video games, see his movies, study and sleep off.

He had a very bad habit that he didn't know how to stop. It was 'stealing.' But he got used to that act because his father never cared to ask him what he needed. He hardly stayed at home and even when he was at home, he was always too busy with Raaluchi, telling stories, laughing raucously, and dinning with her. Those were the only moments Nnanyelugo considered very important and undisturbed. Arinze had approached his father one evening, in the middle of a chat with Raaluchi, just to tell him what he needed for his studies, but Nnanyelugo had looked at him with disdain and had warned him not to disturb his chat with Raaluchi again. For this reason, Arinze would sneak into his parent's room and steal some money from his father's wallet, and with this frequent act of his, he got used to taking things unannounced. His freedom of stealing money from his father, graduated to stealing meats from the pot of food, even after he had his meal with meats.

But one day, Raaluchi caught him in both act of stealing and reported him to Nnnanyelugo who furiously attempted to take him to the police, if not for Raaluchi's special intervention, even after Mummy had intervened, but as usual, was neglected by her husband. Raaluchi pleaded with Nnanyelugo, playing her role of a pacifier, telling him that she would take Arinze to a Priest for counselling and Nnanyelugo hearkened to her plea. Arinze was given a period of grace by Nnanyelugo to change or he would be forced to carry out his threats. Raaluchi had been interceding in prayer for Arinze, just like the Parish Priest told her after counselling Arinze: "Don't leave the prayers for Arinze alone. Always intercede for him." The Parish Priest told Raaluchi and she agreed to do the work, smiling at the Priest for recognizing her holiness, for realizing that she was in the best position to carry out that work for her brother; for realizing that she was different, and most especially, for trusting her to say the prayer to save her brother.

Mummy closed the door of Arinze's room and walked to the kitchen, thinking about her husband and Raaluchi and the fatherly love Nnanyelugo deprived Arinze. The poor boy deserved to be loved too just like Raaluchi and she wasn't happy about it. And what drained her heart in anger was that they were left behind in the house and that her own daughter had taken her place.

That night after dinner, as usual, Raaluchi led the rosary prayer. They knelt down on the floor of the living room, eyes closed and rosaries held. Mummy had discovered that they were only together as a family during their night rosary prayers and Sunday Masses, maybe because they wanted God to pretend to understand that they were a peaceful family bound with togetherness. Raaluchi began to sing a chorus of the Blessed Virgin Mary: *oh lady of Fatima hail...immaculate mother of grace...* with a voice so melodious that it drifted Mummy's mind unconsciously and she remembered their last Sunday Mass before that Saturday night, how they were all sitting together on the church's long bench, dressed on uniforms: blue paper lace with unique designs. They were looking like a peaceful family. She remembered how Nnanyelugo stood up from the seat during donations for the church's project, walked majestically to the altar and donated the sum of one million naira for the church's project in the family's name. The Priest in charge of the Mass almost jumped in excitement when he got up from his seat, and happily laid his hands on Nnanyelugo's head, smiling widely.

Mummy had loved the togetherness and wished it would remain permanent. In between the decades of rosary, Raaluchi prayed that God would keep the togetherness of the family and for God to keep them holy, especially her brother, Arinze, through His grace, so that on the last day, they would all inherit the kingdom of God. In her prayer, she reminded God that she was sinless, reminded Him that Arinze needed His grace and mercy to stop stealing money from their father; and meats from the pot of food, and to also devote his time to Him in Catholic Church Societies. Arinze's calm and wholehearted 'Amen', a response to his sister's prayer, sent a message to the family that he admitted his offence. He admitted that he was a sinner and Mummy was moved with tears. She wondered if Raaluchi would accept her own faults on what she planned to tell her later. Some minutes later, Mummy knocked on Raaluchi's room door as soon as she discovered that she had entered her room to take her night rest. Raaluchi welcomed her mother with smiles. She was sitting on a red plastic chair in front of her dressing mirror oiling her body when Mummy sat down on her bed which was positioned at the right side; just beside the dressing mirror. Her room was not too small but it was very neat and tidy. Raaluchi's room always had a new look and an aura that welcomed anybody with smiles.

But Mummy was not smiling when she entered her daughter's room to talk with her; she wasn't smiling when she gave a clusory look at a framed photograph of Raaluchi and her father smiling in side embrace, and she wasn't smiling when she waited for a moment for her daughter to be through with the oiling of her body. Raaluchi sat down beside her mother and told her delightfully about the places her Daddy took her to in Abatete. Mummy changed the topic immediately, looking very furious. Her forehead revealed wrinkles. Her eyes were dull and pale because she had cried excessively that day, and she was biting her lips.

"Raaluchi, that's enough. I want to discuss a very important issue with you." Raaluchi nodded in acceptance and her facial expression slowly changed to a slight frown when she saw her mother's seriousness. Mummy continued. "Don't you think that you are becoming so unfair and unbearable? Have you for once told your father to reconsider his excessive attention towards you? He doesn't shower the same love to your own brother. It's all about you, you and you. I was supposed to go to that traditional marriage with him but you went with him instead. He always takes you out, leaving your brother and me behind. You always pray for the togetherness of our family but you've been the obstacle to this togetherness that you pray for!" Mummy spoke furiously at her daughter, her eyes filled with tears and her entire body trembled in anxiety.

"Are you jealous of me, Mummy?" Raaluchi asked her mother looking confused with her dimmed eyes, and slightly opened mouth, as though she was innocent of the whole situation, as though she didn't know how much pain she had been inflicting on her mother with her excessive closeness to her father.

"Have you been sleeping with my husband?" Mummy asked her daughter, but the gravity of the words left Raaluchi agape for some minutes. She searched her mind in disarray, as she tried so hard to imagine the possibility of committing incest with her father… *"sleep with Dad? Sleep with…Dad?"* she said in her mind, wavering. Her eyes dimmed in amazement with mouth agape. Mummy kept staring at her daughter for a long moment, looking very serious with her countenance, until Raaluchi began to sob. The way Mummy said *'my husband'* was as though she was claiming the ownership alone, as though Nnanyelugo was hers alone, and for her to have thought that she was committing incest with her father was absolutely disheartening.

"How can you even think about that, Mummy?" Raaluchi asked hoarsely in her profuse tears. Mummy was silent for a short period of time, and then, sympathetically moved closer to pat her daughter's shoulders. She spoke softly to her, trying to reveal the truth she knew to her daughter in a subtle manner.

"I'm sorry my daughter, but I'm only afraid of your father's love for you. He spends more time with you and you are even the one telling me what's going on with my husband. The other day, you told me that your father caught flu and I didn't even know about it and wouldn't have known if you hadn't told me. A day before yesterday, you told me that the doctor restrained your father from eating meats because he has cancer of the liver. How can you be in a position to tell me what's going on with my husband? You have your father all to yourself and you spend all the time with him, leaving your brother and me behind, so young lady, don't blame me for asking you that question because I'm beginning to get uncomfortable with you and your father!" Uncontrollably, Mummy spat her final statement on her daughter, wishing that she could control the anger and jealousy she felt inside her.

This pretty girl beside her was her daughter. She could remember how vibrantly she kicked in her womb when she was pregnant of her, fourteen years ago. She could remember how she nurtured her, how she took turns with her husband to change her diapers at midnights when she cried in her infancy, how Nnanyelugo sang lullaby for her until she fell asleep, how he neglected his business trips only to accompany her for Raaluchi's post natal care, how often he insisted on Raaluchi seeing a doctor over a slight headache. She could vividly remember everything about her, and they were all sweet memories. She had admired this fatherly love in the past, grateful to God for blessing her with a caring husband. But this continuous bond of Nnanyelugo to their daughter was threatening her seriously and it infuriated her. Her needs as a wife had been neglected. Her husband's care for her had vanished. His main concern was for Raaluchi and not even for her. Raaluchi had taken her position as a wife.

"Mummy, my father is your husband and you should be in a better position to talk with him about your family. Daddy is my idol and you can't destroy the bond we have for each other," with that, Raaluchi lay down on her bed and turned her back on her mother, as though she was trying to make her understand that the discussion with her was over and that she needed to take her night rest.

* * * *

Nnanyelugo and Raaluchi's bond continued to blossom. One Saturday morning, as she was cleaning a figurine that she kept on top of her Television set, her mind drifted to Azubuike Agunwa, her classmate in her semi-finals in secondary school, who had been pressurizing her to be his girlfriend. She had a crush on him, considering the fact that the boy was handsome in his light skinned complexion, his oval face with a pointed nose and natural pink lips. He always wore his brown hair in afro style. He was a Mathematician and was nominated the best Mathematics Student in her school and the neatest boy in her class. He was biracial and was endowed with the talent of writing captivating lyric poems, and he had written lots of them for Raaluchi. She liked them because he praised her, most especially, her pretty face. He had described her in one of his poems as: 'an unmethodized creature who God had chosen to create on Monday: the first day of His creation, with a lot of time and concentration, His energetic, innate and impeccable act of creating, resulted to a perfect pretty girl.'

Behold an unmethodized creature
A Monday for her creation, the creator takes
To make a good time with no other eyes but on her
With his powerful hands that gave birth to a golden fish.

Raaluchi would smile at the thoughts of these poetic words whenever she thought of Azubuike. But she was only playing 'hard to get': a game that a girl who is really interested in a *chyker* play so that the boy will not regard her as a cheap girl.

She was just thinking if she should finally agree to date the boy as Nkiruka her friend had suggested to her, before someone else takes the sleep from her eyes. Nkiruka had suggested that she should just date him and not let him see her *things* or even sleep with him if she didn't want to. She was lost in deep thoughts of Azubuike, smiling widely when Nnanyelugo her father shouted her name before entering her room, because he had been calling her but there had been no response. Raaluchi gave a start and just then, the figurine fell from her trembling hands and broke into pieces that it gave her a cut on her feet. Nnanyelugo rushed to carry her and treated her wounds with a first aid box, showering her with so much attention. Ever since the little accident, Nnanyelugo restrained Raaluchi from doing any chores in the house. He employed a house girl that took responsibility for the laundry and cleaning in the house. Her name was Amarachi and she was hardworking and obedient to the core because she was receiving a fat salary. She was of an average height, slim and dark skinned. She was a girl in her late teen. Extremely shy as she was, she would only bend her face to offer her greetings, say 'yes ma' and 'yes sir' whenever she was questioned about the house chores by Nnanyelugo and Mummy, still with her face bent. She was through with her secondary school education and wanted a profitable job to take care of her sick mother and her younger siblings. She never missed her job and was always punctual, as she comes to the house as early as 6:00 am and leaves by 4:00 in the evening.

Nnanyelugo was always at Raaluchi's bedside asking her softly if she felt any pain, and some days after the accident, he took her to the hospital for medical tests and further medications. Mummy was forced to remember the day she had a serious motorcycle accident, her husband had simply employed a Chemist to treat her wounds and the next day after the accident, he started demanding for his food from her, not minding that she was limping. She wished he had treated her exactly the way he did to Raaluchi, wished that he had handled her softly just like he did to their daughter.

Nnanyelugo made sure that Raaluchi never lacked anything and treated her like an egg. Nnanyelugo was the only companion that she had. She loved discussing her experiences in school with her father. They stayed in the veranda to chat every evening except Friday evenings, because they were for her Charismatic Ministry meetings. She never failed to attend them. She would carry her big bible to the church, sneer at girls on trousers on her way to the church, join the Charismatic Choir in their gospel music, nod interestingly to the word of God a preacher shared, chant 'Halleluya' when necessary and when not, and go home with convinctions that she was holier than any other person, and that she was enclosed in salvation. One Monday evening, Raaluchi narrated to her father at the veranda where they stayed to chat, how some girls in her school were caught dancing *awilo* (a dance that moves the waist like a snake) and practicing lesbianism during school hours at the back of their classroom, and their flimsy reason to the teacher who caught them was that they were practicing for a break-dancing competition. She also narrated how an SS3 girl was caught drinking *kai-kai* (an achoholic drink) at the back of her classroom and she confessed to the teacher who caught her that she was trying to abort her unwanted pregnancy.

"They are bad children, and you should really avoid such people in your school," Nnanyelugo said to Raaluchi with a sneer.

"Of course Dad, they are sinners and you know I can't mingle with sinners," Raaluchi replied her father with grimace. The mere thought of her school mates and their acts irritated her.

"Raaluchi they are God's creatures just like you, if you don't like their way of life, you should pray for them and preach to them, and they'll change. Do your part as a Catholic Charismatic Christian to shed light to their lives. Do something to save their souls," Arinze entered the discussion and Nnanyelugo hushed him and sent him out of sight so that he wouldn't eavesdrop on them again.

"Dad, it's a waste of time to pray for and preach to these people. They know what is right and they have refused to do it. Heaven is not for everybody and I don't need population of souls in heaven," Raaluchi said confidently, as though she owned heaven and was entitled to choose the soul that entered and the one that shouldn't. Her father concurred with a nod.

When she finally told her father about Azubuike her crush, her father told her to reject the boy's love advances and to ignore any further distractions from boys. He told his daughter that she was a child of God, and that she shouldn't let the inconsequential thoughts of a crush cross her mind. He told her to be serious with her studies, and that 'crushes' are distractions of an educational success. "You are a shinning star and you need to let your light shine more by working hard to be a famous novelist that you've dreamed of, so don't let the light in you go dim by listening to boys' words of deceit," Nnanyelugo added, and Raaluchi smiled and nodded, but what she couldn't fathom was why her father furiously corrected her. She had noticed his furiousness from his mannerisms: the twisted mouth, the frowned face, the hoarseness of his voice, and the snapped finger. Her father had never been angry with her for any reason. She was also surprised when her father suggested that she skip school the next day and go with him to the hospital, despite Mummy's refusal with reasons that there were time for everything and Raaluchi's school hours must not be disrupted.

After her medical examination, Nnanyelugo gestured at her to wait for him at the hospital reception while he entered the doctor's office to confirm the result. Sooner, he left the doctor's office with a smile on his face. He was happily satisfied with the result. Their drive back home was engulfed with a boring silence. Raaluchi did not play Njideka Okeke's music: '*omalichachukwu*' as she always did with her father's car C.D. and when Nnanyelugo tried to engage her in a funny discussion, she still remained silent. Raaluchi was wallowing in her thoughts, reminiscing what happened in the doctor's office, thirty minutes ago. She didn't remember ever telling her father that she was ill. She had thought that she was accompanying her father for his own check-up.

But she was surprised when her father excused himself and left her alone with the doctor who smiled at her and introduced herself as Doctor Kate, a gynecologist. She had a chocolate skinned complexion, a round beautiful face without make-up, and high cheekbones that revealed when she smiled. She was wearing a gold finger rosary on the fourth finger of her left hand that Raaluchi wondered if she was a Reverend Sister. Most Reverend Sisters she knew in her Parish wore finger rosaries on the fourth finger of their left hands. But she was not wearing a veil. She was simply wearing long bold black braids that she tied to a knot with a white hair band that blended with her white medical long sleeves gown. Doctor Kate's office was spacious and neat. It had a distinct smell of earned effort. Her split unit welcomed her with an abiding air of tranquility. The office was intricately decorated with assorted medical guide: the portrait of female organs and the trimesters of pregnancy, the portrait of a pregnant woman with a bulged belly and stretch marks and the portrait of a woman's cervix and its dilation. The white scan machine was beside her, very close to the examination couch. Her office table for two had two big medical books on it, a packet of examination gloves and a stethoscope.

It was actually Doctor Kate's white gap teeth that magnetized Raaluchi to obey her when she told her to lie down on the examination couch beside her. She watched Doctor Kate wear her white hand gloves, and when she softly told her to remove her underwear and spread her legs, what she could only remember was the movie she had seen last night, about a woman delivering her baby with her legs spread apart. What was this doctor doing to her? She was very sure she was not pregnant, not to talk of delivering a baby. Within a very short time, the doctor was through with her examinations, and Raaluchi quickly dressed up and demanded from the doctor the explanation of what she just did to her, looking bemused.

"Your father wants to know if you have opened your door for strangers," The doctor said to Raaluchi with a smile but she did not smile back and the doctor was pleased that Raaluchi understood what she meant. She was used to speaking that way to her patients; used to reserving the nudity of words with her use of euphemism. Raaluchi's eyes filled with tears as soon as she heard the doctor and she tried not to shed them. *What a flimsy reason to skip school on an English lesson day. Mr. William never repeats his lesson topics.* Raaluchi said in her mind, almost crying.

"Is your mother late?" Doctor Kate asked, and Raaluchi shook her head. The doctor raised her eyebrows in bewilderment. She wanted to say something to Raaluchi about her father but she held her comment.

"So Doctor Kate, have I opened my door for any stranger?"

"Fortunately, you haven't."

As though Nnanyelugo discovered that his daughter was angry with him for what he did, he drove to a popular boutique in New Market Road Onitsha: a place known for good shopping complexes made for the rich only. The boutique Nnanyelugo and Raaluchi visited was known for expensive unique clothes and there, he told Raaluchi to pick the clothes of her choice. Raaluchi chose exquisite long gowns with different styles. On their way back home, Nnanyelugo told Raaluchi not to tell her mother about their visit to Doctor Kate and reassured her that whatever he did was because he loved her very much. He also reassured her that she was too young to date any boy and her studies should be her priority. He finally told her that he would be the person to decide when she would date any boy and Raaluchi agreed with a nod.

Nnanyelugo did not sleep the night that Raaluchi confessed to him about her first crush. He had thought deeply of what to do and suddenly came up with an idea to take Raaluchi to Doctor Kate, a famous gynecologist he had heard of. He had gotten her phone number from Chief Ezeudo, his right hand man; his colleague in the Tailoring Material Business, who had been childless for many years, but was finally blessed with a set of twin baby boys, with the help of Doctor Kate who had taken lots of time to treat his wife. Nnanyelugo made the call very early that morning before he approached Raaluchi in her room and told her to skip school for the day.

The next morning after the visit to Doctor Kate, Raaluchi discovered that she was so weak to get up from her bed and prepare for school. She didn't know if it was the wine she drank last night with her father that made her weak. All she could remember was that she enjoyed the chilled wine and she demanded for more and more glasses of it until she finished a bottle. Nnanyelugo served Raaluchi her breakfast in bed when she discovered how weak she was. He watched her gulp down the warm tea and ate the toasted bread in delight. Afterwards, he told her to lie down and take a rest, and assured her that she would be fine before the end of the day.

"Don't you think that your darling Raaluchi needs to see a doctor?" Mummy asked her husband when he came back to their room to prepare for work.

"No. I think she needs bed rest. She'll be fine before the end of today," Nnanyelugo told Mummy but she was surprised because for the first time, Nnanyelugo did not let Raaluchi see a doctor over a slight sickness. Mummy was tying a wrapper that revealed her cleavages and she was sitting on their large bed. She watched her husband undress from his red robes and wore his white singlet. He frowned as he took a look at himself from his dressing mirror.

"I hope you don't give Amarachi my underwears to wash for me. This one is already loosing its sparkle. I want my underwears and other clothes washed by you and my food cooked by you. You can leave the rest of the chores for Amarachi," Nnanyelugo said and then began to apply his aftershave. It had a spicy perfume and Mummy liked it. Mummy could see from the dressing mirror, his hairy chest above the neck of his singlet, beckoning on her for a caress, and she got up from the bed and walked magnetically close to him. She hugged him from behind with an aching desire for a bodily union.

"I'm also loosing my sparkle, Nkem. Please touch me. I can't remember the last time you touched me and I want you," Mummy said with a voice husky with emotions, caressing his hairy chest and shoulders. Nnanyelugo eased away.

"I don't feel like it. I wish I can… but I just don't feel like it, maybe next time," He said perfunctorily and hurriedly began to dress up. That was not the first time those words came out of his mouth.

Mummy's heart sank as soon as she heard those exact words again. Her aroused sexual desire died instantly and then she wondered how long she was going to tolerate those words from her husband. The mere thought of the fact that her husband does not desire her was like a bomb to her entire body. She took a look at herself through the mirror, undid her wrapper, and stood infront of the dressing mirror, revealing her perfect female organs. She watched herself and smelt herself just to be sure that she didn't have any odour that scared her husband away from her. Nnanyelugo looked at her and still felt nothing. Mummy felt herself wanting to cry. Her heartbeat raced, when she turned to her husband with tears rolling down her cheeks and said: "I'm going to satisfy my sexual urge elsewhere," she said bluntly, expecting to see fright in his eyes, expecting to see him beg her to reconsider and give him sometime, but her husband failed her expectations. He was expressionless when he looked at her again and said: "suit your self." With that, he opened the door and left. Mummy began to cry, a helpless crying. The hoarseness of his voice when he made his last comment, the uncaring and easy meaninglessness of his words, drove her to uncontrollable tears as she sat on the floor and leaned on the wall. "Why did he marry me? Why did he marry me if he did not love me? " Mummy soliloquized in tears, eyes narrow with wonder.

When Nnanyelugo walked downstairs to his car, his chest heaved and he could see the up-down chest movement of his heavy breathing. He was thinking about Raaluchi. He touched his chest and then discovered that even his hand was trembling. He was afraid and at the same time, disappointed at himself for feeling that way. He wanted to come out of this fear that he felt, and as he mumbled his daughter's name repeatedly, he realized that she was who he lived for, and he should never be afraid of anything or what would be the outcome of what he had done to her. Everything that happened was for good; their own good and he had no choice but to do it.

* * * *

It was around 2pm on Wednesday afternoon, after school hours in Giant's Height College Onitsha; Nnanyelugo drove inside the school's large compound, with his black Peugeot 406 that was beautified with a tinted glass. There were two gigantic buidings that stood on the compound. One of them contained all the classrooms, and the other contained the staff rooms, the principals' offices, the Bursar's office, the students' library, and at the far end, the large Assembly Hall. Nnanyelugo alighted from the car and sent for Azubuike Agunwa. He had discovered from Raaluchi that he was the class prefect of her class, and from what he knew about class prefects in their school, they stay back in their classrooms after school hours for ten minutes, just to make sure that the classrooms were tidy and secured, and to secure any misplaced books and learning equipment before they leave the school. Azubuike Agunwa waited until he was done with his duties before he ran downstairs to answer Raaluchi's father. He only wished in his mind that nothing bad has happened to Raaluchi because she had been absent in school and he had thought worriedly about her for the rest of the school hours.

"Good afternoon Sir," Azubuike greeted Nnanyelugo when he bent over to see him face to face from his car. Nnanyelugo gestured at him to enter the front seat of the car and when he did enter, Nnanyelugo yanked his left ear and warned him seriously to stay away from his daughter.

"If I ever hear again that you write love poems for her or that you are disturbing her to be your girlfriend, I'll kill you and feed the dogs with your corpse, now get the hell out of my car!" Azubuike had to jump out of the car because Nnanyelugo had started the car and was already driving off when he spat his last words at him. He fell heavily on the cemented floor of the school compound and had a deep cut on his elbow. Back home, he wrote:

I shall wait for the heal of my wound and let
the scar remind me of my wounded love.
Love and life, which of them can I choose?
Alas! my life is what I need more, for I can love again
If I have my life, but in death, there shall be no love.

Azubuike wrote his poem with tears in his eyes. He closed his notebook and then, hid it under his mattress. His wound still ached, even after he had dressed it and took pain relievers in the Chemist's shop, on his way home. His house and the Chemist's shop were very close to the school. His mother brought his lunch to his room. His mother was an attractive, slim white woman with bold blue eyes, an Australian African who was wearing a strapless orange gown. She wore her brown hair in a ponytail.

"Next time, you should try not to play too much so that you won't have more wounds, okay?"

"Yes Mum." Azubuike replied, knowing full well that he had lied to his mother for the first time because of Raaluchi and her father. His mother watched him eat his food slowly with loss of apetite. She knew that jollof spaghetti with boiled egg was his favourite. He would have eaten it voraciously, but it was different this time. His mother sensed that he was troubled, and wondered what was troubling him and who actually troubled him.

"Are you okay? Did you have a problem in school?" His mother asked him softly, as she moved closer and sat beside him on his bed, striking his hair. Azubuike wanted to share his experience in school with his mother but he knew his mother well enough to make a scene out of it in his school, he knew how uncontrollable her anger could be, especially if it had to do with somebody hurting him. He knew her well enough to fight Nnanyelugo in his school, or even Raaluchi. She had one day fought a Major Seminarian during his days of Cathechism classes for the first Holy Communion, simply because he told her that he received painful strokes of cane on his palm from the Seminarian. She had landed resounding slaps on the young man's cheeks and had held the neck of his Cassock, pushing and shaking him, challenging him to a fight, until a Priest came to his rescue. That particular act ruined his family's reputation and he was disqualified for the first Holy Communion. He knew how badly it would affect Raaluchi if his mother made a scene with her father in the school, that was what he wanted to avoid and so, he held his comment and pretended to be sick from the pains he felt on his elbow. His mother assured him that he would be fine and assured him that she loved him when he pecked him on his right cheek and left his room.

* * * *

Making the decision to reject Azubuike's love advance was too difficult for Raaluchi, considering the fact that he was her first crush and she did like him. She had imagined him kissing her so many times, especially when she read his lyric poems, and somehow, she hated herself for wanting what she should not want, for feeling what sinners feel. She had gone for confession, telling the priest in charge that she had felt 'a passionate lust' and the priest had given her 'twenty decades of rosary' to say for her penance.

Raaluchi abided by her father's words, because she wanted God to smile at her in heaven, for doing exactly what He wanted. She wrote to Azubuike and told him in her letter that she wasn't interested in dating him because she was a child of God, her studies were her major priorities and she didn't want any distraction. Nkiruka her friend told her that she was the biggest fool she had ever seen for rejecting a handsome and intelligent boy, as she watched Raaluchi write the letter one morning in the class room, before the school assembly.

"The guy is very handsome. If he had chosen me, I would have given him a long romantic hug in acceptance, and gladly showed him my *things,* and then, with a gradual process, we'll eat *the food* together," Nkiruka said, smiling at the thoughts of Azubuike, as she stared into spaces with an imaginary phantasm of what she had just said. Raaluchi gave her a defying glance, understanding the euphemistic slangs that worldly girls used for their flirtatious lifestyle. She had usually heard the slangs from the rough girls in her class, girls that she had caught kissing their school boyfriends at the back of their classrooms after school hours; girls that her friend Nkiruka mingled with. "And I let him see my things before we ate the food together..." They would say in their discussion at the back seat of the class room during free periods. Raaluchi hissed loudly at Nkiruka.

"A sinner like you will never understand the values of chastity," Raaluchi said to her friend and began to fold the white paper in such a way that it would enter her small white envelope.

"Really?" Nkiruka replied her with a sneer and shifted to the extreme of the desk just to avoid her.

"Sometimes I wonder why I still keep you as a close friend," Raaluchi said, shaking her head in mock horror. She stood up and left the class room and Nkiruka watched her with uneasiness, knowing that she would apologise to Raaluchi later, for using that slang in her presence. Raaluchi had been her best friend since childhood. They attended the same school right from kindergatten. They played *swell* and *oga* games together during their childhood periods. They studied together in each other's houses. They were very close, until their worlds separated when Nkiruka started giving her time to boys; giving them listening ears and agreeing immediately to have a date with them. They became worlds apart, and none of them wanted to give in to each other's world, and although they differ in a variety of ways, there was something about Raaluchi that made distance impossible to Nkiruka. The last time they quarreled and separated, Nkiruka had felt very lonely and dejected, even when she mixed up with other girls of her kind. Raaluchi was like a carapace that kept her safe; an undefined safety, even though she assumed her character to be the worst she had ever seen, and her Christianity world, a suffocating place she wished not to enter. To Nkiruka, Raaluchi had a way of making 'Christianity' impossible to practice, but she was irresistible. She was like a particular meal that she didn't like but had to eat because it is good to her body. And that was exactly how

Raaluchi felt about her friend Nkiruka. She was a sinner that she should have avoided but could not avoid. They didn't want each other's world, but they needed each other: an undefined safety.

Her rejection letter came into Azubuike's hands after school hours and not during break because Raaluchi wanted it not to disrupt his lesson periods after break. Instead of that usual smile of his, and his joyfully dancing eyes whenever he saw her, she saw terror in his eyes. He looked pale and withdrawn and Raaluchi's heart sank in guilt, wondering if he already knew the contents of the letter before receiving it from her. She walked away as soon as she handed him the letter, feeling very guilty. Still walking away from him, she remembered how he helped her overcome her bullies in school in their Juniour Secondary School days; how he fought with boys who tried to beat her up after school hours simply because she answered questions that they couldn't answer in the class; how often he bought snacks for her in those days, insisting that she saved her money, and how he taught her the best formula to solve a particular Mathematics problem. They had been friends until he started writing her lyric poems, attaching a little red rose on each paper she received; until he began to seek for something more than friendship, something that she just couldn't give to him because of God and Nnanyelugo. God had used her father to make her retrace her steps and she understood. But what baffled Raaluchi was that she did not only loose Azubuike's love advance after the rejection letter, but lost his communication. She had approached him on one of their free periods to teach her Mathematics, but he had ignored her and pretended not to know who she was, and his silence made a fool of her for the students in the class to laugh at.

* * * *

That evening at 7pm, when Raaluchi was eating jollof rice and beans with her father in the dinning room, her father noticed that she was worried because she had only taken a spoon of the food ever since they started eating, and had pushed the rest of the food around the plate. He watched her closely when he raised her face with a raise of her jaw, and with the close watch, he already knew the reason she was worried. He tried so much to control himself when he saw her birth mark again: the black dot on her forehead that took his breath away whenever he saw it.

"You are worried because of Azubuike," Nnanyelugo told her, but she had lowered her eyes in response, not surprised that her father read her feelings and even her thoughts. Her father knew everything about her. To her, it was simply a bond; a desirable bond she shared with her father. The first time she discovered this bond was when she came home from school a year ago, with tears streaming down her cheeks. Her father came home earlier that very day, as though he knew that she was sad and needed company. Raaluchi failed her test on Literature-in-English. To her, it was indeed 'a failure' simply because she didn't get a perfect score. She never missed having her perfect scores whenever she wrote tests and even examinations on her favourite subjects: English Language and Literature in English, and then she scored 10 out of 15 in her test. She felt as though the whole world had crumbled on her. It was so unbearably painful to her, that she had to meet her teacher in the staff room to verify where she had actually gone wrong.

Bianca her Literature-in English teacher was a woman with bleached light and wrinkled skinned complexion who was frowning at the sight of a picture in a magazine she was reading when Raaluchi approached her. "You must be a big fool to consider yourself a perfect person. Who the hell do you think you are? If I see you here again for some stupid reasons, I'm gonna deal with you! Now, get the hell out of this place!" Bianca said rudely to her, with her feigned American accent, using 'gonna' instead of 'going to' simply because she travelled to America on a one month leave and returned with American affectations. Bianca refused to give a second look at the script, telling a colleague in the staff room that she hates it when students go ahead of themselves. Raaluchi came home with tears streaming down her cheeks and she met her father in the living room. "You are crying because you failed your test on Literature- in- English," Nnanyelugo told her without trying to verify the reason to her tears and Raaluchi gave a start. She was very sure that she didn't tell anybody in school about her failure, not even her brother Arinze, and not even her school guardian Mrs. Ekpoma, who her father always called to check up on her. "Your teacher is jealous of your success. She thought that you shouldn't be the only student in your class that performs tremendously in academics, and so, she needed to fail you to satisfy her jealousy. Cheer up my dear," Nnanyelugo said softly to her. That was the way he judged the situation. Raaluchi his daughter could never be wrong. She was a perfect girl and the teacher must have really failed her and not the other way round.

Just when Raaluchi was going to ask him how he knew about her failure, he silenced her by wiping her tears with his white handkerchief. He consoled her more with shawarma and a chilled glass of apple juice. And so, that was the first time Raaluchi discovered their bond. Her inclination about it made it desirable to her. Her father understood her feelings. He knew when she was happy and sad, knew the reason to her laughter even when she did not speak to him about it, knew the reasons to her anger and tears. Nnanyelugo her father knew her very well. Sometimes, she felt so badly that she couldn't reciprocate the thoughts-reading of her father but would only have to ask her father to tell her the reasons of his moodiness whenever he felt moody. And whenever she did ask, her father never failed to give him details. She would then give comforting words to him that would help him relax and feel good.

"Yes Dad, I'm worried because he embarrassed me in the class room. He refused to teach me Mathematics and pretended not to know who I am, simply because I turned down his love advances," Raaluchi said worriedly, her forehead revealed puzzled lines. But Nnanyelugo knew that it wasn't only the reason Azubuike embarrassed her. He didn't want to tell her the other reason and wondered why Azubuike did not tell her. Nnanyelugo only told her softly to forget everything about that boy and concentrate on her studies. Raaluchi nodded and continued her meal with her father. Nnanyelugo hated that Raaluchi worried about her crush, he hated that she could even starve while worrying about him, and most especially, he hated that she thought about him so frequently. Angrily, he made a call in Raaluchi's presence and employed a Mathematician to be Raaluchi's tutor. She was a single lady that had won a Mathematics Competition Award. She was a friend to Chief Ezeudo's sister. Chief Ezeudo had given Nnanyelugo her phone number, incase he needed her to be a tutor to his daughter or anybody else, but he had vaguely saved her number in his cell phone, having the instincts that his daughter was a versatile brilliant girl and wouldn't be needing any tutor. But he guessed he was wrong when he heard from Raaluchi that she wanted Azubuike her crush to teach her Mathematics, but he turned her down.

Raaluchi was ebullient when she heard from her father after the call, that the lady would be tutoring her every Saturday for two hours in the morning until she sat for her West African Examinations Council (WAEC). He also promised to be singing her a lyric poem and folk songs every evening after his moonlight tales. Raaluchi wanted to ask him how he knew that she often thought about Azubuike's powerful words for her in his lyric poems, how he knew that she had been missing his poems ever since she turned down his love advances. He usually walked up to her during break in school, whenever she was alone in the class, to give them to her with smiles on his face. But they no longer existed. Raaluchi did not ask those questions but rather regarded it as that 'desirable bond' she shared with her father. She gave her father a tight hug in ectasy for choosing to replace Azubuike and the rest about her crush became history.

* * * *

The bond between Raaluchi and her father continued to blossom. Raaluchi depended on her father in everything she did, in every decision she made, and the bond was so strong that Mummy couldn't break it. She one day decided to overlook this bond when she read a short note written by an anonymous on a yellow sheet and pasted on the entrance of the chapel in her parish: *The best way to give yourself a peace of mind is to overlook your offender's unchanging fault, even if you have been praying for a change. That is the easiest faith you are showing to God concerning His ability to change that fault, worrying about it can endanger your health, and how can you enjoy that perfect plan of God for a miraculous change without a peace of mind?*

Raaluchi decided to write something about her father's love. She wanted to be a novelist. The urge for it had come when she fell in love with Ifeoma Okoye's novel: *Chimere*. She was mesmerized at the fatherlessness of Chimere the heroine of the novel, and her vigorous struggle to search for her true identity, and know her father. She was also mesmerized at the identification of the needs of fatherhood in a girl's life. Nnanyelugo had bought the novel for her during her Easter holidays. She had read the novel and it mesmerized her. The next day, she told her father about her dream. She wanted to be a novelist, a famous novelist. But she wanted to start with a short story; a story with a first person point view: 'I'. Her father concurred with nods and smiles. And so, when she wrote some words in her diary, she smiled: 'my father's love for me is overwhelming. With him, I feel that there's no other place that I can be… with him, I feel secured.' And she stopped to think before she continued to write with smiles on her face. She was writing every details of her wonderful encounter with her father and the bond they shared.

A month later, Nnanyelugo began to shrink. His head appeared bald and his complexion darkened in such a way that any child can refer to him as a devil; a black skinned devil. One day, a tenant came with his three year old son to visit Nnanyelugo on his sick bed, in his bedroom. The boy refused to offer Nnanyelugo a handshake when he stretched his weak and trembling hand for it. And when the boy's father tried to force him to take the handshake, he fidgeted in tears, saying, "No Daddy, he has changed to a devil." The boy's father quickly apologized to Nnanyelugo and took his son out of the room.

Nnanyelugo stopped driving himself and had to hire a driver from Chief Ezeudo. His name was Stanley, a dark skinned energetic young man in his late twenties, who had highly served Chief Ezeudo. Chief Ezeudo had told Nnanyelugo that the young man can drive any distance without feeling sleepy. The first day Stanley started rendering his service to Nnanyelugo, he appeared shabby in his dirty blue jeans, rumpled red flannel shirt and old big black boots. His hair was over-curly and looked fried. And just without wasting time, he was warned seriously by Nnanyelugo in the living room, never to take a look at Raaluchi his daughter for the rest of his service to him, and he agreed with nods, glancing at Raaluchi and averting his eyes immediately, just to know the person he was not allowed to look at for the rest of his service. Stanley was always punctual every Saturday morning to drive Nnanyelugo and Raaluchi to the hospital for his check up and Chemotherapy medications. They would leave in the morning and return home in the day. One Saturday afternoon, when Raaluchi entered her father's room to check on him, she met him coughing heavily.

"Dad, you need prayers. You need a Priest to pray for you and anoint you. I want to call a priest for you," Raaluchi said softly to him, holding his trembling hand. Nnanyelugo gave Raaluchi a long pitiful look. He wanted to tell her something. Raaluchi sensed that he wanted to speak to her. He wanted to unveil a secret to her but he couldn't, instead, he watched her pitifully, as though he owed her an apology. Suddenly, his facial expression changed. He smiled at her and shook his head, rejecting her idea of calling a priest for him.

"My sweet daughter Raaluchi is God's best friend. She is a keeper of God's commandments and I know she is in a better position to pray for me. Go ahead and say the word. God is listening," Nnanyelugo said like a whisper to her, smiling. Raaluchi smiled back at him, remembering how the Parish Priest recommended her to intercede for her brother Arinze. She smiled at her father for recognizing her holiness, and most especially, for believing in her. She closed her eyes and began to pray for her father: 'Almighty God, I know you cannot fail to answer my prayers because I do your will. I know you cannot fail to answer my prayers because I'm a communicant. I know you love me so much to answer my prayers. I want you to touch my father and heal him through Jesus Christ our lord," Nnanyelugo responded 'Amen.' Mummy, who had entered the room and hovered at the door when Raaluchi started her prayer, cleared her throat and informed Raaluchi that their lunch was ready in the dinning room.

"Mum, have you been standing there for quite sometime?" Raaluchi asked her mother.

"If you really want to know if I heard your prayers for your father, Yes, I did."

"Mum, you did not say 'Amen' to my prayers for Dad," Raaluchi said to her mother, lowering her eyes in confusion, slightly suspecting her mother for being responsible for her father's sickness, for being the unknown witch.

"That is because you did not pray."

"Obiageli, Leave my room." Nnanyelugo said promptly, gesturing at the door for Mummy to make use of it.

"Nkem, please calm down," Mummy said to her husband with pleading gestures, moving closer to him to calm him, so that he wouldn't injure himself out of his furiousness. But Nnanyelugo didn't want her presence. Mummy could see how furious he was. His face was tightened in a deep frown and he was pointing at the door for Mummy to make use of it. "Leave my room!" He shouted out to Mummy, fast-breathing in a furious manner.

Mummy turned her back and left the room. And when she came back later in the evening to check on her husband, he was sleeping noisly: snoring and fast breathing. He watched him for a long time, a long pitiful look. Her eyes filled with tears as she watched him, knowing full well that her husband was slowly passing out. And just when she couldn't stand watching her husband anymore, she left the room and walked to Raaluchi's room. Her room door was open and Mummy met her crying on her bed. Mummy sat beside her and patted her shoulders.

"Crying for your sweetheart will not save his life. Go and call a Priest for your sweetheart. He is dying. Can't you see he's dying? Let him reconcile with God before he dies," Mummy said to her daughter.

"My God is in control. My God will heal him. Dad believes in my prayers. He doesn't want a priest because he believes in my prayers. My father will not die. His faith in my prayers will save him." With that, Raaluchi left her room for her mother alone and headed to the living room. Mummy was staring into spaces, shaking her head in wonder and begging God in her mind to intervene because her husband had rejected a priest to be called for him. Minutes later, she knocked on Arinze's room door and he approved. Arinze was doing his class assignment on his bed. Mummy smiled at him and sat beside him.

"How are you doing?"

"I'm doing good."

Mummy playfully tickled his cheek and Arinze smiled at her and focused on his books. Mummy watched him and was interested to know the textbook he was using for his assignment. It was an English textbook. She took a look at the cover page, flipped it open, and frowned when she saw that the name that was written on the first page of the text book was not her son's.

She darted a questioning glance at her son and Arinze gently took the text book from her.

"Don't worry Mum, I did not steal it. I only borrowed it."

"Are you sure?" Mummy asked him looking worried, her eyes narrowing in doubts, and her hands trembling. Mother and son looked at each other for a short while, before Arinze admitted his sin after he had seen how worried his mother looked; how convinced she was in that look, that he must have stolen the text book.

"I know that I'm a thief. I know that everybody in this house sees me as a thief, but how is that my fault?" Arinze said hoarsely, almost in tears.

"I have told you that there's no justification for sin. I have told you to let me know about your needs, Arinze. You shouldn't have stolen this book. Your father can afford it."

"I know he can afford it. But I'm sick and tired of you begging Raaluchi to talk to my father about my needs. For years, he had been refusing to look at me as his child. For years, he had been treating you like his maid. He doesn't give me his attention and when I take my right by force, he threatens to call the police for me," Arinze said in tears and Mummy was moved to cry with him, drawing him closer to pat on his shoulder.

"You have to let go of this grudge you have for your father. You have to stop hating him," Mummy said in tears, rivers of tears rolled down to her cheeks.

"No Mum, I can't pretend not to hate him."

"Please my son, I beg you to forgive your father. You have to forgive him because he is dying, even though he doesn't know that he needs our forgiveness, I know he does. He needs our mercy because I'm sure he's going to die soon. Please my son, find a place in your heart to forgive him."

Mother and son cried in each other's arms for a moment before Arinze assured his mother of his forgiveness.

"Thank you my son. God smiles at us when we show mercy to an offender. Our Lord Jesus Christ pleaded with His father to forgive His crucifiers, even when they had ravaged His skin. He still showed mercy to them. I want you to know that God is happy with you my son and he's going to forgive you for stealing the text book because you have forgiven your father. Now, let us go and pray for your father."

Mother and son walked hand in hand to Nnanyelugo's room and Arinze started sobbing all over again when he took a look at his father's state of illness. Nnanyelugo was still sleeping noisly. They knelt down on the floor of the room, and Mummy started the prayer after they had made the sign of the cross. In Mummy's prayer, she emphasized on God's mercy, begging God with tears in her eyes, to have mercy on her family and heal her husband with His merciful heart. Arinze's conclusion of prayer coincided with Mummy's, and they both said 'Amen.' Raaluchi hissed. She had been hovering at the door, giving them quizzical looks like people who had committed the most unpardonable sin. She had seen her mother and her brother enter her father's room and she had hurriedly left the living room just to know what Mummy and Arinze wanted to do to her father. She was afraid that her mother was planning something against her father for telling her off in her presence, and for the fact that her mother did not concur to her prayers for her father was abosolutely questionable and suspicious. So, she had hovered at the door to watch them, but her suspicion failed her when she discovered that they had only come to say their prayers for Nnanyelugo.

"What are you doing? You know you are not qualified to pray for Dad. He doesn't need the prayer of a sinner, so please leave," Raaluchi said to Arinze with a sneer. Arinze wanted to talk back at her but Mummy patted on his back and pleaded with him not to say a word. They got up and left the room for Raaluchi and Nnanyelugo. Back to Arinze's room, Mummy instructed Arinze to give the text book back to the owner in his school and he agreed and promised his mother not to steal again.

That night, Mummy decided to sleep in her son's room. She

was scared that Nnanyelugo would not want her presence in their room, and that he may still be mad at her for something that she couldn't actually explain. Nnanyelugo woke up in the middle of the night and started crying. He was reminiscing lots of things, and the more he reminisced, the more he cried. He was pleased to be alone in the room, so he could do whatever he wanted to do without anybody's notice. He opened a drawer at his bedside and brought out a pen and a white paper, and then, he began to write with tears rolling down his cheeks.

* * * *

Chief Nnanyelugo Ezechikwelu kicked the bucket on the day Raaluchi wrote the last paper of her West African Examination Council (WAEC) on the 20th day of May 2005. That very day remained unforgettable to her because what she never expected happened to her. She had been accompanying her father for his treatments and check-ups in the hospital. She had been praying for him. She had not expected him to die so easily and so soon. She came back from school that afternoon only to discover from a tenant that Stanley rushed her father to the hospital with Mummy and Arinze. She made a call and in no time, she was there in the hospital watching her father gasping. Arinze and Mummy were standing beside him and watching him pitifully, with tears in their eyes. He looked helpless and lifeless with the oxygen that was placed on his nose and he was fighting to live. He was shaking his head vigorously, rejecting death. Stanley rushed out of the room to call the doctor. Mummy watched her husband hold Raaluchi's hand unable to leave her, as though he had lived for her. He desperately wanted to say something to Raaluchi but couldn't, because he was gasping, and then finally, he gave up, leaving Raaluchi crumpled on the floor, wailing in profuse tears as though she was Nnanyelugo's widow.

* * * *

Abatete their village was highly equipped with good express roads and gigantic buildings alongside the roads. Mummy, as she watched through the back seat window of her husband's car, smiled wryly at the welcoming exterior view of the village, wishing it was the same with the interior view. She knew full well how different it was with the interior view: the grassy narrow pathways, the rocky roads, the swaying trees, and most of the houses that smelled of pity. Mummy continued to smile wryly until Stanley reduced his driving speed.

"Are you okay, ma?" Stanley asked Mummy and she nodded.

"I'm okay. Take the road at your left side. That is the road that leads to our house."

And when Stanley drove the car to the left side of the road; when he entered the interior side of the village, the car began to jerk, pleading with the rocky roads to have pity.

Mummy and her children were there in Abatete to mourn Nnanyelugo, exactly two months after his death. Some women in T.shirts that revealed their sagging breasts circled Mummy the next morning after her arrival, and shaved her long hair. And they began to give her the rules of a mourning widow: *"You must not eat the food that they'll cook for your husband's burial ceremony… you must not be seen outside when it is 6.00 in the evening…you must wear your white gown always, even in bed…and your face must always look bare."* Mummy nodded, agreeing to keep the rules, her eyes firmly fixed on her long black hair that scattered helplessly on the floor. She mourned anyway; she mourned her past life with Nnanyelugo, before their daughter surfaced, as her mind focused on the very day she first met him. He saw her crying under a tree, wearing an unkempt hair and a battered uniform. He approached her and wanted to help her come out of her misery, unlike other men who passed her and pretended not to see her. Her West African Examination Council fees were stolen from her by some village thugs, on her way to school. They beat her up when she tried to take the money by force. She knew how hard her mother had worked in the farm; how hard she had struggled in the market to sell her farm produce, just to pay her fees. But Nnanyelugo showed up and gave her some money, even more than what she lost. He told her to use the rest of the money to buy new set of uniforms and books. Nnanyelugo was the reason she sat for her examination. After that day, she started dreaming to have a kind man like him as her husband and her dream came true when a week after they met, he came with his father and some kindred to ask for her hand in marriage. She had fallen in love with him because of his kindness and generosity towards her. Apart from her mother, nobody had ever shown her kindness. She was thrilled about it, and didn't hesitate to say 'yes' when he popped the big question.

Mummy cried profusely in her reminiscence. The village women who had shaved her hair watched her pale face streaming with tears and gave her a satisfactory nod. She was indeed mourning.

A day later, a troop of villagers entered the compound to give Nnanyelugo a befitting burial. Loud burial music pervaded the compound. Obiora, Nnanyelugo's younger brother was sitting under a canopy in front of the house, with some of his uncles. He was scribbling some notes on a book, stating the items some people brought for their condolence visit. He was a medical doctor, dark skinned in complexion, and his oval face was not very handsome. He was just a type of person that people can refer as '*being okay.*' And as he stood up from his chair to direct some condolence visitors where to drop their items, his shortness revealed itself. He was wearing a white shirt and a white pair of trousers that were sown with a jean material.

Mummy was sitting with some sympathizers in the room where her husband's body was laid. Her eyes filled with tears that rolled down her cheeks uncontrollably. Some village women on loosed wrappers began to roll on the floor when they saw Nnanyelugo's body lying in the coffin. They began to mention the promises that Nnanyelugo made to them before he died: 'you promised to pull down my mud house and build me a mansion,

Nnanyelugo who will fulfil your promise?' A large-hipped fat woman on a loosed moist wrapper said, as she kept rolling on the floor of the room where Nnanyelugo's body was laid. 'You promised to be paying all my children's school fees and let me rest for some time. Who will fulfil your promise? *Chai! onwu emego m ishe.* Death has dealt with me.' Another fat woman said in Igbo; in Abatete dialect, rolling on the floor.

Nnabueze entered the room with his walking stick on his right hand. He was wearing a white bogus caftan that made him look as though he was inside the caftan. His shriveled hand was trembling on the walking stick. He was a very old man, crying for the death of his son. As he peeked at Nnanyelugo's corpse, he shook his head and said: "I have been begging death to take an old man like me, but it refused to come. Look at Nnanyelugo my son, the Omelora of Abatete, the only son that makes me happy, the only man that throws party for all our youths every New Year. *Onwu amasho ishe.* Death is a fool." Nnabueze said in Igbo; in Abatete dialect, and then, he began to cry loudly. A boy came and took him away.

There were two skinny village women that entered the compound through the backyard with different sizes of foodflasks. Their names were Lotachi and Nwamaka. They headed straight to the site where the food cooking was taking place, to meet their friend that was one of the people responsible for cooking the burial food.

"Nnedi, if I tell you that me and my children have not eaten since yesterday, you won't believe me. When I hear from Mama Chioma that you are one of the people cooking for this burial, I thanked my *chi*," Lotachi said, opening her food flasks immediately, not minding if she was commiting any grammatical error in her English. She had spoken her English like someone who needed to speak it; who may not have lived if she hadn't spoken in English, as though she was treathened by someone to speak English. She was wearing a red gown with a V-neck that exposed her neck bones. Nnedi the cook began to mount jollof rice and chicken chunks inside her foodflasks. She was a fat woman with plumpy cheeks. She was wearing a big yellow T.shirt and a blue wrapper and she was sweating profusely because of the heat of the fire.

There were many people in the food site begging for food with plates and bowls, and hovering at a corner to eat hurriedly, as though someone might enter to snatch the food from them. Nnedi turned to Nwamaka, the other skinny village woman, and gestured at her to open her food flasks, and then, she filled her flasks with the same food.

"Nnedi thank you. I know for sure that with this food, that devil of my husband will not beat me for not keeping food for him… as if he gives me money for food. I'll simply go and save this food in my pot and bring my children for this burial ceremony to eat to their satisfaction," Nwamaka said to Nnedi and she chuckled. Nwamaka was wearing a blue shirt and black tight skirt that exposed her flat buttocks and skinny laps. They left with smiling faces.

When Nnanyelugo's grave was dug, and was laid to rest in the grave, Raaluchi jumped inside the deep grave wailing and hugging the coffine, gesturing at the grave diggers to bury her alive. The men quickly jumped inside the hole and carried her out. They looked at Mummy who was standing by the grave side with Arinze, crying. The look was questioning. It was as though they were asking Mummy why she didn't do the same thing that Raaluchi just did. Raaluchi's act of mourning was obviously different from hers. Some women standing beside Mummy began to sing a dirge in Igbo for Nnanyelugo's spirit to rest in peace: *naba na ndukwa. O ga adilu gi mma… naba na ndukwa.* Go in peace. It shall be well with you …go in peace

Later in the evening, Nnanyelugo's age grade: men on dirty white caftans and red chieftancy caps entered the compound with an elephant masquerade. They danced round the compound as they drummed to the rhythm of a native dirge, asking death why it had taken their brother away so soon. As the dance went on, some women sitting under a canopy began to make arguments about which women group a particular cooler of food belonged to.

"I am telling you that this food belongs to the *umuokpu*."

"And I'm telling you that it belongs to *ndiogoo*"

And just then, they began to fight, dragging the cooler of food and dragging each other out of the canopy. The cooler of food fell heavily from their hands and some jollof rice and fried pieces of chicken scattered on the cemented floor. Angrily, they dragged their hairs, and loosed their head-ties, reaching out for their wrappers to let them loose. Some other women attempted to stop the fight. And then, there became two major scenes to watch for the burial ceremony: the dance and the fight.

* * * *

Ever since Nnanyelugo died, Raaluchi's life became miserable. She restrained from all that made her happy, all the places that she had been to with her father. She was always in her room shedding tears and staring into spaces, lost in thoughts. Mummy felt pity for her, knowing the kind of bond she had shared with her father. Somehow, she wondered if God did finally answer her prayers about the separation she had longed for. That wasn't really the way she had expected the separation to happen. Whenever she watched her daughter in her depressed state, valiantly alone, she got gnawed and wished to help her come out of her situation. The memories of her father gave Raaluchi sleepless nights and she gradually entered into a state of depression despite the love that her mother and Arinze showered on her. Her depression was persistent for over a year until something serious befell her.

PART ONE

UNGRATEFUL HEART

THE YEAR 2009-2010

....

How can one handle big things without learning
how to handle small things first?

....

CHAPTER ONE

HER DEPRESSION BEGAN to oppress her more when she couldn't find her name in the lists of the admitted students in University of Nigeria Nsukka. She had chosen the school as her only choice after three years of search for admission. She had a penchant for the school and couldn't bear to give another school a trial. She was in her late teen and had wanted to get admission into the University before her twentieth birthday. A tight suffocating pressure rose inside her chest as she screened the admission lists over and over again. Her eyes filled with uncontrollable tears that streamed down to her cheeks. Raaluchi was enraged with feelings of bitterness that if she could see God, she would have asked Him why He had chosen to frustrate her ever since her father died. She would have asked Him what sin she had committed to deserve this outrageous punishment. She stood motionless at the administration block in the school, her heartbeat raced and she felt her heart breaking inside her.

Her body trembled in shock as her mind reflected over all the fasting and prayers she indulged in, for the sake of getting admission into a higher institution to further her education. In her reflection, her mind focused on a particular dish she had declined on her fast for admission into the University of her choice: 'pounded yam and chicken *nsala* soup.' This particular dish disappeared from their menu ever since her father died, and so, it appeared in the cooking pot one Sunday afternoon, and she had willingly declined it just for her fast. Mummy had dished out the remanants to her visitors who ate

1

to their satisfaction and praised Mummy for her delicious meal. She missed her mouth watery dish just because of a fast for admission in her desired University. She wept bitterly blaming God for everything. Some people rejoiced at seeing their names in the admission lists and others walked away with heavy hearts as they mumbled words of disappointment. Nkiruka, Raaluchi's bosom friend consoled her with words of encouragement. She was a tall ebony pretty damsel. She was wearing a white T shirt and a tight black jean trouser that revealed her ear-like curved hips, and her tiny braids hung down her shoulders. She advised Raaluchi to try again because the only true failure was when she failed and didn't bother to try again.

"Nkiruka, Is there God? Is there really a God that answers prayers?" Raaluchi's lips trembled in shock as tears streamed down her cheeks. She couldn't believe it. She couldn't believe that she of all people would be in a position to wait for admission. Nkiruka consoled her.

"Raaluchi, please don't blaspheme. Remember the meaning of your name: *leave everything for God*. I'm sure God knows the best," Nkiruka said in tears as she consoled her friend and let Raaluchi's head rest on her bosom. Nkiruka got admission on a first attempt of the Post Jamb Examination. She was offered admission into the same school that Raaluchi wanted to enter at all cost. She was in her third year in school, studying English.

Raaluchi wept bitterly and Nkiruka consoled her again as they walked hand in hand to Nkiruka's hostel. Nkiruka made her settle down comfortably on her bed before she hurriedly prepared noodles and egg for her. Raaluchi rebuffed the food because she had no appetite for it. She couldn't even drink the orange juice that Nkiruka had served her. She was depressed. Her mind wavered in envy for Nkiruka and the voices spoke to her: "Your friend is very much ahead of you in your academic career and you are still battling with admission." And just immediately after the voices ceased, she fumed.

Raaluchi had been the winner right from their primary

and secondary schools education, considering the fact that Nkiruka was not just a friend to her, but her rival in life destiny competition. She had always had the feeling that she was better than Nkiruka and Nkiruka shouldn't get desirable things before her. Nnanyelugo her late father used to tell her that she was better than any other person, she was a shinning star and she was unbeatable and Raaluchi had grown up with those powerful words of her father. She had never lost any opportunity, neither had she waited for anything good in life, and now, her friend was ahead of her and she couldn't stand it as she watched her with feelings of hatred, as though her friend had taken what belonged to her. Nkiruka was moved with pity for her friend and she repeated her consolation with words of encouragement.

"Raaluchi, there is nothing God cannot do. I think you should keep trying and don't give up. I'm sure you'll get admission in your next attempt. I'll fast and pray for you," Nkiruka said softly to Raaluchi and she sneered at the thought of Nkiruka, a big sinner fasting and praying for her. "Can a big sinner fast and pray for you? Fast and pray indeed! Have you seen what she's wearing? Can someone in that manner fast and pray? Oh, what a scumbag! She's just good at spiting people!" The voices echoed again and she infuriated more. It was absurd for a sinner who was wearing trouser; a man's garment, and living a worldly life to be in a position to pray for her, as though her own prayers had been ineffective. Nkiruka was shocked when Raaluchi began to flare up. She had just misunderstood her friend's words of consolation for a means of spiting her.

"I honestly do not blame the fate that kept a long distance in our academic carrier. You are now in a position to spite me simply because you got admission before me. You may be happy that you got admission before me, but it certainly doesn't make you better than me. Go on and spite me!" Raaluchi yelled at Nkiruka not minding the fact that there were people in the hostel and ears were listening. Nkiruka gazed at Raaluchi. She was dumbfounded. Raaluchi angrily took her hand bag from the bed and made a pace until she left the hostel in infuriation. Nkiruka wondered what offence she had committed by giving her friend a word of advice. She reminisced immediately, how Raaluchi had displayed the same envious attitude when she took the first position from Raaluchi for the first time in their Juniour secondary school. Raaluchi had kept malice with Nkiruka for a term before she finally reconciled with her when she regained the first position the subsequent terms. Nkiruka heaved a sigh and lay on her bed, praying that Raaluchi would change from her terrible attitude. Gossips in the hostel entered Nkiruka's corner to know what was amiss but Nkiruka did not utter a word, as she valued her friendship with Raaluchi and wouldn't want to entertain gossips or third party that would destroy her friendship with pieces of bad advice.

Raaluchi was so pleased to be the last person to complete the bus that was going to Onitsha. She sat down and paid her transport fares immediately before the driver drove off. In the bus, she began to murmur and hiss. She blamed God for everything that had happened to her. She blamed God for giving Nkiruka admission instead of her who deserved better, for she prayed three times a day, she belonged to a Catholic Charismatic Ministry and she kept God's commandments, unlike Nkiruka who was a big sinner, who had boyfriends and had even lost her virginity. She blamed God for keeping her at home for three years without education. She blamed God for virtually every misfortune that had befallen her. The bus conductor who was sitting opposite Raaluchi noticed her bitterness and called her *asanwa* (a pretty girl) just to cheer her up but instead of accepting the compliment with a smile, she heaped insults on the poor old man by calling him vulgar names and warned him not to even talk to her at all and that he should mind his business or chat with whoever that cared to listen. The passengers shouted on Raaluchi and told her to control her anger and not display it on a man that was old enough to be her father.

Raaluchi couldn't wait to reach Onitsha. When she finally did, she mounted on the most available motor cycle and told the cyclist her address. Uncontrollably, her tears tickled down to her cheeks. She walked briskly and stalked off upstairs to the third floor. She didn't even greet her mother, but instead, she burst into uncontrollable tears as she ran to her room. She cried loudly just to get relief from her anger. Her mother was not surprised at her behaviour because she knew her daughter well. She knew that greeting was not in her dictionary when she was angry. Mummy had tried so much to correct that flaw of hers but all to no avail. Mummy knocked on her door but she refused to open and so she shrugged and left, feeling worried for her daughter as she heard her loud cry from the living room.

* * * *

Raaluchi's younger brother Arinze came home singing and dancing. He was sixteeen years old but looked older than Raaluchi in his gait and other masculine characteristics. He was very handsome with his chocolate skinned complexion; with the pointed nose on his oval face and with his smiling face that made him look more womanly than male, exactly his father's demeanor. He was thrilled as he flung himself on a sofa in the living room. Mummy asked him what the excitement was all about and he gladly told her that he had been offered admission in Nnamdi Azikiwe University, Awka to study Business administration.

"Oh Mummy I'm so excited, and this great achievement calls for celebration. I can't believe I made it at my first attempt. I've told Uncle Obiora and he promised to give a helping hand to sponsor my university education. Where is Raaluchi? I want to share this good news with her," Arinze said excitedly and he was already at the hallway calling her sister's name when

Mummy hushed him and told him not to tell Raaluchi for fear that she would die of envy.

"I don't think she was offered admission, though I've not asked her. She was in a terrible state when she came home this evening. She didn't even greet me. She locked her room door."

"Oh my God…not again, God please answer my sister's prayers."

"I think your sister is with the key to answers to her prayers. She says the prayer of a Pharisee, like: 'God you know I deserve better because I'm holier than her. I keep your commandments and she doesn't…and so I ask that you answer me because I'm holy and she's a big sinner, can you imagine such a prayer?" Mummy said with a raised eyebrow; a facial expression that showed that the act of Raaluchi was virtually disgusting. Mummy continued after a brief pause. "She's jealous of God's blessings upon her only friend Nkiruka. She always compares herself with others. She thinks she is better than others and that others do not deserve God's blessings. She is self righteous, greedy and very ungrateful."

"Please talk to her Mummy. She needs a change in her life to receive God's blessings," Arinze said sympathetically. Just then, Mummy's cell phone rang. It was Nkiruka calling to know if Raaluchi arrived home safely. She had been calling Raaluchi but her phone was switched off. Nkiruka gave Mummy a graphic detail of what happened in her hostel and Mummy apologized on behalf of Raaluchi and promised to talk to her daughter about the incident.

Raaluchi wept uncontrollably on her bed with puffy eyes. Later in the night, Mummy entered to console her. She had finally unlocked the door. Mummy told her that the best way to receive God's blessings was to give thanks and that she should at least recollect what God had done for her in the past. Her staying alive was a miracle for so many of her age mates had died and decayed in their graves. So many of her age mates could not afford three square meals a day but she could and so many did not even go to school at all. She had all cause to glorify God for she was a blessed child.

"There is no such thing as satisfaction until I become the greatest," Raaluchi said disdainfully in tears and her mother heaved a sigh of controlled anger. She had wanted to slap Raaluchi as soon as those filthy words of arrogance came out of her mouth. As usual, her daughter was very adamant and taking her advice was the last thing she would do. She never agreed with her. Ever since she lost her father, she had always wanted things to work her own way, just her own, and Mummy was scared that her selfishness and impatience would lead her to danger. Raaluchi was being unreasonable and she begged to be left alone, insisting that God had frustrated her enough and she could not possibly thank Him for frustrating her. She had chosen to relinquish her prayers since they had been ineffective and she had also decided to abolish God's commandments since He blessed sinners more than the righteous like her. She had been faithful to God but He abandoned her just to bless sinners and make mockery of her. Nkiruka had boy friends and slept with them right from secondary school but she didn't. She had reserved her virginity for the sake of God. Her body is the temple of the Holy Spirit and shouldn't be defiled with fornication. She had kept that commandment, but God did not value her holiness. Nkiruka was the biggest 'sinner' she had ever seen but God had blessed her making mockery of her that had been 'a faithful one.' To her, that was not fair.

Raaluchi rolled over on her bed with an uttermost peaceless state. Her eyes filled with tears as she remembered the couple of times she had worked for God. She had visited the sick people in the hospital with her friends from the Charismatic Ministry on a very sunny afternoon. They had decided to trek to the General Hospital in Onitsha just to have a penance for their unconscious sins. It was a Lenten season and so they observed their penances in anyway they could. They squinted as they trekked to the hospital, carrying assorted fruits in polyten bags and with the sun beating them mercilessly, they still trekked. And so, they visited the sick people and she led the chorus in their worship songs before the interssesory prayer started. They prayed for all the sick people in different wards before they left. She remembered how they visited houses every Sunday afternoon for their evangelical missions; still with the hurting sun ravaging their skins. She had neglected her siestas and walked house by house with her friends in the ministry, preaching to the people and reviving lost souls.

She also remembered how she visited the Motherless Babies Home and offered cartons of biscuits and drinks to them; how she joyfully carried some babies, played with them on their beds and sang lullabies for them until they fell asleep; how she joined the altar girls in her parish to dress the altar some Saturday mornings; how she entered the parish house with the altar girls to clean the parish house and wash the Reverend Fathers' Cassocks despite her father's warnings not to go to the parish house. She remembered how she rejected her secondary school crush because she wanted to please God. As she remembered the sacrifices she made for God, and the brutal way He responded to those sacrifices, she sobbed openly, tearing her spirit apart. She sobbed uncontrollably, and when she got tired of sobbing, she closed her eyes, begging sleep to take her.

CHAPTER TWO

RAALUCHI PACED UP and down in her room the next morning, looking disheveled. She had cried her eyes out last night. Her puffy eyes savoured the beautiful awards she had received from her Principal and the Minister of Education in her secondary school years. The awards hung line –by-line on the wall and she reached out to them and caressed them with smiles. She was given those awards for emerging the best student in English Language, literature in English and English Essay Writing Competitions. Those awards were the reward of her excellent intelligence.

She remembered Nnanyelugo and his praises for her when she came home with her awards: "Raaluchi you are unbeatable! You are a shinning star and nobody can ever get to see your back. You are better than all of them!" Her eyes filled with tears as her smile changed to a frown; a frown because her intelligence had been put to mockery, to think that she of all people would be in a position of searching for admission in a school where she could have become a lioness: a befitting status for her excellent intelligence. She screamed her father's name in fury, "Nnanyelugo!"

Raaluchi ceased attending Charismatic Ministry meetings in her parish: St. Peter's Catholic Church, Onitsha. She also ceased receiving calls from her friends in the Charismatic Ministry. She was angry with God and she had chosen to live her life without God and the people that reminded her about God. She continued the computer lesson that she had been

9

attending since she graduated from secondary school, decided to give wayward lifestyle a try and to measure up with the people she called 'sinners'. She made wayward friends from the computer school, forced her self to indulge in bad companies: a life style that had never been hers. The wayward friends taught her how to keep boyfriends and make money from them as they discussed in a Pacific Restaurant opposite the Computer School, awash in Wizkid's 'Holla at your boy' a music they considered perfect for their discussion with Raaluchi. They nodded to the rhythm of the music and got chilled with the air conditioning and glasses of wine. It was on a Tuesday sunny afternoon after a computer lesson. They were actually luring Raaluchi into sleeping with a very rich man for she would make a lot of money from him.

Raaluchi in her decency and confused state of mind did not know what to do. She didn't know how it felt like to be with a man in a secret place. And yet, she wanted to belong to the world of waywardness, a world that could enable her to forget God and live a life of iniquity. Most worldly people she knew were very fortunate in life and this seemed to have changed her attitude to life.

"That is prostitution. I can't involve myself in such an abominable act. It's ungodly and I'm still a virgin," Raaluchi blurted out in grimace as she felt irritated from the puff of smoke coming from Peppy's cigarette. Peppy was one of the wayward friends of Raaluchi who was the leader of the group: "The girls on top." She was in her early twenties. She was short, dark skinned, and was wearing an excessive make up that made her look like a scarecrow. She was wearing a pale blue strapless short gown that exposed her fat thighs and *yams* and she wore her hair in dreadlocks.

"That is what you call it. We call it *"Runs!"* Peppy snapped at Raaluchi. Peppy was simply the short form of her real name which is Perpetua. The three wayward girls all abridged their real names and they had chosen a name for Raaluchi since they considered her name so religious and old fashioned. "Anything that has a connection with God is old fashioned," Peppy had said when Raaluchi told them her name the first day she met them. Peppy had released a puff of smoke from her cigarette into Raaluchi's face, to shove Raaluchi of her decency and innocence, to make her realize her new world and where she really belonged. They named her 'Queen' because she looked like a Queen.

"Queen, you've decided to join us so stick to it and don't ruin it by trying to be the 'good one'," Peppy added, looking furious as she wiggled her index finger to Raaluchi's face, warning her to stick to her relationship with them. She hissed loudly and lit another cigarrate. She hated local girls, local, because they exaggerate Christianity with their pretentious attitude of being good, an endearing goodness that made every other person around them unrepentant sinners. Peppy's father was a pastor and to her, the old man simply chose where he belonged. He had his life to live just like she did and she didn't owe anybody any obligation in trying to be good only to please God. She wasn't in to implement the rule of self denial just to please God. She came into the world to enjoy herself and that she was doing and ever going to do until she died. She believed in what she can only see. She believed in the world and nobody can ever lure her into leaving her fun-filled worldly life to a boring life of Christianity; an over bearing bondage, a life style that her father had chosen.

"Don't worry, you'll enjoy it. It's just fun. You'll make a whole lot of money from it and you can take care of yourself. We are in the world of our own, and we have to enjoy it to the fullest. Life is all about happiness, and you have to enjoy your youth. Leave this holy life style of yours, you are too pretty for it and it's never going to make you happy," another one said primly, trying to convince Raaluchi as she stroke Raaluchi's hair and tickled her cheeks with smiles and Raaluchi smiled back. Her name was Jess, a short form of Jessica. She was tall and pretty with a chocolate skinned complexion and an oval face. She wore her braids in a pony tail, and she was wearing a pink sleeveless short gown.

The third one among them was Abby, a short form of Abigail. She was of an average height. She had light skinned complexion that only made her appear glamorous but she wasn't pretty and she wore a spider tattoo on her left leg. She was wearing a white short and a red sleeveless shirt and she dyed her afro red in colour. She was staring at a man in the restaurant who she noticed had been looking lustfully at Raaluchi, an open unabashed looking. She considered the man ugly in his dark skinned complexion, his big bald head and big mouth. He was wearing a black tight Tshirt and a blue jean trouser. Suddenly, Abby wanted to borrow Raaluchi her face just to flirt with the man and make some money from him. Since the act of borrowing a face was impossible, she suddenly came up with a plan and walked straight to the man. He was alone in a neat glass table for two, eating a plate of white rice and chicken sauce, and making sputtering sounds with the food, as though the food was pepperish.

"I'll convince her to spend a night with you if you buy us lunch," Abby said to him with a smile.

"Really?" the man said to Abby, smiling back sheepishly and exposing his huge brown front teeth. There came an instantaneous excitement in him, and in that state, he beckoned the waiter when Abby gave a nod to him in confirmation. Soon, the waiter approached The Girls on Top and they all made their order.

"Abby, I hope you know how expensive the food here is," Peppy said curiously to Abby. "I don't have enough money here to add up to yours and you know that our business has really been poor to the ugly lately. I don't want to be embarrassed here because of food," Peppy added.

"Me too," Jess said, as she entered the discussion just to assure them that she was excluded in the bill. And peppy and

Abby hissed at her and muttered something to her about itching to take from people but hardly gives, even when she earned more in their business.

"You girls should not worry about the payment. That fool over there will make the payment," Abby pointed at the man and they all laughed, except Raaluchi. They praised Abby for being smart and too quick to hook up with a man for food payment, except Raaluchi who only took a look at the man and gave them quizzical looks, wondering what actually made the man a fool for accepting to pay their food bills.

"Abby, you shouldn't have called him a fool. The bible says that anybody that calls a neighbour a fool will be answerable to hell," Raaluchi said, and immediately wished she hadn't said that, she felt that she had disappointed her changing self for defending a God that did not care about her; a God that did not love her. The other three girls laughed at her and mimicked her. Peppy said something to her about the writings in the bible that never existed but were just written for writing sake. She went ahead to assure her that the only God she knew was herself, there was no other God except herself and that anybody that cared to understand, was a God to his or herself. The waiter served them their foods according to their choices of order: fried rice and chicken for Raaluchi, two plates of white rice and chicken sauce for Jess and Peppy, jollof spaghetti and fried eggs and chicken for Abby, and two bottles of chilled Andre wine were standing on their table.

Before they started eating, they convinced Raaluchi again that she was going to enjoy herself if she joined them in their business. Raaluchi agreed with a nod, a slow nod and a confused state of mind. She only wanted to 'punish' God for frustrating her. She had promised God the first time she saw her flower that she would keep her virginity until she got married but the promise was on the verge of breaking. She simply couldn't keep her promise to the God that had hurt her, the God who enjoyed seeing her cry in prayers instead of answering them.

God had made her life so miserable and she didn't care about the promises she made to Him anymore. After all, Nkiruka her friend lost her virginity, had an abortion afterwards but God gave her admission into a university of her choice, making mockery of her; 'the good one'. Arinze her brother was a very big sinner who stole from her father and meats from the pot of food, but God gave him admission into a university of his choice, making her feel abandoned. Jess was right. She can never get the happiness she wanted if she remained in God.

After some minutes, the man that paid their food bills approached them, said 'hi' to all of them, and requested for their names. The three girls gave him fake names, except for Raaluchi who said the truth, simply because she was used to it. Peppy thought immediately how they were going to put much effort to changing Raaluchi. She must be like them if she really wanted to join them. And then, with the man's eyes fixed on Raaluchi, he requested for her phone number but Abby was quick to speak on Raaluchi's behalf. She said that Raaluchi had no phone but intended to buy soon. Raaluchi gazed at Abby. She wanted to tell the man the truth but Jess winked at her, begging her with the sign to co-operate with them.

The man gave Raaluchi his complementary card and told her that he'll be expecting her call. Abby softly told Raaluchi to take the card and she did with trembling hands, surprised at the man's sudden interest in her and unsure if she was going to make the call because the man was very much ugly with his Dracula teeth that she had immediately seen when he gave her his complementary card with a wild smile. She had accepted to defile her body but that would be on her terms. It would be with a handsome man. She can't loose her virginity to a monkey. That would be too degrading of her and the memory would forever remain unpleasant to her. The man smiled a convincing smile and winked at Abby, thanking him with the wink, for a job well done and Abby winked back at him. He left the restaurant, smiling widely. Peppy snatched the complementary card from

Raaluchi's hand, just to take a look at the man's occupation. She read it out to their hearing: "Marcus Ventures Limited. Mr Marcus Nwankwo: dealer of motor-cycle spare parts." They all hissed, long loud hisses, except Raaluchi who was gazing at them, lost in their midsts. Peppy tore the complementary card into pieces.

"I'm sure he must have spent his last cash on our lunch. I saw how he was scratching his head when he was making the payment," Peppy said as she threw the pieces of the complementary card in a trash can behind her and Abby and Jess laughed.

Peppy told Raaluchi the the rules of the *runs* business: *'truths and decent dresses are not allowed. You must make sure that you lure your man into spending lots of money on you first in a boutique of your choice before you let him take you to his house. You must make sure that your man pays you an advance of your agreement with him and that you protect yourself with a condom before you let him see your things. He may be carrying a communicable disease and he may not want to use a condom for what he's actually paying for. You must make sure that your man is rich and highly connected and you must make sure that you don't give your heart to any man. Always bear it in mind that you are playing a game of money and you ought to use your brain and not your heart.'*

Raaluchi gazed at Peppy as she spoke. She felt an instant urge to run away from them, to run and run and run, but when she remembered the God that had hurt her so badly, she regained a determination to join the wayward girls in their business.

"But I don't know how to use a condom," Raaluchi said innocently.

"Don't worry, I'll teach you," Jess told Raaluchi as she patted her shoulder. And Peppy and Abby gave her a surprise stare with their mouths twisted aside and their eyebrows raised, a shieldless surprise, and in their expression was the question: 'how can this full blown pretty girl still be a virgin?'

The wayward girls contacted the rich guy they wanted Raaluchi to make money from. He was Jess's ex-man, a handsome young man who owned a famous factory where ladies hair attachments were made. They sent him Raaluchi's pictures through blackberry messenger. He was interested and he promised to meet Raaluchi for a hundred and fifty thousand naira. They were impressed with the offer and they all had an agreement to share the money when Raaluchi gets it from the rich man and Raaluchi went home with a decision that she would fornicate and live a wayward life just to offend God and pay back for all the sufferings He put her through for three years.

* * * *

On getting home, Raaluchi met a male visitor discussing with her mother. The face of the visitor lit with wild smiles as soon as he sets his eyes on Raaluchi. His teeth reminded him of the man that approached her in the restaurant. She wondered if it was her fate to be meeting men with scary teeth. Raaluchi merely greeted him and headed straight to her room. It took the visitor hours before he finally left and later in the night, Mummy told Raaluchi that the visitor was her suitor and the first- son of Mummy's best friend Eugenia. Eugenia and Mummy had been very close since childhood. They had shared their youthfulness together in Abatete before they got married and moved over to the city. Eugenia's only daughter Ogechi who was Raaluchi's age mate, was happily married to a rich trader that lived in an upper class district area: a place that tolerated no noise---G.R.A Asaba (Government Reserved Area) and her mother always talked about her to Mummy's hearing: "Ogechi said that she's happy with her husband, that she prefers married life to her youth days and that her husband treats her like an egg."

Eugenia always told Mummy that her son- in law had been spoiling her with money to enlarge her Super Market in Ogbo

Ogonogo Market Asaba. And Mummy always felt jealous about her friend. She wished to experience such from her own son-in-law too but Raaluchi had been rejecting her suitors. Raaluchi couldn't wait to hear more words from her mother before she said that she wasn't interested in marriage yet, for she was too young. She was just nineteen years old and even if she was in need of a husband, she wouldn't marry a man whose front teeth were as large as a square-shaped shovel, a dwarf, a man who cannot make a complete statement without committing any grammatical error. Raaluchi had read all his love letters; error-filled love letters, the ones he had only sent to her without approaching her. He was just someone who was not man enough to approach her first.

Besides, she needed time to live her life the way she wanted it, and the least that was on her mind was 'marriage'. She didn't want to be a liability to any man neither did she want to be owned yet, to spend the rest of her life in obedience and submission. All she wanted was to further her education and hold her shoulders high as a self-made success. All she wanted was to make Nnanyelugo proud wherever he was. She wanted to live her life and live it greatly and not being imposed an impromptu marriage. That was old fashioned and she wasn't ready for it yet. She knew her three wayward friends would sneer at it and call it 'an everlasting bondage.' Mummy reasoned with her but she was a little bit worried about Raaluchi her daughter. She knew she had a big flaw and she would have wanted her to marry a gentle man like Olisa, her suitor who could tolerate her bad manners, who was actually a native of Abatete just like them.

Eugenia her friend had told her so much about Olisa. He was just a gentleman that was good at treating a woman like an egg, considering the relationships he had had with his younger sisters. Mummy had found the young man to be so pleasant; pleasant enough to be a good husband to her daughter. Olisa was a Catholic by faith and was a responsible man and even came from a reputable and responsible family. Mummy was sure of that but the least she would do was to force her daughter to marry a man that was not her desire, instead, she would continue to give her advice on the need to marry a good man that could tolerate her. And to make hay while the sun shines, for time waited for nobody and women were like flower which blossomed, because they bring exuberance during full bloom but get discarded when wilted.

Olisa felt dejected when he heard of Raaluchi's refusal to acccept his proposal. It took him lots of time before he moved on with his life and only blamed himself for not daring to approach her first. But the rejected gentleman was only scared of disgracing himself in front of the young lady he was in love with because he cannot speak good English.

* * * *

The rich man cancelled the appointment with Raaluchi for he was traveling to South Africa and the wayward girls were stunned because no man would have rejected a dish served in a golden plate like Raaluchi. They promised to find another man for Raaluchi. While Raaluchi was waiting for another man to defile her, she fell in love instantaneously with a man that rendered her some help, a man that just offered her a ride on a rainy morning. They had exchanged phone numbers and Raaluchi was already in love at first sight simply because the man resembled her late father. She wasn't used to being with worldly men but since she had untied herself from the bondage of Christianity just like her friends had advised her, she guessed it wasn't a bad idea to have a date with this handsome worldly guy she had suddenly fallen in love with. He looked rich in a latest Toyota Avalon which was what mesmerized Raaluchi. Again, he had a nice accent. He had introduced himself as Chiedu and his name kept reeling on Raaluchi's mind.

Through out lesson hours the next day, after her encounter with Chiedu, Raaluchi couldn't concentrate. Her mind kept drifting from the ride Chiedu offered her, the pleasantries, and his smiles with a gorgeous and romantic attraction. Her friends discovered it and when Raaluchi finally opened up to them, they told her to get a lot of money from him by perching on him like a housefly, they told her to remember their rules. "Welcome to our world, Queen," Abby told Raaluchi as she shook her hand and held it a little longer. Without waiting for him to call her first, Raaluchi called him to thank him again for the ride. Aside from that, she wanted to hear his cute voice again. Her heart danced in excitement when he asked her out on phone and praised her beauty. He praised her just like her father and she was mesmerized by it because Chiedu reminded her of the good memories she had shared with Nnanyelugo who had told her that her face looked like the picture of a setting sun, that she was a beauty to behold, a beauty that radiates far the sky. Chiedu had even promised to take her out on a date the next day, and 'yes' was all she needed to say to him. She couldn't dare turn down a prince charming like Chiedu.

Raaluchi had never had a date and she was overwhelmed with joy as she searched her wardrobe for a nice dress to wear but didn't find anyone attractive. All her dresses were long gowns and long skirts and as she watched them with grimace, she imagined her wayward friends laughing at her and calling her *mgbeke (an old fashioned woman)*. She had been with them one day after a computer lesson, just within the premise of the computer school. They were actually rating a lady's attire. Jess had said that the lady was pretty and sophisticated but was just an *mgbeke*, simply because the lady was wearing a long skirt. Raaluchi could hardly wait to see Chiedu again. She loved him and to defile her body with him would be the best way to get even with God for all the pains He had caused her; to defile her body would be the best thing that would ever happen to her new world.

* * * *

19

Chiedu gave Raaluchi a ride at the computer school and he took her to one of the Five Star Restaurants in town. The restaurant was dimly cool, its air scentful and exclusively sweet. P.square's "Do me" was playing loudly in the restaurant. They sat opposite each other in a neat glass table for two and ordered fried potatoes and sausage with fruit juice. They spent time making eye contacts, eating, drinking and chatting till evening before he finally drove her home and invited her to his house. She accepted the offer before she alighted from his car and walked to the stairs, grinning, wishing that her mother would not notice why she was grinning, pleased that her mother locked her provision store at the basement.

That night in her bedroom, she switched on her television and what she saw was a man sweating profusely in a white shirt and black suit as he preached the word of God. He was almost jumping as he moved from one point to another, speaking authoritatively with a microphone. Raaluchi listened to him on the programme that says "Keeping faith in holiness." "Faith is not just believing in God but believing in Him in holiness. Beloved in Christ, don't worsen your situation by living in sin just because of the challenges of life you are facing, because sin is a reproach..." The speaker spoke with his eyes fixed on Raaluchi. It was as though the speaker on TV was actually speaking to her. The talk gave Raaluchi goose-bumps and it made her shiver. Her conscience told her to reconsider her intentions for the road she was about to take was not for her. Raaluchi hardened her heart and refused to oblige. Her mind was made up. God had never been fair to her by frustrating her when she needed Him most.

To Raaluchi, God never loved her. If He did, He would have given her admission into a university of her choice. She had been fasting and praying for it for the past three years. She must defile herself. Her mind was made up. She furiously switched off the TV and the voices echoed: "Go on and do it! God has never been fair to you! It's pay back time!" She got infuriated and yelled in pains, covering her ears with her palms as though by doing that, the voices that she was hearing would stop. In a moment, she was okay. She heaved a sigh of relief and drifted to sleep. Mummy knocked on her door but she didn't open it and then Mummy went back to her own room and dialed Ezenwanyi's phone number. Ezenwanyi was Raaluchi's native doctor who Mummy thought was a specialist in treating cases of spiritual husbands, spiritual wives, and *ogbanje* (marine reincarnation spirit). Ezenwanyi had convinced Mummy that Raaluchi was an *ogbanje* and the voices she was hearing were the voices of her fellow marine spirits.

Mummy had taken Raaluchi to Ezenwanyi about three consecutive times and Ezenwanyi had bathed Raaluchi in the river and had used a pigeon's blood to wash her head after throwing some coins in the river as a pay off for Raaluchi's fellow marine spirits in the river to leave her. Mummy had asked her if she was sure that what she was doing was godly, but Ezenwanyi had answered her bluntly: "remember what the bible says: 'Give to Caesar what belongs to Caesar and to God what belongs to God. I am also a member of the Catholic Women's Organization, so don't doubt my precept,' Ezenwanyi said with great assurance. Ezenwanyi only needed to pay off Raaluchi's fellow witches and to wash her free from them so that she would be delivered from them. Ezenwanyi answered Mummy's call on a second call.

"Ezenwanyi, I think Raaluchi is still hearing those voices, what are we going to do?"

"Bring her to me first thing tomorrow morning. Come with the sum of fifty thousand naira. I'm going to buy some items for the performance of *ogbanje* ritual in the river. They are really very stubborn but we'll continue to sacrifice to them until our daughter is free from them."

Mummy heaved a sigh of helplessness when the line went off. She was going bankrupt because of Raaluchi's spiritual problem. She had spent almost two hundred thousand naira for the same *ogbanje* issue. She had also been fasting and praying to God but all to no avail. She wished that her late husband left money for them before he died but he had died bankrupt. She was yet to understand how a rich man like her husband fell from the sky and crashed. Nnanyelugo had spent all his money for his treatments while struggling to live for Raaluchi, had experienced uncountable business failures: his goods sinking into the water, business partners duping him, so many business disappointments and if not for Doctor Obiora Nnanyelugo's younger brother, Nnanyelugo would not have been given a befitting burial.

Raaluchi had been with the problem of hearing tormenting voices since her father died, when she was just fifteen years old. Mummy knew how close she was to her father and she knew that they shared a bond. Raaluchi's life turned upside down ever since her father died and left her fatherless. She was so depressed until she started to hear the voices: her voice and that of her late father; mixed voices of torment. Ezenwanyi had told Mummy that Raaluchi's fellow witches in the river were using her late father's voice to manipulate their torments on her. A lot of sacrifices had been made by Ezenwanyi. She had been pleading to the *Ogbanjes* in the river to leave Raaluchi in peace.

CHAPTER THREE

RAALUCHI DEVELOPED A feverish feeling on the morning she was to visit Chiedu in his house. She couldn't fathom if the TV programme she had watched the previous night, the conscience that judged her, the sudden change of mind of the rich man that was to defile her and the sudden fever were warnings from God against the sin she was about to commit. She waved the thoughts off her mind. What about her friend Nkiruka who committed the same sin uncountable times but God still gave her His blessings? She felt that she shouldn't feel remorse for what she was about to do because so many people that she was holier than did similar thing and still received God's mercy and favour. It was pointless to feel so worried about what she was going to do but she couldn't help the disturbing feelings that entered into her mind.

Raaluchi refused to be distracted by the feverish feeling and the restless mind. It was on a Saturday morning. Mummy and Arinze went to visit Eugenia in Fegge Housing Estate, Onitsha: a place that forced itself to belong to the upper class district area, but made a useless effort. It had beautiful duplexes and mansions alongside the streets, but the roads were untiled, and there were no gutters to flush down the waters when it rained, and so, the rain formed puddles of muddy water on the roads. Eugenia had returned from Dubai the previous day and had called Mummy to come to her house and take some of the beautiful things she bought before her other friends finished them.

Raaluchi had refused to join them knowing the agenda she

had for the day. She dressed up in a sexy white gown that she had borrowed from Jess, and left for Chiedu's house. She felt uncomfortable in the attire as she struggled with her conscience and forced herself to be comfortable. Her wayward friends had told her that to fit in properly into the group, she would have to change her dressing pattern to sexy attires, but Raaluchi had been battling with her conscience about changing her dressing patterns. Her mother and her conscience were totally against it. But Jess had insisted on a telephone conversation with her, that she must wear something sexy while going to a man's house because that was the only way the man could be attracted to pay well. People who passed Raaluchi on the way, stopped to gaze at her, and some old women who saw her snapped their fingers at her, forbidding her. Her friends from the Charismatic Ministry saw her and shook their heads in disappointment. It was a huge embarrassment to them as they were sure that people would begin to believe that they do not practice what they preach.

Raaluchi's head reeled in excitement as soon as she saw the mansion in 3.3 Housing Estate Onitsha: a place known for its tiled road, clean streets and tranquil environments. Chiedu told her vaguely that the mansion was one of his houses in Onitsha. He teased her for being thrilled over little things. Chiedu welcomed her with a bottle of Smirnoff Ice Drink and a pornographic movie and Raaluchi finally unveiled her *things* and ate the food for sinners on a cushion in the living room, a food that her friend Nkiruka had tasted. It was enjoyably painful for her as she ate the food with Chiedu, who tried so hard to be gentle with her, just to aid her. Minutes later, she relaxed with Chiedu on the cushion, her eyes closed, her door opened, and God forgotten. The law was broken, and she had finally paid back to God every bit of pain He had caused her.

* * * *

Later in the day, Chiedu told Raaluchi that he couldn't drop her off, for his car was in a mechanic workshop. In exhilarating soft voice that melted her heart, he reassured her that he would take her to her destination next time. As a playboy, Chiedu was very perfect. He knew that soft words that meant so little can really get into girls and turn them on. As a playboy, sincerity was certainly not needed and even names had to be forged. He shouldn't just let a girl know that the Toyota Avalon never belonged to him, that he had actually borrowed it from a friend, and the rainy morning he gave her a ride was actually the same morning that he dropped his lover in her house and was on his way to another lover's house before he saw her looking stranded on the road. He shouldn't let her know that he was a jobless and irresponsible man who only depended on the money he received from his Sugar Mummies. The mansion he claimed to be his was not his own. He had actually borrowed it from a friend just to receive Raaluchi his guest, even his enlarged photographs as the owner of the house were supposed to be somewhere in the living room, but they weren't. Raaluchi believed Chiedu's sweet lies as Chiedu gave her a good bye kiss and promised to give her a call and to make their relationship stable.

On her way to the junction where she was going to take a bus, Raaluchi was knocked down mercilessly by an oncoming vehicle and she lay unconscious on the road in a pool of blood. The reckless driver absconded. People gathered and sympathized over Raaluchi, blaming the accident on recklessness. Two boys wearing brown shorts and brown battered singlets rushed to the accident victim. One of them snatched Raaluchi's gold necklace that was shinning around her neck: her last birthday gift from her father. He ran away as soon as he snatched the necklace and the other boy ran after him rejoicing, because he was sure they were going to make lots of money from the necklace.

Some of the sympathizers shouted 'thieves!' as they watched the boys run off vigorously. An old woman wearing a black T.shirt and a Ghana-wax wrapper with a big scapular around her neck walked to the scene and asked why some people were shouting 'thieves!' When she was told what really happened, she shook her head pitifully and mumbled something about the thieves being wicked to an accident victim. She touched her scapular, called the name Jesus and took Raaluchi's handbag that was lying beside her. 'I'll keep this for her,' she said, and headed straight to her shop as the sympathizers watched her with questioning looks, and in their expression was the question: why did she go for the bag first without caring about what to do to the accident victim? They did not go after her because she probably meant well. She was wearing a scapular, she called the name Jesus and for these reasons, she should be trusted. Inside her shop, she went to a tight and hidden corner, opened the handbag and took all the money she laid her hands on. She opened the inner zips and took all the folded naira notes. She mercifully left Raaluchi's phone for her, because it was not a camera phone.

A man called Good Samaritan pulled over as soon as he saw the helpless accident victim lying in a pool of blood. The man was nicknamed Good Samaritan by his friends because he loves to render help to people. He had to convince his friends riding with him in his car to render help to the pathetic accident victim.

The three friends had been best of friends since their Secondary School days. One of them was called Ikenna, an average height plumpy man in his late thirties, whose personality as a voracious eater was remarkable to his friends. Ikenna was a Chemical Engineer who worked in one of the famous oil firms in Port-Harcourt. He was sitting at the front seat of the car eating eggroll and teasing Good Samaritan about being a very active Christian who ought to be ordained a Pope. The other friend of theirs was Barrister Ekpereka, a tall slim man in his late thirties, whose facial expression always looked serious that he was nicknamed by Ikenna and Good Samaritan as *Barrister Ochiabughiuto* (a man that hardly laughs.) He was relaxing at the back seat of the car with an opened newspaper that covered his face as he read. He hissed when Good Samaritan pulled over and he adjusted his spectacle in a way to see with his eyes only, without the help of the spectacle.

He looked at the accident victim and commented: 'situation has to occur for lesson sake…if there's no situation, there certainly will be no lesson to learn.' Good Samaritan and Ikenna turned to look at him from behind as soon as they heard him. They smiled. They weren't surprised at all because Ekpereka was just like that, very serious-minded and they wondered if that was one of the secrets to his success in law court. Barrister Ekpereka had never lost any of his cases. He was very good in Psychology and was even Good Samaritan's tutor in Psychology, a private part-time programme he rendered to Good Samaritan for two years, after his qualification as a pharmacist.

"If you really want to render help to that girl, then it's time to say goodbye because I'm late for this wedding ceremony," Ekpereka said seriously as he closed the newspaper and opened the car door to leave.

"Ochiabughiuto will never change," Good Samaritan said and glanced at Ikenna who mumbled something about being late for a wedding ceremony, and would have left with Ekpereka. He teased Good Samaritan some more about being a very active Christian even when the accident victim was a total stranger. And Good Samaritan reminded him that 'corporal works of mercy must not be taken for granted because it breeds bountiful blessings.' They carried Raaluchi to the car, ready to take her to the hospital for an immediate treatment and the sympathizers on the road watched them with smiles on their faces. They were visibly happy with Good Samaritan for what he was doing. 'This is her handbag. I kept it for her because there are lots of thieves in these area…*ndi ori erika!*' The old woman told Good Samaritan in Igbo language as she handed the bag to him.

"Maama *Daalu*. Thank you," Good Samaritan said in appreciation and stretched some wafts of naira notes as a token for her good work. She smiled sheepishly as she stretched her hand to take the money, revealing her weak black and brown teeth. But Good Samaritan changed his mind, and kept back his money in his shirt pocket, and Ikenna wondered why he did that.

Doctor Emeka in True Vine Specialist Hospital Onitsha, a dark skinned, slim, young man in his early thirtees admitted Raaluchi in a female ward and instructed one of his nurses to clean her up, change her blood stained white gown to a long blue gown: a gown made for patients on emergency. In a short time, a pint of blood and some injections were given to her after the doctor was through with checking her pulse and carrying out series of test on her. Good Samaritan promised to be back and deposited some money in the hospital. After being reassured that Raaluchi would be alright, he left with his friend Ikenna.

* * * *

Mummy and Arinze waited in worried moods for Raaluchi later that evening, after Mummy learned from a tenant that she had seen Raaluchi leaving the yard in a pace, dressed in sexy attire which was very unlike her. They were looking puzzled, and in their puzzledness were distorted faces, legs shaking in anxiety, and right hands beneath their jaws. Arinze recovered first from this mood and mustered courage, believing that his sister was fine wherever she was. Mummy was sniffing in silent tears.

"It is no doubt that the devil has taken possession of my daughter. Raaluchi now flaunts herself on the streets half naked. It is very shameful that the daughter of *Ezinne Ochiora* of CWO is now a prostitute, *e fuo m!* I'm finished!" Mummy said in tears, almost like a scream, her hands on her head.

"Mummy please calm down. She'll soon come home," Arinze said with an arm around his mother's shoulders.

"She must have been raped to death," Mummy said in quick sobs.

"Don't talk like this Mum, where is your faith in God?" Arinze said and sneered at the thought of his sister being raped to death.

"Marriage will definitely solve your sister's problems. She needs a man to show love to her just like her father Nnanyelugo, her sweetheart. Raaluchi doesn't trust us to shower such love to her, and so, she needs a man that will replace Nnanyelugo for her. I'm sure Olisa would have replaced her father's love but she just foolishly rejected his proposal."

"Raaluchi is too young to marry, Mum," Arinze said with a frown. He imagined Raaluchi getting married, exchanging marital vows with Olisa and he brushed off his imagination with a slight hiss.

"She is not too young to marry. I was about her age when I got married to her father. It's just that my *chi* did not bless me with children soon after my wedding. Raaluchi's marriage to a man that will replace Nnanyelugo's love for her will surely regain the joy she had lost in her loss of her father and admission into the higher institution. But how can a sensible man in search of a woman to marry get married to a girl that roams the street half-naked? Raaluchi *egbuo m!* Raaluchi has killed me!" Mummy hiccupped between sobs after she had spoken worriedly in Igbo Language.

* * * *

Good Samaritan visited Raaluchi the next morning. This time, he came alone. Raaluchi was taking a drip to revive her conciousness. He sat close to Raaluchi and watched her closely trying to recollect where he had seen her before. It was as though her face became clear enough to be recognized by him that very morning. His eyes filled with tears as he watched Raaluchi. No doubt, she was the one. She was the one he had been waiting for. He smiled and held her right hand so tightly, as though by the tight hold, he was assuring himself that he would never let her disappear again, especially now that he had finally found her. There was a bandage tied round her forehead which revealed spots of blood. Good Samaritan watched her pitifully, read her psalms and anointed her before he caught a glimpse of her handbag on the floor and remembered that he had forgotten to call her people. He opened it and found her phone. It was switched off and so he had to switch it on to call Raaluchi's mother who answered the call on a first ring. She spoke curiously in Igbo Language, eager to know where Raaluchi was: "Raaluchi *kee ebe I no? Where are you?* And then, she shrieked when she heard that Raaluchi had an accident and had been admitted in a hospital. Mummy promised to be there right away before she hung up.

"God will bless you abundantly my son. I don't know that people like you still exist in this world," Mummy spoke gratefully with a slight smile. Her whole body was trembling in anxiety. She hadn't recovered from the shock about her daughter's accident.

"It was nothing Mum, what are Christians for?" Good Samaritan introduced himself to Mummy as Onyeka Ibekwe, a pharmacist. Onyeka was tall and looked cute in a black jean trouser, a white shirt and a brown blazer. He was discussing with Mummy on how he had settled the hospital bills before Raaluchi stared and said 'Chiedu' in a weak voice.

Mummy thanked God that she had stared but wondered who this Chiedu was, if the accident had affected her brain. She notified the doctor but the doctor told them that Raaluchi was only sleep-talking. The only bad news about Raaluchi's accident was that she had a closed fracture. She wouldn't be able to walk for some time. But with constant treatment for three months, she would walk again. The doctor recommended a wheel chair for Raaluchi. She had refused to use the POP, complaining that it would make her legs look terrible. She should be on a wheel chair just for some time until she was medically okay to walk again.

CHAPTER FOUR

ARINZE VOLUNTEERED TO remain at home to push Raaluchi around until he was ready to leave for school. Raaluchi had remained silent and had refused to open up to her mother about Chiedu and about her sudden change of dressing. Mummy carried everything to God in prayer, begging Him to forgive her daughter if she had erred and uphold her faith in Him for she was sure that she lacked it. Raaluchi still blamed God for her condition in a wheel chair. To her, it was all God's fault that she had an accident. God had only intensified His hatred for her. She knew that God had never loved her. Nkiruka committed the same sin but she didn't have an accident. She was pardoned and was blessed, but hers was totally different, just one step of sin and a huge punishment followed suit. She nagged at everybody that sympathized with her, even her mother and her younger brother. She loved to be alone in her room, seeing a movie that had the setting of a university education. She would see the movie with tears streaming down her cheeks, and she would think in comparison. "You are stuck on a wheel chair while your mates are all in school. You are a disappointment!" The voices would echoe in her. First was the female's voice: her voice and the other was a male's voice: her father's.

The voices were right. She agreed with the voices. Her mates were all in school receiving lectures and she was at home, stuck in a wheel chair. She hated her life. She hated her life because she had disappointed her father. She hated herself and she felt so useless. One day, she exhibited her cantankerous attitude to tenants that visited her to sympathize with her and pray for her condition.

"Why is everybody chanting sorry for me? Is this sorry said to comfort me or to make me irritated and feel worse than I've already been? Will you all get out of my sight? I just want to be alone! " and Mummy had to offer them pleading gestures, talking to them in low tones to understand and forgive her daughter for her ill manners and they understood and left the house.

* * * *

Raaluchi felt the urge to cry when Chiedu did not reply her incessant text messages about her accident and her terrible condition. She was always with her phone, only to be sure that she didn't miss his call. She would feel jumpy whenever she received a text message in her phone and she would get annoyed when the sender was not who she expected. Raaluchi's wayward friends sent her sympathy text messages when Raaluchi told them about her condition, but they were very much concerned on how much money she got from Chiedu for sleeping with him. When they discovered that Raaluchi didn't get a dime from Chiedu, they sent her hurtful text messages, telling her that she was a complete fool, because she allowed someone to eat her food without paying. They told her that her foolishness was the reason she had an accident, and that it served her right to be in a wheel chair, where fools belong. Raaluchi swung to self pity believing in the fact that she was really a fool and a disappointment and that no one loved her and nothing good would ever come out of her.

Chiedu was with his friend Atinga who was very skinny and ugly, and his shriveled body looked like it needed watering. They were smoking and drinking beer in a dirty joint when Raaluchi's twelfth text message came in. They were sweating profusely. The joint had poor ventilation because it was built with planks. There were flies perching on the wood tables with brown liquid stains of pepper soup, and on the bush meats that some men were eating. The gutter infront of the joint was filled with refuse, and there were black liquid substances that gave the environment a bad odour. Chiedu laughed raucously and mimicked the voice of the text message. Raaluchi had written in her last sentence that she loved him so much and couldn't bear to lose him.

"Who's she?" Atinga asked Chiedu as he smoked, it was as though he was draining the water in his body with the cigarette and leaving himself so dry and shriveled.

"She's just the innocent girl I met few days ago. I just hate eating food with innocent girls because they will never let you be. They'll keep bugging you with their annoying text messages and calls. She had an accident, so what? What has that got to do with me? Does she think I have time to push a cripple around?" Chiedu hissed and released a puff of smoke.

"Just do as you normally do your things. Change your sim card," Atinga said and chuckled before he waggled his left hand to drive away a fly that was perching on the tumbler of his drink.

"I can't do that for sometime. There's this new chick that I met yesterday and she has this phone number. As soon as I'm done with her, I'll change my sim card."

"You are a bad man!" Atinga uttered in amusement.

"It's not my fault that some fishes fall for this good looking face. My outlook may be cool but I'm not a cool guy."

And the rest of things became hilarious as they drank and smoked in stupor.

* * * *

Onyeka visited Raaluchi at home every evening to know how she fared and Raaluchi couldn't help but wonder if he was actually the careless driver that knocked her down and was just pretending to be a Good Samaritan. She accepted the apples he gave her and listened noncommittally to the word of God he preached to her from Matthew 9:1-2: where Christ healed a paralyzed man by assuring him first that his sins were forgiven. *My sins are forgiven indeed...let Him make me walk then, why is He delaying?* Raaluchi said in her mind, as she nodded, pretending to understand what Onyeka was preaching to her. She remained silent about the questions Onyeka asked her concerning the moral lessons of the gospel: why did Christ heal the paralyzed man? Why is the sin of the paralyzed man a hindrance to his healing? What exactly did you learn from this gospel? But Onyeka did not mind and understood her silence as frustration. He knew she was hurting inside; that there were somethings that she was angry with God for, he wanted to know about them but didn't know how to get the answers from her with her silence.

Onyeka was always there for Raaluchi as a friend and a companion who calmed her bad moods with funny stories whenever she rejected the word of God from him. He would tell her stories about an illetrate First Class Graduate who couldn't defend her certificate in public, and a Further Mathematics lecturer who couldn't solve a linear equation for his students and had to force his students to take the Mathematics problem as an assignment. Mummy was surprised that Raaluchi was changing gradually. At least her daughter had begun to smile and laugh; what she hadn't done for so long. Onyeka took her for her weekly check-ups and pushed her around to so many places that she wished to go for sight seeing just to make her happy and avoid the feelings of dejection in her condition. He took her to chapels and prayed for God's mercy and her healing with tears rolling down his cheeks.

One day, outside the chapel, at the church premises, he finally asked her what had been on his mind the day he watched her closely in her sick bed. He asked her if she belonged to a Charismatic Ministry in her parish. Raaluchi replied in affirmation and he reminded her the day she sang in a Charismatic Ministry crusade. He had been invited to the crusade by his cousin Amaechi, and he confessed that he enjoyed the crusade, most especially, her melodious voice. He confessed to her that he had visited the crusade ground repeatedly but didn't see her again. He had asked about her and Amaechi had told him that she had quit the Charismatic Ministry.

"I don't know your reasons for quitting the Charismatic Ministry, but, one thing I can assure you is that God without man is still the almighty God but one without God is nothing."

Raaluchi was dumbfounded. Who was this man that had been so caring to her, praying for her, preaching the gospel to her? Could he be an angel? The last thing she wanted was to hear about God's goodness. God had never been good. If He had, He wouldn't have frustrated her for three years. He had chosen Nkiruka her friend over her who never missed Charismatic Ministry meetings, who never ceased praying three times a day, who never ceased receiving communion at Holy Masses. He had chosen Arinze her brother over her, Arinze that did not even devote his time to Him, Arinze that did not even belong to any Catholic Church Ministry. No! God can never be good. God is wicked! Her mind wavered in doubts as she compared herself with her friend and her brother.

What Good Samaritan had been preaching made no sense to her because it was obvious that God did not love her. Onyeka promised himself that he would never stop until he reassured Raaluchi of God's love for humanity, until he restored Raaluchi's faith, until he brightened those sorrowful eyes that excruciated, until he made her happy. He couldn't understand why he was so committed to this girl but there was this feeling in him that assured him that he had a huge responsibility to take for Raaluchi as the first woman that he had ever recognized.

Onyeka thought about Raaluchi in his house as he watched the art work he had made for himself the very night he set his eyes on her. He had painted her as soon as he got home. He had painted her from his mind's eye. He had captured her looks with his mind and he had painted her so perfectly. She was singing so magnificently that night with her sorrowful eyes that released tears that coursed down her cheeks. He had studied her mien and he discovered that she was depressed. Raaluchi was the first woman he had ever recognized, maybe because she left an impact to cherish. She exuded what he wanted, what he had ever desired from a woman he would call his own.

He had never felt that way before but he knew that very night, as his heart beat raced, that Raaluchi was his and he was going to see her again, and now that he had finally met her, he doubted if he could ever let her go. The girl he had nurtured in his heart for months was finally close to him and he wasn't ever going to let her go. He would do anything in his power to make her his. He watched her portrait all night. He committed his falling in love with her to God in prayers, pouring his heart to God that he wanted Raaluchi as a wife, even though she was crippled. He told his friend Ikenna, that he was in love with Raaluchi and wished to marry her and he sneered.

"You mean you are already in love with that cripple? Onyeka, you should get real, that girl is highly irresponsible. The indecent dress she was putting on that day exposed the height of her irresponsibility. She's only good in bed and not good for marriage, unless you want to be like us, then I can advise you to take some bites and throw away the rest."

"I don't think she's irresponsible. I think she's frustrated. She is depressed and she is forcing herself to be who she's not. I studied psychology, you know. Besides, she's the same girl that I told you about…the first girl I've ever recognized. "

"The one you painted?"

"Yes"

Onyeka smiled as his mind focused on the art work. Ikenna chuckled as he watched him.

"I always believed that I was going to see her again and now I feel that fate has brought her to me. I'm so happy that I can never loose this opportunity. I will make her happy for the rest of her life."

"Have you told her about your feelings for her?"

"No. It's too soon and I don't want to scare her, not with that horrible mood of hers that I'm trying so hard to change…I don't want her to suspect me as someone who wants to take advantage of her and run away. She's still a kid and I'd rather wait for the right time," Onyeka said primly to his friend and his friend chuckled in a startled manner after he had sipped his glass of beer.

"I wonder why you should be falling in love with a kid, Onyeka. That's incredible. If you had told this to Ekpereka, I'm sure he would have given you a slap in response to awaken your senses."

"Love does not choose, Ikenna. Love is not about age range and you can't tell my heart who to love."

Ikenna laughed raucously as soon as he heard his friend, as soon as he imagined a relationship between an elephant and a lizard. And he wondered how blind love can become for the fools who have refused to see clearly. It was foolish enough that his friend could not see this Raaluchi he was in love with so clearly; could not realize that this Raaluchi was only good in bed and not marriage.

The two men got chilled with the fresh air that came from Onyeka's veranda and Onyeka nodded to the rhythm of *chinwike:* a soft gospel music playing from his phone. They discussed some other things about pharmaceutical companies and open drug markets. Onyeka insisted that the open drug markets should be banned in Nigeria because those were the reasons why so many people had lost their lives in an untimely death because of cheap fake drugs. Ikenna disagreed with the reason that not all open drug markets sell fake drugs and that Onyeka should be considerate by placing himself in their shoes. They cannot make a good living and take care of their children if they are being denied of their rights. That would be injustice. The best way to solve the problem of fake drugs was that NAFDAC should continue to search thoroughly for fake drugs in the open markets and close down shops that are subjects to them.

It was almost 8pm when the argument ended and Ikenna was ready to leave. He had the last gulp of his beer and stood up to go and Onyeka saw him off. After they climbed downstairs, he watched him drive off in his red Toyota Camry 2.2. Ikenna was on six weeks leave and he still had enough time to tour Asaba. He had refused to lodge in Onyeka's house telling him that although they were best of friends, there were limits to everything. He'd rather have his privacy with his new-caught fish in a hotel than share his house with him. Onyeka also understood that he didn't want to hear his word of God and join him in his fasting and prayers, because he had confessed to him that they piss him off. But Onyeka had never given up on his friends. He believed that he can change them to be better through prayers.

Mummy was so grateful to God for Onyeka who had been a source of strength to her sick daughter. A man who could abandon his job just to push a sick girl around on a wheel chair must have truly loved her. Onyeka was really a nice man and she pondered over his companionship with her daughter and wondered if God had finally answered her prayers for a nice man that could tolerate her daughter in marriage. She had known a lot about Onyeka. He had revealed himself totally to Mummy one of the evenings when he brought Raaluchi home from their outing. He was a native of Umudioka in Dunukofia local government area. He was the only man in his father's house besides four women. His sisters were all married with children and his parents were still alive and healthy and were devoted Catholics.

Onyeka was a successful pharmacist and Mummy wished he would end up getting married to her daughter. Marriage according to Mummy would change her daughter's life completely, not only on her own terms or selfish reasons. It would make her completely independent and strip her of her over-bearing juvenile delinquency. Raaluchi only needed a tolerant husband that can tolerate her bad attitudes since she had tried to change those bad attitudes in her but she was very incorrigible and she didn't really know what to do about her. Mummy thought that Raaluchi needed an active Christian as a husband because only an active Christian can be a true friend to his wife. Mummy believed that only those who fear the Lord keep true friendships. To Mummy, Onyeka was in a better position to cast out those demons in Raaluchi since he was very godly. Mummy had gone on her knees begging God for a man that can tolerate her daughter in marriage since she had tried her best as a mother. She had promised God to kill a cow for Him if He answered her prayers.

CHAPTER FIVE

THE DAY THAT Raaluchi finally walked was a miracle day. She had completed her dose of injections and tablets and had finally walked on the sixth month after she had lost hope of ever walking again. Onyeka encouraged her to trust God for He could do all things. Raaluchi doubted. God did not give her admission in a university of her choice, how then can He possibly make her walk? She always had the negative things in her life to blame God for, and didn't thank God for the good ones she experienced. She had been with Onyeka in a chapel when Onyeka encouraged her to try to walk by faith, for he believed she could walk again even if she attempted and failed. Raaluchi laughed the kind of laugh that Sarah laughed when she was told by the visitors that she would conceive and bear a son. Onyeka pleaded with her to give it a trial to walk.

Raaluchi was thrilled when she finally staggered and attempted to walk, and then walked. She thereafter thanked Onyeka with a safe platonic hug and thumped him on the back twice as though he actually peformed the healing. She was happily smiling widely.

"Is it God or the medications?" Raaluchi asked Onyeka.

"It is God…it has always been God in the medications, but God wanted your healing to come differently and miraculously just to uphold your faith in Him," Onyeka responded to her with a gentle touch on her shoulder. Raaluchi was happy and astonished at the same time. She kept watching her legs to know if they would tremble and make her fall but they didn't. They strolled hand in hand to so many places in the church premises before Onyeka finally took her home. Mummy was so happy, she lacked words to express her excitement and she booked a thanksgiving mass in their parish. She wished that Arinze was around to testify to what God had done for Raaluchi through Onyeka's faith, but unfortunately he had gone back to school.

Raaluchi resumed computer school after two weeks of the miracle. Her wayward friends had all graduated from the computer school, and the computer school environment reminded Raaluchi so much about them and each time she remembered them, she fumed for the mean words they said to her. Onyeka was always there to pick her up from the computer school and take her home every day. Sometimes, he would take her out for lunch in a restaurant of her choice. Sometimes, he would take her to boutiques and buy clothes of her choice for her. He took her to so many places of her choice but the only thing he never did was to take her to his house. He rather took her to his pharmaceutical company and introduced her to his staff as his best friend and they all cheered for their boss. Onyeka never ceased praying for Raaluchi telling God that he wanted to marry her and take care of her and make her happy.

* * * *

One Thursday morning, after Onyeka had driven Raaluchi to school for her computer lessons, Raaluchi met Chiedu at the second floor of the building. She was actually running the stairs to the third floor, to her class, when she saw him. Her heart raced for him. She couldn't believe she still had feelings for him after what he did to her. She almost lost her life because of him and even when she needed him most, he didn't show up. She ran up the stairs before Chiedu held her hand and made her stop. The first thing he did was to watch her legs and when he was sure that she wasn't crippled anymore, he smiled at her, "I like your shoes", he flattered her just to cover up his mischief. He smiled warmly at her, that particular smile that swept her feet, that particular smile that reminded her so much about her father. Her heart raced more for him and her legs trembled. He watched her looking gorgeous on a blue gown which Onyeka bought for her. Her hair hung down her shoulders and her face glamoured in a light make up. She was looking strikingly pretty and he longed to have her again and to the best of his strategies as a playboy, he was sure he would.

"Baby, I've searched everywhere for you. I've been coming here everyday to look for you…where have you been?"

"You ask me such stupid question? What about my frequent text messages? What about my phone calls? What happened to them? Chiedu, I almost died because of you, and you abandoned me like pieces of rags," Raaluchi said, almost crying. She was befuddled, and the new shrillness in her voice just because of Chiedu annoyed her. She wanted to feel different in his presence. She wanted to be mean to him but she found herself feeling weak in his presence, as though he had taken full control of her. She could see her father from his face and suddenly, she wanted nothing else but to be with him.

"You almost died? Baby, we need to talk."

Chiedu had actually come to the computer school to catch another fish because he had heard that the computer school was the centre for golden fishes (pretty girls) and fortunately for him, he met the previous one he had caught and this previous fish was not wise to run away from this fisherman, was not wise to know that a fisherman who catches fish has no other intention apart from selling the fish or eating the fish. Chiedu had decided to finish the fish he had previously caught and he was ready to lure this fish into his net so that it wouldn't escape, since this fish happened to add a lot of weight just within few months. He was thankful to whoever that had fed this fish in his absence. He couldn't tarry longer to eat this fish again.

Soon, they sat opposite each other in a restaurant opposite the computer school; exactly the place she had stayed with her wayward friends and the place reminded her about them

again. A waiter approachd Chiedu and Raaluchi at their table
and Chiedu ordered for fruit juice, without giving Raaluchi a
chance to make her choice of order. Chiedu told her that he
lost his phone that same evening that she left his house. He had
strolled to a neighbour's house and was attacked by thugs on
his way back. They couldn't find his wallet so they left with his
'blackberry bold 4', which was the latest blackberry in the year
2009, in that year. As he spoke fluently in sweet lies, he prayed
in his mind that his phone would not ring in his jean trouser
pocket and just immediately, he excused himself, saying he was
pressed and inside the rest room, he switched it off. He was
wearing a big T. shirt so she could hardly notice that there was a
phone lying in his pocket. He chuckled in the toilet and praised
himself for being so smart. "Girls and their fish brains...*ha ha
ha...*" He chuckled some more until he was ready to leave the
rest room and meet his long lost fish.

"Baby, I'm so sorry. You know I love you very much. I'm so
sorry I couldn't find you when you needed my help. I should
have come to your house but I was only scared of your Mum
considering the fact that she didn't know me and our affair was
supposed to be secret," Raaluchi believed him. He showered
words of love on her, prophesying undiluted love for her and
her head reeled in excitement, with all manner of emotions
churning inside her and he drove her to a hotel where she
opened her door for him again. The computer lesson was
forgotten for the day and she saw the room swaying around
her as they ate the food together.

* * * *

When Onyeka came back to the computer school at four
in the evening to drive Raaluchi home, he didn't find her. He
called her but her phone was switched off. He decided to go
to her house and there, he met her Mummy at the basement,
in her provision store. Mummy welcomed him with smiles and
seemed shocked when she heard that Onyeka didn't see her

daughter at the computer school. It was in his eagerness to see Raaluchi that he admitted to Mummy that he was in love with her and wanted to marry her. According to Onyeka, he would not stand to see any evil befall her. Mummy danced in her shop and thanked God for answering her prayers.

Just then, a flashy red jeep pulled in opposite Mummy's shop and even without Raaluchi realizing that her mother and Onyeka were around and watching her, she accepted Chiedu's goodbye kiss and waved at him after she alighted. Onyeka's heart beat raced in pain as soon as he saw them. He was hurt from the deepest part of his heart and he left without saying any other thing to Mummy. Raaluchi saw him, and the mere sight of him startled her. She wondered why she felt that way; to be startled in the presence of a man she didn't care about was really a crazy thing. She greeted him casually before realizing immediately that he was angry because he did not respond to her greeting, but she wasn't bothered. He was angry because he had chosen to be. For all she cared, she owed him nothing. She owed him no explanations for being with the man she loved.

Mummy's eyes were filled with tears and she wept angrily. She locked her shop in anger and rushed home to cast out those demons in Raaluchi, and she was sure she would.

"Raaluchi! Raaluchi!" Mummy screamed her name. Raaluchi finally opened the door and she immediately descended on her. She slapped, spanked and kicked her, calling the name Jesus in between each slap and kick until Raaluchi wept.

"Raaluchi, you are a disgrace. You are very wicked and ungrateful and I'm sure that God sitting on His throne will be very disappointed in you. For how long has this been going on? For how long have you been fornicating?"

"I love him Mummy. His name is Chiedu. I knew him before the accident… and he's so lovely," Raaluchi said in tears.

"So where has he been when you were lying critically ill on the hospital bed? Where was he when Onyeka was pushing you around in your wheel chair, abandoning his work just to make you happy? Raaluchi, where was he? You know who your real friend is, in troubled times. Raaluchi, you don't have a conscience." Mummy wept bitterly and begged God to forgive her daughter.

"Raaluchi, God loves you so much but you keep breaking with your distrust and ingratitude, the sweetest heart of Jesus. What hasn't God done for you? He sent you a companion when you were sick. He made you walk again. Why must you fornicate? He knows when to fulfil your dreams of furthering your education. His time is the best. God loves you. I love you. Onyeka loves you and he even wants to marry you."

"He never told me he was in love with me," Raaluchi said, her face streaming down crocodile tears. She was only crying because of the beatings her mother gave her and not for any other reason. The slaps hurt her cheeks so badly. She wasn't sorry for anything. She didn't see any reason why she should feel sorry for whatever she did and she didn't care if she was becoming evil. She was just living her life and that was the way God wanted it, since He chose to bless sinners, and chose them over the righteous. And as for Onyeka, how could he be so naïve not to notice that she was just using him to console herself for her loss of admission and her loss of Chiedu. And now she had finally had Chiedu back, she wouldn't let him leave her anymore. She felt that she couldn't possibly leave the only man that reminded her so much about her sweet father. How could Onyeka be so naïve not to notice that he disgusted her and whatever he preached to her about God was like an unquenchable fire to her for she can never come in good terms with the person who acknowledges God; a God that had never loved her.

"Are you a goat? Didn't you notice? Which man in his right senses would push a cripple around, abandoning his work, just to make her happy, if he doesn't love her? Which man in his right senses would take a girl to so many places of her choice if he doesn't love her? Onyeka told me few minutes ago that he wanted to marry you and now you have made him change his mind."

"But Mum, I don't love him. And when is this marriage tale ever going to end? Mummy, I'm not ready for marriage! I just want to be with who I love for now."

"You are a big fool and you don't even know what love is. True love is divine…it is kind…it is sacrificial…it is not selfish. I'm sure that it is exactly what Onyeka has for you but you prefer to wallow in fornication and live in darkness, claiming to be in love. Tell me Raaluchi, fornication and marital bodily union, which one is right in the eyes of God? That man you claim to love only wants what is under your skirt and not who you are. But soon you'll regret it because I'm sure he's not genuine, if he is, he would have shown himself to me from the very start."

"I won't regret it because I'm sure Chiedu loves me. The fact that Onyeka saved my life doesn't mean I owe him my entire life. I owe him no obligations. And I think it'll do him a whole lot of good if he stops bugging me, pretending to care for me. I have my life to live, Mummy, so please don't just meddle with my affairs!" Raaluchi said furiously and headed to her room, grumbling. She slammed her room door after she had entered and groaned in fury. She was wrecked in infuriation as she watched the frame of Jesus Christ that hung on the wall. She watched it in uttermost hatred and the voices echoed: "Shatter it! Shatter it! He ruined your life!" Raaluchi uttered a statement in her depressed state: "You know I wouldn't have been this bad if you had saved my father's life for me, if you had answered my prayers for my admission into a university of my choice. You made a fool of me for three years! You hated me! You took the two precious things in my life! You took away my happiness! and I'm fornicating because you pushed me to it. You kept me hopeless and frustrated me for three years! I hate you! You ruined my life! "

And just then, she grabbed the frame and smashed it into pieces, just to intensify her animosity. Mummy rushed to the scene and gazed at her daughter whose face had totally turned red in complexion and who was panting in fury. She also gazed at the shattered frame on the floor. Her heart raced in fear as she ran out of the room. She was sure that the devil had taken possession of Raaluchi but she must do something to cast him out of her daughter this time, before he killed her daughter.

* * * *

Mummy dialed her brother-in-law's phone number with trembling hands and she was lucky that he answered the call on the first ring because he was a very busy person, a medical doctor in Enugu and he was the only person she could lean on at that time, even though she knew he wasn't spiritual just like her. She was crying as she spoke to him and he was calming her down in a mellow voice but she cried harder.

"The *Ogbanjes* are still after my daughter, Obiora can't you see? Please how can I see this spiritual Father Gilbert? I heard he resides in Enugu. I think Raaluchi needs deliverance prayers."

"Calm down Mama Raaluchi. There's no *Ogbanje* in Raaluchi's life. She needs medication. She's sick in the head."

"Obiora, my daughter is possessed with the evil spirit and you are telling me to calm down? You need to see what she did in her room simply because she hasn't gotten admission. She is proud of her sins and she is blaspheming. I don't know why this girl can never be grateful to God for once in her life. I just want deliverance prayers for her and let her also get married so that I'll have peace of mind."

"She's too young for marriage and even if she gets married, she still can't be happy because she's psychotic and she needs medication. Bring her to Enugu so that I can arrange for a psychiatrist to take care of her mental sickness," Doctor Obiora reassured Mummy. Mummy refuted the idea that her daughter was suffering from mental sickness. She was convinced that Raaluchi was suffering from *Ogbanje* problems, and why would she listen to Obiora while he wasn't spiritual? Why would she listen to someone that only believes in the power of science and not of God?

"Obiora, my daughter needs deliverance prayers. She is not mad."

Obiora chuckled and only advised his late brother's wife to calm down for his niece was just sick and not demonic. She probably did not need any deliverance prayers because she had no demons in her and he would be glad if his sister-in law stopped giving her conclusions on spiritual matters only. She should be realistic sometimes and learn to take some things ordinarily like a learned person and not like a fanatical human being whose judgments are based only on spirituality of a problem and not on the ordinary fact of it. To Obiora, Raaluchi needed urgent medication before the dangerous sickness destroys her. Obiora tried to convince Mummy that it was still God doing His work through the medications, but Mummy refused, still convinced that her daughter was going through a spiritual problem and she would fight the devil with the very last drop of her blood if he refused to leave her daughter's body.

"Obiora, I know that I'm not educated enough like you but I'm right in this matter." Mummy insisted that she would want to stay in touch with Father Gilbert the exorcist of the Diocese and Obiora promised to send her the address of his Adoration Ministry but refused to be involved with going there for Raaluchi's deliverance knowing full well that Raaluchi his niece needed a psychiatrist and not an exorcist.

"Science will lead you astray one day, Obiora. *Oke akwukwo ajoka!* It's too bad to be too knowledgeable because, it can take you away from your God," Mummy said to Obiora but he hung up after telling her that he had a patient to attend to urgently. Mummy heaved a sigh and went on her knees in tears, telling God to come to her aid and calm Raaluchi's storm like he calmed the storm that frightened his disciples in the boat.

* * * *

Onyeka couldn't sleep that very night even after he had demolished three bottles of beer, what he had never done before. He wept bitterly and staggered and blabbed. He propped up from his bed as soon as he lay. He couldn't sleep. To him, the fact that he had never taken Raaluchi to his house or a hotel should have given Raaluchi the clue that he truly loved her and wasn't lusting after her unlike Chiedu. He had studied him immediately he saw him kissing Raaluchi in his car and waving her goodbye with his fake charming smile that Raaluchi had fallen for. He had studied his mien and had discovered that he was just a playboy. It pained him to see Raaluchi in the hands of a man who never loved her but was only taking advantage of her. The fact that he exposed his relationship with Raaluchi should have also made her to understand that he had no skeleton in his cupboard because he knew that 'a clandestine relationship is a total deceit and a shadow of darkness for what is hidden certainly has no light.' He knew that 'a genuine relationship is an open one for whatever that is uncovered breeds light for God is light.' Onyeka's intention had been genuine but he was wrong. He was wrong to have fallen helplessly in love with a girl that did not even like him not to talk of loving him. It was so painful to love someone that doesn't appreciate your love and love you in return.

In his E-mail box, Onyeka meditated on these words: *"Onyeka, It's a grievous experience to love someone that never loves you in return. This is exactly what God experienced with His children too. His love for His children made him give up his life so endlessly, that His children may have life and be happy. God gave everything He had to give, especially His word so that His children may be safe and free from the enemy of their salvation. But what did He get in return for His goodness? He got betrayal and all manners of sinfulness. So many Christians claim to love God but love Satan, the enemy because they obey Him by living sinful lives. I understand how you feel and always know that God experiences that pain too. Onyeka, what is yours would definitely come. If Raaluchi is yours, she would be with you in the end, come what may. You should stop hurting and give yourself a treat. You are more precious than gold and don't you ever forget that."*

Onyeka smiled as soon as he finished reading his mail. The mail was from his spiritual director, a Catholic priest, his very good Facebook friend and a pen pal. His name was Father Pius Lim from Boston. Onyeka never missed reading his interesting homilies that he always publish in the internet and he had accepted without any delay to be Onyeka's spiritual director when Onyeka asked him for it.

CHAPTER SIX

"I TOLD YOU that that girl is irresponsible but you didn't believe me; now, see what she has done to you. You now live in misery and isolation. You no longer report to work and your staff are complaining," Ikenna, spoke in a sad tone, pacing around his friend's spacious room. He had been angry when Onyeka gave him the details of Raaluchi's disappointment. This was a girl he abandoned his company and went to take care of, just for her sake. He wished she was present so he could beat her up and force her to eat shit and even flush her down the toilet if he had to. He couldn't fathom what Onyeka had actually seen in this Raaluchi that had succeeded in driving him insane. To him, Onyeka his friend was going nuts because of a girl, a girl that he had regarded worthless, and he couldn't just fold his hands and watch his friend drain in isolation and depression simply because of a girl, a girl that had never deserved his friend. He knew that Onyeka had been starving, and so, he went to his kitchen and cooked for him. He cooked noodles and fried eggs. He ate a portion in the kitchen before he brought some for his friend. But Onyeka did not eat it. He didn't want to eat. He had lost his appetite. His weakness just because of a woman infuriated Ikenna but he controlled himself. He wanted to be nice to him.

"Good Samaritan, you need to freshen up and stop crying like a baby. I know you love her so much but you can't kill yourself because of her. She doesn't deserve you, and she's not even aware that you feel this way," Ikenna said softly to his friend, patting him on his shoulder. He wanted to tell him that it was painful being a Christian and practicing Christianity. To him, active Christians give out their hearts easily and they get hurt easily. They are too soft and emotional. He wanted to tell him to quit being an active Christian. He wanted to tell him to be like him. Pretty girls flocked around him, he used them as he wished but he didn't give his heart to any of them. But when he gave him a second look, he was reaching out for his bible beside his pillow with tears still rolling down from his eyes, and then Ikenna knew that he would never give in to him. Onyeka was addicted to Jesus.

"Can you read out Psalm 125 for me? That particular psalm gives me strength," Onyeka said to Ikenna and he gazed at him, wondering if he knew exactly what he was requesting from him. He wanted to tell him that he would rather call a priest for him but he read out the portion of bible for him, he read it out noncommittally, trying so hard not to hear himself as he read the portion of the bible. Ikenna wanted to please him. He wanted Onyeka to recover from his depression and live his life like a normal human being and if reading out a portion of the bible would help him recover, then, he would do that for him.

With constant advice from Ikenna for Onyeka to freshen up, and adhering to Father Pius's mail, Onyeka finally hearkened and freshened up and resumed work, struggling to forget Raaluchi, but the obsession was still there because Raaluchi had been registered in his brain, and he dreamt about her every night. He took the heartbreak as one of the lessons of life but couldn't resist the cause of the heartbreak. Maybe Raaluchi wasn't the right woman for him, the right woman to make him happy for the rest of his life, but why was he so obsessed with her? Love must be so cruel to fall for someone that never cared about him.

* * * *

Just to be sure that his friend returned to his senses and moved on with his life, Ikenna introduced Onyeka to an ebony beauty in her early thirties and advised him to build a serious relationship with her and marry her. She was slender and tall and had an oval face with a small mouth that looked like a dot. She was Ikenna's cousin. Ikenna insisted that Onyeka deserved a matured woman for marriage and not someone who was so naïve like Raaluchi. Martha was a very nice lady who was caring to the core. She spent weekends in Onyeka's house doing his laundries, cleaning his entire apartment, cooking for him and bringing him his lunch in his office during weekdays. She adored Onyeka like someone who may have truly loved him or someone who was only trying to hold unto a great opportunity of getting married to one of the richest men in town. But Onyeka had no feelings for her even though she was good to him and that was the only reason she allowed her to be in his house. He had no feelings for her.

Onyeka had only agreed to date Martha just to please his friend Ikenna and leave him with a feign conviction that he had moved on with his life so that he wouldn't have to worry about him anymore, but he still couldn't forget Raaluchi, even though she broke his heart. He was willing to wait for Raaluchi. He believed she was for him and she would come back to him. Onyeka broke up with Martha when she began to ask more than Onyeka could afford to give her. To her, if she got Onyeka to impregnate her, he would have no choice but to marry her and forget about Raaluchi who never cared about him. And so, she began to monitor her ovulation periods, to wear bomb shorts that exposed her curved hips and strapless tops that exposed her flat belly and navel, just for the eyes of Onyeka to see, but, he had seen them and had refused to fall for them. Somehow, Martha wondered if he was a stone or a human being.

One Friday night, on her ovulation, she decided to go to Onyeka's room since she had waited for him to make a move to her but to no avail. She entered the room when Onyeka approved her knock. He looked at her and then looked away, regaining his focus on the newspaper he was reading before she entered his room. He was lying on his back and was engulfed with the information he was getting on the first page of his newspaper about the death of Muhammed Yusuf: Nigeria's Boko Haram Chief. Again, he failed to notice her short white night gown with a spaghetti hand and a V.neck that revealed her cleavages and big breasts. She walked psychedelically to Onyeka and lay beside him on his large bed. That was the first time she had dared to enter his room and lie beside him. He murmured something, a vague tacit objection, as she moved closer to him and slowly closed his newspaper and took his hand in hers. He was aware of her intentions, and he muttered: 'I'm in love with someone else," with that, he turned his back on her.

"How long are you going to tell me that you are in love with someone else? Why are you even keeping faith for her? We are supposed to get married and I love you. When will you stop deluding yourself by waiting for that girl to come back to you? She doesn't love you. Please, get that into your head," Martha spoke furiously in Onyeka's bedroom when she couldn't get Onyeka's attention. She was frowning and murmuring something about Onyeka keeping faith for a girl that did not care about him, and then, she rolled over to the edge of the bed, their backs facing each other.

"I was only in this relationship because of my friend and not that I have feelings for you. I never proposed to you, Martha. I appreciate the fact that you are good to me but it still does not change the fact that I don't want to marry you because I'm in love with another."

"Onyeka, please I love you very much and I promise to be a good wife. You'll get to love me soon. Please let's get married." Martha diverted her furiousness to gentility, moving closer to onyeka to face him.

"Martha, I can't marry you. You are a good woman and I'm sure you'll find love in the future."

"Onyeka, please don't do this to me. Just make love to me and pretend that I'm Raaluchi. I can even answer Raaluchi for your sake, if that's what you want," She spoke softly to him, caressing his face, then his neck and his hairy chest.

"Martha, we are not bound by any legal rights to do this. Please forget about it. I can't do what you want from me, I'm sorry. I can't make love to you and I can't get married to you while my heart is longing for someone else. I shouldn't have started this relationship at all. It's all because of Ikenna my friend who thinks he's only doing me a favour. You are a good woman and I'm sure you'll find love in the future." Onyeka's words were like a bomb to her. No man had ever turned her down in bed and she also knew full well that he was breaking up with her.

"Go to hell," Martha spat the words to his face and burst in tears. With that, she briskly walked out of his bedroom and slammed the door. Onyeka wanted to go after her and console her but he didn't. He did the right thing, he presumed. Martha was not his and can never be his. Martha dialed Ikenna's phone number in the guest room and spoke vehemently to him without minding if she was shouting at that late hour of the night.

"What kind of bush man did you introduce me to? Oh gosh, he just turned down my sex appeal...what I'm sure men want from women...what kind of man will need a certificate before making love to a woman? Are you sure he's okay? He's such a bush man!" Martha spoke in exasperation. She flung her hair net as far away as possible and ruffled her scruffy braids, looking haggard. When she hung up without trying to hear a word from Ikenna, the words of her mother rang a bell to her ears: "you better find a rich man to hook up with you in marriage this year, because we can't share the same roof from next year. You didn't make a good result in school and you can't get a job. You have become a liability to me." Martha heaved a long sigh of frustration. After series of heartbreak from the men she had dated, she had approached her cousin Ikenna to help her find someone to settle down with her, and Ikenna did help, but it wasn't working. It just wasn't working. Martha left

Onyeka's house very early in the morning and never came back again and Onyeka heaved a sigh of relief and hoped she would understand.

* * * *

Mummy was in her provision store when Mama Echezona, one of the tenants came to her with a beaming face and announced the miracle which God performed for her only child who had a hole in the heart. Mama Echezona was a very plumpy woman who was always wearing native wears: abada gowns and long skirts with matching scarfs. She was a hair stylist and had a beauty salon beside Mummy's provision store. She was dark complexioned and she had large brown front teeth that she wasn't ashamed to hide whenever she talked and laughed too much in her usual gossip with some women in her salon. She always gossiped about fat mothers who forced themselves to be like teenagers in their dressing patterns; who preferred to wear tight trousers that revealed their big buttocks, to wearing free gowns. As she gossiped, she would point at the women she was referring to: fat women on trousers, passing by the road.

She was in Mummy's shop, telling her that she had been to several hospitals but the doctors told her that her son needed surgery for the heart to be corrected. She had forbidden all of them because she was sure that her son would be healed by the God of Pastor Jacob and her faith had really saved her. The woman danced in Mummy's shop and her buttocks heaved up and down in a funny way.

"Let my enemies come and see what Ja has done for me. The God of Pastor Jacob has finally healed my son. He doesn't gasp anymore," Mama Echezona said happily as she danced.

Mummy was attracted to this miracle that God performed on Echezona, a boy of twelve years old and Mummy took the address of the church from Mama Echezona. If God had used this -Pastor Jacob to heal a twelve year old boy, she was convinced that her daughter's demons must be cast out by him.

"Mama Echezona, I'm so happy for you," Mummy said happily, smiling widely at Mama Echezona who started dancing all over again, singing praises in Igbo Language to the God of Pastor Jacob: *Jehova bu Onye oma mu o, Onye oma mu o...Jehova bu Ogwo oria mu o...Onye oma mu o. Jehova is my helper...my helper... Jehova is my healer...my helper.*

"So, you cannot spray money on me for dancing, *eh*, Mama Raaluchi," Mama Echezona said to Mummy in a fast-breathing manner. She sat down on a plastic chair in Mummy's shop, still fast breathing, trying to recover from her dance that had taken her breath away. She was trying to muster up her strength. She was sweating profusely. Mummy opened her small fridge and offered Mama Echezona a chilled bottle of Malt.

"Mama Raaluchi, you have gums in your hand o." Mama Echezona said, as soon as she took the drink from Mummy. Mummy looked at her palm, curious to see the gums on it, but Mama Echezona laughed at her, and then, Mummy understood what she meant, and told her that she couldn't give her money to her just because of a dance, and if she must answer a stingy woman because of it, then, so be it. Just then, a skinny dark skinned teenage girl on a tight black trouser and a red *show back* top entered Mummy's shop looking annoyingly anxious. She didn't greet the women. She just started speaking to Mama Echezona, grimacing and touching her newly styled Ghana Weaving.

"I've been waiting in your salon. Someone told me to meet you here. I need to loose this weaving and fix a weavon. I saw my enemy in a Super Market this morning, and I noticed that she was wearing my hair style. I don't want her to feel that I copied her style. I don't want her to feel that I like her too much or want to make peace with her. So please, let's start. I want to go back to the Super Market today and show off my new style of hair to her, because I'm sure she'll still be there," The girl said fastly, as though she was talking to her mate. She was rolling her eyes, moving her legs in anxiety and flaunting her black designer hand bag.

"Eziokwu? Really? You really think I have that kind of time to play stupid games with you. Look at this tiny thing o. So, because you saw your enemy with your style of hair, you want me to loose this fine weaving that I made this morning and start all over again with a weavon? You are very stupid. Get out of here, before you spoil my mood." Mama Echezona said, and hissed loudly before taking a sip of her drink.

"Won't I pay you for it?" The girl said, sizing Mama Echezona with her strong questioning look, dissing, her artificial eye lashes moving up and down. And in her facial expression, was the question: 'Am I not trying to help you come out of your poverty?'

"You want to buy my time for stupid reasons. I'm very perfect in what I do. I don't look for customers and I don't need your money. Get out of this place before I kill you and give your enemy to eat!" Mama Echezona yelled at her, wishing to break the bottle of Malt on her head. The girl hissed and left, muttering something about a lazy woman who prefers leisure to making money.

"Can I say that children of this modern age lack respect, or that our jobs lack respect? Mummy said, and stood up to attend to a customer that entered to buy a tin of milk. The next moment, she sat beside Mama Echezona asking her curiously about the miracle that God of Pastor Jacob peformed on her son and how the miracle happened.

"Mama Raaluchi, Ja Jehova the God of Pastor Jacob is a very powerful God. His prayer warriors prayed for my son after they held a dry fasting for him. When we finally met Pastor Jacob, he gave my son a big bottle of Olive Oil to drink, and told us to go home and testify. My son is healed. The God of Pastor Jacob has indeed healed my son. He is no more gasping. He is totally healed," Mama Echezona said in excitement, revealing her huge front teeth that begged to be hidden. Mummy watched her with smiles, moved by her testimony and curious to take Raaluchi there.

* * * *

Raaluchi refused to go with Mummy to meet Pastor Jacob but after Mummy pleaded with her to understand that they were only seeking for a solution to her problems, she agreed. At the gate of the church, the address of the church was boldly engraved in coloured letters, on a white cloth that lay horizontally on the gate: "PASTOR JACOB'S MIRACULOUS MINISTRY". Raaluchi noticed that they had come on a testimony day because she had read the inscription at the church entrance: *'You are welcome to our evening of great testimonies'.* It was on a Wednesday, one of the days in the month of September 2009.

In the church, the drummers drummed to the rhythm of the song that some women were singing. It was almost half an hour before a woman came up to the altar and danced. Her body looked shriveled and her moist wrapper looked as though it was slowly loosening from her waist. She signaled to the drummers and singers to stop and there was an absolute silence in the church before she spoke through the microphone: "Praise Ja! Papa Adaora, my husband always beat me up whenever the soup I prepared got sour, because he doesn't joke with his big belly at all. He would give me blows on my cheeks that I would look for a good chemist store to treat my wounds. Early this morning, I hurriedly left for the market. I was almost at the market square when I remembered that I did not warm the soup I cooked last night. I couldn't go back home because the road was too far and I would have made a bad market if I had decided to go back home, but Ja saved me from what would have been another traumatic blow from my husband. Earlier this evening, as soon as I was sure that I've made a good sum for today's market, I rushed home to check the soup, but to my greatest surprise, the soup did not get sour! It did not sour o! praise Ja!!" The woman shouted in excitement, waving her right hand for Ja, and the congregation chanted "Halleluya!"

Raaluchi chuckled and wondered how sarcastic and funny a testimony in Pastor Jacob's church could be. Somehow, she became discouraged. After the series of testimonies, Mummy asked some people in the church how to see Pastor Jacob privately for some deliverance prayers and she was told to meet Pastor Jacob's prayer warriors first for one cannot go to the doctor without meeting a nurse first. The prayer warriors in the church were hungry-looking. They were wearing extra large shirts in their skinny bodies and their trousers were drawn up, just on their bellies, and were tied up tightly with belts. And they were carrying heavy bibles. Mummy had to be informed by one of the prayer warriors that she had to pay the sum of sixty thousand naira; money for the three days dry fasting which the prayer warriors would hold for Raaluchi and the rest of the money was consultation fee to see the mighty Pastor Jacob. Mummy paid immediately and they were asked to return after three days.

After three days, the prayer warriors circled Raaluchi and shouted an intercessory prayer to her ears: "You stubborn marine spirits, you must leave this body whether you like it or not! Die in the name of Ja! Ja Jehova!" and they hit her head and ears with their heavy bibles that gave her a wracked headache and ear pain that aggravated the voices. The voices began to scream in her, repeating after the prayer warriors every word of prayer they were saying, that Raaluchi had to scream along. Mummy smiled to herself, grateful to God that at least the demons were responding to the prayers and soon, they would all leave her daughter's body. On the third day of the deliverance prayer, Raaluchi and Mummy saw Pastor Jacob in his office. As they settled down inside the office, Raaluchi savoured the puny office and noticed that the calendars with the faces of Jesus Christ and St Michael the arch angel were hung line by line on the wall. Pastor Jacob gave Raaluchi a big bottle of Olive oil to drink the contents in his presence and instructed her to shout 'Ja!' in between the gulps of Olive oil. Raaluchi hesitated, but Mummy assured her that it was a blessed sacramental and that she should not be afraid. Raaluchi nodded and did just as she was instructed by Pastor Jacob.

"Say Ja!" Pastor Jacob instructed Raaluchi after she had drunk the big bottle of Olive oil.

"Ja!" Raaluchi shouted and the voices shouted back at her and Raaluchi gave a start because she discovered that the prayers did not yield any changes, because she was still hearing the voices. Raaluchi had to speak up to Pastor Jacob and he laughed and simply told her to have faith for Ja was in control and he wouldn't hear the voices after that very day. Raaluchi believed and went home with Mummy, but the voices did not disappear as Pastor Jacob said. Mummy was shattered and confused.

Two weeks after Mama Echezona came to testify to Mummy about the miracle that God of Pastor Jacob performed on her son, she came back to Mummy's shop with tears. It was a very grievous morning for her as she wept bitterly in Mummy's shop. Echezona her son had kicked the bucket last night. A neighbour had volunteered to take the corpse to DIVINE HEALTH SPECIALIST HOSPITAL in Odoakpu Onitsha, a hospital known for the best attention anyone desires to have and for its affordable rate. Some people referred to it as 'a small heaven' that God gave to the poor and the rich. In the hospital, a Post Mortem was carried out, and it was discovered that Echezona had died of a severe hole in the heart. Doctor Kene, the doctor that carried out the Post Mortem happened to be the same doctor that advised Mama Echezona to attempt a surgery on her son but Mama Echezona refused, claiming that the God of Pastor Jacob was in control. Papa Echezona almost strangled his wife in the hospital for the death of their son. He had returned from Italy after hearing the terrible news. To him, the most painful part of it was that he sent money for his son's medical treatment without the slightest idea that his wife squandered the money on Pastor Jacob's Prayer Ministry.

"Woman, your faith is so blind. We the doctors are agents in the hands of God. God only heals humanly impossible ailments. You ought to be shaved of your ignorance," Doctor Kene said furiously to Mama Echezona, his eyes blinking consistently. He was furious at Mama Echezona's mentality about 'science and religion.' Doctor Kene had an average height, and was red skinned in complexion because he was born with albinism. Mama Echezona started rolling on the floor of the hospital, with tears streaming down her cheeks. Doctor Kene left her to roll on the floor of his hospital's hallway and then, entered his office to get busy with other things. He was still furious, and so, he couldn't concentrate on anything in his office. He was good at surgery, and he knew full well that he would have saved Echezona's life if only he was given a chance. He hissed loudly in deep furiousity, and then, he reached out to his Blackberry cell phone and posted a note on his Facebook page, just to set his heart free from this furiousity, very sure that his friends would comfort him with useful comments: *I lost my patient; a twelve year old boy because of his mother's archaic mentality about science. Some people in this modern era believe that science is demonic and poisonous, and so, they wait on their pastors to cure them with 'prophesy and sacramentals.' I ask myself these questions: 'If all aiments are cured with prophesy and sacramentals, then why is there a hospital and why does God still breed doctors in this world?'*

To add salt to the injury, Papa Echezona ordered his wife to pack her things and leave his house.

CHAPTER SEVEN

RAALUCHI CONTINUED FLIRTING with Chiedu. She had stopped the flirting for sometime because Mummy pleaded with her to stop her affair with Chiedu so that the God of Pastor Jacob can deliver her quickly. To her, since the deliverance prayers did not yield any positive result, she continued with her affair with Chiedu. On the fourteenth day of October 2009, she decided to pay Chiedu a surprise visit in his house just to cook a meal for two and have a romantic day with him to mark her late father's birthday. Raaluchi never missed celebrating her father's birthday, even though her father was dead and since Chiedu reminded her so much about her late father, she felt it was a good thing to celebrate her late father's birthday with him because it would be as though she was actually celebrating it with her father.

When she got to that same house she had been to, the gate man refused her entry in an arrogant manner. That was the same gate man that was there the first time she visited. He was from the Hausa ethnic tribe and he spoke his language very fast with a deep fury like someone who was about to strangle a defenseless person. He ordered Raaluchi to leave. She snapped back at the gateman for such an insult and called him names. Her voice was so loud that the owner of the mansion came out to verify what was amiss. He made it clear to Raaluchi that the house never belonged to Chiedu, and that he lent him the house few months ago just to receive his guest. Raaluchi's heart sank. Her legs trembled so much that she couldn't walk. She called Chiedu on the new line that he gave her and when he heard her speaking in tears, he discovered that she had found out his tricks and then he hissed and hung up.

Just to be sure that the owner of the mansion was not lying to her, she waited through out the day but Chiedu did not show up and she was led by her perception to go in search of him in the hotel he seldom took her to. The receptionist confirmed his presence in Room 2 and she caught him in the act with another girl. She tried to fight with the girl and Chiedu pounced on her with brutal blows and kicks for ruining his fun. The situation was untenable for Raaluchi. Chiedu pushed her heavily out of the room and she landed on the hallway floor with a banging head that she didn't believe she actually survived it, and then, she was convinced that the only man she had thought that loved her in return, the only man that had reminded her so much of her dear father was just a beast.

She felt like the most stupid girl in the world as she walked slowly and shamefully out of the hotel, with a battered face and trembling legs, praying she wouldn't be knocked down by a vehicle again. She was completely deranged. She finally mounted a motor cycle and went home. She attempted suicide by hanging herself in her room. To her, life had been so unfair to her, God hated her and nobody loves her. The only person that loved her was Nnanyelugo but he was gone and never to come back to her, and now she wanted nothing else but to join her father wherever he was. It was pointless to remain alive. She was so lucky to be rescued by her mother who had entered her room just at the right time.

"Why do you want to kill yourself Raaluchi? So, if I haven't entered your room, you would have killed yourself?" Mummy startled with a frown when she saw the bruises on her daughter's face. "Oh my God, what happened to your face?"

"The world is wicked, Mum," Raaluchi said mournfully. She was holding the rope that she had attempted suicide with.

Her chest ached and her eyes filled with tears. She had been squashed to a very painful limit.

"So are you," Mummy spoke up plainly looking straight into her eyes and Raaluchi hiccupped between sobs that she had difficulty with breathing and Mummy was moved to console her when she saw how breathless she looked in shedding tears. She made her sit down on her bed to hear her out, and was also moved with tears after she heard her story.

"Raaluchi God loves you so much…right from the onset, but you were so blind to realize it because you had been very depressed, you were so ungrateful to God and you were faithless."

"If God loves me, then why did He take away my father? Why did He give my friend admission into the university and ignored me knowing full well that I'm holier than her?"

"Raaluchi my daughter, please listen carefully to what I'm about to tell you so that you can stop comparing yourself with others." Tears rolled down Raaluchi's cheeks when Mummy told her to watch her fingers and see if they were equal. Raaluchi did and shook her head and then Mummy smiled and heaved a sigh. She took her daughter's hand in hers and began to shed light to her dark mind. Mummy had a long talk with her daughter and for once, Raaluchi was willing to listen and obey without grumbling and walking out.

"The fact is that if we are not grateful concerning our own worth as unique individuals, we will find ourselves competing with anyone who appears to be successful. Life is a wind of destiny and it blows in different directions but the blast we receive from it is never permanent, for everybody receives the test of hard and good times in different ways. The word of God in Galatians 5:26 can be a food for thought for you Raaluchi. This entails the need for Christians to strip themselves from the dress of vain glory, competitive mind and a heart of envy for they are big impediments to our salvation."

Mummy had to shed light on Raaluchi's dark mind by

teaching her the word of God. She told her that God is a God of patience and faith and that, anybody who wanted to worship Him must acquire those qualities. She told her that those qualities were fruits of the Holy Spirit that a true Christian must acquire to carry a cross and follow Jesus Christ in spirit and truth. Mummy told Raaluchi that one can carry a cross through the challenges of life he or she faces. She told her that Jesus Christ carried His heavy cross with faith and patience as He fell three times on His way to calvary but got up and continued His journey, refusing to give up, but, Raaluchi fell with her light cross and gave up, refusing to get up and move on. Mummy made Raaluchi to understand that God loves appreciation and the best way to force Him to action was to praise Him with a grateful heart.

"My dear, showing a heart of gratitude to God is the easiest way of carrying a cross and the greatest faith one can show to God," Mummy said to her daughter with an arm around her shoulders.

"But what can I appreciate God for? Raaluchi asked her mother. She was ready to give her mother a chance to counsel her. She was ready to submit to her mother. Apart from the pains she was feeling from the bruises that Chiedu gave her, she felt as though Mummy's words were loosing some tangled knots in her. She felt freedom in herself.

"Those things you think are not worth appreciating God are the most important things to God. How can you expect greater things from God when you cannot handle small things first?" Mummy asked her daughter softly and tears began to tickle from Raaluchi's eyes as she listened to her mother. Mummy continued: "Raaluchi, your life is a miracle. If you go to the mortuary, you will understand what I mean. The food you eat is a miracle. There are so many beggars along the streets begging for food. You attended a secondary school and you came home with three awards for your excellence. Have you thanked God for them?" Mummy asked her daughter but she looked at her mother with her mouth agape and tears streamed down to her cheeks. Mummy continued.

Mummy told Raaluchi that God loves His children and He has better plans for them. She told Raaluchi that she should have been grateful because she had all course to glorify God but she quickly gave up just because of a little test of faith. She told her that God had really wanted to know if she really belonged to Him, if she truly served Him in truth or she was just worshiping Him with her lips and not with her heart, and He had delayed the most precious thing in her life: her education, knowing full well that Raaluchi never joked with her studies. He did that just to test her faith.

Also, being a loving God, He knew the best for Raaluchi and was ready to bless her at the appointed time but her mind of comparison and her foolishness just to challenge God disrupted God's plan for her because nobody ever challenged God. Mummy told her daughter that her foolishness had forced her to take the wrong way, a way that God had been avoiding for her just like He warned Adam and Eve to avoid the forbidden fruit but they disobeyed. Raaluchi had disobeyed God by taking the wrong decision that led her to sin: the sin of fornication, an intentional sin. Raaluchi had challenged God with her heart of jealousy, envy and comparison: the common traits of the insecure Christian.

Again, Mummy told Raaluchi the need to strip from the dress of self-righteousness. She told her that a self-righteous person lacks love and cannever show love to a neighbour. She continued to shed light to her.

"True love breeds true repentance, and so, it requires a wholehearted feeling. It requires showing love without discrimination," Mummy said softly to her daughter and she nodded with a feeling of freedom. Mummy continued.

"A self-righteous person lives a life of comparison. A self-righteous person is judgemental. A self- righteous person is a proud person because, 'a show of humility is pride in disguise.'

Mummy also made her to understand the word of God in John 9:41: where Christ stated the need for Christians to maintain their blindness in God and stop claiming to see and understand things that are above their human understanding; the need for Christians to stop taking the position of God by becoming too judgemental in their self-righteousness. Mummy made her daughter to understand that a true Christian ought to follow God with a humble heart (blindness) knowing that He is the Superior God and the perfect Judge.

Mummy told Raaluchi that she should not love anybody more than God because God is the creator of everything and the giver of everything good. He alone decides what to do with his creatures. Mummy further told her that she did not belong to the worldly life; that was why she couldn't escape the disaster she experienced in the hands of her wayward friends in the computer school and Chiedu who all joined to ruin her life. They knew all the strategies of wayward living and they succeeded, but she didn't because she simply didn't belong there. She told Raaluchi that the temptation was of course from the devil and a weapon to destroy her but God wanted to use the temptation which she couldn't overcome to develop her and to teach her that she simply did not belong where she was going…the worldly fun…the beautiful roads of darkness. She belonged to God.

Mummy told her daughter that God is a lover of goodness and what He did, He did for good with no intention to hurt His children. He knew the best for Raaluchi but Raaluchi lacked faith in Him. That was why she didn't observe patience to receive God's blessings: the will of God. Finally, she told her the need for Christians to love God wholeheartedly. She told her that when a Christian loves God wholeheartedly, the person would give God what he/she has to offer Him wholeheartedly, without expecting anything in return, knowing that God is capable of enriching givers with unexpected blessings, without the giver reminding Him of his/her reward.

Mummy and daughter had a long discussion for four hours before they realized that it was late to prepare dinner. They only ate some fruits and went to bed and Mummy promised to take her to the Chemist the next day to treat her bruises without any slightest idea that Raaluchi was excruciating with the bruises and had begun to feel feverish. Mummy couldn't do anything to retaliate what Chiedu did to her daughter because Raaluchi didn't even know where he lived. She had been lost in delusion with her lover and Chiedu had taken advantage of her naivety.

Raaluchi lay beside her Mummy, awash in the words she had fed her with. The words were like a beautiful bright light shimmering all over her body and untangling the knots of darkness in her. That night, she decided to go for a sacrament of reconciliation the next day, to stabilize her relationship with God, but she fainted in the middle of the night because she was so weak and the beatings Chiedu gave her were very severe. Mummy rushed her to DIVINE HEALTH SPECIALIST HOSPITAL by 3.00 am in the morning, saying her 'Divine Mercy Prayer' in her mind, for that time was the hour of mercy. A tenant had actually volunteered to take them to the hospital and Mummy was so grateful to him. Raaluchi was administered a drip in no time and Mummy sat opposite her in the female ward watching her daughter with tears streaming down her cheeks.

Onyeka was actually in the same hospital at that time. He had knocked down an old man, a pedestrian at 9pm, earlier last night. He was careless in driving because he was busy thinking about Raaluchi and wasn't focusing. Mummy saw him at the hospital hallway and gave a start. She was going to check and know if the doctor was free in his office when she saw him. Tears streamed down Mummy's cheeks as she watched him and said: "My son." Onyeka stood up to console her and wondered what she was doing in the hospital at that late hour.

"What is it Mummy, why are you crying? What are you doing here?" Onyeka asked curiously and Mummy kept pointing at

Raaluchi's ward without saying anything but shedding tears and then it dawned on him that Raaluchi might be in danger. He rushed inside the ward and gasped in shock as he saw Raaluchi struggling with her life, looking battered. "Oh my God," he said in shock, clasping a hand over his mouth. His eyes filled with tears. Mummy tapped his shoulder in consolation.

"Who did this to her?" Onyeka asked in fury, tears coursing down his eyes. He wept because he wasn't given a chance to protect her. If only Raaluchi had loved him in return, if only she had chosen him, she wouldn't have been in danger of giving herself to an animal. He couldn't bear to watch the only person he had ever loved lying so lifeless in her sick bed and he wept harder as he moved closer to her bedside.

"Calm down my son…just pull yourself together. I know how much you love her."

"I'm going to sue him to court. That animal has no right to do this to her. This is a young girl that has a future. Does he want to kill her? It was not enough that he took advantage of her… he went ahead to beat her up, abusing her womanhood. Why?"

"Calm down my son"

"No Mummy, don't ask me to calm down. I'm going to do everything to make sure that that idiot rots in jail."

But Mummy told Onyeka that he couldn't do that because Raaluchi had no idea of where he actually lived and didn't know him well enough. She had only fallen helplessly in love with him because he reminded Raaluchi so much of her late father. His name may have even been forged. Raaluchi her daughter knew absolutely nothing about the man that ruined her life.

Onyeka settled the bills for the two patients in the hospital and was always at Raaluchi's bedside talking softly to her, telling her how much he loved her and praying for her. He hoped she heard her in her spirit even though she was unconscious. Onyeka visited Raaluchi regularly for a week buying her provisions, 'get well soon cards' and roses until Raaluchi regained consciousness one Sunday morning. And when she did and saw Onyeka at her side, she froze in guilt and didn't know how to react in his presence. Onyeka was like rays of light shimmering all over her and she was so uncomfortable. Mummy smiled up to her and told her that Onyeka had been by her side and had never left her. She showed her the roses and the provisions he bought for her and Mummy was startled with her mouth agape when Raaluchi screamed for help with her little strength. She screamed in tears. Her scream alerted the nurses at the reception and they came to verify what was amiss.

"I want him out of this place. Tell this man to leave. I don't want to see him," Raaluchi spoke in between sobs.

"Raaluchi, you know I can't leave you like this. Raaluchi I love you and I'll do anything to make you happy…" Onyeka pleaded with tears but Raaluchi locked her eyes and didn't want to look at him anymore. The light was too bright for her and made her very uncomfortable. She insisted that she didn't need Onyeka's presence and the nurses asked him to leave. One of them wondered if he had something to do with the patient's condition just like he almost killed an old man in the male ward. The nurses considered him to be a jerk since all he did was to hurt people.

Onyeka kept calling Mummy on phone to know how Raaluchi fared with her health and Mummy assured him that she was fine but was still on her medications. Mummy told Onyeka that Raaluchi confessed to her that she appreciated what he did for her but she couldn't stand his presence because he made her uncomfortable with mixed feelings of guilt and fear. His presence reminded her of the fact that she went back to her vomit even after God had used him to heal her legs. She considered him too good for her. She had said that she wasn't ready for another relationship, since she had been through a lot, even though she knew Onyeka was totally different from Chiedu. She didn't need a man in her life anymore. All she wanted was to further her education and she wished that God would grant her that. But Onyeka refused to give up on

Raaluchi. She told Mummy that he was willing to wait and that he even wanted her to have the best education in life. He wanted the best for her, anything that would make her happy. He was ready to give her the best in life. All he needed was her friendship, since she didn't want a relationship. He cannot focus without Raaluchi. He wanted to be with her and put a smile on her face and make up for all the pains she had been through in life and in the hands of Chiedu.

* * * *

Raaluchi confessed her sins through the grille and the priest softly gave her a word of advice. The priest was a man blessed with a soft voice, a voice so soft that it was almost like a melody. The priest advised Raaluchi to keep her mind and body holy by avoiding erotic thoughts and daydreams. The priest also advised her to embrace patience in life, depend on God and make friends with godly people that can show the light of a true Christian life and finally, he gave her a penance to do and she left with a free heart as though she had off loaded the heaviest thing in her heart. That night in her dream, she saw rays of light coming from above and shinning down on her. She woke up a happy girl, so pleased that she had regained her friendship with God, for God is light.

CHAPTER EIGHT

RAALUCHI RESUMED CHARISMATIC Ministry meetings and the Ministry threw her a little 'welcome back party' like a prodigal son who had been lost but was finally found. Raaluchi appreciated what they did for her: they never gave up on her, because they still valued her as a member, and they confirmed God's answered prayers for her. They had been fasting and praying for her to come back and she finally did. Raaluchi traveled to Nsukka to apologise to her best friend Nkiruka for all the hurtful words she blurted out on her in her hostel, and Nkiruka accepted her apology with smiles and hugs. Nkiruka admitted how much she had missed Raaluchi in her life. Her life had been empty without her. She also admitted that she never stopped praying for her. They took time discussing about their childhood, and laughed out loud when a particular discussion called for it. Hours later, Raaluchi finally left her friend's hostel, telling her that she had a choir practice to attend at home, for the oncoming charismatic crusade.

That evening, in her room, she recited the song that she had composed for the crusade. The song was titled: TRUE LOVE MAKES A WAY FOR A CHANGE. And in the song, she expressed that everybody is one in God, no matter the difference, and that it is only by showing love to any kind of person, that one can make a change. She expressed that Jesus healed a sick man who had been enslaved in the hands of leprosy. He would have avoided the sick man just like any other person, so as not to contact the disease, but he chose to show love, and with this true love, the sick man was made whole and clean. Raaluchi also went as far as expressing in her song that Jesus showed love to Mary Magdalene the adulterer, even when He would have judged her a sinner and allowed her to die in her sins, just like any other person, but, He made a way for a change by saving her life, and she gave her life to Him and repented from her sins. When she presented the song at the crusade ground that night, she saw tears rolling down the eyes of many people, even the members of the Charismatic Ministry.

* * * *

Onyeka took Amaechi his cousin to Mr Biggs: a fast food joint alongside Nnebisi Road Asaba: a road known for traffics and noisy honks of cars. They settled down for fried rice and chicken and orange juice. The fast food joint was a neat puny building with white marble floor, corralled with tables on white table clothes, and people eating and drinking and talking. Amaechi was a boy in his late teens, easygoing, loving and prayereful. In a few moment of togetherness with Onyeka, Onyeka had come to realize how much Amaechi was like him in his prayer life. They would go to chapel together every Saturday, read and analyze the bible together every night and attend Mass together every Sunday. He did all these willingly, without Onyeka telling him to do them. Amaechi had come to spend the weekend with him in his house again, and since Martha was not available for their meal anymore, Onyeka took him out for dinner. As they enjoyed their food, they talked. Amaechi told him to get married so that he could at least stop eating out, but, Onyeka said that he hadn't found a wife yet. Amaechi chuckled as his mind reached out to Martha in remembrance. He wondered why things didn't work out well between Martha and Onyeka. Martha was a good cook and he had really enjoyed her *ora* soup on one of the weekends he had spent in his cousin's house. He knew that good cooking was one of the qualities of a good wife. To him, the important thing for a man was to feed well. Other flaws can either be tolerated or corrected by the husband. As he thought about Martha, he wondered what must have disqualified her in winning his brother's heart, and then he focused on her prayer life. Amaechi knew that Martha detested prayers and every detail of it. He knew she joined them in prayers just to please Onyeka. He could remember the night they said the twenty decades of rosary in the living room. She had heaved deep sighes, and finally muttered: 'are we not supposed to be concluding this prayer?'

"What happened between you and Martha?" Amaechi asked Onyeka after he took a sip of his orange juice.

"She just left the house because she couldn't stand the heat in my house, besides, I don't love her," Onyeka said. His mind reached out to Raaluchi again, the only one he loves. His chest heaved and his heart began to race. He remembered the first time he saw her. As though Amaechi saw the picture in his mind, he suddenly began to talk about Raaluchi.

"That runaway girl in my parish is back to Charismatic Ministry and we threw a welcome back party for her," Amaechi said to his cousin as he tried to cut his chicken with his knife and his fork held it so tight to prevent it from falling from his plate. "She really surprised me when she sang impressively with biblical passages at the crusade ground last week. Her song really moved me and I couldn't help but cry," Amaechi added.

Onyeka heaved a sigh of helplessness as he remembered her. She had refused to see him or even speak to him when he visited her at home. She didn't want any other man in her life but he was willing to wait for her until she was ready. The rest of the things Amaechi told him landed on deaf ears of an absent minded person. Onyeka was staring into spaces with dancing eyes and all manner of emotions churning inside him. Raaluchi's picture kept revealing itself in his mind as he battled with his emotions. All of a sudden, his head ached painfully and he smiled sheepishly and everything around him suddenly became Raaluchi, Raaluchi dinning with him, Raaluchi moving around the restaurant, Raaluchi smiling at him, revealing her dimples and dim eyes, Raaluchi thanking him in a boutique with brief hugs and Raaluchi sleeping off in his car after a long day outing. He shrieked in pains with fire in his eyes that everybody in the restaurant gazed at him. And just before Amaechi reached over to his cousin, he slumped and fainted. Amaechi was confused as he watched his brother spread on the floor like pieces of rags. He pleaded for help. He didn't know how to carry his tall and plump elder brother alone. Some men at the restaurant helped to carry Onyeka to his car and Amaechi drove him to a nearby hospital alongside Nnebisi Road, and at the entrance of the hospital was an inscription: SPECIAL CARE SPECIALIST HOSPITAL, ASABA.

Onyeka lay critically ill after he had revived his consciousness through the help of the drip he had taken. The only name he could call was Raaluchi. Amaechi watched him, looking puzzled with puzzled lines on his forehead. He wondered if he had known Raaluchi, his sister in Christ, if she had been the reason for his faint. He reported it to the doctor. The doctor was a young man with pimpled face and a nice accent. His name was Dr. Chima. Later at night, he confirmed that Onyeka was love sick and he must have been madly in love with someone that his brain had been affected due to a frequent thought about that particular person. Dr. Chima had carried out an Xray on Onyeka and he was able to reveal his discovery about Onyeka's damaged brain to Amaechi. The doctor explained to Amaechi that the 'dopamine' in his brain gave him the focus on Raaluchi due to his excessive thoughts about her. He explained that Onyeka had been obsessed with Raaluchi. He also explained that when someone is in love, the brain circulating is linked with 'panic' and 'anxiety' and the release of 'dopamine' and 'cortisol' divert blood away from the gut. Sometimes, it affects the normal heart beat because of the level of obsession, and when the heart beat is affected, it leads to 'syncope' as a result of quickened heart rate. That was exactly what caused Onyeka's unconsciousness.

"That is the nature of love. Your brother is just being love sick and you better find that Raaluchi because that is the only medicine to his sickness," Dr. Chima said.

Amaechi had to go to Raaluchi's house with the direction of a friend in the Charismatic Ministry first thing the next morning and he was lucky to see Raaluchi coming back from morning mass. She was humming a song, her missal and rosary in her left hand. Raaluchi welcomed Amaechi with smiles and teased him for sleeping like a log of wood that he forgot to attend the morning mass and they had a chat. Amaechi gave her his testimony from the song that she presented at the crusade ground: he was deeply moved and converted to see a bight light that he had never seen in the Charismatic Ministry. Raaluchi thanked God. Amaechi and Raaluchi were age mates and so they got along very well. They had talked for twenty minutes before Amaechi finally asked her if she knew his cousin and described Onyeka. He even called his name and Raaluchi concurred with an odd expression, wondering how little the world can be for Amaechi to be Onyeka's brother. Her mind drifted into reminiscing what Onyeka had told her about a cousin of his that invited him to the Charismatic Ministry crusade. She believed that cousin of his to be Amaechi.

Raaluchi had been thinking of going to Onyeka's company to see him and have a talk with him, and explain things better to him, but, she changed her mind knowing full well that Onyeka will never let her leave his office without her accepting to be friend with him. Amaechi pleaded with Raaluchi to save his brother's life for he was madly in love with her. He explained the previous night incidence just because he was obsessed with her and Raaluchi agreed to go with him to the hospital after refusing for personal reasons. Mummy had joined in the plea, telling her daughter that it was rather time for her to reciprocate what Onyeka did for her by saving her life in a serious accident.

Mummy danced in the kitchen when Raaluchi finally agreed to go to the hospital with Amaechi. She muttered something about destiny being delayed but never denied as she made custard for breakfast.

Raaluchi left with Amaechi to the hospital after they had eaten fried plantain and custard for breakfast. She thought of Onyeka on their way to the hospital. She liked him as a person, he was godly and she knew he loved her, but she cannot possibly accept to be in a relationship with him. She cannot give him anything more than friendship. She learned a lesson from her previous mistake of letting someone take advantage of her naivety and innocence simply because of her frustration, her anger with God: the anger that had made her act on impulse. Raaluchi was moved to tears as soon as she saw Onyeka lying critically helpless on his bed and just immediately, Onyeka stared, as though he felt her presence. He was on a second drip, a drip to calm his heart rate. Onyeka smiled widely as soon as he saw Raaluchi. His belly churned and his heart danced in excitement.

Raaluchi sat down at his bedside and smiled at him saying, "I'm here for you now." Onyeka touched her fingers and tears dripped down his eyes.

"I love you Raaluchi…what can I do to make you love me? What can I do to make you care? Please tell me and I'll do it," Onyeka spoke hoarsely. Raaluchi was speechless and he reached over and wiped his tears. Amaechi watched them and confirmed that Onyeka his brother must have truly fallen in love with Raaluchi that he shed tears for her - what men hardly do. The doctor discharged Onyeka as soon as he was done with his second drip. He also had a talk with Raaluchi about Onyeka's condition, repeating exactly what he told Amaechi and Raaluchi promised to handle the situation well so that he wouldn't have to go back to syncope. She promised to make him happy except where it will lead to sin against God. She wasn't ready for that, even though she knew Onyeka to be a godly person.

CHAPTER NINE

RAALUCHI AND ONYEKA continued their chapel visitation, committing their friendship to God in prayer, and other outings that made them very happy, especially Onyeka who couldn't let a day pass by without spending it with Raaluchi. Gradually, they became fond of each other but Raaluchi was being too careful not to open her heart for intimacy by letting the beautiful places Onyeka took her to and his sensational words get into her and turn her on. Onyeka's syncope ceased and he was happier than ever. He was grateful to God for bringing Raaluchi back to his life, at least he can improve her faith in God and he can also make her happy. Onyeka offered Raaluchi a job in his company as his Personal Assistant, since she had passed out of computer school. He did it to keep her busy so that she wouldn't have the time to stay at home and think of how useless she was for not being in school with her mates. Raaluchi became the Personal Assistant to the C.E.O of Fanco Pharmaceutical Company Asaba, a job to hold unto, until she gained admission into a university.

Raaluchi was very happy and she shared the good news with her mother who danced and praised God and reminded Raaluchi that Onyeka really meant well so she should prepare to answer the wedding bells. Raaluchi only smiled at her mother as she watched her dance. Mummy was shaking her waist and she bent so low that her wrapper let loose. Raaluchi wasn't surprised at all about her mother's continuous happiness ever since she regained her friendship with Onyeka. To her, her mother was just 'a Marriage Freak.' And she knew that she desperately wanted her to get married to Onyeka.

* * * *

Raaluchi's main duty as Onyeka's Personal Assistant was to help him go through his company files and go out with him for lunch. Raaluchi was alone in Onyeka's office one Friday morning when she received a call from Onyeka. He told her that he had to dash to the pharmacists' monthly meeting in Enugu. He promised her not to be long. She had actually come to Onyeka's office to keep some files and for once, Raaluchi felt like staying in his office in his absence just to feel the warmth and richness of the luxurious spacious office. She had nothing to do for Onyeka that morning, and so, she began to open his drawers searching for what she was unsure of. She had opened the third drawer when she saw a big album. It was a very beautiful album, green in colour and decorated with red hearts. She smiled at the attractiveness of the album and was tempted to flip the pages of the album open. She gasped when she saw her picture painted so perfectly.

The art work revealed a vivid description of a depressed damsel singing in tears with a microphone. She was moved to tears as she watched it. She couldn't believe that Onyeka had actually painted her and had been with the picture as a personal belonging. She flipped more pages to know if she would see another picture but she didn't. Her picture was the only one in the big album. Her tears began to tickle when she read the note inscribed just below the picture.

Is love this racing heartbeat I felt the first time I set my eyes on you? Is it this frequent uncontrollable feeling of a huge responsibility for you? Is it this exciting conviction to know that the most beautiful encounters are those with painful tears waiting for the right person to wipe them off and make them happy?

Raaluchi reread the words over and over again and her tears dripped on the page like a wet leaf dropping water on the sandy floor. For an instant, she was touched. The words moved her heart. She wished she wasn't touched by those powerful words but she was and for some moment, she remembered Chiedu and wondered if Onyeka was also trying to play tricks on her, but she doubted that and took it as a misconception because she hadn't stayed in Onyeka's office, simply because she was avoiding being alone with him and Onyeka had been with this album for a long time, since she sang on the crusade ground on the nineteenth day of December 2008. That day was her birthday and she had volunteered to sing for her birthday. She wiped her tears, placed back the album in the drawer and went back to her office thinking about those powerful words and Onyeka.

* * * *

Raaluchi took ill and missed work for some weeks. Her absence was such that Onyeka became so worried. He never ceased visiting her at home every evening and buying her roses and a 'get well soon' card. Raaluchi had refused to go to the hospital, telling Onyeka that it was just a minor sickness that she could handle but Onyeka was worried about her. One afternoon, Mummy was flapping Raaluchi's washed clothes and was placing them in her box as Raaluchi watched her, looking pale on her sick bed. There were noises coming from the next yard. A woman would stand on her veranda and call someone living upstairs on the third floor. She would shout the name and deliver her message even when she got no response: "Mama Ada! Please come and take your money! I did not see *okpa* in the market…you better be fast before I use the money for my children's tea!" The woman living downstairs would shout so loudly as though it was a big offence to go upstairs and deliver her message to Mama Ada.

"I wonder why we can never live without noise in this area. This is one of the reasons I want you to get married, so that you can live comfortably as a landlady in a rich man's house, a house where you wouldn't be distracted by noises," Mummy said confidently, as though she was sure that Onyeka was rich enough to own a mansion; a mansion that tolerated no noise. She carried Raaluchi's box to the wardrobe and just then, Raaluchi got up from the bed, eager to throw up. Just before she could get to the bathroom, she threw up on the terrazzo floor. Mummy watched her closely. "Did Onyeka touch you?" Mummy finally asked her daughter curiously, after she had hesitated for so long to let loose the question from her trap, after she had noticed how different her daughter looked." *Gwanu m,* tell me," Mummy said in Igbo language.

"No, Mum. Onyeka had told me since I decided to have a serious relationship with him that he wouldn't touch me until we are married…"

"*Ezigbo nwoke!* Good man! That man is a godly gentle man and I like him for you," Mummy took words from Raaluchi without allowing the girl to finish up what she was saying.

"But I have a bad news for him."

"*E kwuzina.* Stop saying that. What bad news?"

"I'm pregnant for Chiedu."

"*I si gini?* What did you just say?"

Mummy released her entire body and landed forcefully on Raaluchi's plastic chair, in such a way that the chair jerked, pleading with Mummy to handle it with care. She wept bitterly with her hands on her head. Raaluchi watched her mournfully, wishing that she could change situations. Raaluchi had actually conceived on her last romantic meeting with Chiedu, on one of the days in the month of September. Chiedu had taken her to a hotel, after lying to her that his elder sister's kids were on holiday in his house and they would be a big distraction to them, without any slightest idea that the house wasn't Chiedu's. Raaluchi had agreed in her little world of naivety and false love. Mummy contemplated on her keeping the baby and getting rid of it. Keeping the baby would be a big impediment to her getting married to Onyeka and getting rid of the baby was a mortal sin. She shrieked in confusion as tears streamed down her cheeks.

To Raaluchi, life was a stage and her performance had ended. There was absolutely no way she could get married to a man who was crazy about her and who she had finally wanted to marry, with another man's baby in her womb. To her, God was unfair to her again because He could have as well washed away the baby like He washed away her sins with His precious blood. She lost faith and wavered in doubts. As she wavered in doubts and got furious at God, she discovered that a knot was forming inside her and holding her captive. The voices echoed: 'You are a big disgrace! You are worthless and nothing good will ever come out of you!' Raaluchi got more infuriated, believing in the voices. She screamed out her anger and Mummy rushed to her and held her. She had disappointed her father again. She was indeed worthless. She thought.

Raaluchi stopped receiving Onyeka's phone calls after Mummy warned her seriously not to kill the innocent baby in her womb for she wouldn't stand the implications if she did. Mummy told her daughter to allow the will of God to be done. Onyeka's syncope repeated when he finally received Raaluchi's text message putting an end to their relationship. Raaluchi had written that she never deserved him, and that they weren't meant to be together. Onyeka ended up in a hospital and pleaded with Amaechi to tell Raaluchi that he would die if she didn't come to see him and Amaechi carried out the message. Raaluchi and Mummy went to see him and just with Raaluchi beside him on his love sick bed, offering him a feigned smile, he felt relieved and recovered from his syncope.

* * * *

Raaluchi finally opened up to Onyeka about her pregnancy a week after Onyeka's recovery from the syncope and Onyeka was completely deranged as he listened to Raaluchi. His eyes filled with tears and it dropped slowly, like a wet leaf dripping water on a sandy floor. They were in his office, sitting opposite each other, their hands enclosed in each other's, and their wet faces facing each other so close that it was almost like a kiss magnet. Raaluchi wanted to be with him in his office, to observe a special moment with him because she knew for sure that she would be leaving him soon, for good. If she was going to remember her last meeting with him, she wanted to remember it in his luxurious office.

"This is the reason I wrote that we weren't made for each other. Onyeka, I'm so sorry. I can't marry you," Raaluchi told him softly with tears rolling down to her cheeks, praying that Onyeka wouldn't faint again or even die because of her. Onyeka wept. He tore his heart in tears begging God in his mind to take control for he could never live without Raaluchi. Life without Raaluchi was a huge punishment to him. Raaluchi was irreplaceable and with tears streaming down to their cheeks, Raaluchi left his office as Onyeka watched her with drained heart. He couldn't help it. *"Why am I this unlucky? Just when Raaluchi had finally begun to build a relationship with me, this unwanted pregnancy came up to be an obstacle."* He said in his mind. He was shattered and confused. He had blur visions and he quit work for that day, notifying the staff that he was indisposed.

Onyeka did not wink an eye that night. He couldn't sleep. He needed to talk to someone and he couldn't even count on Ikenna for he had detested Raaluchi right from the start, and he had been furious with Onyeka when he discovered his reunion with Raaluchi. Ikenna had accused him of being a weak man. He remembered Father Pius and sent him an E-mail telling him exactly how he felt about the problem that wanted to be an obstacle to his relationship with Raaluchi. He waited for Father Pius's reply and when he finally did, he smiled at what he sent to him.

Love has a price to pay and a sacrifice to make. Christ wasn't responsible for our sins but he died for them so that we can share in his righteousness.

Onyeka understood exactly what Father Pius meant and he searched his heart and discovered that it was what his heart wanted for the woman he loved. He wasn't responsible for Raaluchi's pregnancy but he must accept her in that condition and marry her so that he can shed light to her dark life as a responsibility to carry out for her. He would do it because he loved her.

Raaluchi on her side couldn't sleep. Her pillow was wet with tears and she had refused to answer Onyeka's calls. He had been calling her since 8pm and it was 12 mid night when he finally stopped. Raaluchi was very scared that she wondered if he had syncope again. She wished she could go to his house but she didn't know where he lived.

* * * *

Raaluchi was startled when she saw Onyeka sitting on a plastic chair opposite her bed and she wondered how he got in before she remembered that she left her room door unlocked. She didn't even realize that it was dawn and that Onyeka had been in her room since 6am watching her sleep with her swollen eyes.

"Good morning," Raaluchi said, stifling a yawn. She was so weak.

"Good morning my beloved, how was your night?"

"Awful…I was so worried that you would faint again until I prayed for you before I finally slept off. How was your night?"

"It was terrible. The worst night I've ever had. I didn't sleep at all, not when you did not pick my calls."

Raaluchi watched him sympathetically and pleaded with him to try and forget her for she could never get married to him with another man's baby lying in her womb. She was going to give the baby up for adoption when she was due. She was going to stay calm and wait for God to decide what he wanted to do with her life.

"Do you still love Chiedu?" Onyeka asked her searchingly,

searching her eyes to know if they would react and dance in excitement like someone who nurtured feelings but they didn't and he heaved a sigh of relief.

"No…not after what he did to me."

"Oh gosh, I'm so sorry, you are such a baby and you don't even know what love is. I shouldn't have asked," Onyeka chuckled after he had spoken to Raaluchi and she mimicked him. Her mimicry made her face look funny: the twisted mouth and the wrinkled forehead appeared funny.

"You are silly, Onyeka," Raaluchi said and chuckled too and Onyeka watched her fixedly and searchingly for a moment, regaining a serious mood. Their eyes met and held for a moment before Raaluchi quickly withdrew hers. Onyeka opened her room door, as widely open as possible, trying so hard to control his emotions.

"Raaluchi, I'm sure you know what a true love is when you experience it. Love is not to be said often just to fantasize someone. It is to be expressed. You get to know if someone loves you by what he does for you, if he makes you cry or makes you happy, if he wants to be with you or to be with your body. Love is holy…It is not selfish …it is not arrogant…it is sacrificial…it is patient and God is love. Believe me Raalu, when I say that I love you for who you are and I want to make you happy. I know you are young, and that is the more reason I want to be with you. I want to protect you from the cruelties of the world, because you don't belong to the world, and I don't ever want to see you get hurt by the world. You are my heartbeat Raalu, and you are the only love of my life. You are the first woman I've ever recognized and I want to be with you for the rest of my life even if it means fathering that baby." The last word rang a bell in Raaluchi's ears, in such a way that she got up forcefully from her bed and sat down.

"What?" Raaluchi expressed her shock with quivering lips like someone who was going through a severe cold. Her shock gave her goosebumps and uncontrollable tears ran down from her eyes.

"Why are you doing this, Onyeka?" Raaluchi asked him in bewilderment.

"I'm doing it because I can't live without you, because I love you and life without you is going to be a punishment to me. Raalu, I love you. You don't marry someone you can live without; you marry the person who you cannot live without. Raalu, I can't live without you."

Raaluchi hugged him so tight with smiles on her face and tears of joy streamed down their cheeks. She did not only love the words he had heard him say, she also loved the way he had said them, even the way he had abridged her name. Mummy entered the room and smiled at them and imagined what a wonderful couple they would have become if not for Raaluchi's unwanted pregnancy. She was thrilled when Raaluchi told her what Onyeka said and Mummy confessed that she had never seen such a man like Onyeka in her entire life. Mummy thanked God because what Onyeka had done would have taken a special grace of God not just the fact that he loved Raaluchi.

* * * *

Raaluchi and Onyeka registered for a marriage course in Onyeka's parish in Asaba: St Lucy Catholic Church Asaba. They took time attending it every Monday, Wednesday and Friday for a month and a week, before they finally distributed their wedding invitation cards. Their wedding was going to hold on 19th December 2009. Onyeka actually chose the date so that it would mark a one year anniversary of his love for her and also a birthday gift to the woman he loves. He had actually explained this intention to the Parish Priest: Father Emma Iweka, and that was why he was allowed to wed without completing the three months marriage course, although it wasn't easy convincing him to accept their intentions and wed them.

Nkiruka was happy for her friend and was even happier

when Raaluchi told her that she was going to be her Chief Bride's Maid. Onyeka took Raaluchi and Nkiruka to the biggest boutique in Asaba and they shopped for the wedding. The boutique was spacious enough to contain assorted London wedding gowns, liccra gowns, high heel slippers, shoes, bags, etc. They all hung line by line in their sites. After shopping, they all had lunch together in a restaurant beside the boutique. It was spacious, neat, and air conditioned. The waitresses were wearing smiling faces, attending to customers in a welcoming manner. As they settled down in a neat glasss table for three, they made their order. Raaluchi ordered for semovita and chicken nsala soup and Onyeka went for the same, except Nkiruka who ordered for jollof rice and chicken. As they enjoyed their meal, Onyeka told Raaluchi that their honey moon was going to be in America. Father Pius his Facebook pal in America had been anxious to meet the love of his life, the girl who drove Onyeka insane and he had sent them an invitation letter. Nkiruka was so happy for her friend. She smiled at them as she watched them talk intimately. She wished she was in Raaluchi's shoes and prayed in her mind for a caring husband like Raaluchi's. Onyeka popped a bottle of wine: San Cassiano Amarone 2006. Their wine glasses clinked in unison as they toasted for a better future ahead.

CHAPTER TEN

RAALUCHI HAD A miscarriage two days before the wedding day. She had just had her bath and was about to step out of the bath tub when she missed her step and fell heavily in the tub. She screamed for help and her mother rushed to her rescue and carried her to her room before she alerted Onyeka who took her to DIVINE HEALTH SPECIALIST HOSPITAL in Odoakpu Onitsha. Dr. Kene discharged her after a medical treatment.

Back home, Mummy popped a bottle of Chamdor wine for Raaluchi's miscarriage and she danced to the rhythm of Sister Chinyere Udoma's '*mkpologwu m,* my pillar'. Her buttocks shook as she danced and Onyeka laughed. They prayed together and thanked God for his wonderful intervention. Mummy was sure that it was just the will of God. She was sure that God didn't want a stain in the white garments He had decided to dress the couple in. No doubt, the baby would have been a pain in the ass especially if he inherited his biological father's waywardness.

* * * *

The wedding Mass was a huge success. The priest that administered the sacrament of their matrimony was Father Joe Ezeka: the assistant parish priest of St. Lucy Catholic Church Asaba. It was him because the parish priest: Father Emma Iweka, who the couple thought would have wedded them because he knew their intentions of not being able to complete the three months marriage course travelled to Rome on a priestly errand,

89

and so his assistant had to wed the couple and two other couples who were also wedding on that same day. The vows the couple had taken kept reciting itself on Raaluchi's mind. She couldn't believe that she just got married on her nineteenth birthday. The couple spent time taking photographs with friends and relatives outside the church. The speech Onyeka presented to the wedding guests at the reception hall was emotional and fantastic to those who heard him. He said that meeting Raaluchi for the first time was like a dream come true to him. He had told God that his attraction to his wife would come with a melodious song because he loved music, and Raaluchi exhibited it so perfectly well that he desired to meet her. He had also told God in his prayers that he would love to be attracted to his wife in a church and God really answered his prayers. He said that Raaluchi was like a bright morning sun radiating in a real beauty when she sang, but he studied her, and from her eyes he discovered she was depressed and there was something pulling her down and that evening, he promised himself that whatever reason for her depression, he would love to be involved in lighting up those sorrowful eyes that excruciated. He would love to be involved in making her happy even if it had something to do with all he had. But unfortunately, she disappeared in the crowd after the crusade and he believed that fate would bring her to him again if they were destined to be together.

The wedding guests applauded with glistened smiles and there were tears in Raaluchi's eyes as she listened to her husband's speech. Onyeka gave her a long passionate hug and they danced to the rhythm of P.Square's *Onyinye* as it played loudly in the reception hall. The guests ate assorted food and drank assorted wines to their satisfaction. Nkiruka was envious of her friend as she watched her dance with her husband in her dazzling white wedding gown, she imagined her own husband dancing with her on her wedding day and making a promise to take her to America for their honeymoon. She imagined herself in America exploring all the states in America. She would tell her husband that he would have to let her decide where to be for their honeymoon on her terms. She would choose Las Vegas because she had read so much about that place, she had read that it is the entertainment city of the world and the most populous city in the U.S of Nevada and it is famous for its consolidated casino-hotels. That she imagined, was a befitting atmosphere for honey moon.

As she watched the good matched couple, she decided to break up her relationship with Nonso her boy friend in school, a final year student in Marketing Department. She wasn't going to wait for someone that still depended on his parents for financial assistance. Nonso still had a long way to go and she just couldn't wait for him. She needed a fast-moving vehicle in her life and not traffic. To her, Nonso was just 'traffic' and she just couldn't tolerate his delay. She was going to get married to a rich man just like Raaluchi's husband and she would have to accomplish her dream of touring Las Vegas for her honeymoon soon.

Okpanam Asaba was a new site for different set of edifices; a home for a diverse range of people. It was a tranquil environment; a place contented with itself. Onyeka's house was situated in Okpanam. It was a well structured brick duplex resting in a cemented compound filled with flowers. That evening, Raaluchi spent time admiring her new home, the interior decations were splendid and the rooms were spacious enough. She was pleased to be living there. She got acquainted with the tenants that lived at the basement of the duplex; who had actually visited her just to welcome her. That night, before the couple went to bed, they had a toast with a bottle of champaigne in their bedroom. The toast was for a fruitful marriage and beautiful laughter in a glamorous happiness and as they cuddled each other in bed, making love in ecstatic desire, Onyeka whispered 'Raalu' to her ears. It pleased her to hear her abridged name from him in such a romantic way. Afterwards, with their bodies suffused in peace, they slept peacefully, knowing within their hearts that they shared a common destiny as deep as a bond.

CHAPTER ELEVEN

THE COUPLE'S HONEY moon in Boston, Massachusetts State of America was exquisite and elaborate. They lodged in Father Pius's Parish house in Hyde Park neighbourhood: an urban location with suburban characteristics. Father Pius had actually accommodated Raaluchi and Onyeka in the parish house and they enjoyed the hospitality of the Reverend Father. The house was elaborately structured and dimly cool. Father Pius was very lively, benevolent, cheerful and fun to be with. He talked too fast with fluent American accent that sometimes, Raaluchi felt like a fool listening to him and he questioned a lot. There were other fascinating priests that warmed the house with their high pitched laughter as they cracked jokes. But when the priests were in the mood of novena prayers, the house would be silent and boring. The snow discomforted Raaluchi, as she had to leave the house on a winter jacket and big boots.

The couple never missed morning Masses and even Raaluchi was surprised when she discovered that the women that attended Mass didn't cover their heads, and they even wore trousers to church. She had once listened to Amaechi bring up a topic in the Charismatic meetings, about women wearing trousers. He had expressed that there was nothing sinful about it and exemplified his fact by involving the whites, but the Charismatic members hushed him and accused him of having too much to drink which was totally unacceptable. She had actually agreed that it was sinful. And now, she watched them as they walked to the altar to give offerings. She watched them like people who had committed an unpardonable sin, and that they had no reason to defile the altar of God even if the weather was cold. Thick gowns, socks, big boots and parkas were available in the boutiques. They just had nobody to speak up for what was right simply because they were so stupid and have no regards for God. She sneered at them as she watched, forgetting that she was in the house of God.

The people exhibited the sign of peace by hugging each other with wild smiles, giggles and tickling of cheeks and Raaluchi was mesmerized. She watched them receive communion with smiles on their faces, like pictures of little children in her bible story book, where the kids came to be blessed by Jesus and the disciples stopped them, but, Jesus told them to let them be for the kingdom of God belonged to them and the minds that are like theirs. She remembered the pictures in her bible story book, a book she handled when she was just six years old.

Raaluchi was engrossed about their expression of peace and she learned immediately, eager to exhibit it in Nigeria and then wondered if Father Emma Iweka in her new parish in Asaba that was easily angered, would just skip her and give communion to the next person. She had known how easily angered he was when the parishioners that were present on a Sunday evening Mass did not respond 'Amen' to the *collect* (Mass opening prayer). Father Emma had bluntly told them that God's door of blessings would not open if they refuse to respond and they would all go home the same way they came. He had considered everybody in the church totally unprepared for the Mass. She smiled as she watched the American Communicants.

One of the white women said 'Merry Christmas' to Raaluchi after the Mass and her voice was like the sound of a buzzing hungry mosquito. Raaluchi said 'Merry Christmas' in return and smiled back at her, and admired the cute baby girl she was carrying with a baby carrier. As though the baby noticed that she was admiring her, she smiled and Raaluchi tickled her little cheeks and longed to have her own baby very soon, very certain that she had conceived. The woman extended her hand for a hand shake and an introduction and Raaluchi shook it respectfully, enclosing her hand in hers.

"I'm Lisa Scott," She said. Her smile was glamorous, matching with her complexion, her red lip stick and her blonde hair.

"I'm Raaluchi Ibekwe"

Lisa raised an eye brow in wonder as she hadn't heard that kind of name and so she asked for the meaning.

"It means, leave everything for God," Raaluchi answered her, and just then a car pulled up to a stop and honked. It was Father Pius and her husband Onyeka occupying the front seats. Lisa greeted Father Pius and commended him on the interesting homilies and he smiled in response and muttered something about being God's doing and not his. Raaluchi entered the car and waved good bye to her new friend, Lisa, and hoped to see her again in the church.

"I got to know how shameless the women here are. They don't have regards for God and so they have to wear trousers to church and uncover their heads. Oh gosh! That's absolutely unacceptable," Raaluchi said to her husband as they were undressing in the room. She expressed vehemently of her disapproval of their culture by shaking her head continuously, and her husband smiled at her.

"It is really good if we keep God's word in the bible but very bad to exhibit the attitude of a self righteous person who only finds faults with others, condemn and pass judgment on them. Even the scripture in Matthew 7:1 and 2 warned against that. The devil loves to keep our minds busy by mentally judging the faults of others and that way, we never see or deal with what is wrong in us. When we have our thoughts and conversations on what is wrong with others, we are usually being deceived about our own conduct. Jesus commanded that we should not concern ourselves with what is wrong with others but in humility allow God to judge them and deal with our own faults first, for nobody is perfect and is entitled to pass judgment on others. By doing so, we lack love for one another which is the first commandment of Jesus who appealed that we should love one another just like he loves us."

Raaluchi stood motionless staring at her husband after he had spoken. Those words reminded her of her mother, and again, she felt a knot untangling inside her. She was speechless. She remained speechless even after breakfast and Onyeka had to take her out for strolling in the afternoon. They strolled down the lanes of Washington streets where they had sight seeing and laughter. In the evening, Raaluchi enjoyed their outings to Santa Claus. They watched kids' laughter and giggles with Father Christmas and when they came home, she felt a gentle tranquility inside her, as though she was being transformed. She felt relaxed and free from the voices.

Raaluchi missed her favourite African dishes; pounded yam and *nsala* soup. Father Pius had always promised to take them to an African restaurant in Boston but never did. Later, she realized that the African foods in the restaurant were very expensive and that Father Pius could not possibly afford to squander his parish money just to entertain his guests. The cook in the parish house was a single lady who was fat and busty. She had blue eyes and red hair. She looked glamorous in her white skinned nature but she wasn't pretty. Her name was Molly. Raaluchi, as she watched her serve them mashed potatoes and hot dogs, realized that she was not far from the resemblance of a doll she once handled as a kid. Father Pius loved to tease Molly and so he teased her about getting a husband for her who he was sure would really love to marry a good cook like her and she scowled her face and left after she was done with her service.

Father Pius told the couple as they ate, that Molly detested marriage a lot and hated to even hear about it. Molly had come from a very miserable home. Her parents were just a replica of a bad marriage. They nagged and fought everyday and called corps for each other until they finally separated. Molly lived in the parish house and her mother had relocated to Atlanta and her brothers lived with her father in Boise. Molly had gotten a job as a cook in the parish house and had been on it for four months and sometimes, Father Pius tried to talk her into settling down but she had totally refused. She preferred to stay single to ending up in a bad marriage. Father Pius told them that Molly only needed a psychologist to enlighten her mind and make her understand that all marriages were not the same; that she could fall in love, she could be loved and that she could enjoy the beauty of marriage. Raaluchi felt pity for Molly and wished she could reconsider her decisions about remaining single for the rest of her life simply because she was brought up in a bad marriage.

* * * *

Onyeka volunteered the next day to be Molly's psychologist and although Raaluchi frowned at it, she however accepted this role of her husband. Father Pius was happy and he informed Molly about this. On Onyeka's third day in his counseling career to Molly, he confided on his wife that Molly's case was pathetic and that she had had an outrageous childhood. Molly had confessed that she was a victim of child abuse and molestation and that her father was totally responsible for it. She had told Onyeka that she had had repeated abortions for her father when she was in her early teens and that her mother got to find out this. Her mother lost the case when she sewed her husband to court. She had to close her bank account just to be sure her husband rots in jail, but, Molly's father being a very wealthy and influential man made his way out with his lawyers through the use of bribery and other crooked means because there was actually no evidence against him.

Molly had actually been the reason for her parent's marital war and separation and she had lied to Father Pius over the matter because she never involved herself to be the reason but had actually feigned a helpless and pathetic young woman who had intentionally hidden her terrible sins and even lied to a priest just to achieve her ambition of getting a job as a cook in the parish house: a place where she could stay away from her parents, especially her father. Raaluchi would have said that the lady was so dangerous, evil, an opportunist, and a big liar but she didn't. She just gave her husband a puzzled look.

"She just had to confide in me first…as a psychologist, you know." Onyeka winked at Raaluchi playfully but she did not smile.

"I want you to quit being Molly's psychologist."

"But we are not doing anything wrong, so why should I stop giving a listening ear to her problems?"

"Not when that Molly or whatever she is called, sheds crocodile tears for my husband just to move him to wipe them away with his handkerchief and soft words that were meant for his wife. Are you attracted to her?" Onyeka smiled as soon as he heard Raaluchi his wife. He sensed that Raaluchi had actually been watching them and was possibly eavesdropping on his discussion with Molly, but never said a word about it until he finally told her.

"Are you jealous of Molly?" Onyeka asked her. His heart danced and her jealousy pleased him. Raaluchi did not utter any word for an answer to the question instead she sat down on the luxurious couch in their bedroom and began to murmur. Onyeka reached out to her and stroked her shoulders.

"Now I know how much you love me… I thought I'm the only lover in this love story," Onyeka said and tickled her sides. Raaluchi was forced to laugh. Her eyes shut, her dimples dancing in full glamour, and her chest heaving. Onyeka tickled her cheeks and she laughed more and more. Raaluchi told her husband again that he should quit further counseling for Molly for she did not like the way she stared at him whenever they talked and that she was really very jealous of Molly.

"I think Molly already has a crush on my husband," Raaluchi said and Onyeka mimicked her and they laughed together.

Later in the night, Raaluchi sang for her husband, a song composed by her. She would just let out the words with right rhythm and sometimes, Onyeka wondered how she did it. Her melodious voice put him to sleep and he murmured her name repeatedly as he fell asleep and Raaluchi watched him for a long time with wide smiles, before settling him on the bed and lying beside him.

Her mind reached out to Nnanyelugo with deep thoughts and she smiled as she remembered his folk songs for her. She wavered in thoughts of him and wondered if he was happy wherever he was with her decision of marriage to Onyeka. She knew that if her father was alive, he wouldn't have consented to her marriage to any man, until she was through with her education. But she knew that Onyeka was different from some other men and considerate too. Ogechi may have a caring husband that treated her like an egg, but he deprived her of furthering her education and turned her into a 'baby factory' instead, not only because he wanted her to stay back home and give him children but because he didn't want her to go to the university at all.

When Ogechi told her this on phone, she had wondered what her husband's reasons were, for depriving a young woman her freedom of education. But Ogechi wasn't bothered. She had told Raaluchi that she wasn't bothered because she lived in affluence. "What is the use of education, my friend, when most people don't get jobs after graduation?" Ogechi had asked Raaluchi. Raaluchi had laughed at her through the phone because Ogechi only regarded 'education' as something that only put food on the table and not to impact knowledge and widen horizons for the poor and the rich. She had met Ogechi for the first time when she came to her house with her mother few days after she turned down Olisa's marriage proposal. "I have come to see the girl that broke my brother's heart," She said jokingly to Raaluchi with a beaming face and a winkle of an eye. And it was that act of friendliness that Raaluchi liked about her. She was the kind of person that made her way into someone's life, whether the person cared or not. Later, she engaged Raaluchi in a discussion about the benefits of marrying a rich man, and then, about her brother Olisa, gently and tactically convincing Raaluchi to accept her brother's marriage proposal. They exchanged phone numbers and since then, she had been the one calling Raaluchi, and even attended her wedding, just to assure her that she was pleased with her choice of partner.

But Onyeka her husband was not like Ogechi's husband. He valued her education and was already tutoring her for her JAMB Examinations (Joint Admission and Matriulation Board). She knew that Onyeka loves her and also wants the best for her. She knew that her marriage to Onyeka was never a mistake. It was what she wanted. And just then, her head ached, and it was as though her head was about to rupture. She looked back at her husband and the voices echoed, urging her to leave Onyeka and go back to her isolated room in Odoakpu Onitsha. That was where she belonged since she was a complete disappointment to her father to consider 'marriage' first over her education. 'You are a disappointment! You are worthless!' The voice of her father and another female voice shouted in her. Her head ached and uncontrollably, she screamed out loud as she forcefully pulled her hair net from her head, flung it on the floor, and ruffled her hair looking like a harassed mad woman.

Onyeka woke up immediately and held her so that she couldn't run away from the room to God knows where. She struggled for Onyeka to let go of her, but Onyeka held her, praying in his mind for God to come to his aid. Raaluchi's eyes blazed as they suddenly turned red in colour. Onyeka prayed incessantly in his mind before Raaluchi finally relaxed, heaved a sigh and lay back on the bed. Her headache calmed. She realized what she had done in a brief moment because Onyeka had been gazing at her: a scary gaze. She wondered if Onyeka would hate her for it, if his love for her would change.

"Are you okay?" Onyeka asked her and she smiled in response after a brief moment and nodded.

"I just had a nightmare. I'm sorry if I disturbed you," Raaluchi lied as soon as she remembered how seriously her mother had warned her when she decided to marry Onyeka, never to tell Onyeka about the voices she was hearing.

"It's okay," Onyeka said softly to her and made her head rest on his chest and then she stroked her hair until she fell asleep. He searched his mind wondering what was really wrong with his wife. He knew she was depressed and God knows he had been trying so hard to make her happy. He heaved a sigh and concluded that it was just a nightmare after all, but he couldn't help but admit within him that Raaluchi scared him with those blazing eyes. He wanted to know what was really wrong with his wife, if she needed a doctor. But he became desperately convinced that there was nothing wrong with his wife as he forced his suspicions out of his mind and believed that his wife was okay and that it was just a normal nightmare which anybody could have. He loved his wife so much to consider her to be psychotic.

Raaluchi wanted to pay a visit to her new friend Lisa Scott in Charlestown neighborhood and she went with her husband on a Sunday afternoon. Lisa's kids, three boys between the ages of four and six years, flung themselves on Raaluchi and her husband. And Onyeka ruffled their shiny brown hairs and they giggled. The oldest among them complimented Raaluchi on her beauty and asked her to be his wife. Just then, Lisa entered the living room and invited them to the dinning room for lunch and the kids hastened to the dinning room first with fast questions that were thrown at Raaluchi. The youngest one asked her which country she came from, and the younger one asked her why her beauty was so unique; why she dims her eyes while smiling and finally, the oldest among them asked her when she would get married to him and Lisa laughed and talked about spanking him if he didn't shut up but he muttered something to his Mum about talking so much of spanking but never did. The rest of things became hilarious with the kids giggling and talking very fast in a fluent American accent like birds chirping on the trees, and they all had a wonderful lunch: fruit salad and soups.

Raaluchi felt free inside her. She felt something untangling deep inside her, like a relief and freedom from claustrophobia. She was happy and relaxed. No doubt, the change of environment did her real good. All thanks to her husband who was exposing her to places with the hope of making her to learn more about happiness, about laughter and about the joy of togetherness which were fruits of a long life.

The baby in the nursery cried. Lisa hurried to carry her and when she was brought to the dinning room, she began to laugh and took part in the laughter that came from Onyeka's teases to the three boys, as though she understood their conversations. Raauchi yearned for a beautiful daughter like her and she was certain she had conceived as she caressed her belly.

"A day without engaging in one activity or the other that will bring happiness is like a phone call to depression and that is the devil's fastest means of evil manifestations. A good Christian should have the key of happiness at all times and never forget to thank God for the day that had been spent, hoping for a brighter day. No problem deserves worry or a call to depression. Our happiness is in our hands and God has given us laughter to sweep off the sorrows in our lives, preparing ourselves for a better future," Onyeka said to his wife as the parish driver drove them home and she did nothing else but grin, thanking her husband for making her life so beautiful. Onyeka was trying to make up for Raaluchi's depression and frustration for three years by telling her inspirational words that would strengthen her weaknesses and keep her strong for her bright future, his responsibility to her.

* * * *

The rest of the weeks in Boston flew very fast but they enjoyed every bit of their stay. They decided to travel back to Nigeria. Before then, they took time to visit the African restaurant in Newton, just for Raaluchi to satisfy her curiosity for the food. The restaurant was a small one, but, it had a neat appearance with its cool air. The couple discovered that only the blacks were eating in the restaurant and the waitresses were blacks. Onyeka giggled as he watched his wife eat voraciously and discovered that she had starved of '*nsala soup*' for a long time. A black waitress who had served them the food chortled as she watched Raaluchi by the counter. Minutes later, the black waitress approached them outside the restaurant and shook hands with Raaluchi. Onyeka waved 'hi' to her and walked to the car and his manner of distance pleased Raaluchi.

"I'm Sochima, a Nigerian." She said in American accent. She was chocolate skinned, and was wearing brown tiny braids that hung down her shoulders. She wasn't beautiful, neither was she attractive but Raaluchi liked her because of her friendliness.

"I'm Raaluchi, Nigerian too," Raaluchi said, returning her smile. Her hand was still enclosed in hers.

"This is my little earned enterprise. I'm actually selling what I make. I'm glad you enjoyed my food," Sochima said to Raaluchi, releasing her hand from Raaluchi's, and again, she asked her if she was in the country for good and said she would love to stay in touch; would love to see her come some other time to enjoy her african dishes but her exciting looking face, slowly changed to a slight frown when Raaluchi told her that they were leaving soon. Finally, she waved goodbye at them as Father Pius's driver drove out.

The couple took time to visit a Cinema in Hyde Park and giggled while watching the comedy, with Raaluchi's head resting on her husband's shoulder. They took time to shop. Raaluchi shopped for herself, her mother, her brother and her friend Nkiruka, enjoying her husband's wealth. Even Molly cried when the couple were about to leave the parish house on New Year's day and Raaluchi felt like hushing her with a handful of sand in her mouth. She hated her for flirting with her husband and hiding on the shadow of her problems. Onyeka had met her shortly and privately in the kitchen the previous evening and had told her to make her confessions to Father Pius and she promised Onyeka that she would.

Father Pius gave them a ride to the airport. He promised to keep in touch with them before the announcement of their air line came on air and the couple dashed to board the plane. It was Emirate Air Line, flying from America to Lagos, Nigeria. As the plane taxied, the couple smiled to each other talking through their mannerisms that they had a wonderful honey moon.

"Making you happy is my priority," Onyeka said almost like a whisper to her.

"Thank you very much. You've made my life so beautiful," Raaluchi said softly and smiled at him and he watched her and remembered how this particular smile had registered in his dopamine and how this beautiful woman had taken his senses away and he thanked God in his heart for giving him such a pretty woman that would bear beautiful kids for him, promising God that he would give her everything she desired. He loved her so much to do that for her.

* * * *

The couple's tenants in Asaba welcomed them back from their honeymoon trip the next day after they arrived home. Raaluchi cooked delicious *jollof* rice and chicken and they all ate and drank wine and fruit juice to their satisfaction. Ego, one of the tenants, felt so relaxed in the living room as she crossed her legs and questioned Onyeka a lot about the weather in America and his experiences in the aeroplane. Onyeka kept explaining like a seer that led blind people, and they were all so engrossed as they listened to Onyeka, although he was pissed off by Ego, knowing full well that she was being too inquisitive to get on his nerve and also put off his wife because she never allowed Raaluchi to speak also, or join in the conversation. He was convinced that Ego had not changed, that was why she didn't attend his wedding even when other tenants did. He had been misled by her sudden change of dressing; wearing only maxi gowns without make up on her face, her evangelical mission to him and all the tenants, some months before Armed robbers entered his house in the middle of the night, took his money, and shattered his close circuit camera. Later, Onyeka gave the tenants tooth pastes and face towels as gifts he brought back from America when they asked him for it. He didn't really shop for the tenants and they wouldn't have known about their honeymoon in America if Raaluchi didn't tell Ego, the woman in her early thirties, living downstairs in Onyeka's duplex. Raaluchi did almost all the shopping and Onyeka couldn't displease his wife just to please other people. The tenants showed gratitude by thanking the couple immensely, except Ego who had to look at the tooth paste as though it was a piece of shit that she just had to walk away without saying 'thank you.'

"What an insult! So Onyeka traveled a long distance to America just to give me tooth paste and face towel, *nji eme gini?* What should I do with these things? Ego hissed loudly as she soliloquized in Igbo language and then threw the gifts in the gutter outside the gate before entering her house. "I know that I'm poor but at least I know when I'm insulted by the rich," she added in her soliloquy and hissed loudly again, burning in fury. When she got to her room, she sat down, lost in thoughts. She was thinking of what to do to the newly married couple whom she knew were so much happy together. Some couple of times she had seen them, before they traveled abroad, they were talking and laughing excitedly in the car as Onyeka drove inside the compound. She had felt jealous and now all she thought of was how she was going to ruin their happiness. "I'm going to deal with Onyeka...I'm going to use his wife and deal with him. They will all wallow in misery. *Ndi ala! Unu na enyem sooso tooth paste na towel...* mad people! You people are only giving me toothpaste and towel," She soliloquized, snapped her fingers, bit her lips as she fumed and hissed loudly again that her husband had to approach her and asked her what was worrying her. He was actually reading a newspaper in the next room and his wife's loud hisses were disturbing him.

"What do you care? You are a useless poor man. Your mates are taking their wives abroad and you are here struggling Garri and Soup with me. Get out of my sight," Ego said to her husband, dissing. Her husband went back to his room without saying any other thing, as though his wife had henpecked him. Ego's kids circled her, like children playing '*kpa kpa nkolo*'(a game played by children while running in a circle.) They circled to search her bag to know if she brought back something eatable as she promised them.

"Olaedo, I didn't bring back anything. The landlord did not give me anything 'at all', so please take your brothers to the room." Olaedo, the eldest among Ego's three children scowled her face and murmured as she took her siblings, the two boys to their room.

"Olaedo, don't let me squeeze that your mouth," Ego said angrily feeling worse than she had already been.

* * * *

That night in the couple's bed, Onyeka had a long talk with his wife as though he felt Ego's dangerous anger. He told her to stay away from the tenant women and stop visiting them in their houses if she still wanted to have her respect as the land-lady. He told her that "Humility is based on honour and respect" but that should be exhibited whenever she saw her elders and not by going to their houses and talking with them, especially Ego her closest among them.

"Jobless women have nothing useful to do but to gossip and destroy marriages. Don't allow Ego into this place anymore.

My perception tells me she's not a good woman and you saw how she frowned as soon as I gave her gift, as though she gave me money to buy something for her and I didn't. People that are ungrateful are known to be very wicked and you need to avoid her."

Ego and her family had lived in Onyeka's house for four years and they still owe him house rents. Onyeka had been patient with them considering Ego's husband who had been sweating as a petit- trader to make a good living and pay his house rents. The poor man Ubaka, would kneel in front of Onyeka and weep profusely, beating his chest each time Onyeka suggested that they rather moved out of the house and find a smaller place to live and manage their income. Onyeka would be moved with pity for the man and permit him and his family to stay some more.

"But Onyeka, don't you think you are being misled by a misconception?" Raaluchi asked her husband as she doubted what her husband had said about Ego. To her, Ego was a nice woman and she had showed her nothing but kindness since she came in as a land lady. She had no concrete reason to drive her away when she visited.

"Raalu, I don't want to argue with you. If you value the love we have for each other and if you trust me as your husband, you'll obey me. And you know I can never deceive you. Please don't let Ego into this house. She's not a good woman to make a friend and she's not your mate," Onyeka spoke softly as he stroked Raaluchi's hair and she smiled and nodded but her mind wavered in reasoning before she finally fell asleep.

The advice that Onyeka gave his wife all fell on deaf ears when she let Ego into her matrimonial home for the second time on a Saturday morning, in the month of April. Onyeka had traveled to the village and Raaluchi had refused to go with him saying she caught flu. Ego had noticed Onyeka's absence. She had watched him drive out alone and then she was convinced that Raaluchi was alone in the house. Ego pretended to be nice by bringing Raaluchi's washed clothes upstairs to her.

"Aunty Ego, you shouldn't have bothered yourself. I was going to bring them in myself," Raaluchi said to Ego, returning the smile she gave her. Ego smiled widely and told her that it was nothing if she brought in her clothes and that she was like a younger sister to her. She even volunteered to wash Raaluchi's dirty clothes since she was sick and Raaluchi was so grateful and presumed that her husband was absolutely wrong about Ego. To her, Ego was a nice woman, a humble one for that matter to even wash her clothes for her. Raaluchi sat and watched her wash her clothes in the laundry room.

"I hope your sickness is a good one? *Ya burukwa ezigbo aru* so that I can come and drink hot water," Ego said in Igbo language and Raaluchi chuckled and wished she was right. Ego cooked lunch and they ate in Raluchi's dinning table and Raaluchi was so grateful to her but she told her to stop thanking her for helping her younger sister. The clandestine friendship between Raaluchi and Ego extended, and Ego succeeded in corrupting Raaluchi's mind by telling her so many things that can ruin her marriage and Raaluchi fell for it because she had a reason to believe and that was the picture: the evidence that Ego had shown her. As she looked at the picture, she became infuriated, and the voices echoed, telling her that she had married the wrong man. Raaluchi hated her husband for fooling her with lies, making her believe that she was his first love while she wasn't and she suspected that the reason Onyeka had told her to avoid Ego was obviously the fact that she knew his secret and didn't want her to disclose it to her.

CHAPTER TWELVE

THINGS FELL COMPLETELY apart and the atmosphere between the couple became tense when Raaluchi couldn't get pregnant just five months after they got married. She believed that God had disappointed her again; that God did not love her because, He had been delaying the most precious things in her life. She had been crying her hearts out even when her husband had encouraged her to have patience for the fruit will come in its time, but Raaluchi would blurt out hurtful words to him in anger for all the lies he had told her, for the deceit, and each time she did that, Onyeka would get so confused. Raaluchi felt humiliated and began to question her faith. That was not the kind of life she had envisaged for herself. Patience had never been in her dictionary and the traffic in her life began when she stayed without admission in a university of her choice for three solid years.

She had never waited for any success, ranging from her primary school level to the secondary. Why was God so unfair to her? Why would He continue to delay the precious things in her life? Her admission to a university of her choice was delayed and now another thing that can make her happy while waiting for admission had also been delayed. Onyeka her husband who she had regarded as a very nice man was a complete liar that had fooled her just to marry her. Why did she have such a bad luck in life? Why was she experiencing this traffic in her life? How on earth could she possibly wait for these two things she desired to manifest in her life? She was not really a patient person and yet God was forcing her to be one. Does He want her to die before these dreams come true in her life?

Her mind wavered again and she compared herself with the couples that wedded together with them on their wedding day. She had seen the two women's protruding bellies at mass. Why must her own be totally different? She continued to weep profusely one morning after Onyeka had consoled her but to no avail. He had begun to dress up for work when Raaluchi attacked him by grabbing his collar and heaping insults on him. The voices spoke in her and her head ached. She was completely deranged as she repeated after the voices 'You are a cheat! You are a liar! You ruined my life! You used me! You are just a user!" and just then, like a force, as though she was controlled by the voices she was hearing, she rushed to the dressing mirror, took the available bottle of perfume on the mirror cupboard, and broke it on the marble floor. Just when Onyeka rushed to stop her from using the broken bottle on him, she stabbed Onyeka on his belly and ran away from the room.

Onyeka was in pains for some time. His white shirt was stained with blood. He groveled to the next room and helped himself with a first aid box. He cancelled his work for the day and stayed back home to get some rest. He had to lock the room to make sure that Raaluchi couldn't come and make more troubles. He didn't dare call anybody for help. He didn't want anybody to think bad about his wife. He didn't want to give anybody the impression that he had married the wrong woman. He loved his wife and he had promised to be with her for the rest of his life: for better or worse. He was sure that God was with him and with God, he would make Raaluchi happy.

* * * *

Onyeka was in his office one Wednesday afternoon when he decided to go home to his wife and sort things out with her. He hadn't been concentrating on his work ever since the outrageous incidence with her. He had been avoiding her, but he felt that he just couldn't continue with that attitude with the woman he loves. True love should be tolerant. He just needed to make peace with his wife and know just how he had cheated on her and how he had used her. Those words Raaluchi had blurted out before she stabbed him really gave him sleepless nights. He didn't know why Raaluchi had been so angry with him that she had suddenly begun to hurt him. She no longer sang for him, that melodious voice of hers that always put him to sleep, that aroused him to love her endlessly, that reminded him of the first time he set his eyes on her: the night he was arrested by love. It was obvious that they weren't happy anymore because Raaluchi was angry with him. They no longer shared the same bed except when she approached him on her ovulation periods, just on her terms. She only wanted nothing but to conceive his child even when she wasn't happy with him. Onyeka just needed to resolve the situation before she started thinking about leaving him. Raaluchi was his heartbeat, his life and he loved her so very much.

* * * *

Ego and Raaluchi were gossiping as usual, about Raaluchi's marriage when they heard Onyeka's horn and Ego escaped from the house and fastly ran down the stairs to the basement, to meet another tenant, so that Onyeka would not see her or even catch a glimpse of her. Her plans were definitely falling into place and when she would be done dealing with the new couple, Onyeka would wish he were dead. It wasn't her fault that he married a naïve woman who was ready to be fooled by her, and it wasn't also her fault that his precious wife did not trust him. Onyeka met his wife frowning as she saw a movie in the living room. He smiled at her and handed her the beautiful roses he had bought for her. There was a little white card with a red heart design and an inscription that was bodly engraved MY HEARTBEAT on it. If Raaluchi had opened the card, she would have read the words in it; the words that her husband had composed for her with tears in his eyes, the words that he had written down on a paper and had given a card designer to design for his wife: *My heart has never longed for a bond until it noticed you … my heart races in excitement when it hears your melodious voice. It loves to see you happy cos it feeds in your happiness. It loves to share your sadness, cos it wants nothing but your happiness. You hurt us when you break my heart because you live in my heart and we are entangled in one heart... I'll be lifeless without you in my heart cos you are MY HEARTBEAT.* Raaluchi sneered at the bouquet of white and red roses with a little card. She flung it on the floor and at the same time, her mind wavered, remembering what Ego told her about men.

"Men are so cunny. The only reason why they give you roses or any other gift is to buy your heart so that they can have you in bed because that is the only thing they think you are good at, and with their sweet words, they take your mind far away from knowing their secrets. Men are unfaithful in nature. Marriage is a game…so you learn to play along and don't be so trusting with your husband."

"If you think you can buy my heart with those roses, then you are making a very big mistake," Raaluchi said to her husband and Onyeka watched her in pains. His eyes filled with tears, his chest was aching, and he just stood in front of his wife looking mournful, watching her and begging her with his mournful look to unbreak his heart.

"Raalu, we need to talk. Why are you being so unfair to me? What have I done wrong?"

"I don't have anything to say to you, so please get out of my sight!"

"I don't like it when I see you moody. Won't you at least tell me what I did?" Onyeka shouted back at her before he regained himself and moved towards her to calm her down but she pushed him away and left the living room, stepping on the bouquet of roses with the little romantic card on it. Ego could hear their shouting voices from her house and then she laughed out loud and celebrated her successful plan with a bottle of Fanta. Onyeka concluded that Raaluchi's inability to conceive had been the reason for her anger towards him and so he met with her mother and told her what he had been undergoing in the hands of Raaluchi and begged Mummy to talk to her daughter. Mummy promised to talk to her daughter and pleaded with Onyeka to be patient with her. When Onyeka left the house, Mummy sat down and was lost in thoughts. She knew that the voices Raaluchi had been hearing had something to do with her dangerous mood, to have attempted to kill her own husband. She began to cry and asked God when He would cast out those demons that had been disturbing her daughter, those demons that had taken away her daughter's happiness.

* * * *

Raaluchi leaned on the veranda pillar of Onyeka's bungalow in Umudioka and listened to Mama her mother- in- law with a frowned face that looked like a heap of faeces. The atmosphere between Onyeka and Raaluchi had been tensed that the marital bliss had collapsed. Her mother- in- law spoke very slowly and primly as though she was being too careful in the words she used; too careful not to appear implausible before her daughter- in -law. It was on the eve of New Yam Festival in August and there was a cold blast of air outside the house. The rain was not heavy but came with cold. Rain drops slid down the leaves and the air smelt of wet soil. The birds chirped on the trees. Onyeka had actually wanted to spend the brief holiday with his parents in the village and so he was able to convince his nagging wife after he pleaded repeatedly for days before she agreed to come with him. They had come the previous day which was Thursday. Previously, before their wedding, when Onyeka introduced Raaluchi to his mother, Raaluchi spent some time with Mama in the kitchen , saying ' Mama *rapuba*. I can slize the *arigbe*. I can cook the food. Mama biko *rapuba*. Go and rest," she said in Igbo language and humbly cooked the rice and vegetable stew for Mama, who did not go inside the room to rest, but sat on a kitchen stool, watching Raaluchi cook the food, nodding in confirmation. The kitchen was spacious and airy enough and so, she didn't get bored watching and waiting on Raaluchi to finish the cooking. Mama had eaten three plates of the rice and vegetable stew, confirming to Onyeka as they ate in the dinning table, how delicious the food was. Later that evening, before Onyeka left the house with Raaluchi, Mama said to her son privately, under a gmelina tree in the spacious compound: "that girl is a wife material. When are you paying her bride price?"

But since the couple arrived for the New Yam Festival, Raaluchi had not bothered to enter the kitchen to cook. She had intentionally left all the cooking for Mama. She would lie down on the bed and watch TV, she would complain of headache and menstrual pain to Mama whenever Mama entered the room to check on her, as though to prepare the woman's mind not to expect a grand child from her yet. Raaluchi understood that Mama's constant visit to her matrimonial room was to tell her to help her out in the kitchen. But Mama was not straightforward. She kept gesturing without pointing. "*Nne, kedu ka i mee?* How do you feel? I've just put a pot of meat on the fire. I want to cook okro soup," Mama would say, and Raaluchi would nod and mutter something about the pain reducing, but wasn't gone entirely. Raaluchi was too depressed to cook any meal. She was scared that she would burn the food or mess up the cooking with wrong spices, because she was simply indisposed. And so, that Friday evening, Mama knocked on their room door and required for Raaluchi's presence at the veranda. She obeyed. The couple had been lying separately on the bed when Mama called Raaluchi. Onyeka lay on his back, reading his mail from his auditors with his phone, while Raaluchi lay sideways humming a song, just to distract him.

"You don't understand how much my son loves you, Raaluchi. I heard that you weep every month. You weep profusely when you see your period as though God has killed you. It is just seven months of your marriage and you already want to kill yourself, *gbo?* Are you God that gives children?"

Raaluchi was silent. She fake-coughed, unable to say anything but mustered how to face Onyeka later, for daring to tell his mother about her. For all she cared, if there was anybody who needed counselling, it should be Onyeka who was a very big liar and who had fooled her in so many ways. Mama cleared her throat and spat out through the veranda pillars and then watched Raaluchi with love in her eyes and beckoned her to come closer and when Raaluchi did, she made Raaluchi's head lie on her weak laps and she stroked Raaluchi's hair. Mama told Raaluchi a story that entailed: "A fast runner doesn't always win the race." It was a moon light tale about the dog and tortoise. They were set on a running competition and the dog made caricature of the tortoise's slow movement and ran very fast without any idea that the tortoise had kept some pieces of bones for the dog under a tree. When the dog caught a glimpse of the bones, he mounted on them and began to eat them voraciously, while the tortoise continued with his journey, knowing full well that the dog must need some sleep after eating the plenty bones. The dog fell asleep under a tree and then forgot about the race competition only to realize his mistakes when it was already too late; when the tortoise won the competition.

The birds chirped on the trees continuously, as though they were enjoying the tale, and that particular tale reminded Raaluchi about Nnanyelugo and his interesting folk tales for her. After the tale, Mama pleaded with Raaluchi to embrace patience and prayers for those were the only solutions to her problems. Mama told Raaluchi that those who walk slowly through the roads of their destinies do not make mistakes of falling because they are careful with their steps and so, their being cautious prevents them from falling, but those who run or even walk too fast end up falling. Mama told Raaluchi that she waited on the Lord for eight years before she finally began to have children. She told her that good things don't come easily and the most important thing to be grateful to God for is "life" for God keeping his children alive, has a better plan, a brighter future for them, for when life is in abundance, hope grows and yields moving faith that breeds expectant results.

"Thank you Mama. I find your advice soothing but...I don't know why my own pattern of life should be different. My best friend is in her final year in school while I'm yet to get admission and she is even married and is obviously pregnant. She is so much ahead of me and I don't like it. Sometimes I feel that God is being so mean to me by delaying my blessings."

"Raaluchi my daughter, God loves you. He is only waiting for the right time to bless you. Your mother was right when she told me that you challenge God a lot by comparing yourself with others. Life is not a competition and you'll make a terrible mistake if you end up imposing people's destinies on yourself, a life that is not made for you, a life style that withdraws you from your own track of life thereby making you fall into temptation to sin against your creator."

Raaluchi began to cry. She couldn't believe there was a brighter future for her. She was a complete disappointment and nobody loved her, Onyeka had been making a fool of her, just like Chiedu and even God had abandoned her. She shouldn't continue to listen to solemn words of advice that had yielded no positive results for her. She was tired of hearing about God and Patience. She wavered in her faithless mind as she concentrated on Nkiruka's success. She focused her mind on Nkiruka's final year in school, her wedding in March and her protruding belly four months after her wedding. Nkiruka had all the good lucks following her, even when she was a huge sinner, but with her own life, the reverse was the case. She said good night to Mama and headed to her matrimonial room with her face streaming with tears. Mama's piece of advice that had lasted almost an hour disappeared into the thin air and did not bear fruit in the life of Raaluchi because she didn't accept it. As she stepped inside her matrimonial room and watched her husband, her mind pondered on what Ego had told her in one of her frequent visits to her matrimonial home and the picture she had shown her as an evidence of the truth she was telling her.

"Did he tell you that you are his first love? Ha ha ha...and you believed him? I've been his tenant for years and I know him well. Onyeka had numerous girlfriends and they spent the night in his house... My dear, shine your eyes o, he's just using you. Men are so domineering and they don't deserve respect at all. He may have contacted a severe infection from his fornications that must have rendered him impotent, that is why you cannot conceive and he can never admit it...I pity you my sister, you don't know who men are."

She sat at the foot of the bed and watched Onyeka snore in his sleep. Her head began to ache and the voices echoed, calling her husband "an impotent man." She watched him disgustingly with a raging hatred. She watched him for a long time wondering if he was really a man or he was impotent. Onyeka loved to keep the light on while sleeping and it had been his habit since childhood and Raaluchi knew it but she turned off the light just to wake him up and Onyeka woke up immediately. Raaluchi wasn't satisfied with the test they had carried out a month before and two months after their wedding. There was certainly something wrong with her husband. Ego was right. She wavered in her mind and concluded that the doctor they had seen for fertility test may have deluded her by telling her that there was nothing wrong with her husband, just to protect her husband. Her mind wavered, and as it wavered, her head ached and aggravated the voices. *"You've once gotten pregnant, you are okay but he's not! He's impotent! He's impotent!"*. The voices spoke in her as though they interpreted her thoughts. She was totally alright but for Onyeka, she wasn't sure.

She needed him to carry out another test in another hospital. She was going to tell him about it in the morning when Onyeka woke up and stifled a yawn and felt her presence beside him. His mind raced as he saw those blazing eyes again and he began to pray in his mind, begging God to save him. And because he was still in love with her, he demanded to know what was wrong again because there had always been problems to complain about; the issues of pregnancy and admission into the higher institution. She couldn't even wait for the right time before she spelt it out like a pregnant woman who was in labour and couldn't wait to deliver. "Are you impotent?"

"Please get a night rest," Onyeka said stoically and heaved a sigh as he controlled his temper. He didn't know how to express his anger because he was absolutely angry, and so he controlled it. He loved Raaluchi and telling her right in her face that she disgusted him and had been ever since her pregnancy madness started, would hurt her and even him because he couldn't afford to insult a woman he loved so much, come what may, they were still one and she lived in him. He had been angry ever since the issue of pregnancy and admission took away their marital happiness, ever since Raaluchi began to nag so annoyingly, ever since she stopped sharing her feelings with him. Before their marital bliss collapsed, Raaluchi would stay in her office and text him, would share her feelings with him: *I'm having mood swings. I need you.* The next minute, Onyeka would suspend his work and come to her in her office, and they would chat and laugh and make love on her office table.

Raaluchi ceased smiling for him, those smiles that he loved to watch, those smiles that made his heart dance so lustily. She stopped singing, those sweet melodious songs that magnetized him to her each time he listened to them. Raaluchi stopped working in his company and preferred to stay alone in the house crying her hearts out and thinking in comparison. Raaluchi felt worse whenever she saw pregnant women. She blamed God and questioned Him for blessing those pregnant women instead of her that deserved it. She had even displayed a very bad attitude of a distressed damsel when Onyeka's colleagues visited them one of the weekends in May, with their pregnant wives. Raaluchi had felt dejected and had refused to utter a word or join in the flowing conversation that was mingled with jokes and elicited laughter. The pregnant women were stunned that they had to ask their husbands after the visit, if Raaluchi was abnormal and Onyeka was furious when one of his colleagues asked him on phone if his wife was abnormal. He didn't blame his colleague neither did he blame the question he asked because his wife was really behaving like an abnormal person and exposing her stupidity and shamelessness, embarrassing her husband and making mockery of their marital love just because she had chosen to be faithless.

Raaluchi began to make mistakes in her cooking and her meal tasted so badly because she lacked concentration when she cooked, because her mind was always busy every minute of the day, comparing and contrasting. Raaluchi stopped performing her matrimonial duties of coition except on her ovulation periods and even after that, she would still give in to anxiety and fear of seeing her period again and that would jeopardize her chances of conception. Onyeka had been angry and had been conflicted with his painful desire to send Raaluchi back to her parent's house or to keep talking to God about her. He loved Raaluchi so much, but if his love for her would take away his peace of mind and his own life, then it had gotten to the extent where they would give themselves breathing spaces so that they could at least have peace. He hated to think about leaving Raaluchi, but he really had no choice. He knew just within him, that he had tried to make his wife happy by carrying out his responsibility for her but she was very incorrigible.

Onyeka had confided on Raaluchi's mother about Raaluchi's terrible attitude but her mother had been pleading for patience and tolerance, unable to disclose Raaluchi's problems to Onyeka. Mummy was so scared that Onyeka, the nicest man she had ever known would leave her daughter once he found out about Raaluchi's condition. As a mother, she had even talked to Raaluchi but being that same incorrigible person, she had refused to accept her mother's advice. Mummy had to tell Onyeka's mother who had talked to Raaluchi but she was still adamant.

"If we must discuss anything, it must be now, or are you afraid of admitting to your wife that you are impotent? Raaluchi said scornfully. The words rang loudly on Onyeka's ears, like a school bell alerting pupils for assembly. The sleep disappeared from Onyeka's eyes and he heaved a sigh of exhaustion and anger, the kind of anger that had to be controlled so that it wouldn't cause harm to its victim, as it died slowly inside the heart.

"Raaluchi, what offence have I committed in marrying you? Is it an offence to fall in love with you? Why can't I have peace in my own house? Why have you decided to toil with my emotions, piercing my heart with your mean words…Raalu, why?" Onyeka said bitterly, his eyes filled with tears as he fought them and lay back on the bed leaving Raaluchi dumbfounded. She left the room and made her way to the living room where she murmured. She murmured about how cunning her husband can be especially when she raised the pregnancy topic. Ego was right. Men are so cunny. She murmured about his impotency and his cunning refusal to admit it. Onyeka wept in his bed begging God to take control. He wanted to regret ever falling in love with Raaluchi, but he couldn't because he knew that a part of her had made him very happy.

"Love is wicked to make me fall for someone that doesn't care about me," he muttered sorrowfully and wished he could go back to sleep but he wasn't feeling sleepy anymore. He turned on the light believing it would put him to sleep but the sleep had disappeared from his eyes and then he stared into the space and finally his eyes fixed on the wall where their wedding picture was hung. In it, Raaluchi's smile glistened with arms spread apart as he carried her to his chest, and as he watched the enlarged photograph, he wondered when he would ever see those smiles again, he wondered if his Raaluchi would ever change. He was heads over heels in love with his wife but he was unsure if she felt the same for him. He wanted to fall out of love with her, because she seemed to be so ungrateful to him and to God, but he couldn't.

True love was supposed to be like a house that was built with trust but he had just discovered that Raaluchi did not trust him. She did not trust him, even when he had confessed to her that she was the only woman he had ever slept with. She did not trust him, even when he had given her almost everything he had, just to put a smile on her face. She still did not trust him even when he gave her frequent phone calls just to know how she fared at home, since she stopped work and even came home on time to put a smile on her face but she always turned him down. She always turned down his roses for her, his offer to take her out, and so many other things that were capable of making a woman happy.

His life as the only son of his father before he got married had been a complete devotion to God. He served Masses until he gained admission into the higher institution and before then, he made a vow to God that he would remain a virgin until he got married and he kept it, irrespective of the temptation he underwent in school because of his over-exalted intellectualism and his handsomeness. Raaluchi did not trust him. Instead, she toiled with his emotions knowing full well how much he loved her. "Should I quit this marriage before I die in it?" Onyeka soliloquized in confusion. But his marital vows recited in his mind like a school anthem: *'I promise to be with you in good times and in bad...till death do us part.'* and he sighed in dismay.

CHAPTER THIRTEEN

THE FIRST THING that Onyeka did as soon as they got back to Asaba was to take Raaluchi with him to the hospital, another hospital, a hospital of her choice. In the doctor's office, Onyeka excused himself for the doctor to have a talk with his wife so that he wouldn't be accused of influencing the doctor to manipulate the result. The doctor said to the hearing of Raaluchi that her husband was very much okay, that she only needed to be patient with God, waiting in happiness and obedience. The long drive back home was strained with silence of heated anger in Onyeka's mind. Raaluchi watched him unable to figure out the polite way to render an apology to her husband. For once, she thought of doing what is right without wavering to find answers from Ego's advice. If she had wavered, she would have known that Ego had said that 'apology is not needed in marriage because it gives men the ability to hurt their wives continuously.' She placed her left hand on his lap and he waggled free, pretending to change the car gear.

"I love you," Raaluchi muttered, almost breathless. She meant to say she was sorry.

"I hate bare faced flatteries, especially when they are made to fool me. Raaluchi, there is no need for that pretence." Onyeka hissed in anger as he joined the traffic and blasted his horn in fury. His belly churned in hunger. He longed for his mother's food since his wife was no more a good cook. He didn't take breakfast in the village since he was so eager to satisfy Raaluchi's curiosity and give her proof that he wasn't impotent

121

and that if he was, he wouldn't have considered marriage at all. He was going to visit Mummy later in the evening to eat food, and afterwards, he would lodge in a hotel to mollify his anger and decide what next to do with Raaluchi. His mother had even admitted to him that he had lost so much weight and that had been as a result of Raaluchi's depression, even when he tried to make her happy.

He knew that he could never be happy in his matrimonial home when his wife was not happy either. He didn't know what other ways to tackle Raaluchi's problems. For all he knew, Raaluchi lacked nothing but had chosen to be depressed because of things that were beyond her control. Raaluchi had wanted her husband to bribe the Vice Chancellor and lecturers for her admission in the University which she was curious to attend but he had refused considering the fact that it was a sin and he couldn't afford to sin against God to prove to his wife how much he loved her. Onyeka had advised her to believe that she would get admission on merit because what was actually hers must definitely come with merit, but she had wavered as she used to, not sure of it, instead she accused Onyeka of not willing to offer a helping hand.

Raaluchi in her overwhelming pride, refused to tender more apologies to her husband, believing in Ego's words and hoping he would come back to her and shower her with soft words like he used to and buy her roses that she always rebuffed, just to play with his emotions and feel very important and punish him for daring to lie to her. She adhered to Ego's words: 'Men are domineering and deserves no respect. A woman is a queen in her marriage.' She was the queen in her marriage and queens don't go beyond their limits in apologizing to men they knew were so much in love with them. She had never been the one apologizing. Onyeka had always been doing that even when she was always the offender. She knew he loved her and couldn't resist her, but she may be wrong this time because Onyeka did not notify her of his going away until she watched him drive off just an hour after they had come home.

He had refused to wait for Raaluchi's food after she had told him vaguely that she had put a pot of rice on fire. Onyeka knowing full well that it was going to be one hell of shit as usual couldn't continue with that. Minutes later, after Raaluchi had seen her husband drive off, her heart raced. She didn't know why she felt that way but she did. Previously, when she was in good terms with her husband, before Onyeka would leave the house, he would give her a goodbye kiss but it no longer existed. She wanted it that way. She wanted things to change between them until he wallowed in guilt and opened up to her about his lies and deceits. The voices spoke in her, they convinced her that she was doing the right thing and that Ego was right about everything she had told her. Raaluchi believed in her late father's voice as it shouted on her. To her, Onyeka was just the second Chiedu in her life. Onyeka was even worse than Chiedu because Chiedu proved himself to be a beast by what he did to her but Onyeka was a friendly enemy who in his love hurt her with his lies and didn't bother to tell her the truth when she began to change towards him. She came off the thought with a hiss and got busy with her cooking, the one she always messed up while wavering in her endless thoughts. Ego knocked briefly and Raaluchi let her in with a brief hug.

"You came just on time. My jollof rice is almost ready," Raaluchi said as she stirred the tomato stew and then sat down in one of the plastic chairs in the kitchen and Ego pulled the other chair and sat beside her.

"Has Onyeka finally opened up to you?" Ego asked Raaluchi but she shook her head. That was what Ego wanted to hear. Her plans would be ruined if the couple finally reconciled. It was a good thing that Raaluchi was helping her put her plans into place because she seemed to be obeying her pieces of advice: the weapons that could only destroy her. To her, she wouldn't stop until she destroyed the young marriage completely and have her revenge for what Onyeka did to her. Ego was sure that using Raaluchi to destroy Onyeka was very easy because she was sure that Raaluchi was naïve and stupid because she couldn't keep marital secrets and she believed in stupid things. Ego had lured her into telling her what attracted Onyeka to her and she had told her the complete detail without knowing that she had given Ego the key to her husband's heart.

* * * *

Mummy made *egusi* soup with chicken and pounded yam for her son- in- law and she almost cried as she watched him pitifully. She watched Onyeka eat hungrily knowing full well that Raaluchi had been starving her husband. Onyeka explained to Mummy the reason he would be lodging in a hotel for some days and Mummy nodded in agreement, at least it would bring back Raaluchi's senses, if she really had any.

"If you show a woman that you cannot live without her, she would play games with your emotions. I want her to look for me…let her feel my absence for some days and let me know if her madness will stop. I also want to get some rest. I've missed that for so long. "

Later in the afternoon, on the 29th day of August 2010, Onyeka withdrew some money from his account and shopped in a boutique. He bought casual wears and toiletries and then drove to **BEST VIEW HOTEL**: an exquisite hotel in G.R.A Asaba; a place highly structured and equipped with fancy things anyone can think of. He got chilled in a luxurious room. The blast from the air conditioner welcomed him as he sighed and sat down to enjoy the chilling air he got from the air conditioner. For once, he could cool his head and be free from Raaluchi's naggings. He called his General Manager and announced that he would be absent from work for some days, for personal reasons, and he concurred. Onyeka gave him the address of the hotel he was lodging, incase he wanted to see him for something urgent.

"True love never lies. It reveals itself completely for a woman that is so lucky to experience it. The love is true because it offers everything, everything that gladdens the heart, everything that is true and worthy of emulation and appreciation but an ingrate is an enemy to this true love because no matter how hard this true love tries to make the ingrate happy, it would never be appreciated. It would be like a black ink destroying the innocence of the clean water as it penetrates it," Onyeka soliloquized and heaved a sigh before lying down to get some rest.

* * * *

Raaluchi waited for her husband to come home but waited in vain. She called his phone numbers but he did not answer the calls. She became afraid when she finally called her mother at twelve mid- night to verify if she had seen her husband.

"Mrs Raaluchi Ibekwe, you'll never know what you have until you lose it. Don't even try to use the evil voices you hear as an excuse because you are with the key to your recovery. God gave you a precious gift, a gift as precious as gold, but you threw it in the gutters. Keep acting like a fool. I have not seen your husband and please don't call this number again."

"Mummy please wait... wait..." She didn't speak further before Mummy hung up on her and she heaved a sigh and forced herself to sleep. 'Onyeka will come back to me because I'm absolutely sure that Onyeka cannot do without me,' Raaluchi said to herself in consolation and reminded herself that she shouldn't be worried about Onyeka's absence. Raaluchi regained herself from worrying about Onyeka and the voices didn't speak to her. She felt peace within her and she was startled with this sudden peace of mind, and in that peaceful state, she drifted to sleep. In her dream that night, her wedding ring was missing and she was crying profusely, looking for it, ransacking the whole house because of it and then, she saw Ego laughing at her, a devilish laughter with an impish grin. She showed Raaluchi her missing wedding ring and when Raaluchi rushed to take the ring from her, Ego threw the ring into a blazing fire and Raaluchi screamed and wept bitterly. Raaluchi woke up with a scream. "Was it just a dream or a revelation?" Raaluchi asked herself and concluded that it was a revelation because she didn't think about Ego at all before going to bed and yet she featured in her dream.

She went into a deep thought. She asked herself how Ego happened to get the picture of her husband and a lady smiling widely in embrace. She asked herself why Ego had to meddle in her husband's life and why she should show her the picture, saying nasty things about her husband and marriage just to poison her mind. She asked herself why she did not verify the truth from her husband first before quarrelling with him. She also asked herself why she was angry with her husband over what he did not even know about. She knew she had a problem that had been affecting her reasoning, but she didn't know how to help herself come out of her problems. She concluded that she must have been a fool to listen to Ego and to let her lure her to destroy her marriage. She suspected that Ego was angry with her husband over something she was unsure of but knew that it must have really hurt her and she had used her naivety and stupidity to take revenge on her husband. Raaluchi wept, blaming herself for everything. She needed to see her husband. It was as though the revelation opened her right sense of judgement, as though it stopped the voices from controlling her for some time, as though it came with a positive impact that stripped her of her overbearing stupidity.

The next things Raaluchi did that morning were to take a shower, dress up, and take a bus to Onitsha: to her mother's house, and there, she pleaded with her mother to tell her where to find her husband, if she really knew and Mummy refused to say anything. She wanted Raaluchi to suffer for the pains she had caused her husband simply because Onyeka truly loved her and had been trying to make her happy. For all she knew,

Raaluchi her daughter was very ungrateful and she blamed her late husband, Nnanyelugo for misleading Raaluchi with words of pride and insatiable desire. Raaluchi had inherited that dreadful character from Nnanyelugo, her father.

"I don't know where your husband is. Begin to say your prayers… just pray that he doesn't come home with another woman that will take your place," Mummy spoke angrily to her daughter who had been getting on her nerves and had refused to change.

The thought of Onyeka coming home with another woman scared Raaluchi, even though she was sure that her husband was incapable of such an act because she knew he loved her so much and that he was godly. She hastened out of the house immediately with a heavy heart. On her way, she called her husband incessantly but he did not answer the calls. She sent him lovely text messages but got no reply. She was worried and she had to dash to her husband's company to know if he was there, but Jerry the General Manager realizing just immediately that Onyeka's wife had no idea about his absence, guessed that Onyeka's absence was a secret to his wife and he would be in trouble if he disclosed it without Onyeka's consent. He had to excuse himself pretending to be pressed and called his boss in one of the rest rooms in the company. Onyeka gave him an order not to disclose any information to Raaluchi and he agreed. Raaluchi cried silently as she left the company and traveled to Nsukka to see her friend and take solace in her. She couldn't bear to lose her husband after she had discovered in her revelation the previous night that Ego had fooled her and had come between her and her husband.

Just as the bus sped to Nsukka, she reminisced how lovely her husband had been to her and tears tickled down her cheeks. "What has she been doing?" She asked herself but she wished she could get the correct answers to her question, not until she saw Onyeka, not until she looked him deep in his eyes and tell him how sorry she was to have caused him so much pain, to have mingled with Ego, to have allowed the issue of pregnancy, her pride and her mind of comparison to disrupt the love they had for each other, especially Onyeka who had made her life so beautiful, who had shown her what true love really meant, who was there for her in her bad times. How could she have been so mean to the only man who truly loved her? She couldn't believe that she never thought of that before allowing Ego to fool her.

It was as though her eyes became clear and her mind became sound enough in that peaceful state she was in last night, before she drifted to sleep. She believed that it was the peace of God that revealed the truth to her through the revelation. The issue of pregnancy and her faithlessness had pulled her down so much even when Onyeka's people were not bothered, considering the fact that Onyeka was the only son of his father. She sniffed in tears and the old woman that was sitting very close to her in the bus, was moved to console her like her own daughter and advised her that whatever reason for her crying should not take away her happiness and she should just commit her problems to God in prayers. But Raaluchi couldn't remember the last time she had prayed. She had been angry with God and had been questioning her fate and so, she suspended her prayers as usual.

* * * *

Raaluchi saw Ikogu street in Nsukka a scrappy place, forlon, and faded with its sandy roads. Market women were selling fruits and vegetables by the roads, and there were some people hovering by the side and pricing them. Shops stood side by side in shappy views. Most of the buildings were bungalows joined to one another in sliding rows. She walked cautiously; cautious enough not to pull down a market woman's goods by mistake, and be forced to pay for it. She kept walking until she entered Nkiruka's house: a beautiful bungalow facing tired bungalows in a large compound. Nkiruka was pounding yam in the kitchen with her condition of pregnancy. Her face was battered with bruises. Raaluchi was shocked as she watched her with mouth agape and squinted eyes. She had actually come to seek solace from Nkiruka but Nkiruka's condition seemed to be worse than hers, making it difficult to give her attention.

"Nkiruka, what happened to you? Why are you pounding yam in your pregnancy? Don't you have a house help anymore?" Nkiruka answered her with tears running down her cheeks. Raaluchi had always been telling her through telephone conversation that she wished she was in her shoes just because Nkiruka was almost through with her school, had gotten married and had gotten pregnant shortly after her wedding. Raaluchi had wished to be in her shoes without realizing that Nkiruka had married a man who redesigned her face with blows and hot slaps anytime she asked for money for her toiletries.

"Raaluchi, I married a beast. Jekwu is just a devil. He almost raped my house girl to death before I finally sent her back to her parent's house. *O di egwu,* It's wonderful. I wanted a man like your husband and I married a devil who convinced me that he was very rich while he didn't even have a dime…*kobo, o nwero!*" Nkiruka snapped her fingers to show the seriousness of the situation; about her husband not having a dime. She continued. "Do you know he had actually borrowed money for my wedding ceremony and the lenders are now on his neck? They had even threatened to sell our house if he did not pay back in three months. Raaluchi my friend, just take a look at me. Take a look at the person you want to be in her shoes." Nkiruka burst into an uncontrollable tears and Raaluchi was moved to console her.

"How did you meet this Jekwu your husband?" Raaluchi asked her friend as she allowed Nkiruka's head to rest on her left shoulder.

"I met him in school. He gave me a ride in a flashy jeep that I was not sure if it was his or he borrowed from someone just to entice me. We became friends afterwards. He bought me so many good things. I was only mesmerized about the goodies he showered on me before I accepted to marry him and I thought I had finally gotten a rich man that can help me actualize my dream of touring Las Vegas. I thought that he was a successful international business man like he told me, while he hasn't even been to Lagos, *ifukwa?*

"My goodness, Nkiruka, don't tell me that you barely know the man that you married?

"Raaluchi my sister, I just discovered that I did not know the man I married, and this is my fault o…I married him out of curiousity. You were going to travel to America with your husband for your honey moon and I wanted the same for myself. The money he showered on me blindfolded me and I thought he was actually a rich man. He lied to me. He told me that he imports computers from America and I believed him because he looked so wealthy and comfortable, until our Armada Jeep disappeared from the compound a week after our wedding and did not appear again, until some men tried to fight him in our living room one Sunday morning, urging him to pay his depts. Raaluchi my sister, the truth of the matter is that I don't know who my husband is. I cannot say anything good about Mr. Chukwujekwu Okafor. He is a liar, a drunkard, a rapist, and a brutal fighter. Look at where my long throat has landed me into; just because I was curious to marry a man like your husband, a man that can take me to *Obodo oyibo* just like your husband did for you," Nkiruka spoke in tears and Raaluchi consoled her as she reminisced over her relationship with Chiedu and how she lost her virginity to a man who was just a beast and then, her mind finally settled on Onyeka, the sunshine in her life, a precious gift from God that she had fiddled with and she wished desperately that he would come back to her. She was willing to change.

Raaluchi was admiring Nkiruka's destiny without knowing that Nkiruka had been longing to be in her own shoes. Raaluchi just realized that she never knew the value of what she had. Her heart beat very fast as she thought of going to see the priest that administered the sacrament of their matrimony and blessed their marriage. She was going to plead with him to talk to her husband to come back home. She was willing to change. Raaluchi wept, saying to herself that she should have been grateful to God for giving her a man that had a compendium of goodness and lacked nothing. She should have been grateful to God that Onyeka really loved her and had been tolerating her bad moods and naggings but never raised his hands on her, unlike Nkiruka's husband. She should have been grateful to God because her husband had been trying to make her happy despite the fact that she wasn't good to him at all, but had been taking his love for granted and feeling very important in her pride. She should be grateful to God because her marriage was far too good to be compared with Nkiruka's, her friend and her rival.

Raaluchi went home looking devastated. She had no appetite to eat, and just then, she reminisced again how lovely Onyeka had been to her right from the onset and she blamed herself for treating her husband with so much contempt, a man that had truly loved her. She promised herself to change if her husband finally returned. Just then, she switched on the television and the news flashed that the jamb results for the year 2010 was out and she smiled and remembered how Onyeka had taught her some subjects, the sleepless nights they had had when Onyeka was trying to make sure that she had the best result. That was in February, the second month after their honeymoon before her pregnancy madness started. She wished she could turn the hands of time. She called her husband again for the fifteenth time but he did not answer the call.

* * * *

The raging voice which Ego heard behind her startled her. She had been soliloquizing and smiling to herself about her deceit on Raaluchi and how her plans had been successful. She didn't realize that she had left the kitchen door open and

Raaluchi had been listening to her from behind. *'It was true. It was a revelation after all, not just a dream.'* Raaluchi said in her mind. She was convinced. Ego had indeed used her. Fear gripped Ego when she saw Raaluchi's blazing eyes.

"You devil! You used me! You deceived me! You are the reason why my husband has left me! I hate you!" Raaluchi shouted furiously on Ego as she made a move towards her. The voices screamed in her, urging her to stab Ego for ruining her marriage and she was about to stab Ego with a kitchen knife that she had hidden at her waist, just between her skirt and her sleeveless top. Ego struggled with Raaluchi for the knife until she got it from her and threw it away.

"And so what if I used you? People use their fellow people to get what they want, isn't it? Is it my fault that you were such a big fool and that you don't even trust your man?" Ego said to Raaluchi with an impish grin, and Raaluchi noticed that it was exactly the same grin she had seen in her revelation. The urge to kill Ego came to her and Raaluchi grabbed her hair until she pulled her down. The two women engaged in a fight and Raaluchi made sure that she smashed Ego's face. Ego finally took control of the fight and she pushed Raaluchi out of her house and bolted her door. She leaned on the kitchen door and gasped, holding her chest, before she finally ran to her room and watched her face through her dressing mirror. Raaluchi had just designed her face with bruises.

"You have finally stepped on my toes Raaluchi, and because of these bruises you gave me, I'll go ahead with my Plan B. I'll never stop until I see you wallow in misery," Ego soliloquized as she watched herself through her dressing mirror.

PART TWO

SPEAKING IN SILENCE

THE YEAR 2012

Silence is a painful disease that has a magical
key to unlock every closed iron door.

CHAPTER FOURTEEN

BOBO CRAWLED ON the floor and babbled 'Mummy see' as he pointed at a picture on the television. Raaluchi laughed when she discovered that the picture was 'Barney and friends': a play song for kids. Bobo laughed along as he watched Barney, a dinosaur, move his ear-like curved hips in a funny way, with slight jumps and wiggles. Nanny Nene was ready to sweep the filthy floor of the living room where Bobo had just messed up with biscuits. Nanny Nene was a fat light skinned woman in her late thirties who did nothing but work diligently without grumbling. She was employed by Onyeka, a month after Bobo's birth, which was in June 2011. Raaluchi couldn't resist admiring Bobo and every time she stared at him, it was just like staring at her husband. It was half past seven in the evening and she had just returned from school. She was a two hundred level student of Delta State University, Asaba campus.

She made her way to the Master's Bedroom to meet her husband, the Master's Bedroom, because that was where her husband slept without her, and there she saw him busy with his lap top. He smiled up to her, a wry smile, as response to her greeting. Silence surpassed between them and Onyeka spoke to her in his mind, not to dare come closer for he couldn't offer her anything more than a fake smile. And she understood. She understood him when she moved forward to hug him but didn't get his attention. She had not given up on him yet. She must not give up on him. She must continue to be nice until she won back his love. The priest had told her not to give up and so she must not give up.

Just then, Onyeka's cell phone rang, and he stared at Raaluchi and then ignored the call. The phone rang for the second time and this time, Onyeka answered it and told the caller that he would return the call later and added that he loved her.

"Is she still calling you?"Raaluchi asked immediately. Her mind raced vigorously as she watched her husband continue to work on his lap top. He couldn't even look at her. He didn't want to look at her, nor talk to her. Raaluchi was not sure what the shriveling in her stomach and the racing in her chest meant, but she knew she was hurt. She was hurt because Onyeka could profess love for a woman in her presence. She only wished she could bear it. And if she couldn't, what will she do? Leave her marriage? No way!

"Onyeka, I'm talking to you…"

Onyeka remained silent, an offensive silence, as though she was a big fool. Bobo yelled in a long cry and Raaluchi dashed to the living room to meet him and he pointed at Nanny Nene, reporting her to Raaluchi for sweeping off his pieces of biscuits. Raaluchi cuddled him and playfully told Nanny Nene that she would beat her so mercilessly for making her baby yell in tears.

It seemed very painful and unbearable to Raaluchi that her husband had not spoken to her for over one year before Bobo was born, that was after their meeting with Father Joe the priest that administered the sacrament of marriage to them. His silence pierced her heart like a sharp sword. But she must be patient. She was forced to be patient because she had no choice; she had realized that she was the architect of her misfortune and she was also trying to make up for her foolishness that had destroyed her marriage. She must continue to pray, Father Joe had encouraged her to pray in patience if she must win back Onyeka's love. She had been crying to Jesus in the Blessed Sacrament, begging Him to have mercy on her and give her a second chance to change and be a submissive wife and not a nagger. She wondered as she served breakfast in the dinning room, at the dinning table, when that day would be, a day when her husband would at least say 'hello' to her. She would be the happiest woman when that day comes.

One morning, Onyeka settled down for breakfast. The only thing that gave her hope in her prayers was that Onyeka had started eating her food after he had rejected it for a long time. She had rejoiced when Nanny told her one Saturday afternoon that Onyeka called the house phone. He wanted Raaluchi to prepare *ora* soup for him. She had prepared a very delicious *ora* soup for her husband, happily, and she had watched him eat although he didn't talk to her or even commend her for her delicious meal. She had waited every night to welcome him from work and try to make him talk to her when he ate, but all to no avail. Whenever she spoke, she got an offensive silence as a response.

She had tried seducing him by going naked in front of him, but he only walked away and didn't fall for it. Raaluchi had been crying her hearts out, wondering when that day would come, a day when she would win back her husband's love. Her matrimonial home was becoming a dysfunctional atmosphere for her. Raaluchi had wanted to hear her husband's voice, to hear him speak to her when she asked him if he wanted his bread toasted or not, knowing full well that Onyeka her husband eats only toasted bread. Onyeka ignored her and got up to leave for work, before Raaluchi held him and begged him not to go for she had already served him some toasted bread. Onyeka sat back and enjoyed his breakfast in silence.

* * * *

Jekwu came home at 10pm in the night humming a song and dancing in front of his wife, shaking his buttocks in a funny way that he farted but didn't spoil the air. Nkiruka couldn't help but sneer at him and at the same time, she blamed herself for falling so cheaply for a drunkard and a rapist because of money. Her parents warned her when she was about to get married to Jekwu but she refused to listen to them because she was only blindfolded that she couldn't look beyond what she had seen in a man that she wanted to give the rest of her life to. She was done with her youth service and was still looking for a job but all to no avail. She considered her life with Jekwu a total bad luck.

"I bought you *suya,* you'll like it, *O di oyi! di uso!* It's good and delicious." Jekwu spoke his Igbo so proudly, like someone who can bet to tell his wife how proud he was of his language. He was from Nsukka and his dialect had a strong rural accent.

"Eat your *suya* alone. If you think you can have me just for some pieces of meat, then you must be out of your mind, *onye anuluma!* Drunkard! You are just a bad luck!"

Jekwu did not think twice before he pounced on her with some blows and kicks until she was forced to apologize in tears. Their baby cried in the room and Jekwu went to carry her but was stopped by Nkiruka who snatched the baby from him.

"Give me my baby! I hate you! Go away!"

"Nky, I'm sorry. I didn't mean to beat you," Jekwu said with pleading gestures, recovering from what he did.

"I hate you! Useless man!"

Nkiruka cried bitterly as she held her one year old baby girl in her arms. Again, she remembered her parents who had been totally against her marriage to Jekwu but had no choice to yield to their daughter's plea to get married to him because they thought she loved him and really knew him. Jekwu left the house and went to Madam Caro's bar to drink his sorrows away. Madam Caro was a palmwine seller. She was very fat, large-hipped and busty. She tolerated no nonsense from anybody, that people around the neighbourhood, especially her customers nicknamed her 'Action woman.' She never sold her drinks on credit and would lock any drunkard that refused to pay her inside her bar until dawn. Her bar was an old inferior building that had louvers for its small window. Her bar had inscriptions that gave some people pops of laughter when they read them: *Madam Caro the action woman tolerates no nonsense. She gives drinks to everybody in the bar but locks up those who have lost their senses to pay.*

Jekwu was used to getting locked up in Madam Caro's bar. He would stay there in his drunken state and sleep off and then, pay his bills in the morning. Sometimes, he would be bullied and beaten by his fellow drunkards who spent the night with him in the bar, whenever he farted unconsciously in his sleep. He would scream in pains and beg for the dawn to come and rescue him. That night, he ordered for three bottles of palm wine. There was a boulder in his chest and a stinging in his throat. His eyes filled with tears. He began to gulp down the first bottle, trusting the palmwine to make him feel better. He was crying inside him and as he slept on a bench in Madam Caro's bar later at mid night, flying cockroaches welcomed him as they perched on his ears and on his opened mouth, leaking his saliva. He was snoring heavily in his sleep that he didn't notice the cockroaches as they feasted on him.

CHAPTER FIFTEEN

JUST LIKE HE did every week, he went to see Ifeoma. It was on a sunny Friday afternoon and he had taken some time off in his office just to be with her. He was longing for her embrace, her songs and her bodily union. Ifeoma welcomed him with a glass of Orange juice and he enjoyed the juice with a striping look at her but she was indisposed. Previously, she would welcome him with kisses, hungry passionate kisses and they would make love in the living room. She would sing for him to fall asleep; songs she was used to singing, songs that already existed before she knew about them. And again, he would call her Raalu before falling asleep. Later, she would go inside the kitchen to get something for him to eat and drink. But now, things seemed to have changed and this change displeased Onyeka. Ifeoma had welcomed him with just a chubby hug, asked him how his day went, and served him a chilled Orange juice with a displeasing indifference, as though it was just yesterday they last saw each other.

Ifeoma was going to tell him that she wouldn't continue with the sinful relationship anymore and that she had given her life to Christ and also that she couldn't bear his wife's incessant text messages, pleading with her to leave her husband alone. Ifeoma had come to understand that she was a woman just like his wife and she had realized that if she ever got married and her husband got hooked with a mistress, she would not be happy. She had to put a stop to her affair with Onyeka. She owed the Ibekwe's family nothing anymore.

"What is wrong with you? I'm sure you don't look bright," Onyeka asked Ifeoma very softly as he moved closer to her, but she moved to the extreme of the sofa just to avoid him.

"Do you need more money? Do you want another car? Please Ify, talk to me. You know I hate it when you look sad."

"Onyeka, I can't continue with this…I'll forever be haunted by my conscience knowing that what we are doing is wrong. Raaluchi your wife still loves you and I think its time for you to forgive her for whatever she has done to you."

Onyeka's heart raced in fury as he frowned and infuriated and furiously, he shattered the glass of juice on the floor and Ifeoma held him and begged him to calm down.

"So tell me, has she been calling you?"

A brief silence held the question hanging.

"Speak up now!"

"She has not been calling me. I just feel for her. If I were in her shoes, I wouldn't be happy. Onyeka please for the sake of God, forgive her and move on with her. I know you still love her and I'm sure she loves you. If she doesn't, she would have left your house a long time ago."

"And who cares if she leaves my house? I've fallen out of love with her. She's a pain in the ass…she ruined my life."

"Onyeka I want to change for the better. I've given my life to Christ."

Onyeka laughed raucously until he flung himself on a sofa. There was a brief silence after the laugh as he remembered how Raaluchi changed him. He had always thought that it was all lies about what he heard people say about the negative changes some wives bring out in their husbands, to think that he of all people could abandon his faith just because of a woman. To him, Raaluchi was just a Delilah in his life who had shaved his hair after he had been trapped in her beauty and the passionate love he had for her. The thought of it infuriated him and made him detest Raaluchi more. He beckoned on Ifeoma and she sat down beside him. He asked her softly why she wanted to quit the relationship, he asked her again if his wife had been talking to her but she lied, a jocose lie just to save the life of a marriage that she had ruined. She was regretting everything now. She couldn't bear that she was riding a jeep and lived alone in a comfortable bungalow while his own wife had nothing and took a taxi to school. It was as though she had stolen everything from Raaluchi, she had stolen her man, her happiness, her comfort and as far as she was still alive with a conscience, she owed her an apology.

"Look Ify, this is not time to feel pity for anybody. You make me happy and I refuse to quit this relationship."

"But Onyeka…"

"Sing for me. A soft music that can put me to sleep," Onyeka said, taking off his shirt and then he lay on the long sofa, his head on Ifeoma's laps. Ifeoma obeyed deciding within her to take things easy and leave him quietly. She had to leave him. She must leave him. She had caused so much pain to Raaluchi. How could Onyeka be so mean? Raaluchi, his wife was taking good care of Bobo, his own baby. That was a good reason to forgive her.

* * * *

Raaluchi visited Mummy on a Sunday afternoon. She took Bobo with her. That was the only Onyeka she had now, and when Bobo talked to her, it was as though Onyeka was finally talking to her and making up for his long silence. Arinze hugged his sister so tight, unable to let go of the hug. He had heard from Mummy about Raaluchi's marital problems and he had felt pity for her. It had been long since they saw each other and so, he held unto the hug for a long time, fighting his tears. He lifted Bobo up and down in a playful way and he chortled. His crackled laughter pleased Arinze and when he put him down, he held unto his hand, begging him to lift him up some more, and he did, until Raaluchi told Bobo to let Arinze rest. They all settled down for lunch in the dinning room. It was rice and chicken stew and Raaluchi fed Bobo as she ate.

"Mummy has never stopped being a good cook," Raaluchi commended Mummy and stifled a smile and even Bobo smiled, as though he understood.

"It's a far cry from what I eat in school. Mummy's food is surely the best," Arinze said, eating voraciously. He took permission from Mummy to get more chickens from the pot and Mummy concurred. Raaluchi gave a slight start. She gave Mummy a quizzical look and Mummy understood and nodded.

"He has changed," Mummy said to Raaluchi and she nodded a slow nod with an odd facial expression, and in her mind, was full of words restrained.

Arinze came back from the kitchen with a plate of two chicken laps and Raaluchi watched him closely and differently, with her eyes fixed on his eyes, as though she was absorbing the change in him. Arinze continued to eat voraciously. He would take a scoop of rice, chew fastly and take a bite of the chicken. He enjoyed the food.

"Make sure you don't eat like this in public," Raaluchi said to her brother and chuckled, amused at the manner he was eating the food, as though the food was running away.

"I know. I'm just feeling free in my house," Arinze said and gulped down a chilled glass of water.

Mummy watched her daughter and the deep affection she had for Bobo, as she often asked Bobo if he's okay, if he wants to eat any other thing. Mummy watched Raaluchi's body and discovered that she was looking skinny. She knew exactly what Raaluchi was going through. It was a pity that things turned out so badly for her. If only she had listened to her, if only she had hearkened to the advice of her loved ones, even her mother-in-law, if only she had observed wisdom and patience in life, she wouldn't have suffered much. She was so impatient to wait on God for her admission and now that she had finally gotten it, her marital happiness was missing. Everything seemed to be so incomplete because of her impatience and stupidity.

Mummy knew that that was not what God planned for her but her lack of faith and patience pushed her to the wrong track. But Mummy was happy all the same because her daughter had hoped that things would turn out for good in the nearest future. This Father Joe must be so powerful to have succeeded in changing her daughter to be so patient with her husband: a seed of faith, something that had never been in her daughter's dictionary.

CHAPTER SIXTEEN

RAALUCHI WAITED FOR Father Joe at the church pavement. It was after a Saturday morning mass and people had gathered for the blessings of their sacramentals and to book appointments with him. Two women hovered at a corner as they spoke in low tones, eyeing Father Joe. One was very old and the other was very much younger. Raaluchi chuckled as she listened to them and watched one of them snap her fingers in a startled expression as she spoke.

"*O na asu ka ndi ocha.* He speaks like the white men. He should learn how to speak Igbo so that we wouldn't have to feel like outcasts when he speaks. We should really pray for him so that souls wouldn't have to perish because he cannot speak his mother tongue," Ekemma, the old woman spoke in Igbo as she snapped her fingers, chewed her chewing stick and spat out on the sandy floor: some pale yellow saliva. She was very short and her body was so shriveled. The smell of her moist wrapper was unpleasant, and her white T –shirt that revealed her sagging breasts had an inscription "*ADIEU PAPA*" on it.

"Mama, I heard that part of his life as a *fada* had been in… what should I call it? Is it Romeo or Romo?" The other woman, Orjiugo said in English as she thought for a while, her eyes closed in a way that people do when they could not remember something that is within the reach of their memories. Ekemma sneered at her. She had just been insulted. Who does Orjiugo think she is to speak English to her after she had just complained about Father Joe's own that she could barely hear,

145

not to talk of understanding? Ekemma controlled her temper, smiling in pretence as she waited for Orjiugo to finish her statement before she asked a question that had been on her mind as soon as Orjiugo let her English flow freely out of her mouth, just to spite her.

"Is your son through with his University education? *O gusigo?*"

Ekemma asked Orjiugo in Igbo and Orjiugo nodded in return.

"And he has started teaching you how to speak English, *o kwa ya?*" Orjiugo nodded again.

"Very good… I'm sure he must have also taught you how to insult an old woman by making her look like an *'onuku',* a fool, simply because you speak the language she cannot speak," Ekemma spoke in infuriation, a silent infuriation, the kind that pretended to be happy by exposing her teeth, while her heart boiled in deep fury.

"No Mama, I didn't mean to insult you o. I was just trying to practice my English lessons." Orjiugo replied in Igbo.

"Of course you didn't mean to insult me. You were just practicing your idea on a poor old woman after all. *Ikpe amaro gi,* It's not your fault," Ekemma spoke, still faking a smile as she walked away and her slippers made a clattering noise. Orjiugo followed suit, trying to get her attention by pleading for pardon but Ekemma did not stop. Raaluchi smiled at them as she watched them leave the church's compound.

Raaluchi followed Father Joe to the parish house and they sat down in the living room to talk about her marriage. The remembrance of her marital problems drove her to tears. Raaluchi narrated her experiences: her husband's unbearable silence, his late nights coupled with his affairs with his mistress. She narrated in tears as she spoke hoarsely.

"Father, I'm loosing hope. I don't think I can ever win back his love," Raaluchi sniffed in tears as she wiped them with her handkerchief.

"You don't have to loose hope. You should keep your hope high for that day. When he'll speak to you will definitely come."

"But Father…"

"You must not stop praying. Your prayers are working. The fact that he has started eating your food is enough sign of your answered prayers. You must not give up."

Raaluchi nodded and sniffed in tears.

"By the way, have you been sending text messages to his mistress, like I told you?"

The hearing of her husband's mistress saddened her more. She began to cry all over again.

"Have you been pleading in the text messages or have you been threatening her to leave your husband alone?"

"Father, I've been pleading with her. But I really think it's better to start threatening her because she may be taking my pleas for granted."

Father Joe giggled at Raaluchi and advised her to be wise. Threatening her husband's mistress would worsen situations. The best thing to do was to plead with her, using bible quotations because, soft words are kind and easy to speak but their echoes are endless and last forever. Father Joe advised Raaluchi that soft words are powerful to the conscience, and shouldn't be taken for granted. He advised her to remain soft with her husband's mistress.

"What attracted your husband to you?" Father Joe asked Raaluchi and the question reminded her about Ego, the enemy that had participated in ruining her marriage. Somehow, she didn't want to answer Father Joe but she did answer because Father Joe was a priest and definitely had nothing serious to do with what he had asked her.

"My singing voice, my youngness and my beauty," These are the primary things I know that attracted him to me."

"Have you been doing that in his presence, I mean, have you been looking beautiful for him and singing for him?"

"Father, I've been doing that but he doesn't look at me at

all, even my songs don't impress him anymore. He's just being too silent and it's breaking my heart. I don't know the charm this Ifeoma used on my husband that is so difficult to leave my husband's eyes."

"You must not give up. I have this feeling that you'll smile soon, and please when you do smile again, hold what you have so tight and appreciate it."

"Father, I've learned my lessons. This is just an eye opener for me," Raaluchi said hoarsely as she sniffed in tears.

Father Joe consoled her and assured her of his prayers and even took her to the chapel and prayed for her before she left. Bobo was crying in his father's arms when Raaluchi reached home. Onyeka was singing a song for him but he cried harder, he cried because his father's voice was croaked. As soon as he saw Raaluchi, he stretched his arms for an embrace and Raaluchi carried him with smiles on her face and greeted her husband who was lost in thoughts while looking at them, how Bobo giggled softly as soon as Raaluchi carried him and ruffled his hair and sang him a song, a song so melodious: *'Bobo is a fine boy, iya iya ooo…"* Onyeka was forced to reminisce the first time he met her on a crusade ground. He couldn't help smiling so widely, so glamorously, that Raaluchi stood watching him and smiling back at him. Father Joe's prayers had finally worked just so soon. She moved forward to feel his warmth before he realized their distance and walked away, refusing to fall for it, to fall for that melodious voice and that glamorous smile that revealed her dimples and dim eyes. Raaluchi almost cried. Her belly clenched. She looked suddenly pale and her entire body was trembling in rejection. She held Bobo tightly, as though she was begging him not to walk away from her too. Still trembling, she realized that she was slowly walking into the world of the dead. The detritus of her marital life: a life of rejection and depression was slowly taking her. She remembered Father Joe and revived her strenghth. She took Bobo to the nursery and sang him more songs and finally, she got him settled on his bed and talked to him.

"I want your father to talk to me. What will I do to make him speak to me? What will I do to win back his love? Bobo my darling, just give me a sign, I'll understand. You just have to help Mummy win back Daddy's love."

And just then, Bobo pointed at a mobile phone charging at the wall socket and Raaluchi realized that it was hers. She was actually charging the phone last night when he sang lullaby for Bobo. Raaluchi watched him point continuously at the phone and she went for it and noticed that she had a text message. Surprisingly, it was from Ifeoma: her husband's mistress. She told Raaluchi in the text message that she was willing to leave her husband alone. She apologized for causing her so much pain by taking what belonged to her. She begged to see Raaluchi in her school on Monday to tell her what to do to win back Onyeka's love. Raaluchi smiled and tears of joy streamed down her cheeks. She clutched Bobo in her arms and kissed his cheek and then he chuckled and babbled: 'Mummy' and just then she realized the truth in what people say about children being angels of God.

Raaluchi replied the text message, promising to meet her in her school on Monday. Just immediately after she had sent the text, her phone rang. It was Nkiruka calling her. She was crying and she begged Raaluchi to accommodate her and her baby girl in her matrimonial house until she discovered where else to stay away from Jekwu. Raaluchi practically refused, considering the fact that she had been through a lot, she wasn't on speaking terms with her husband and she didn't want Jekwu to start causing troubles in her house simply because she was harboring his family.

"Nkiruka, marriage is not a bed of roses. You appended your signature for it and you just have to endure and make it work," Raaluchi replied softly and Nkiruka gave a start as she listened to her. She didn't expect to hear such words from Raaluchi her friend.

"Make it work? How can I possibly make it work? You know the kind of man I married, don't you? He's going to kill me if I continue to live with him and my parents are not even helping matters. They've refused to harbor me."

"You can make it work through prayers. Nkiruka, go down on your knees and pray. You are married to Jekwu and the fact will remain for the rest of your life. It's inevitable. You have made the mistake of making riches your prerequisite for love, and now, you only need to correct your mistakes by stooping to conquer. You already have a child with Jekwu, and even if you decide to leave your marriage, you'll remain a second hand material and no sensible man would ever want to marry a woman that had been married. He would always be afraid with the thoughts that you may have done something wrong for you to have left your matrimonial home. Nkiruka, you can change situations with prayers and humility. You can never conquer without stooping."

"What are you saying to me, Raaluchi?" Nkiruka asked in bewilderment. She was bewildered because the Raaluchi she knew was just as proud as a peacock but this Raaluchi that was speaking to her seemed to be totally different. She sounded like a humble angel.

"Listen to me Nkiruka, the beauty of your marriage is in your hands. You hold the key to the changes you want in your husband. He loves you so much to have married you. You will be happy in your marriage, if you focus on the good characters of your husband instead of his flaws. You are not a saint either and we are all faced with our imperfections. He can stop being a drunkard and a rapist if you pray for him and respect him. Life is too short and things change with time. He may be the richest man in the world tomorrow, who knows? Love him now for whom he is and enjoy your marriage."

"But Raaluchi...If I stoop for him, he'll put me in his pocket."

"If he put you in his pocket, you eat what is in his pocket. Nkiruka please reflect on what I've just told you and put it into practice. I'll like you to get this book in any available book shop: **The Beauty in Humility.** It was given to me by Father Joe, my spiritual director, who is also the author. The book has really changed me. It will change your marriage. You don't just run away from your marriage like a coward, you face it with boldness. Marriage is a 'stick and stay' relationship and not a 'hit and run' relationship"

The line went off and Nkiruka heaved a sigh on her bed and began to ponder on what Raaluchi had told her. She wondered if those words of wisdom actually came from Raaluchi her arrogant friend. She had just packed her things and, as a matter of fact, she was ready to leave her husband's house with her daughter. She was going to leave Jekwu for good and to hell with the marriage if it would strangle her to death. She had better things to do with her life than to get hooked in a marriage that offered her nothing but sorrows. As she looked at her luggage, she heaved a deep sigh of hopelessness. She didn't know where else to go. Raaluchi was her only hope, and now she had turned her down, and she blamed herself for not asking her first before packing their things. She had hoped that Raaluchi would send her address to her as soon as she asked her for help, but it didn't just work out the way she had hoped. She thought of going to Nneoma's house. It wasn't far from the University.

Nneoma was her course mate in school and was living alone in a room apartment. She had not graduated because she still had so many carry over courses to write. She would definitely harbour them in her house, but she changed her mind when she thought of how she had boasted about her husband to her hearing, few days before her wedding with Jekwu. She had told Nneoma that she had finally gotten a rich man that would help her actualize her dreams, and that her man was fun to be with and was also the richest man in Nigeria. She felt ashamed to go back to that same Nneoma and expose her marital problems to her, to let her know that the man whom she had actually boasted about was not who she thought he was. Nneoma would mock her. She would laugh at her and tell her that she would rather remain single, than marry such a person. She knew Nneoma very well to do that to her. She didn't want to expose her problems to someone who cannot help her solve them. She didn't want to expose her problems to someone who would only worsen her situation by mocking her and exposing her problems to other people's ears. She knew Nneoma well to do that to her.

She had one day boasted about Nonso, her school boyfriend's parents to be rich and well connected politicians, until Nonso's mother showed up in school one broad day light and sent Nneoma to call her. She had come to sell her knitted hair nets to female students who were interested to buy. Nkiruka had felt very ashamed; ashamed that Nonso actually gave her name to his mother for her to supply customers for her. And so, it became Nneoma's subject of mockery in her hostel, in her department, in school canteens, virtually everywhere they met. She mocked her about becoming a daughter-in-law to 'a hair net seller' and unbearably, she broke up with Nonso some days after Raaluchi's wedding. She didn't want poverty in her life. It was a big disease to her. She had dated Nonso because she was receiving from him, everything she needed for her upkeep in school, without caring to know how he got the money. But she just couldn't bear the shame of dating a boy whose parents were still struggling for livelihood. It was a big embarrassement to her and she was a big girl in campus…the '*Nky baby oku.*' She broke up with Nonso.

Nkiruka wanted an experienced married woman or even a priest to counsel her; someone who can understand how she felt, and help her to solve her problems without exposing them. She pondered continuously on what Raaluchi told her and soliloquized in tears. "How can I possibly stay married to a man that tricked me into marrying him? How can I stay married to a poor stricken man, a fighter, a rapist, an animal? Oh God, help me."

For Raaluchi to have spoken to her with so much wisdom and enlightenment, Nkiruka took an overwhelming decision to buy this mysterious book that had really changed her friend. She carried her daughter on her back, made her way to the University Book Shop and searched for the book but to no avail. It was when she was on her way home that she saw another book shop that sold inspirational books. She hurried inside the bookshop and asked for the book and the seller gave it to her. The seller increased the price of the book as soon as he saw the curiosity in Nkiruka's face but she did not mind giving the seller the only money she had left, just to read this book that had really changed Raaluchi. Back home, she opened the book and what she saw on the preface was an instruction by the author. He was instructing the reader of his book to spend at least one hour in a Catholic Church, gazing at the crucifix. She wondered if Raaluchi had obeyed the author before reading other pages of the book. She attended Mass every Sunday but she never for once gazed at the crucifix, because there was nothing so special about it, if not that Christ died for humanity and there was an evidence of his death on the cross. And now, she was instructed in the book to gaze at it for at least one hour.

She obeyed because she was sure that Raaluchi had obeyed the author. Her baby was still sleeping. She carried her on her back again with a wrapper and left for St. Vincent de Paul Catholic Church. It was a stone throw to her house. The church had an indispensable silence for prayer and meditation. She saw a little girl of about five years old, kneeling at the altar with outstretched arms and absolute wholeheartedness. She was mumbling prayers and her eyes were shut. She was inside the church's indispensable silence and she was safe in this silence. Nkiruka looked around to know if she had come with her parents, but she was alone in the big church with this little girl. She guessed that her mother may have brought her and left, hoping to come back for her later. To her, that was an outrageous faith; for a mother to leave her daughter alone in the church, believing that she was safe. She was moved to tears as she saw her. What went through her mind as she gazed at the little girl was that: *if this little girl had so much faith to have known what God was capable of doing, what about a grown up like her?*

She raised her face to the crucifix and began to gaze at it. She didn't plan to meditate on it, but she found herself meditating on it as she gazed at it. She meditated on the crown of thorns that was hung on the head of Jesus, the blood that oozed out of His head, the pain that He must have felt with that crown of thorns ravaging his head. She meditated on His outstretched arms on the cross, the nails that pierced His palms; the blood that oozed out from His palms. She meditated on His bleeding left side, His knees and His feet. She began to imagine how awful it must have been for Him as He went through the pains on the cross. He volunteered himself to go through a punishment that He didn't deserve. He went through the punishment that would have been for humanity simply because of 'love.' He humbled himself and went through pains on the cross simply because of 'love.'

Nkiruka continued to meditate on the crucifix, and then, she found herself apologizing to Jesus for all her sins: her fornications in Secondary School and University, her series of abortion. She was crying and rendering her apologies when the little girl's mother entered the church and tapped her daughter's shoulder to wake up from her sleep. The little girl had slept off in the altar after her prayers. After an hour, Nkiruka went home to read the mysterious book.

* * * *

The book: The Beauty in Humility.

Day One: The writer discusses the victory derived in patient waiting. Pride prevents patient waiting because the proud person thinks so highly of himself that he believes he should never be inconvenienced in anyway. He discusses that if we get the idea in our heads that everything concerning us; our circumstances, marriage and relationships should always be perfect... no inconveniences, no unlovely people to deal with... then we are setting ourselves up for a fall. He discusses that we live in an imperfect world, full of imperfect people. Finally, he discusses the need to be realistic enough to realize ahead of time that very few things in life are ever perfect.

Nkiruka heaved a sigh of relief when she was done reading the Day One part of the book. She pondered on it and learned that it was better to wait patiently on her husband and not to give up because of Pride. She also had her own shortcomings, not only her husband. She was expecting perfection from her husband but she wasn't perfect either. She also knew that her husband was also expecting somethings from her, but the problem was that nobody was willing to stoop first for those expectations. She yearned to conquer her marital problems but she couldn't do that without stooping in humility. The world is full of imperfect people, and so, she must stoop to conquer. She unpacked her bags and said her prayers, thanking God for the book she was reading. If this book had really changed her friend, she was sure that it would change her too and help change her marriage too.

CHAPTER SEVENTEEN

RAALUCHI MET IFEOMA inside a restaurant in her school. The restaurant was spacious enough to contain lots of wood tables and chairs. The doors and windows were open to aid ventilation. There were some inscriptions pasted on the wall of the counter: *OKOCHA ONCE ATE FROM MY POT. NO EXTRA PLATE FOR SAME AMOUNT. NO FOOD ON CREDIT.* There were some students hovering at the counter and making orders for their food, and some were eating and drinking and chatting at the table.

Ifeoma was light skinned and pretty and a female student that had been staring at her from the next table, couldn't help but ask Raaluchi if they were sisters, because they had the same height, the same slim weight and the same complexion. But the difference was that Raaluchi was far more beautiful. Raaluchi admired her red designer gown, her gold ear rings and necklace, and feelings of jealousy went through her. Those things she was putting on were supposed to be hers. She didn't want to be engulfed with the feelings that Ifeoma stole her man from her. She had come to meet this lady in peace because she knew that she alone had the solution to her problem.

"Raaluchi, I apologize again for all the pains that I've caused you and all the nasty things I said to you in the past. I'm sure you'll believe me if I tell you that my conscience has never been at rest since I started reading your text messages. I won't deny the fact that I love your husband. I love him because he's a very caring person. But I don't have the right to keep him because he doesn't belong to me. Raaluchi, he belongs to you because you are his lawfully wedded wife," Ifeoma's eyes filled with tears as she spoke so softly, almost like a whisper. She took Raaluchi's hand in hers and tears coursed down Raaluchi's cheeks. Ifeoma continued to speak.

"I say to myself, 'what will I gain from keeping someone's husband to myself knowing full well that I would feel bad if another woman happened to do the same thing to me. Raaluchi…to be honest, Onyeka still loves you. Many a time, he called me Raalu, the moments when I sang for him. Raaluchi, I don't really want to probe into the personal life you both shared before I surfaced but I'm sure you must have been a very good singer and that must have been one of the reasons why he fell in love with you."

Raaluchi sniffed in tears as she listened to Ifeoma.

"I'm giving you a glorious opportunity to win back your husband's love."

"What will I do, Ifeoma? Please tell me because I'm willing to do anything within my powers to win back my husband's love. I want him to see the Raalu he used to know in me… his wife… and not in someone else. Please Ifeoma, you need to help me. I love my husband," Raaluchi spoke in silent tears.

Ifeoma told Raaluchi that Onyeka had invited her to sing in a 'Dinner party and Singing Competition' organized by all the Pharmaceutical Companies in Nigeria. It was going to hold in Abuja on Friday of that week. Ifeoma thought it'll be a golden opportunity for her to win back her husband's love if she volunteered to sing for him in public, not just for the people there and for his Pharmaceutical Company, but to show him how much she still loved and cared about him. Raaluchi smiled at the suggestion and considered it to be a very good one. She would do anything to win back Onyeka's love and she was going to make use of her talent.

"I'll be going to Abuja with Onyeka on Thursday evening. I'll go with him so that he won't suspect anything. You can travel on your own as soon as we leave," Ifeoma said and sipped her glass of orange juice.

"Thank you very much, Ifeoma."

Ifeoma smiled in response, opened her big hand bag and handed Raaluchi a dress wrapped in white proof. Raaluchi was amazed as she watched the dress after she had been allowed to unseal the proof by Ifeoma. It was a beautiful blue dinner gown and Raaluchi knew it was very expensive. It was a designer gown by Vivian Westhood.

"Onyeka bought the gown for me to use for the singing competition. I'm giving it to you because I'm sure it belongs to you. You'll wear it on that Friday night. You are a very pretty woman and I'm sure you wouldn't hesitate to look attractive for your husband," Ifeoma smiled as she spoke and Raaluchi returned the smile and thanked her again.

The two women talked on about Onyeka and his love for songs, that Raaluchi forgot she had lectures by 2pm that afternoon. Winning back her husband's love was the greatest thing that had been on her mind since a year, and with that, she knew she would do better in school. Ifeoma advised her to make her song emotional. Her song was not supposed to impress her husband alone but people around. It was the people that would commend her and her husband would be proud of her for pleasing the audience. The theme of the song should be concisely about her husband and he alone would understand the song and he would never be the same again.

Raaluchi thanked her again and they engaged themselves in further chats until Ifeoma was ready to go. Raaluchi walked her to her car. She drove off and honked good bye to her. Raaluchi couldn't help to feel so jealous of Ifeoma who was riding a jeep, a twenty one year old girl who enjoyed her husband's wealth. She regained herself from the thoughts of jealousy as she remembered the mysterious book: Beauty in humility. She had read that 'envy could cause a person to behave callously and crudely.' She waved the envy aside because she didn't want it to penetrate her heart and make her feel perturbed about it. She didn't want to hate Ifeoma because she knew that she needed her so much to accomplish her success. All she wanted was to win back her husband's love and after that, all those material things she had seen with Ifeoma would be hers.

She was sure she would smile at last and all thanks to Ifeoma who had told her what to do. She had to practice for the occasion. She had to compose an emotional song with a very slow and soft rhythm, the kind that moved the heart and forced tears from the eyes. She thought about how she would travel. She would leave Bobo with Nanny Nene. She knew it was going to be very difficult because Bobo was fond of her but she had to do it. She had to do something to unite her marriage. Ifeoma had promised to send her the address of the event. She had told her to lodge in a hotel in Maitama: a town in Abuja, a town where the event would hold. Raaluchi knew it was expensive but Ifeoma had promised to send her some money.

* * * *

When Raaluchi got home that evening, Bobo was crying in the arms of Nanny Nene and Raaluchi carried him and sang for him before he fell asleep. As she watched Bobo sleep soundly in his bed, she remembered the honeymoon with her husband in America, the nights she put him to sleep with songs. "Blood is thicker than water," Raaluchi said, and then, she pecked Bobo on his cheeks. Bobo was just the small Onyeka. There was nothing different. He loved melodious songs just like his father. Raaluchi waited for her husband to return from work after she had prepared and served dinner. Onyeka finally returned at 10 pm that night and as Raaluchi watched him closely, he looked completely disheveled in his white shirt that he had buttoned in a wrong way, probably because he was in a hurry, and she saw a mark of red lip stick on his white shirt. Raaluchi's heart sank as she saw it and already knew who was responsible for it. She went ahead to hug her husband but he avoided her. She tried to take his portfolio but he refused. She called him by name and he stopped to look at her. He looked at her as though he didn't know her, as though she was a total stranger and not his wife. Tears began to trickle from Raaluchi's eyes and for an instance, Onyeka was moved, and he wanted to wipe her tears but decided not to fall for it. *I'm sorry my dear wife...but if what I'm doing is hurting you, just know that you pushed me to it.* Onyeka spoke in his mind as he walked to the bedroom with his portfolio at his right hand and his black suit hanging on his left hand.

Raaluchi flung herself on the sofa in the living room and wept, tearing her heart in sorrows. The voices tortured her, reminded her of how useless she was; reminded her that nothing good would ever come out of her again because she was just a looser. Nanny Nene had to take her to her room and there she consoled her and told her to be patient with her husband. She told Raaluchi that she experienced the same pains in her own marriage until her husband got fed up and asked for forgiveness. She told Raaluchi that she was praying for her marriage; that crying would not solve the problem but would only endanger her health. When Nanny Nene left, Raaluchi picked her phone and dialed Ifeoma's number. She just couldn't bear the pains she felt and to think they had a long talk in her school and she had trusted her to help her win back her husband's love.

"You slept with my husband this night." Raaluchi blurted out. It wasn't a question. It was a direct statement of fact. Ifeoma was speechless and the line was silent. She began to stutter.

"Ifeoma, I'm talking to you, so speak."

"Raalu, please calm down. It wasn't my intention. He forced me. He sees you in me...and that is just the problem."

"Just how many times are you going to tell me that? Here I am leaning on you to help me win back my husband's love and there you are, sleeping with him and taking him far away from me. You know what? You really are in love with my husband

and I'm going to have an annulment so that you can marry him since that is what you want!" Raaluchi said furiously and hung up. She couldn't bear the boils she felt in her heart and so she wept all over again and she was prompted to send a text message to her husband and prayed that he would be moved by it.

You promised me that I'll never be alone, and that you'll protect me from the cruelties of the world…but you are already lost in the world and you have shown me the cruelties. If I had pushed you to the world… Please my darling husband, forgive me. Let's start all over again. Your silence is causing me heartache. Onyeka, you don't belong to the world. No matter what, you remain my husband and I'll wait for your return.

Onyeka's Blackberry phone beeped and the red light blinked, indicating an unread message, but he was fast asleep in his room that he couldn't read the message. He had slept on his shirt and trousers. He didn't bother to take his bath and have his dinner. Ifeoma stared at her silent phone for a long time, shaken. She didn't want to do what she did. She was doing it because she wanted to leave Onyeka slowly, that was why she couldn't reject him when he barged into her house at 7pm earlier that night. Ifeoma had just returned from a friend's house and was resting on a sofa when Onyeka barged into her living room and forced himself on her, and as usual in his sexual satisfaction, he called her 'Raalu'. Onyeka had the spare key of her bungalow and so she didn't even have her privacy. She was deeply sorry.

CHAPTER EIGHTEEN

JEKWU STAGGERED INTO the house. He was foaming from the consumed liquid contents of palmwine and as he belched, the room was filled with the smell of palmwine and Nkiruka went to hold him so that he would be steady and not fall and injure himself. A neighbour had paid for his drinks in Madam Caro's bar and had brought him home. Nkiruka thanked the kind man and offered to give him a drink, but the man rebuffed the idea with an upward flick of his palm, and left the house immediately. "If I give you my back hand, you'll faint," Jekwu spoke to his wife incoherently and staggered to the room. Nkiruka watched him as he snored heavily on the bed. She sat down and was lost in thought about what to do, savoring the pages of the 'mysterious book' in her mind. She finally got the solution to her problem in 'Day Seven and Eight' where the writer discusses *'the danger that is seen in the greedy eyes, and the need for wives to submit to their husbands.'* He sifts that the reason the eyes shed tears so often is because, it is very greedy.

Nkiruka understood and learned that the reason she had cried so much in her marriage was because she had been greedy. She wanted to marry a rich man that could actualize her dream of touring Las Vegas. Money was her pre-requisite for love, and so, she believed in just what she could only see. Nkiruka soliloquized as she watched her husband snore heavily in his drunken state. "He tricked you because you wouldn't have accepted marrying a poor man, he knew what you wanted. He knew that money was your prerequisite for love, and so, he

162

disguised himself to give you the prerequisite, and he married you because he loves you. He became a rapist when you stopped performing your matrimonial duties as a wife. He beat you up because you kept insulting him, knowing full well that he's hot-tempered. Nkiruka, you can make your marriage work by submitting whole heartedly to your husband. Take the writer's advice. Running away is never a solution in marriage. Marriage is a life time commitment and you don't just run away from your commitment, come what may." Nkiruka spoke softly to herself.

And then, finally, she focused her mind on the 'Day Nine.' There, the writer discusses that *'evil does not beget evil and people should not let the negativities of other people become a part of their response.'* The writer explained further that: 'when a neighbour offends you with a slap, you should show the person the other cheek to complete the slap.' This means that you should be humble enough to reciprocate with love. It is only through this love, that the offender would be forced to repent. Love remains the most important commandment of Christ because it conquers all things. It stenghthens the weak and humbles the proud. It is not enough to profess our love for God. We show that love for God by loving our neighbour. Nkiruka decided to show love to her husband.

Jekwu woke up very early in the morning, sound and back to his senses. He stifled a long yawn. He expected to wake up in Madam Caro's bar but was startled to see himself in his room. He was about to prop up from the bed when he saw his wife lying beside him. He gave a start and woke her up by calling her name repeatedly.

"You slept here?" Jekwu asked in a startled manner, with mouth agape and lowered eyes.

"Yes. I couldn't leave you alone in your drunkenness…I care about you."

Jekwu cleared his eyes as soon as he heard her and watched her closely, to know if she really was the Nkiruka he married or someone else. Nkiruka had stopped sharing the same bed with her husband when she discovered that Jekwu tricked her into marrying him, because in the real sense, he was poor and claimed to be rich. She heaped insults on him whenever he demanded for food and told him to cook it himself if he was really hungry. Jekwu had been enduring her but couldn't control his temper anymore. Nkiruka received severe beatings from her husband whenever she asked him for money, because she didn't ask well, but always insulted him by comparing him with his fellow men. She lacked the manner of approach and she had been hurting inside her ever since she discovered that her husband disguised himself to be rich just to marry her.

"I need just fifteen thousand naira for my toiletries, *kita kita,* now now!" Nkiruka would tell her husband furiously by stretching her hand for the money to be placed on her palm, and when he tried to explain the reason he could not give her the exact amount, she would start flaring up, comparing him with his mates who worked harder to make money, not him who disguised himself as a rich man, just to have a woman that was not his class.

"You know what Jekwu? The reason you just couldn't make money but chose to borrow from people to entice me is because you are just so lazy. You are a lazy baboon!" Nkiruka would blurt out and Jekwu would angrily beat her up before she could release another bomb from her mouth.

"And you know what Nkiruka? The reason you ended up being my wife is because of your long throat...your huge appetite to consume money! I loved you enough to marry you and that was why I had to satisfy you with money because I knew that was what you wanted, *akpili ego!* Now you are married to me, you really have to cut down your expenses and get this fact that I'm just a Petty-trader, not a 'money making machine'.

"You knew you couldn't take care of me and you married me for some stupid love. You should have left me with my parents instead of wearing a clothe that is not your size!"

"This is no longer courtship, Nkiruka. This is marriage and

you really have to live with it, money or no money. Marriage is for better or worse."

"You forced me into poverty and I'll never give you peace in this house until you take me back to my parents."

"And you'll continue to see the beast in me until you humble your self."

And the couple had been living like enemies, fighting like cat and dog until Raaluchi spoke to Nkiruka, until Nkiruka read the mysterious book. Nkiruka had decided to submit herself to her husband and be happy. She was tired of fighting with her husband and alerting the neighborhood. Nkiruka prepared break fast for her husband for the first time after so many months of anger and disunity. She prepared yam porridge with stock fishes. And before Jekwu took his breakfast, he prayed repeatedly. He just couldn't fathom what had come over his wife. She may be a good actress but he shouldn't be so stupid to think that she woke up one morning and decided to be a changed person. And if it was true that she had changed, then he should be the happiest man on earth.

* * * *

Onyeka couldn't concentrate on anything in his office. It was on a Tuesday morning, on the 20th day of August, Raluchi's text messages kept reciting in his mind, and it made him feel so uncomfortable. He scrambled out of his chair and paced round his office table. No doubt, he loved his wife but had seen Raalu, the Raalu that drove him insane in another woman, and he just couldn't help it. Raaluchi had never loved him, but had hurt him so badly, and sometimes he wondered if he really forced her into marrying him, if his love for her had driven him insane; had been so blind for him not to have known that Raaluchi never loved him, even when he gave her everything. But Ifeoma had been there for him when he needed a friend to lean on. The priest, Father Joe had preached forgiveness to him on phone, but it wasn't easy to forgive. Raaluchi just proved to him beyond reasonable doubts that she did not trust him; that he really had used her and that was just too much for him to bear.

He knew that what he had been doing with Ifeoma was a very big sin: a sin of adultery, but he wouldn't have been living in that sin if Raaluchi didn't push him to it, if she hadn't abused his love and made mockery of his godliness. He had come a long way with Ifeoma, the Raalu that made him happy. He had come a long way to leave Ifeoma for Raaluchi his wife, who had tormented him so much. All he needed was happiness and he had found that in Ifeoma. And why was Raaluchi writing to him to remind him of his promises to her when she never thought of that before making his life miserable. He deleted the text message and called Ifeoma on phone, just to have someone to keep him company and make him forget the haunting memories of Raaluchi's text message. But Ifeoma didn't answer the call. He decided to pay her a visit in her bungalow.

* * * *

The shouting and the exchange of words between the two women in Ifeoma's room revealed their secrets to Onyeka as he eavesdropped. He had to stop to eavesdrop because the discussions were pointedly about him. His heart ached as he listened to them and peeked at them. They were Ifeoma and Ego. Onyeka had just discovered from their discussion that they were sisters and Ego was the one who sent Ifeoma to him. In their discussion, Ego was pressurizing Ifeoma to remain in the relationship with Onyeka just to receive money and other material things from him. She called Ifeoma 'a big fool' for reconsidering the situation just because of a mere text message from Raaluchi, a mere religious sympathy that was absolutely not needed in business.

"I don't know why you have remained the biggest fool I've ever seen in my life. So, just because, Raaluchi preached God's message for you, you are already giving your beautiful

166

relationship with Onyeka a second thought. You think God will destroy all the sinners in this world just to please Raaluchi? The world will not end just because of a single idiot like Raaluchi. In this world, people are busy grabbing opportunities and making good use of them, and you already have a golden one, but foolishly want to throw it away. You want to go back to our forsaking village and suffer with our mother? Wake up from your sleep my sister, and use what you have to get what you want," Ego said to Ifeoma in anger, with a fast-breathing expression of infuriation.

Ego was using Ifeoma her sister to get back at Onyeka and have her revenge for what Onyeka did to her. Aside from that, she was also using her sister to cater for her family. Onyeka crept out of the house and drove home. He couldn't believe what he had heard. He didn't know why all these terrible things had to happen to him and Onyeka knew from the two women's discussion that the same Ego had been responsible for corrupting his wife to turn against him. What offence had he committed to experience such heartache in life? He locked himself in his bedroom and wept bitterly.

"Ego will never go unpunished for what she did to me, that devil!" Onyeka spoke in a raging temper and his tears tickled down from his eyes as he remembered the first time he met his wife. He had had the instinct to be responsible for making her life so beautiful. He had wanted to change her but the reverse was the case. He wept bitterly.

* * * *

Raaluchi began her singing practice. She had to borrow some money from her mother just to register in a music school in Asaba and practice for two days. She made friends with two women who were good singers too and they taught her the steps of a good performance in an emotional song. Raaluchi had sleepless nights reciting the song she composed for her husband. She wondered why Ifeoma did not call her or even send her an apology text for what she did. She considered Ifeoma her husband's mistress, unreliable. A lady who had told her face to face that she loved her husband must not be trusted. She would do anything to win back her husband's love. With her prayers and the song she was going to present, she had faith that she would win back her husband's love. She shouldn't depend on Ifeoma to send her some money as she had promised. She still had some money that she had borrowed from her mother and she just prayed that it would sustain her in Abuja. But the problem was that she didn't know the address of the event.

* * * *

On Thursday evening, Ifeoma called Onyeka to inform him that she was ready to travel with him to Abuja, but Onyeka in his rage about what he had heard from her discussion with Ego, pretended to be in good terms with her and take back what she had given to her before she ran away with his property. Left to him, he didn't want to attend the party anymore because he was very much indisposed, but he had to attend it for the sake of his own company. His presence was needed. Ifeoma and Onyeka left for Abuja in a 5pm flight, and it was 5: 40pm in the evening when they landed at the Abuja airport and took a cab to a hotel.

Ifeoma had a perception that Raaluchi would call her and she put her phone in silence for the rest of the day. She had changed her mind in helping her win back her husband's love. She couldn't just give up now, and how could she have been a fool to tell Raaluchi the secret to the renewal of her marital love, knowing full well that she would be the looser at the end? Ego her sister had talked senses into her, and she had bought her idea. She should not be done with Onyeka's wealth and if Raaluchi finally reconciled with her husband, she would be the looser. She loved her life with Onyeka and it was all a mistake that she had wanted to back out. She would sing for Onyeka, and Onyeka would love her more, and she would end up marrying him and kicking Raaluchi out of his house, after all, she got what it takes to be a wife and Raaluchi had none. She would give Onyeka more of what she wanted from her, not just her songs. It was a good thing that she didn't tell Raaluchi the address of the party and for all she cared, Raaluchi should get lost and sing a dirge for herself because her loss was already her gain.

* * * *

Raaluchi took an 8:00 am flight to Abuja on that Friday morning and in the plane, she prayed that God would grant her request. She had endured her feelings of dejection and loneliness for over a year. Her marital problems all started with her and it was going to end with her. For the first time in her life, she had this moving faith that her plans would be successful and at last, she would reunite her marriage with Onyeka, and would hold him so tight so that he wouldn't have to slip from her hands again. She would have her husband as her only true friend and God as her ally. To her, if there was a lesson to learn from this problem of hers, it was just that she shouldn't trust anybody else apart from God and her husband. She shouldn't reveal what should be a secret to anybody. She shouldn't underestimate her enemies and judge from physical appearance. She should be obedient. If she had obeyed her husband by staying away from Ego, all her marital problems wouldn't have occurred. She should ask God for wisdom in her prayers and she should be humble with cringing submission.

Her mind reached out to Father Joe, her spiritual director and a true friend. She reminisced over how he had been of immense help to her when she was drowning in sorrows. As she remembered him, she smiled, grateful that he had helped to brighten her life by letting her draw her strength from him. She soliloquized in her smiles: 'According to our lord Jesus Christ, the greatest person on earth is he who humbles himself like a servant. A woman's power is in her submission to her husband,' she soliloquized as she remembered the statement which Father

Joe had dropped for her when she asked him for help to save her marriage, when she gave her the mysterious book. As the plane taxied after landing smoothly, she peeked through the window, wondering what her stay in Abuja would be like, but believing that things would work out her own way, and that was winning back her husband's love.

At the Arrival Exit, many Airport taxi drivers were approaching people with pleading gestures, just to take them to their destinations. One of the taxi drivers approached Raaluchi, and just before Raaluchi agreed to ride with him, he took Raaluchi's box from her hand and sooner, he was already walking briskly to the Car Lot with the small pink box jerking on his head.

"I'm going to Maitama. How much will I pay you?" Raaluchi asked the Taxi driver who raised his hands high enough to show his shirt holes under his arm. His arm-pit odour smelled of poverty and the profuse sweat that streamed down his face revealed in him a man struggling to feed his family.

"Just five thousand naira, ma," The driver said in his hand-raised expression, as though the amount was just too affordable, and he would kindly accept it because he wasn't greedy. Raaluchi looked at him, lowering her eyes in disagreement. But she decided to patronize him for his hardwork.

Maitama smelled of freedom and luxury. The air was cool and exclusively green. Raaluchi, as she looked at the gigantic buildings through the car, and the fresh green masquerade trees that stood by the roads, smiled in satisfaction. The driver was speeding, probably because there was no traffic. As the driver drove down the road of Aguiyi Ironsi Street, Raaluchi told the driver to slow down, she surveyed the environment, watching curiously to see a hotel that indicated a cheap one, and at last, she smiled, wishing that the simple duplex her eyes had caught was cheap indeed.

CHAPTER NINETEEN

RAALUCHI CALLED IFEOMA for a number of times, to let her know that she has arrived Maitama, and to get the address of the event from her, but she intentionally ignored it and then, Raaluchi understood that her premonition was right after all. Ifeoma didn't want her to reconcile with her husband. A woman who had told her right in her face that she was in love with her husband, had no intentions of leaving him, not after what she was getting from her husband. She owed her thanks to God, who had used Ifeoma to give her a clue of what she would do to reunite her marriage with Onyeka.

Just at the reception where she was taking a drink later in the day, she heard some men discussing on the blast occasion that would hold in 'Treasure Island' hotel in IBB Express way, for all the pharmacists in Nigeria. She absorbed the address and thanked God for making a way for her. She rebuffed the request of a date from one of the men that were discussing the event and afterwards, she went upstairs to her room to practice her song.

* * * *

Ifeoma noticed that Onyeka had been so cold to her and didn't crave her attention as he used to. She wondered what was wrong. Her mind wavered and she wondered if Raaluchi had finally reconciled with her husband. That night as she dressed for the occasion in a white strapless dinner gown and wore her make up, she looked so beautiful and she swayed in front of Onyeka just to show off her dress and get his attention.

"I'm sorry, honey, I didn't bring the blue gown along. I prefer to be in white and sing for you like an angel. I hope you don't mind?" She asked Onyeka in a sensational smile but Onyeka forced a smile in return and didn't comment on her good looks. He dressed up in a blue shirt and milk colored designer suit that made him look like a charming prince. Ifeoma couldn't help but reach out to him in a tight hug and perceived his perfume. He smelled and looked so sweet.

"Oh honey, you look like a charming prince and I love you,"

"Let's go", Onyeka said sternly, adjusting his milk coloured tie as he made his way to the door, trying to leave first. Ifeoma's heart raced in thoughts about what was going on and she only prayed in her mind that Raaluchi would not show her face at the party. Her legs trembled as she walked and she hoped she wouldn't embarrass herself by missing a step with her high heel slippers. Ifeoma fumed when Onyeka introduced her to his colleagues as his friend and was jealous when his staff asked about Raaluchi his wife with so much curiosity and interest. They had missed her so much in the company ever since she stopped work.

More guests began arriving at the lounge shortly after eight o'clock. A handful of well known socialites, pharmacists and movie stars were there, and waiters in red dinner jackets were serving champagne on silver trays. Celine Dion's 'Because You Love me' played in the background, and one can only hear the clinging of wine glasses and the soft giggles and discussions that came mostly from the ladies.

"Music is medicinal. It cures all ills of life," A dark skinned lady in a peach dinner gown said to her friend as they nodded to the soft music. Raaluchi was just in a corner where she knew she would not be noticed. She was looking gorgeous and strikingly pretty on her blue dinner gown. She had already seen Ifeoma feeling at place with her husband and she couldn't help but admire her husband, the man who had loved her so much. She believed that tonight Onyeka would be back in her arms again.

* * * *

The singing competition began with singers from Abuja Pharmaceutical Companies, and the ladies performed marvelously great, and the guests applauded. Waiters began to serve dinner but Raaluchi in her dark corner, rejected hers. She didn't want to eat and loose her melodious voice. She had been taught in her music school that if she needed to sing melodiously, she would have to abstain from food three hours before the song, she would take a hot cup of Lipton tea to soften her throat, so that it wouldn't crack as she sang. She was just abiding by the rules that her teachers had given her. She waited for so many singers to sing, and when Ifeoma was called up, she was attacked by stage fright.

The spacious luxurious hall was corralled with a congregation of people present for the occassion and they were watching her with annoying gazes and slight hisses. Some eyes averted as soon as they saw her and some ladies began to whisper to themselves, giggling and gesturing at her, darting annoying glances. Ifeoma's legs trembled in fright and all of a sudden, she forgot the rhythm of the song she composed and then found herself singing Celine Dion's 'Faith Artist.' A female judge giggled a bell of disqualification and Ifeoma was disqualified instantly. According to the rule of the competition, a song that is ready for presentation must be unique. Ifeoma muttered 'I'm sorry' through the microphone and walked out of the stage with trembling legs and eyes downcast. She was abashed of her failure. Onyeka was disappointed. He bent his head in disappointment, his eyes downcast. His heart ached in uttermost discomfort. He couldn't afford to loose the thirty thousand dollars award that would be given to the best singer for a Pharmaceutical Company.

"There's one more singer for Fanco Pharmaceutical

Company Asaba, one more singer please!" Raaluchi notified as she came up in her dazzling beauty, and the guests gaped at her, even the judges. Onyeka was stunned and he gazed at Raaluchi his wife and wondered how she knew about the competition. But he felt relieved anyway, because it was a good thing that Ifeoma was replaced. Ifeoma got infuriated as she watched Raaluchi.

"I'm sorry Miss, we only permit one singer for a company," One of the female judges said to Raaluchi. She was misled by her misconception to regard Raaluchi as 'A miss' because of her beautiful youngness. Onyeka craved to hug his wife. He didn't know why the anxiety for the hug came, maybe it was clearer to him to reconcile with his wife since his mistress had betrayed him. He had never seen Raaluchi look that beautiful and the more he looked at her, the longer he craved for her hug. She looked exclusively beautiful. Raaluchi was radiating in a cool blue beauty and even when Onyeka knew that they were still speaking in silence, he longed for her hug.

"Lets give her a chance to perform," The leader of the judges, a man in a gray suit said in conclusion and Raaluchi smiled, her heart untangling from panicking. She had just panicked when she was turned down by the female judge. Raaluchi introduced herself as Raaluchi Ibekwe but didn't give details of the introduction, as no one actually knew if she was married or single. She presented the title of her song as 'WAITING FOR YOUR LOVE' Raaluchi hummed to the rhythm first, walked majestically in a psychedelically measured steps. She sang magnificently and the people present admired her voice and were engrossed with the music; even Onyeka was moved as he listened to the words of the song. His eyes filled with tears as he listened, knowing full well that the song was just for him. Raaluchi had expressed the urge of waiting for his love no matter how long it was going to take. She had told him in the song that they were made for each other and when she finally won back his love, she would cherish him forever; she would make him understand that she was the only woman for him and him, the only man she would ever love.

And Raaluchi sang so marvelously and melodiously, a song that was so emotional, a song that pierced the heart of whom it was actually sung for. The song was an apology. Raaluchi was obviously sorry for taking his love for granted; it was obvious because her tears coursed down to her cheeks as she sang and her eyes met with his and interlocked. Onyeka was forced to remember the first time he met her on a crusade ground singing in tears. His heart raced and ached for her. How could he explain the fact that he was sorry for being so mean? How could he explain the fact that he had been lost in the seductive body of a mistress that he had chosen to take as his own Raalu? His tears streamed down to his cheeks and he was so quick to wipe them off. Ifeoma watched Onyeka and felt jumpy as she rose from her seat and sat back forcefully in a deep infuriation.

"Oh my God, this pretty damsel is a wonderful singer. I'm going to ask her out tonight," A man, light skinned in complexion: one of the guests that was sitting beside Onyeka said in excitement, mesmerized with Raaluchi's beauty and her wonderful performance. Onyeka watched him, fuming in jealousy. He fumed more when he heard many men praising Raaluchi and planning to ask her out. The guests applauded Raaluchi and she gave a beautiful smile complimented with her dimples and her dimming eyes, a self-satisfied smile. Ifeoma infuriated. She watched Onyeka walk magnetically towards his wife to give her a long tight hug. He held on in his hug unable to leave Raaluchi. It was so long a hug, a desirable hug, a hug that he had craved for. Raaluchi thought she was dreaming. She wanted to wake up from this dream. It had been over one year since she felt her husband's warm hug. All manner of emotions churned in her. She thanked God in her heart as she felt safe in her husband's warm hug. It was as though she had finally found something so precious that had been missing in her life. She thanked God for making her dreams come true. She thanked God for using Ifeoma, the kind part of her that gave her a way to win back her husband's love. She thanked Bobo, her little angel that led the way, and she also thanked Father Joe for his mysterious book. She would forever remain thankful and grateful to these people who had helped in putting smiles on her face again.

That night, the 24th day of August 2012 was the night that Raaluchi would never forget, a night when she won back her long lost husband.

"I love you Raaluchi and I'm sorry for hurting you. Wait no more for my love because I'll never leave you again."

"I love you more Onyeka and I'm sorry for hurting you too. I'll never let you leave me anymore." They spoke in whispers to each other and Onyeka stroke her hair and their eyes filled with tears as it rolled down to their cheeks. The guests applauded and the judges announced the winner of the singing competition. It was Raaluchi. They thought she deserved it because her song appeared so unique, melodious, impressive and emotional and they had also discovered that she had sung the song for her husband. Raaluchi received her award with trembling hands and the staff of Fanco Pharmaceutical Company shrieked in excitement. They couldn't believe that their company finally won the singing competition. All thanks to Raaluchi who made it possible and who had marked a very impressive and unforgettable record for the company. Ifeoma cried as she watched the couple in their lovely embrace and she stumped out of the lounge in mixed feelings of infuriation and jealousy. She entered a rest room and wept in front of the large wall mirror. And then, she noticed that her underpants were very wet. She slid up her white long gown and then she saw it. Her monthly visitor had visited her unexpectedly and it had come profusely that it had stained her white dinner gown and her underpants. She wept more in shame until there were no more tears to shed.

Afterwards, she left the hotel with her personal effects, unannounced to Onyeka. She was very bitter and eager to break the news of the reconciliation to Ego, her sister. When Onyeka entered the hotel room that he lodged with Ifeoma, he noticed that her personal effects weren't there anymore and he chuckled, convinced that she must have left out of jealousy. That night, Raaluchi checked out from her hotel room and joined Onyeka in his. They spent time strolling around the spacious compound of the hotel and sang by the swimming pool, repeating the award winning song of Raaluchi with Raaluchi's head resting on Onyeka's shoulder. And Raaluchi was surprised at how easily Onyeka absorbed the song. "You are a genius Raalu. You should really release your album one of these days. You made me proud tonight." Onyeka commended her and kissed her on her cheek and she smiled. They unconsciously drifted to different thoughts, knowing where the rain started to beat them and ready to correct their mistakes.

PART THREE

BEFRORE THE SILENCE: HIS SIN

THE YEAR 2010- 2011

In a world of imperfection, a sin is bent on occurring...

CHAPTER TWENTY

IT DAWNED ON the 30th day of August 2010. Onyeka was still depressed even though he had caught some sleep. He had seen Raaluchi's missed calls and text messages but he couldn't just give in to them, at least not so soon. What Raaluchi had done to him deserved some punishments. He had tolerated her enough, but he couldn't bear to live in his matrimonial house without peace of mind. He needed peace. He needed it more than any other thing. He had to remain in the hotel to cool off before thinking of going back to Raaluchi, her nagging and arrogant wife. The truth was that he was falling out of love with her, the offensive part of her that made him hate her while she was still in love with the gentle part of her, the melodious voice that attracted him to her. He couldn't fathom what had actually gotten into Raaluchi ever since they returned from their honeymoon. Her over bearing disobedience, her craving desire to do her own will by not taking advice and her endless arguments that symbolized distrust in its subtlest forms were heartaching. He was missing the Raaluchi he used to know, the Raaluchi that smiled so innocently, that sang so marvelously, her youngness, her beauty and his longing desire to give her everything she wanted.

Onyeka had stayed in the luxurious hotel for three days, missing the good part of his wife, his love feelings reaching out to her and wanting to see her, her beautiful face, and the other hurtful feeling that hated her for what she had done to him urged him to remain in the hotel and punish her severely for what she did, for all the sleepless nights she had caused him, for making his life so miserable. On the second day of September, he was in his room engrossed in an interesting American soap opera, when someone called his cell phone and he answered. It was Jerry his General Manager. He had actually called to inform him that his mother-in-law wanted to see him. She had introduced herself as Mrs Oby Ezechikwelu and wished to know the address of the hotel he was lodging and Onyeka approved. That was his mother-in-law. Onyeka heaved a sigh and dressed up in a white T-shirt and a blue jean trouser and sat on the cushion to wait for his mother-in-law. He already knew the reason she was visiting. He knew she wanted to plead on Raaluchi's behalf and make him reconsider his decision and go back to his matrimonial home but he couldn't do that, at least not now. Raaluchi had caused him so much pain and at least he was relaxed in this tranquil environment. He waited for his mother- in- law for hours and he called her but her phone was switched off. He decided in his mind that she must have changed her mind.

Mummy really changed her mind because Jerry gave her a wrong message. Jerry told her that Onyeka did not want to see her, and that he needed to be alone, and the poor woman left the company with a heavy heart, wishing she met Onyeka. She didn't know the address of the hotel Onyeka was lodging. His MTN line had been switched off, she didn't have his other phone contacts, and she was also refused to pay a visit. She thought that she would have told Onyeka about Raaluchi's condition when she payed a visit but she too wasn't given a chance. When she reached home, she switched off her phone and began to say her prayers. Onyeka received another call, this time, it was his hotel phone and the receptionist informed him that he was invited to the third year anniversary of the hotel. It was going to be a dinner party that would hold at the lounge and Onyeka concurred and promised to be there. At the reception, he felt lonely because he couldn't bear the oppressive feelings that went through him when he saw most couples dinning together, winning, laughing and chatting in excitement, enjoying their togetherness. He thought about Raaluchi but what he could only remember about her was the way she had hurt him so terribly. Angrily, he requested for a chilled bottle of champagne and drank it all in one gulp, as though he was used to drinking that way. His heart was heavy and he was depressed.

It was that night at the hotel lounge that Onyeka met Ifeoma, his Raalu. She had entertained the guests by singing so good. She was one of the waitresses in the hotel. She looked exquisite on her waitress uniform; a red T-shirt and a short blue flay skirt. It was that night that Onyeka fell into temptation out of drunkeness. He was aroused to meet her, to talk to her and to have her. As she sang more, he couldn't take it anymore. All manner of emotions churned in him. It was as though Raaluchi was actually there. She looked so much like Raaluchi. To him, she was Raaluchi, Raaluchi his precious wife, Raaluchi his singer, his beautiful queen. He couldn't remember the last time he had slept with his wife and now looking at this second Raaluchi, he couldn't take his eyes off her. He was tempted to touch her, and her singing voice aroused him more. He couldn't let go of what he felt inside. For the first time in his life, he couldn't overcome a temptation. His obsession for the good Raalu he fell in love with aroused him more and for all he knew, that young lady was his Raalu.

When she held him and walked him to his room that night, after the party, he held her tightly, unable to leave her. She left the room, and minutes later, he saw her looking sexily attractive on her short pink night gown with a V- neck that revealed her cleavages. She was carrying a bag: her small bag that had a design of a teddy bear. She smiled at him, an attractive lop-sided smile and her dancing eyes seduced him. She was irresistible, and he was magnetized to her, and he made love to her just immediately he let her inside his room. To him, he was making love to the woman he fell in love with, the good part of her. He whispered his wife's name in Ifeoma's ears, as he had her piece of flesh with satisfaction. Onyeka fell asleep beside Ifeoma and she watched him. She hadn't seen a man so handsome like him. She knew she shouldn't have done what she did but she needed to do it and she didn't regret it.

* * * *

The bright light of dawn shimmered inside the room and Onyeka sleepily rolled over to face Ifeoma, and he stared at Ifeoma with his sleepy eyes. Ifeoma was looking directly into his eyes, wondering what a fool his wife must have been for leaving her husband alone in a dangerous cave and now he was trapped because he can never escape from her, for she was the cave.

"You sang so beautifully, Raalu, and I love you," Onyeka said softly and sleepily to Ifeoma and she smiled.

"Thanks. But I'm not this Raalu you've been calling me since last night. My name is Ifeoma. I'm a waitress in this hotel. I knew you wanted me last night from the way you stared at me, that was why I came," Ifeoma spoke with a voice husky with emotion. Onyeka sprang from the bed and watched her closely. She wasn't Raaluchi but there was a close resemblance. He was still naked and as he watched himself, he was filled with shame, and the enormity of what he did dawned on him. He had defiled himself, and it was all Raaluchi's fault that he did it. He didn't control his passion last night, and he had mistaken the pretty lady to be Raaluchi, his wife. And that night, he swore to himself that he would never forgive Raaluchi for pushing him out of his matrimonial home and for pushing him to sin, a sexual sin, a sin of adultery because she had deprived him of his right, his right as her husband. Onyeka's eyes filled with tears but he didn't dare shed it.

"Please Ifeoma, leave my room. I want to be alone," Onyeka said scornfully. His anger was not on Ifeoma but on Raaluchi who caused it and now he had enough reason to remain far away from her.

"I'm sorry it happened," Ifeoma spoke softly and dressed up on her waitress uniform. But before she left, she dropped her phone number on the bed and told Onyeka to call her if he needed her, and Onyeka remained silent until she left, and then he wept. He wept because he knew he had sinned against his creator. He had never done that before. The first person he had done it with was his wife, and he couldn't help thinking that he had avoided fornication in his youth, but had ended up with adultery, the enormous part of sexual sins. He wept until he was completely drained in his sorrowful tears, until he was exhausted. He didn't order for breakfast, neither did he order for lunch, and in the evening, Ifeoma came back to his room with a tray of salad and two cups of ice cream. She watched him look like hell and she discovered that he had been crying. She moved forward to him after she had dropped the tray of food on the table. She knelt down in front of him and asked him for forgiveness with tears rolling down her cheeks.

"Please Sir, forgive me. I didn't mean to do it…I didn't know you are a married man," she sniffed in her tears as she spoke so softly with her eyes fixed on his gold wedding ring, and Onyeka watched her, not sure of what he should do to her. "Last night when I sang, I saw how you looked at me in admiration and lust…I was attracted to you. I didn't know what came over me… maybe I was drunk…maybe I was insane…I only needed to meet you, so I asked for your room number. Please Sir, forgive me. I'm not as bad as you think. I only allowed my emotions to take over my sense of reasoning," Ifeoma cried after she had spoken so softly, so innocently that Onyeka fell for it and was moved to console her and hug her, and in this hug, she grinned, an impish grin. She had gotten him.

Onyeka allowed her to eat with him after she had told him her touching story. She told him that she was an orphan, and she lived with her uncle whose wife maltreated her so much that she had to leave and squat with her friends who happened to be waitresses in the hotel, and they helped her get a job as a waitress. She said she had dropped out of school when her parents died and since then, she couldn't continue because she had no one to sponsor her University education. Onyeka bought her story and since then, they became friends, and it graduated to a relationship, and Ifeoma ceased Raaluchi's husband in the hotel for over a month until Onyeka received another call from Father Joe who pleaded with him to come back home at least, instead of staying in a hotel. Onyeka agreed. Before he left, Ifeoma told him that she was pregnant and showed him the laboratory result.

Onyeka promised never to leave her alone with the pregnancy. He would do anything to keep her and his baby. He cherished the moments he shared with Ifeoma, the moments in his hotel room, the songs she sang for him all the time, her funny gists and laughter. They were sweet memories, unlike the sad memories of Raaluchi's arrogance and how she had pushed him to sin. He was sorry he sinned, but he just couldn't let go of this woman he had committed adultery with, because she happened to be the one to make him happy, to put back smiles on his face. He was never going to leave her, and now that she was carrying his baby, he promised her that she would never lack anything and Ifeoma was so overwhelmed in ecstasy. To Onyeka, he was going to use the baby Ifeoma was carrying to get even with Raaluchi and make her pay dearly for all the terrible things she did and said to him.

CHAPTER TWENTY-ONE

RAALUCHI HAD CRIED her hearts out, begging Father Joe to help her talk to her husband to come back home, and when Onyeka finally came back home, it was as though she had lost him. She caught him several times answering long-stay- calls mingled with excitement, and when she searched his phone one night, she discovered that the frequent caller was a lady. What pained her mostly that she almost fainted, was when she read his received text message and discovered that this lady called Ifeoma was pregnant for her husband: *Onyi, to say that I love you is a practical understatement. I adore you, my charming prince. Our baby is fine. He's longing for his father. When are you coming to spend some time with us?* She couldn't stand it as she wept in her room one night after she had taken her husband's phone from the wall socket in the living room; after she had discovered and had known what was needed to know.

"What have I done to myself? I've been childless for some months and now this intruder is already pregnant for my husband just for a month and three weeks of his absence in his matrimonial home. Ego...Ego...Ego...you have killed me," Raaluchi soliloquized with quivering lips. She tore her feelings in tears that night and awoke the tormenting voices in her. They mocked her, and again, the voice of her late father reminded her of how useless she was, and that nothing good would ever come out of her. Raaluchi believed she had failed her father again. She suffered from insomnia, and when she bumped into Father Joe's office the next morning; on Tuesday morning, she

187

looked like a harassed mad woman. She didn't let Father Joe speak to her before she cried out uncontrollably and Father Joe waited until she was done with her cry and was ready to speak.

"Father, he che---ated ---on me---," Raaluchi said in between her sobs.

"Raaluchi, stop crying and talk to me. Pull yourself together. What happened?"

"He hasn't been speaking to me since he returned and when I tried to talk to him, he rebuked me. He's been angry with me. He engaged himself for a long time in one particular call...and later, I got to discover that the caller was a woman, and what drove me crazy was that this woman is already pregnant for my husband. Father, I'm finished. It's so painful to see another woman take my place," Raaluchi spoke hoarsely and Father Joe consoled her.

"It's okay Raaluchi. There is no problem that has no solution in the eyes of God. But Raaluchi, where have you been? How could you have allowed another woman to take your place? How could you have allowed your husband to slip from your hands?"

Raaluchi answered his questions with more sobs that tore her heart completely, as though the priest aggravated her depression by asking her those questions. Father Joe heaved a long sigh. He didn't really know what to do to stop Raaluchi from sobbing and he didn't want someone to enter his office and think that he actually made her cry. It was an embarrassment to him. He consoled her and offered to drive her home but she refused and said she would manage to walk home, as though she wanted the world to see how heartbroken she was. Father Joe promised to invite her husband. He promised to take care of the situation with his limited ability, and leave the rest for God to handle. And Raaluchi thanked him and went home with puffy eyes and swollen face.

* * * *

Nkiruka was in her seventh month of pregnancy and each

time she looked at the bulged belly, she felt helpless. She was seeing a Nollywood movie in the living room when the bulb blinked and the light went off. She got furious and began to murmur. 'What kind of heartbreaking life is this? What have I really done to myself?' There was no generator in the house and now, she couldn't get enough air in her pregnancy. All she had envisaged for herself was an easygoing lifestyle, a life style full of riches and goodies, not poverty… certainly not poverty! She began to moan with tears coursing down her cheeks. The living room began to heat up. It was too small to aid ventilation. The sofas were clustering each other, begging to be changed. The bungalow was built well. It had an exterior attraction, but the interior was very unpleasant. To Nkiruka, the house painted a vivid picture of her husband who claimed to be who he wasn't.

She tried to pace round the living room, but there were no space for pacing. She had just finished drinking a cup of water, and furiously, she flung the rubber cup on the wall. She searched for a hand fan but found an old newspaper on a plastic chair beside the TV stand and then she made use of it to give herself some hot air. She couldn't go outside because she didn't want to greet her neighbours that she knew must be hanging around outside. She wanted to be on her own with her bulged belly. It was already 8.00 pm in the night, and she was still infuriated with the poor ventilated living room when Jekwu came home.

"Is there no light here?" He asked, sounding annoyingly jaunty, as though he had kept light in the house before leaving, as though he had strictly instructed light to stay on until he said otherwise. Nkiruka hissed loudly and continued to fan herself. Jekwu lit the small touch in his pocket. Nkiruka looked at him and sneered. Jekwu handed him a gift with smiling face. He knew she would like it and it would change her bad mood. She opened the gift and set her eyes on a leather wrist watch.

"I saw it in one of the boutiques in University areas and I bought it for you to show you how much I love you and how happy I am to be your husband. Nky, I love you so much. How's my baby doing in there?" Jekwu happily caressed her bulged belly and she furiously pulled off his hands from her belly and flung the wrist watch on him. It was a good thing that it was still in a wristwatch case and so it didn't smash into pieces.

"My- oh- My… How the mighty has fallen! This is just like a fall from the sky, to think that I can descend this low…from a gold wrist watch to a fake leather wrist watch. Jekwu you are worthless! So you know you are a wretched poor man and you tricked me into marrying you?"

"Enough Nkiruka, else you'll get it from me again. What I did, I did for love. I love you enough to marry you and true love is not materialistic. You should love me for who I am and not for money."

"Nonso my school boyfriend was just a student, but he lived up to my expectations. As for you, you don't even know how to satisfy a woman. You made a fool of me for making me believe that you are one big millionaire. Who told you that I'm a subject to poverty? Who told you that I belong to the slums like you do? What have you gained for tricking me?"

"I gained a lot of things Nkiruka. I'm married to you and you are carrying my baby. We are going to live together as one happy family, managing what we have and begging God to give us more, besides, we don't need lots of money to make us happy, do we?"

Jekwu smiled sheepishly as he spoke and he tickled his wife's cheeks but she smacked him and spat on him.

"That will be in your dreams! I can't stay married to you anymore, Mr Jekwu Okafor. I need a divorce!" Nkiruka spat on him again and he gave her a small painful slap and warned her to watch her back and that she shouldn't do that again.

"You are a mad man, Jekwu!" Nkiruka blurted out and she began to cry, blaming herself for everything. After shedding tears, she fell asleep on the cushion and Jekwu watched her for a long time, a long lovely watch engulfed with admiration. He carried her to her room and placed her quietly on her bed. He would have taken her to their matrimonial room, but he knew how she was going to react if she woke up and found herself there. She would heap insults on him and he would be forced to lay his hands on her, and that, he didn't want to do anymore. He loved his wife so much to keep hurting her, but he was only sorry that he couldn't control his temper each time she insulted him, and mostly, he was sorry that he couldn't really give her all she wanted, the extravagant life, the Las Vegas fun.

She had told him uncountable times, shortly after their wedding to take her to Las Vegas but he had been postponing the trip and also postponing to take her to their new mansion as he had lied to her, until she found out the truth about him when his lenders barged into their matrimonial home one Sunday morning and demanded for their money in front of his wife. They embarrassed him and called him 'a church rat' who claimed to be 'an elephant' simply because of a woman. Jekwu watched his wife in her sleep. He longed to have her piece of flesh, but he didn't dare. She would never give in to him. She would only scream and alert the neighbours that he was raping her, he was raping his wife. He said a short prayer for her before he left her room, battling with his emotions, and at the same time, with his conscience, wondering if he did the right thing by tricking her, and the other side of him assured him that he did it for love, he did it because he wanted to marry her desperately and sooner or later, she would adjust to his low- life class. He wished he could see God to explain to Him face to face how much he loved Nkiruka and how sorry he was for being selfish, but unfortunately God was invisible and so he prayed and told God to forgive him and bring peace in his marriage with Nkiruka. He didn't know how He was going to do it, but he believed He would do it since He is God.

CHAPTER TWENTY-TWO

"THE SIN OF disobedience is the worst sin on earth because it is the reason why God drove Adam and Eve out of the Garden of Eden, for eating the forbidden fruit, a wage for their sin, and also the reason why Lot's wife turned to a bag of salt for looking back on the day God destroyed Sodom and Gomorrah," Father Joe said to Raaluchi after the couple had narrated their own sides of the story. He blamed Raaluchi for her disobedience in mingling with a woman that her husband warned her to avoid. When Raaluchi brought up the picture, Father Joe blamed her more for her distrust and for not telling her husband about it but rather chose to use it as a pillar to her baseless and useless anger.

"I know you are very intelligent but I don't know that you are so stupid to trust an outsider instead of me. You took my love for granted and you are going to pay for all the terrible things that you did to me," Onyeka spoke furiously to Raaluchi and she began to cry and turned to face her husband.

"You hurt me terribly by cheating on me and impregnating your mistress and I'll never forgive you for your adultery," Raaluchi spoke in tears.

"And who cares if you don't? Are you God? At least you know full well that I'm not impotent after all. You pushed me to that sin and you should be reprimanded for it."

Father Joe hit his hands on his table to hush the couple for their arguments.

"Enough! How dare you brag in your sin?" Father Joe said

to Onyeka but he was still fuming. He wanted to leave the office and go home. He shouldn't remain there to hear Raaluchi's stupid reason for changing from one gentle young lady to a nagger. And all those while he was condoning her bad manners, he had misunderstood her reason to be 'frustration' because she had been waiting for admission into a higher institution, and because she couldn't get pregnant. He didn't know that she had been harboring a grudge against him simply because she didn't trust him.

"A sin remains a sin, no matter how hard we try to justify it. Nagging is a fruit of pride and pride will destroy any marriage. The nagging wife needs to apologise to her husband. The child in question is innocent and has a right to the father but the mother of the child has no right in the marriage. Nagging doesn't justify infidelity and so the man needs to apologize to the wife and to God with a sincere heart. Submissive wife will win her husband. A woman's power is in her submission to her husband. Complete care must be taken for a nagging wife because there are other vices in pride such as laziness, wickedness and prayerlessness. God hates pride and the nagging wife needs urgent deliverance prayers. It is God who gives fruit of the womb and it comes in peaceful and humble atmosphere. The more the nagging, the more the gift is delayed," Father Joe gave his final judgement and gave the couple a moment of privacy to make their reconciliation. They sat in silence, still angry with each other. Nobody was willing to take the first step of apology. Minutes later, Father Joe entered for a closing prayer.

Back home, Onyeka didn't bother to aplogise to his wife. He was still fuming and he did not need to render an apology to the woman who ruined his life. He shouldn't have come. He shouldn't have honoured Father Joe's invitation if he had known that he wasn't going to get the justification he needed from him. He should not have expected a round-faced voluntary eunuch in white robes to be in a position to understand how he felt. Father Joe had spoken so easily, so predictably because he was only a priest and did not know how it felt to be in love and to be hurt by love, and he did not need to have come to hear his priestly judgement. Raaluchi was very ungrateful, and she made his life so miserable. He offered her love but she spat on his face. She didn't deserve his love. Ifeoma deserved it.

Raaluchi cried in her room. To her, she would have wholeheartedly apologized to Onyeka if he hadn't gone as far as cheating on her and impregnating his mistress. He had paid her back in a very painful way, so it was useless apologizing to him. She once again, thought of how useless her life had been ever since Nnanyelugo died. She didn't understand her life anymore; didn't understand what was happening to her and didn't even know how to help herself come out of her problems. She felt an instant urge to pack her things and leave her marriage. But on a second thought, she remembered her husband's mistress and imagined how joyfully she would move into her matrimonial home to take her place, as soon as she discovered her absence. She heaved a long sigh. She didn't want to be a looser. She appended her signature on her marriage certificate. She was the legal wife and she would never surrender her right to any other woman. She mustered courage and promised herself to go through any amount of pain in her marriage and overcome it victoriously. To Raaluchi, Onyeka is her destiny and she would never let another woman take her destiny. She must wait. She would only be a corward if she ran away… but no, she must wait.

Before his silence, the last thing Onyeka told his wife was that he didn't love her anymore and he should bear it in mind that the fact that they were still married to each other was just because they had to stay married to keep the biblical law and not because of love. Raaluchi couldn't bear to live like an outcast in her matrimonial home. She felt bereft especially when she knew that her marital love and happiness were missing and Onyeka's love was lying in the heart of another woman that had stolen him from her. Onyeka in his awful silence, didn't bother to give her a call to know how she felt as he used to, and when he finally got home by 9pm every night, he would shrug off her warm hug and would only head to the bedroom without having his dinner and this attitude depressed Raaluchi that the voices never failed to torment her. One Saturday morning, Raaluchi was able to trace her husband to verify where he visited his mistress, and she felt like barging into the bungalow when Ifeoma came out of it and embraced her husband before leading him inside with an arm around his shoulders. She wept for a brief moment in jealousy before she went home in a taxi.

* * * *

Onyeka's silence was suffocating and repetitive to Raaluchi, and just unbearable. On Monday evening, she took a taxi to Ifeoma's bungalow. She just needed to fight for what belonged to her. She didn't want to stay back home and do nothing but shed tears when she knew well enough that she could do something to stop the game from playing. She only wished that Ifeoma was at home when she pressed the bell to the entrance door. She had stood for ten minutes before someone in a black bomb short and pink T-shirt unlocked the door and gave her a quizzical look.

"I'm Mrs. Raaluchi Ibekwe, Onyeka's wife." Raaluchi said proudly as she let herself inside the house and was already looking around the house in admiration before she sat down in one of the luxurious red sofas. The floor was covered with black tiles. The ceiling had a POP decoration merging with an attractive chandelier. The plasma TV was showing a music video in Channel O, with half naked girls shaking their asses as they danced. Ifeoma was watching Raaluchi, looking very surprised. Her eyes continued to narrow in wonder. She was wondering what she had come for. If she had come for peace, she would give her peace but if she had come to warn her to leave her husband alone, then she was asking for war for she would never do such a thing. They sat staring at each other for a brief moment before Raaluchi broke the silence.

"Won't you offer me something to drink?" Raaluchi asked her with a feigned smile as she tried to be relaxed and feel comfortable with this pretty young woman that had stolen Onyeka from her.

"And why will I do such a thing? I can't remember inviting you to my house."

Raaluchi laughed a slight provocative laugh that regained her seriousness afterwards. She glared at Ifeoma. At first, she wanted to beat her up and concentrate more on her pregnant belly until she miscarried, but something in her held her and begged her not to make a scene.

"Don't feel so comfortable with what you have now, because, it's never going to last, since you are a thief to take what does not belong to you."

"You may call me a thief, but, I don't bloody care because, that is not who I am. I only took the precious gold that you threw in the gutters. I only took what you abandoned, and that does not make me a thief."

"You've got guts to speak to me in that manner. How dare you?" Raaluchi fumed as she stood up forcefully, and Ifeoma stood up too. The two young women stood facing each other and glaring at each other. The clock in the living room ticked, it was six o'clock and then furiously, Raaluchi turned to leave. But she stopped as soon as she heard another blow from Ifeoma.

"I am not perturbed by your anger. If you really want to apportion blames, you should apportion such blames on your stupidity. A man like Onyeka needs to be guarded jealously because he is a blessing from above. He is one of the richest pharmacists in Nigeria and he is very handsome and responsible. Oh gosh! What were you thinking? You hurt him so much by fiddling with his heart. I'm sorry if you feel terribly bad but it's good you know that his love now lies in me; the mother of his child... a child that you cannot offer!" Ifeoma released the hurtful words very fast, as though she had been saving them for Raaluchi in her mind. Raaluchi's eyes were filled with tears. The tumultuous surging of anger and pain that shot through her, made her turn back and pounce on Ifeoma with two painful slaps that landed her on a long sofa. Ifeoma screamed for help but Raaluchi did not want to stop dealing with her. She kicked her on her belly, and was squeezing her mouth, squeezing and twisting so hardly as though she was tying a knot. She spat on her and was giving her knocks with the heel of her shoe before someone entered and stopped the fight.

Raaluchi trembled in her room that evening. Onyeka was mad at her for what she did. Even though he didn't speak to her when he got home, she knew from the way he glared at her when he stopped the fight in Ifeoma's bungalow, from the way he slapped her so hard on her right cheek that she almost lost her sight, she also knew from the way she defended Ifeoma by asking her if she was hurt, if she was bleeding. Raaluchi was sure about what would come next and so she packed her things and waited for Onyeka to voice it out. She waited for him to ask her to leave his house for attempting to kill his unborn baby.

She cried as she paced in her room and then walked slowly to the front of her dressing mirror and savagely squeezed her belly with both hands. The pain reminded her of how useless she was; reminded her that a child nestled now in a stranger's body instead of in hers. She cried uncontrollably as she sat down on the floor and looked at her self through her dressing mirror, knowing full well that she was hurt and that a lot had changed about her: she had lost so much weight and she was slowly passing out in a tormenting depression, and it had taken her beauty away. The voices began to torment her and she cried bitterly when they reminded her again of how useless she was.

From the master's bedroom, Onyeka heard her crying voice and felt sorry for her and made a move to go to her, console her and apologise to her for daring to lay his hands on her, what he had never done to her. But the other feelings of hatred, grudges and the urge to retaliate for all the terrible things Raaluchi did to him held him back. She should as well go through the pains just like he did. For all he knew, what was happening to her now was a big lesson which she needed to learn and he shouldn't feel sorry for her. For all he knew, Raaluchi pushed him to the kind of life he was now living.

CHAPTER TWENTY-THREE

IT WAS A big duty for Raaluchi, a duty that she enjoyed doing just to unite her marriage. She had made it a necessary duty to visit Onyeka's parents with gifts and plead with her mother-in-law to talk to Onyeka. Each time she came for the same purpose, Mama would cuddle her in a warm embrace, and would tell her to pray for her husband. Mama did not know why she loved Raaluchi so much not to blame her for what was happening in her marriage, but she knew that Raaluchi had faced so much challenges in life and needed to be loved, no matter what.

"Mama he had stopped eating my food, he doesn't call me on phone anymore and he comes back late everyday. Mama I can't bear this anymore. That woman has succeeded in charming my husband," Raaluchi would say hoarsely in tears and Mama would cuddle her and console her. Mama would assure her that she was only waiting for her son's mistress to finally deliver the baby so that she would personally tell her off. Mama knew she couldn't do that now that Ifeoma was heavily pregnant. The baby was Onyeka's and had the blood of the Ibekwe family and so she couldn't possibly tell her off in her pregnancy. Raaluchi would have to be patient and persevere until Ifeoma delivered the baby. Mama had assured Raaluchi that she would personally talk Ifeoma into leaving Onyeka for good.

* * * *

A week later, about 6am on a Friday morning, Mama called Onyeka and announced that she would be visiting his office and Onyeka concurred. He heaved a sigh of relief when he searched his schedule for the day and discovered that he didn't have lots of work for the day. He would have used his free time with Ifeoma if not for his mother's visit. He propped up from his bed and was heading to the toilet to powder his nose when he heard Raaluchi's loud intercessory prayer.

"Oh God, any woman that has succeeded in snatching my husband from me, Holy Ghost fire destroy her! Holy Ghost fire! destroy her!"

Onyeka chortled as he heard her prayer, convinced that God would not answer such a prayer. An hour later, he was ready for work and he left without taking his breakfast. It was about 10am in the morning when Onyeka heard a soft knock on his office door and he approved it. His secretary, a light skinned languorous man with a serious face announced his mother's presence and he nooded, signaling to the man to let her in. Mama walked inside his son's office and looked around in admiration, trying to remember the last time she had visited her son in his office. Onyeka couldn't help but admire his mother's attire: a well sown skirt and blouse with a sky blue hollandis *abada*. She was looking gorgeous on the attire that matched with her beautiful silver slippers and clutch bag. He watched her in admiration, recognizing the hollandis *abada*. He had given it to her during her Mothering Sunday feast in his father's house in Umudioka.

"Mama *nno*. Welcome," Onyeka said softly to her as he went to give her a warm hug, before she made herself comfortable with one of the beautiful office chairs. Mother and son exchanged pleasantries but Onyeka's countenance changed to a slight frown when Mama asked him about Raaluchi. But Mama understood him and didn't say something about Raaluchi anymore. She also wondered when her son would finally reconcile with his wife, when those pains he felt and the grudges he had for his wife would all die. Onyeka called his secretary through his office phone and requested for fresh snacks for Mama but his mother told him immediately not to bother himself and Onyeka quickly told his secretary to forget about going to the company's bakery.

"Onyekachukwu, my son."

"Yes Mama." Onyeka looked at his mother. He knew that his mother only called his name in full if she had something serious to discuss with him. He turned off his computer, ready to listen to what his mother had to say.

"What plans do you have for your baby after the delivery?"

Onyeka heaved a sigh of helplessness as soon as he heard his mother. He had actually been thinking towards that direction and he hadn't come up with a conclusion. The first time he discussed it with Ifeoma, she refused vehemently, insisting that Onyeka did not pay her bride price and so, the baby belonged to her.

"You must look for a way to talk her into giving the baby to you. That woman cannot bring up a baby. She is a prostitute."

"Mama, Raaluchi is not a saint either, besides, a mother has the right to her child, married or single," Onyeka told his mother angrily. He was pissed because of Mama's blind love for Raaluchi, a woman who ruined his life.

"I hope you are not planning to marry that girl. I will not encourage polygamy in our family. You better stop any further relationship with her and reconcile with your wife who has been craving for your attention," Mama blurted in anger, placing her shriveled hand under her jaw and Onyeka watched her with scoffs. He wished that his mother understood how he felt. He wished that his mother knew that Ifeoma was his Raalu now, the woman that regained his happiness.

* * * *

Ifeoma delivered a bouncing baby boy on the 14th day of June, 2011. Onyeka employed Nanny Nene to assist Ifeoma in bringing up the baby. The Nanny was recommended by his mother. She was from Umudioka and her mother was a very good friend of Mama. Mama told Onyeka that she would be relaxed if Nanny Nene assisted Ifeoma in raising the baby because she was homely to the core. Nanny Nene had been a Nanny for so six years, ever since she became a childless widow. To her, she understood her state of childlessness to be the fact that she was to cater for other people's children. She was simply a mother of all children that she came in contact with. She was very good at her job. The last place she worked as a Nanny was in Awka. There, she met a stingy couple who would want her to give them her best without paying her well. She resigned from the job and fortunately for her, she got what she wanted for her selfless service when Onyeka employed her.

Nanny Nene lived in Ifeoma's bungalow. She helped to wash the baby's clothes, take the baby to his mother for breastfeeding, whenever he cried in hunger and cooed the baby to sleep whenever he needed it. But Nany Nene observed something strange about Ifeoma: her horrible mood whenever she was carrying the baby. She would watch the baby with sadness and then she would give a start and forcefully drop the baby on the bed. She had done this repeatedly and each time, she did it, the baby would cry.

One day, she was carrying the baby, and again, her mind drifted to her past, her past life experience with her guardian's baby, the past that had chosen to torment her ever since she carried her own child in her arms. She remembered it vividly. She was only eleven years old then, when her mother brought her to Lagos to become a housegirl to her friend's daughter Aunty Nkechi: a banker who delivered a baby and was already through with her six weeks maternity leave. She remembered that she was instructed by Aunty Nkechi to give the baby a 2.5 metre of Paracetamol Syrup at 12. 0' clock in the afternoon, five minutes after feeding him with baby formula milk. She had over slept that afternoon only to wake up when the baby cried.

She looked at the wall clock. It was 1. 30 pm. Out of curiousity and panick of not yielding to Aunty Nkechi's instruction, she brought out the baby's basket of medicine, and gave the baby a metilated spirit, thinking it was paracetamol syrup. When she realized her mistake, she began to cry and made for the house phone to call Aunty Nkechi who left everything she was doing in the bank and headed home. But before she got to the house, the baby died on Ifeoma, who wailed in shock.

Aunty Nkechi came back and descended on her with kicks and slaps, and as though the punishments were not enough, she broke a wood stool on her head and she fainted in her own pool of blood. She didn't know what happened next, but what she was sure of was that she regained herself in a hospital bed. The person that brought her there was not Aunty Nkechi but a man he barely knew. Ever since this unfortunate incidence, any time that Ifeoma carried a baby, she would be forced to reminisce about that sorrowful day and this moved her to fear and shock. This was exactly what she was passing through whenever she carried her baby in her arms. Unbearably, just in the middle of one night, she made away with her baby, and dumped him on the doorsteps of an old building. She didn't realize that Nanny Nene followed her when she left the house with the baby, and after Ifeoma left for the house, Nanny Nene carried the baby and reported the incident to Onyeka on phone.

Ifeoma was surprised when Onyeka came the following morning and requested to take the baby with a raging voice.

"Ifeoma, I want to take my baby now!" Onyeka raged, peered all the rooms for the baby until he found Nanny Nene carrying the baby, sitting on a chair at the veranda of the back yard.

"No! I thought we had an agreement. The baby belongs to me, since I'm not married to you. You are free to pay him a visit but you can't take him away from me," Ifeoma said disdainfully walking behind Onyeka.

"So you would rather dump my baby on a doorstep than let me have him? You are impossible and I think you don't love this baby. I would rather have him than watch you abandon him to God knows where," and with that, Onyeka, ordered Nanny Nene to pack their things and bring them to his car outside, while he carried his baby so tightly, unable to let go of him. Soon, Onyeka drove out with Nanny Nene and his baby, together with their personal effects. Ifeoma watched them with tears streaming down her cheeks.

* * * *

Onyeka was extremely happy to have the baby and he named the baby after him, but the name 'Bobo' stole his name because that was what Mama called him. Mama spent a month in Onyeka's house just for the baby, and Raaluchi finally fell in love with the baby. She would cuddle the baby and coo him when he howled and she would watch him closely in admiration. The baby had an obvious resemblance with his father. The full head of softy curled black hair and the dark skin and the widely spaced eyes were unmistakable. He looked like Onyeka. Onyeka expected anger from Raaluchi, an unmitigated jealousy and the inevitable urge to leave the house but he was deadly startled that Raaluchi fell in love with the baby and spent more time with him. Mama did just as she had promised Raaluchi. She told Ifeoma off. It was a good time to do that, since she discovered from Nanny Nene what Ifeoma did to her own baby. Mama left the house but before she left, Raaluchi held her tightly and begged her not to go.

"My child, you don't need to worry anymore. Just enjoy your marriage. I've talked to my son and he promised never to have anything to do with that Ifeoma again. I also told Ifeoma off and so she wouldn't dare interfere with your marriage anymore, *inugo?*" Mama spoke softly to Raaluchi, so softly in a low tone that Onyeka couldn't hear her, and she nodded in tears. Perspiration dampened Raaluchi's palms before she finally let go of holding Mama. She watched Mama enter the car and Onyeka drove off. She waved at Mama and Mama waved back. She wondered if she could trust Mama's words: that she could enjoy her marriage and that the intruder had been told off. But Mama was wrong because, Onyeka's silence continued, coupled with his clandestine relationships with Ifeoma. Raaluchi was jealous about how easily Onyeka forgave Ifeoma for abandoning their child in the middle of the night, how easily they re-established their relationship and how often they talked on phone. She had to meet Father Joe, and he gave her prayers and the mysterious book to save her marriage.

PART FOUR

THE BURNING BACHELOR (*O NA AGBA OKU*)

THE YEAR 2007-2008

....

A bachelor who is too handsome to a fault, must be
ready to face the consequences of his handsomeness.

....

CHAPTER TWENTY-FOUR

EGO ALWAYS PEEKED through the window every morning just to watch Onyeka drive off to work. She made it a daily duty to watch him every nine o'clock in the morning, even though her baby needed her attention. She would stick out her head and watch him in lustful admiration, blaming her *chi* for not giving her a befitting husband like Onyeka, who was really handsome and rich in every aspect and would have taken good care of her if she had waited for some years. But all the same, she knew she wouldn't have seen Onyeka if she had stayed married to her husband in Onitsha, if her husband hadn't decided that they moved into Onyeka's house in Asaba because his friends all resided in Asaba and he just couldn't be an exception, even though he knew he didn't have enough money. To Ego, she deserved Onyeka. She deserved to be married to a rich man and not hooked to a poverty stricken husband of hers.

As she watched him every morning, she told herself that she would do everything just to have him and make him love her and take care of her, even though she was married. Jobless as she was, she would waste the money for feeding her children, to trace Onyeka to his office, and then, to other places he went, just to know if he was meeting up with any woman. She got a chance to meet him in his house when one of the female tenants reported her to Onyeka the landlord, for no longer taking her turns to sweep the compound. Onyeka sent for Ego one Sunday evening and she took time re-applying her make up and dancing in front of her dressing mirror like someone who was given a golden opportunity to meet the president. Ego was the kind of woman that was very confident of her beauty, a kind of woman that would put up a fight to anybody that would tell the bitter truth of her obvious ugliness.

"Mummy, I want food," Olaedo her daughter told her as she stood beside her, crying and holding her mother's dress so tight as though she knew she was about to leave the house and the little girl was dying of hunger. Ego quietly removed her daughter's hand from her dress, the only beautiful dress that she had been saving to wear to Onyeka's house. She just couldn't bear to see it rumpled. It sure would look unpleasant to Onyeka and she just didn't want that to happen. Ego pushed her daughter aside and made her way upstairs to Onyeka's house. Olaedo landed on the floor with profuse tears.

Minutes later, Ego stood in front of Onyeka and watched him lustfully. The questions Onyeka asked her about no longer participating in sweeping the compound were unanswered. She did nothing but gazed at him, and then, she began to smile a mysterious smile.

"Mrs Ego Mmaduka, are you okay?" Onyeka asked her but she didn't answer, instead she began to stutter. She stood motionless, and her legs trembled. She was a plain village woman that had been mesmerized by the sight of a handsome man in his rich world and she thought she looked so attractive on her over makeup: a red lipstick and green eyeshadow. She was wearing a green silk gown and her dark skinned complexion was shinning from an over-used oily cream. Her green gown had the length end above her knees. She didn't know why she felt so uneasy standing in front of the man that had swept off her feet, but all she wanted was to stay there forever and denounce her husband and children for his sake. He was so fresh-looking; fresh-looking enough that she could see her face from his face.

"Mrs Ego Mmaduka!" Onyeka had to shout her name to bring back her sanity if she had lost it by entering his house.

"Sir?" Ego answered and moved breathtakingly closer to him. Onyeka stood up and asked her to leave. He gestured at the door for her and then she began to cry. Onyeka heaved a sigh of confusion as he watched her and wondered what the woman had planned to do with him in his house. She was married and he shouldn't be answerable to anybody's pathetic and immature emotion. He just didn't know what her husband would say if he entered his house and found his wife crying in front of him. He just didn't want to take responsibility for making a woman cry.

"Woman, I said you should leave my house."

Ego held Onyeka's legs in her crocodile tears as she knelt down in front of him.

"Sir please I need you, just let me be with you much longer, *biko*. My husband is not coming back today. I can cook for you and I'm ready to give you anything you want from me," Ego begged him in tears and Onyeka shook her hands off his legs.

"You need Jesus, not me. Get the hell out of my house now or I'll be forced to push you out!" Onyeka exclaimed. He was furious and very much disappointed. Ego was a shame to womanhood and he couldn't possibly think that Ubaka, her husband left his children and his house in her care without realizing the fact that Ego his wife was a shameless flirt who had chosen to flirt, to taking care of her children; a devil looking for who to devour.

Ego finally stood up and left after Onyeka shrieked angrily at her again and Onyeka heaved a sigh of relief. He thought of what to do to Ego and his mind wavered in contemplation of what to decide. He wanted to tell Ego's husband and later he would give them quit notice. He wanted to have peace in his house and feel relaxed and not so uncomfortable and restless knowing full well that someone may enter his house one day and rape him.

* * * *

Ego cleared the table after her husband was done with his food. It was half past seven in the evening and Ubaka had just returned from his yesterday's journey to the village. He pulled out the meat particles that stuck in between his teeth with tooth pick. Ego sat beside him and watched him, wondering if the landlord called him on phone and told him something. She was about to ask him when Ubaka spoke up first.

"The landlord wants to see me this evening."

Ego's heart raced in fear for she was sure that Onyeka was going to tell her husband about her deeds. She must stop her husband from answering the landlord. She would be finished if her husband sent her back to her mother in the village, with her mission of having Onyeka unaccomplished. She must look for a way to pin her husband in the house so that he wouldn't know anything about what happened between her and Onyeka the previous evening. She knew what to do to make him powerless, and that was satisfying him in bed.

* * * *

Onyeka was working in his office when Amaka his secretary entered to inform him that a woman was looking for him. Amaka was a woman with hungry eyes, yearning for any man's attention. She also had her hungry eyes on Onyeka and had been waiting for him to notice her first. Onyeka approved vaguely because he was engrossed in his work that he didn't bother to know if he was actually expecting someone. Ego entered his office dressed in a pink long gown and a big scarf like someone who planned to go to the church but changed her mind on her way. Onyeka was startled to see her and he asked her who gave her his office address and she began to stutter. She wanted to be his friend but his overwhelming burst of anger displayed an awed fear in her whenever she was with him.

"Speak up!"

"I…I picked your complementary card in the compound."

"Leave my office."

Ego knelt down and streamed her crocodile tears. She begged him to forgive her and that he shouldn't tell her husband about what she said to him in his house. Onyeka glared at her in uttermost disgust. He hated women who are very unfaithful to their husbands, women who don't know God.

"You know you should be very ashamed of yourself. I mean, how can a married woman like you, a mother of three be so sluttish? You are just a slut in your husband's house craving for men to satisfy your unsatisfied urge. You are what our people call '*ono na di acho di*.' Onyeka said in Igbo.

"I'm sorry Sir. It won't happen again, please forgive me." Ego spoke hoarsely in tears and Onyeka gave her a long mournful look.

"I forgive you. Go and sin no more. By the way, where is your baby?" Onyeka asked her, just to remind her that she was a mother and what her duty as a mother is.

"I left him with Mama Chigozie, the woman that lives at the left basement," Ego said with eyes downcast, unwilling to hear his answer or even see his reaction to her reply. She thanked him and briskly walked out of his office. But the thought of the hurtful words Onyeka blurted out to her infuriated her, simply because she had been yearning for him. No man had ever turned her down. She was an ebony pretty lady. Just outside Onyeka's company, Amaka approached her. She had been eavesdropping on her boss's discussion with Ego and she had left the company before Ego, to tell her off.

"Hey, stop there please. You this *old cargo*, you better remove your eyes from my man Onyeka. He is mine. You should be concentrating more on breastfeeding your baby and taking care of your family, instead of itching for a man," Amaka said angrily to Ego wiggling her index finger to Ego's face, warning her to remove her eyes from her man. Ego ignored her and shamefully left her presence. She had wanted to fight Amaka but the reason for their fight to whoever that may come to rescue Amaka, would be very embarrassing to her as a mother, and so, she ignored her and walked away.

Ego promised herself that she would do anything within her powers to make Onyeka pay for all the terrible things he said to her, and for turning her down. But she didn't keep that promise when she set her eyes on Onyeka again as she peeped through the window the next morning. All she thought of was how to convince him to have an affair with her. She hadn't desired any man the way she desired to have Onyeka by all means. She came up with a plan to make Onyeka come home that afternoon and she succeeded.

Onyeka was having a board meeting in his office when his cell phone rang and the caller informed him that his apartment was on fire. Onyeka hurriedly postponed the meeting and dashed out of the company. He was heading to his apartment when he saw a half naked woman sitting on his door steps, unaware of a hidden camera watching her. At first, he didn't know what came into him and he approached Ego by walking slowly to her but he suddenly realized himself when he was almost so close to Ego and shouted the name 'Jesus'. He got infuriated and pushed Ego out of his sight. To Onyeka, Ego was impossible if she was still insisting on having an affair with him and to think that he left his important office meeting just to fall into Ego's trap of animalistic urge. He decided instantly that he would tell Ego's husband since his wife was getting out of control.

CHAPTER TWENTY-FIVE

UBAKA EXPRESSED HIS disappointment when Onyeka showed him the camera: the close circuit camera that monitored what happened both inside and outside his house. In his outraged anger, he sent Ego back to the village where she came from. Ego left her matrimonial house on the 21st day of July 2007 and when she arrived at her mother's house in Mbaise, her mother made sure that she blurted painful words to her; words that made her suffer from isolation and constant remembrance of how loose she was for her not to be satisfied with her husband alone. Ego hated Onyeka for putting her in a sorrowful condition, even when she was still a nursing mother. Ubaka had deprived her of seeing her children and her mother was making life very difficult for her, even the villagers had heard her story and they took her to be a disgrace to womanhood. They mocked her everywhere she went, called her *akwunakwuna* (a prostitute) and all other bad names for a flirtatious woman, in Igbo expressions, and the market women refused to sell things to her because of the abominable crime that she committed. Ego always sobbed because she had been degraded and embarrassed.

Ego swore to herself that she must revenge what Onyeka had done to her even if she knew she loved him, she must make him pay so much for rejecting her love and for publicly disgracing her. Her obsession to revenge made her take devious steps to visiting a native doctor: Ndagwuiyi, a very dangerous native doctor that was capable of taking lives of people, tying up peoples' destinies and so many other devilish things. Ndagwuiyi's instructions on how Ego could end up henpecking her husband, and taking his senses away did not depart from Ego, as she regularly performed the ritual of calling her husband's name every mid-night, and the breaking of eggs after each call. She was successful in winning back her husband's heart, that Ubaka came for her and took her back home just after few weeks of her incarceration in the village.

Ego's mother was surprised and had no objection to make. Left for her, Ubaka would have allowed her to stay longer in the village so that she would teach her daughter a serious lesson. Back home in Asaba, nothing changed Onyeka's feelings towards her and she felt disappointed in Ndagwuiyi's charm because, Onyeka still hated her. Ndagwuiyi had assured her after he killed a white cock, and made the call of Onyeka's name in his shrine that Onyeka will reciprocate her love and then with that, she would get him too easy to deal with. She was even more disappointed that she had to offer her body to Ndagwuiyi, as payment for the jobs he did for her since she had no money.

Onyeka exhibited his hatred by not responding to her greetings; by pretending not to hear them when she greeted him. Ndagwuiyi had assured him that Onyeka would crave for her attention, and reciprocate her love feelings but that was a lie because, Onyeka didn't show any interest at all. Nothing had changed. He was still the burning bachelor that she longed to possess but could not, and because of that, she directed her passion to hatred. She thought of paying every bit of pains and shame which she underwent in the hands of Onyeka. If Onyeka cannot love her in return, then he must be ready to experience the consequences of his stubbornness.

* * * *

Other women that craved to have Onyeka to love and possibly marry them were numerous that they even quarreled with one another, warning one another to stay away from Onyeka. The

216

second woman after Ego was Amaka his Secretary: She had one day entered Onyeka's office and unbearably planted a passionate kiss on Onyeka's lips. Onyeka rebuked her and had to sack her for sexual harassments in his office. Others were his business colleagues. There was one of them, a rich famous Pharmacist in Enugu, who promised Onyeka to give him fifty thousand dollars if he only accepted to spend a night with her. Another one promised to abandon her job and become a caring house wife just for his sake, if he married her, and others wrote endless love letters, attaching their complementary cards and waiting for Onyeka's call. But Onyeka didn't give in to any of them, instead he fastened the seatbelt of his prayer life, telling God what he wanted in a life partner and believing that God would do it for him. He wanted to take a huge responsibility of wiping the sorrowful tears of a distressed damsel in a godly manner. The last among the hungry women that craved for the burning bachelor was Martha.

PART FIVE

WHEN LOVE IS TESTED

THE YEAR 2012-2013.

Love is not real until it is tested.

CHAPTER TWENTY-SIX

THE THINGS ONYEKA did when he returned home with his wife from the award night, were executing his plans of terminating Ifeoma's tenancy in the bungalow rented to her and giving Ubaka's family a quit notice. The couple spent time talking at the verandah. Onyeka told Raaluchi the details of his encounter with Ego and so many other women in the past. He didn't tell her earlier because he thought it was irrelevant. He also told Raaluchi about his eavesdropping on Ego's discussion with Ifeoma, and hoped that Raaluchi wouldn't think that it was his reason for accepting to forgive her. He apologized to Raaluchi for his adultery with tears in his eyes and they promised each other to resolve their mistakes after a long hug. Nanny Nene was happy with the re-union when she peeped from the window and saw them in a romantic hug. She smiled a slow long smile, admiring them. Raaluchi had never been so peaceful in her life. Her reconciliation with her husband was like a dream come true for her.

Onyeka wanted to make things right. He longed to confess his sins to a priest and be free from the guilt that tormented him; the guilt that made him remember just how unworthy he was to be with Raaluchi, and on that night of the 25th of August 2012, just unbearably, he told Raaluchi to accompany him to the church. He wanted to see Father Joe for a sacrament of reconciliation and re-establish his union with his father in heaven. Just like the prodigal son, he was tired and wanted to make peace with his heavenly father. They were on their way to the church when a speeding car, a black Mercedes 190 with a rough rider overtook them, and blocked their way from moving forward. Mean looking men in black alighted from the car and released some steam with their guns that Onyeka was frightened. Pedestrians began to run as fast as they could, and opened shops along the road, started closing for the night.

The men all covered their faces with masks making it difficult for Onyeka to recognize them. Two of the men pulled the couple out of the front seats of their car: Xtera jeep, and pushed them inside the back of the car. The couple struggled with the kidnappers and immediately, the kidnappers made them fall asleep with a poisonous handkerchief that they had inhaled, before they sped off in Onyeka's Xtera, and the other set of kidnappers followed suit in their Mercedes 190. In an uncompleted building, they were tied up. Raaluchi pleaded for mercy in tears but the men hushed her by pointing a gun at her. Raaluchi feared for her life.

Onyeka begged them for mercy, promising to give them anything they wanted but the kidnappers did not oblige. Onyeka wondered who must have sent the deadly kidnappers to torture them. The newly reconciled couple spent a disastrous time in a dolorous uncompleted building. What they fed on were only small loaves of bread and satchets of water, and Onyeka was already having a hard time with the bread. He prayed in his mind, asking God for mercy and a way to escape from the hell they were in. Somehow, he wondered if that was a punishment from God to correct his mistakes. His heart ached but he didn't shed tears.

Raaluchi was so depressed that the evil voices began to shout on her again, reminding her of how miserable her life was, and that she would never have a chance of happiness because, she was doomed to a big bad luck. Nnanyelugo's voice screamed at her, reminding her that she was always in trouble and that her life was full of troubles. She screamed in fury that she scared everybody in the uncompleted building including Onyeka her husband who was forced to reminisce about their honeymoon in America; that awful night when Raaluchi scared him to death with those blazing eyes of hers. Something is wrong with his wife and he was eager to find out what that is. One of the kidnappers released a bullet in the air to shut Raaluchi up, and then, she stopped screaming and began to cry. Onyeka felt for her. He wanted to hold her and console her but he couldn't. He wondered why they were passing through these pains just when they had finally reconciled with each other; now that their love was rekindled.

The couple stayed in the dark hands of the kidnappers for three days, before Ego finally showed up as the mastermind of the whole situation. She was wearing a black T-shirt and a black pair of jean trousers, just like the rest of the kidnappers. As soon as Onyeka saw her, he suspected that she was a member of the "Black Axe": a very dangerous cult. But one thing he knew was that he must never be afraid of her, and he would survive the ordeal with his wife. He was going to have a second chance of happiness with Raaluchi and nobody, not even Ego, could separate them again.

"You devil! Don't you ever get tired of tormenting me?" Raaluchi spoke up in fury. She struggled to let go of herself from the tight tie but she couldn't. The men laughed at her; at her inability to escape from the tight tie.

"I will never get tired of tormenting both of you. As a matter of fact, I've decided to make that my hobby," Ego said and began to whip Raaluchi's back right in front of Onyeka. Raaluchi screamed in tears and it tore Onyeka's heart that his wife was in pains right in front of him, but he couldn't save her. Ego whipped harder that Onyeka began to plead, but Ego did not stop. Raaluchi wept in pains, and the evil voices echoed in her. Her entire body was on fire. She was so much in pains, that the voices tormented her. The pains were unbearable. She was depressed and distressed.

"You should whip me. Leave Raaluchi out of your misery.

She has done nothing wrong to you," Onyeka said almost in tears. He had been watching Raaluchi wallow in pains and he couldn't bear it anymore.

"So now you know how much pain you caused me, Onyeka. The painful tears your wife is shedding now were exactly the kind I shedded just because of you. You were the reason I lived a mockery life of isolation in the village four years ago and you are the reason I've become so evil that I can kill. I offered you my body and my heart but you spat on my face; you turned me down as if I was a refuse dump and now, I'll make sure that you can never be a happy man because, I'm going to kill your wife right in front of you!"

"May God have mercy on you, Ego"

Ego laughed after Onyeka had spoken and she mimicked him.

"You should be the one seeking for mercy from God. Look at you Onyeka, you need God's mercy. The way you rejected me four years ago, I thought that you were really a saint. But you proved me wrong by falling for my sister's seduction, sleeping with her, and impregnating her. I want you to know that I always bounce back on people who say no to me. I don't ever loose my games because I play them well." Just then, the police men released gun shots in the air and announced to everyone in the uncompleted building of their presence, and also announced that everybody should freeze.

The stubborn black- axe men tried to shoot back and they were overpowered and shot down one after the other by the policemen. The policemen entered the uncompleted building and Onyeka thanked God in his heart, and also to whoever that was responsible for alerting the police on their behalf. The police men untied the victims and arrested Ego. She was the only one alive among the kidnappers. Just then, the voices urged Raaluchi to grab a gun from the policeman's back-pocket, and she did that immediately as though the voices controlled her actions.

Unknown to the other policemen who were busy inspecting

the uncompleted building, to know if there were more kidnappers hiding somewhere, Raaluchi had pulled the trigger and shot Ego dead. She shot her several times on her back, as though she made sure that the bullets went straight to her chest to penetrate her wicked heart and kill her instantly. The voices had urged her to kill Ego for ruining her love life in marriage. Raaluchi fell down after the act, and began to cry, a horrible cry: horrible because she had just been used by the voices again. The policemen were angry at what Raaluchi did and they arrested her immediately for murder.

* * * *

They all headed to Asaba Police Station after a policeman made some calls on how to take the corpses to the mortuary for their people to claim. In the police station, Raaluchi was locked up in a female cell, despite Onyeka's pleadings with the policemen. They only told Onyeka that the law must take its full course, and even accused Raaluchi of being an accomplice to the kidnap for killing the culprit. Onyeka called Raaluchi's mother and she answered the call on the first ring. Mummy was grateful to God that they had finally been rescued from the kidnappers. When Nanny Nene informed her that the newly reconciled couple was missing, she got very worried and informed her in-laws who reported the matter to the police and also to the Broadcasting Network Service in Delta State. The Ibekwe family was willing to offer the sum of two hundred thousand naira to anybody with useful information that would lead to finding the missing couple.

It happened that some students that lived in Anwai traced the kidnappers to an uncompleted building and reported to the police, not sure if they were the wanted missing couple. It turned out that they were, and the students were still hovering at the police-station for their reward, not knowing that the music had changed its tune. Mummy shrieked on the phone when she heard from Onyeka that Raaluchi had been arrested by the police for murder. She promised Onyeka to be at the police station in no time. Onyeka was waiting for the arrival of Mummy, when the police called Ifeoma and reported everything to her. They had been trying to reach out to Ego's husband on phone, but he wasn't picking his calls and so they had to contact her sister after they had copied the contact from Ego's phone. Ifeoma entered the police station in less than thirty minutes and she began to sob when she heard about her sister's death. She promised Onyeka that she would do all she could to make sure that Raaluchi rots in jail, even if it was going to cause the last drop of her blood.

Raaluchi had been crying her hearts out in the cell and when she saw her mother again at the visitor's corner the next day, her heart sank in shame. She had disappointed her mother, she had committed a huge crime, and she knew she deserved the punishment she was going through in a gloomy cell.

"I didn't mean to do it, Mummy. It's the voices… the voices forced me to do it," Raaluchi said hoarsely in tears and her mother believed her. She gave her a warm hug and promised her that she will never abandon her to go through her pains alone. She told herself that it was high time she told Onyeka about the problems her daughter had been having before he married her. She was ready to let go the fear that Onyeka would leave her daughter because she has a problem of hearing voices. She was ready to let go the fear that she would loose a perfect husband for her daughter. She would reveal the truth to Onyeka. If he really loved her daughter, he would never leave her, but if he didn't, she didn't care if he left her, all she knew was that she was going to do all she could to save her daughter's life and give her the happiness that she really needed even if it meant closing down her shop.

* * * *

Nanny Nene opened the door for Mummy to enter and

Mummy sat down on the most available sofa in the living room before she asked of Onyeka.

"Mummy, I'm afraid that Sir Onyeka is really depreciating. Ever since Madam Raaluchi was taken by the police, he has never eaten anything." Nanny Nene reported to Mummy with a worried frown.

"Where is he?"

Nanny Nene gestured at the door of his bedroom. Just then, Onyeka came out from the room looking very skinny and completely worn out.

"My in-law, you can't continue like this. You have to eat something. I'll cook a delicious *nsala* soup for you," Mummy said and made Onyeka to relax on a sofa while she headed to the kitchen to meet Nanny Nene for soup spices. In an hour, the soup was ready and he watched Onyeka eat to his satisfaction, although Onyeka ate just to please Mummy, left for him, he had completely lost his appetite. After the meal, Mummy led him to the center of the living room and made him settle down on a sofa before she asked about Ifeoma. Onyeka told her that Ifeoma had filed a case against Raaluchi for the murder of her sister, and that he was sorry he wasn't convinced if Raaluchi could get away with what she had done because he knew how difficult it was to win a murder case. Raaluchi is guilty and even if he employed the best lawyer for her case, it wouldn't make her win.

The mention of Ifeoma made Onyeka reminisce over the last meeting he had with her when he went to her to plead on Raaluchi's behalf. The conditions she had given him in order to withdraw the charges on Raaluchi were for him to denounce the love he had for Raaluchi, and marry her, the mother of his son. He couldn't believe he was actually giving the conditions a thought when Mummy recovered his senses by tapping on his shoulder. He was worried and he had been pondering over how to save the woman he loves. Mummy made sure he calmed him down first before she told him about Raaluchi's problems.

"She will not succeed again. All I want to do is to save the woman I love from the punishment she's going through in that hell of a cell. But I don't have enough evidence that can set her free," Onyeka spoke mournfully, his eyes filled with tears. Mummy, hearing 'the evidence that can set her daughter free' began to cry as she narrated Raaluchi's problems of hearing voices, and how it had affected her social and spiritual life ever since she lost her father when she was fifteen years old. She narrated how she had taken her to the river because she was convinced that she was having a spiritual problem, how she had taken her to a pastor who made her drink a full bottle of olive oil, but the voices did not stop. Onyeka gazed at Mummy with mouth agape, shocked about what he just heard. It was as though the whole world crumbled against him as soon as he heard what Mummy said.

"My son, you can put the blame on me for not telling you on time, but I was only afraid that you may change your mind about marrying my daughter and you know, I liked and trusted you to take care of my daughter. I wanted to narrate this to you the day after you left your matrimonial home to observe peace in a hotel room but your General Manager told me that you did not want to see me. My brother-in-law Doctor Obiora said that Raaluchi was suffering from depression: a psychological trauma, but I didn't believe him because I thought it was a spiritual problem. Now I think that Obiora my brother-in-law may be right, because I've prayed and fasted for her condition for years, I've done everything I could apart from taking her to the hospital for treatment. I'm so sorry Onyeka."

Onyeka gazed at Mummy. What went through his mind as tears tickled down his cheeks was that he had been ignorant of her wife's psychological problems, and to think that he had treated her with contempt, in retaliation of what she did to him, what he now understood quite well that wasn't her fault because she was sick in the mind. He still couldn't believe that he had been married to a psychotic woman. He excused himself from

Mummy and headed to his bedroom in silence. He did not come out from his bedroom until it was dark at 10pm, when Mummy told Nanny Nene to check on him and remind him that she was still waiting in the living room, Onyeka told Nanny Nene that he needed to be alone and that he was done talking to Mummy. Mummy left with a heavy heart that night, blaming herself for keeping the secret.

* * * *

Onyeka took some time off and visited a chapel, the same chapel he had been taking Raaluchi to, before he finally got married to her, the chapel where God blessed their friendship. There, he soul-searched and prayed, and each time he came up with a decision to quit the marriage with Raaluchi, his wedding vows recited itself to his ears: *"In sickness and in health…for better or worse…"* and then again, the words of his prayer for a life partner recited itself to his ears: *I want to take a full responsibility of wiping the sorrowful tears of a distressed damsel.* He left the chapel with the thought of consulting Father Pius for counseling. No doubt, he loves Raaluchi but he was deceived because nobody, not even Raaluchi told him that she was hearing voices. His marriage to Raaluchi was like a building on the verge of collapsing, because it was founded on deceit.

He had thought that the only obstacle he battled with were Raaluchi's educational challenges, her father's death, her mistakes with Chiedu and her unwanted pregnancy, that all contributed to her depression. But Mummy had told him the main truth about Raaluchi, the truth that had turned him upside down with heartaches the very moment he heard them. How could he continue to stay married to a psychotic woman? This question continued to wallow in his mind and he also wavered and reminisced about the incident at home with Raaluchi: when she stabbed him with a smashed bottle of perfume. She was indeed psychotic to have done that to him. He loved Raaluchi, but, can he put himself together to accept her after knowing the truth about her? Can he risk his life for her? Onyeka sent Father Pius a mail and told him what he recently discovered about Raaluchi, and Father Pius did not give him a reply immediately but waited till after three days, because he sought God for wisdom to reveal the truth to Onyeka and for the will of God to prevail in the life of Onyeka and Raaluchi.

Deceit and mental illness are part of impediments in marriage. A man who is getting married to a woman he loves has the right to know everything about the woman. You were manipulated by your mother-in-law, because she was the one that instructed her daughter not to tell you about her mental illness. She deliberately concealed a disruptive quality which by its very nature can gravely disturb the partnership of conjugal life. The truth is that this could be basis for annulment of your marriage. But since you love Raaluchi so much; since what drove you to love her was her depressive state, instead of seeking for annulment because of this new problem of hers that you discovered, giving her a helping hand to overcome her period of sorrows in her gloomy cell, and her psychological trauma, would be very wonderful and God would love you for it. This is because her condition was as a result of the depression she felt about her father's demise and the delay in her admission into a university of her choice. You have to forgive your mother-in-law because whatever she did in her ignorance was because she loved you for her daughter.

Onyeka heaved a deep sigh after he read the mail that Father Pius sent to him. He wondered if Raaluchi's inability to conceive all these years was a sign for him to know that his marriage was void. But the truth was that there was a part of him that longed for Raaluchi and had been, even when they were speaking in silence. He hadn't visited Raaluchi in her cell for the past three days, ever since Mummy revealed the truth to him. His mind reminisced the first time he saw her singing with tears, the racing heartbeat he felt as he watched her sing then, the instantaneous attraction for her, the urge he felt then, to be responsible to wiping those tears of hers, moved him to see her again. He was touched to help her for the sake of his love for her, even if he was having doubts of marrying her again.

Onyeka made up his mind in his isolation to do everything possible to save the life of the woman he loves. Raaluchi his love can't possibly rot in jail. He can't let that horrible thing happen to her. Although he was angry with Mummy for not telling him about Raaluchi's condition when he was asking for her hand in marriage, he also understood that Mummy did what she did because she wanted him for her daughter. Mummy and Onyeka decided to pay a visit to Doctor Obiora after Mummy had spoken to him on phone. Luckily for them, the doctor was on leave. They arrived at Enugu in two hours and Onyeka drove speedily to Independence Layout with Mummy's direction. That was exactly where Doctor Obiora lived. The roads there were all tiled, and there were well trimmed green flowers inbetween the roads. Doctor Obiora's house was a very pacific bungalow and the visitors sat down comfortably on the upholsteries while waiting for the doctor.

Uchendu served them cold drinks, and immediately corked the bottles of Smirnoff and Coke that stood still on a silver tray, waiting to be taken by the visitors. Uchendu was Obiora's houseboy in his late teen. He was of an average height, dark in complexion and looked very serious. He was a kind of person that hardly laughs, but elicits laughter. He was wearing only a red short, and was sweating profusely, because he was always busy with house chores, and his arm pit odour filled the living room as soon as he served the drinks. He left the living room still looking very serious. In the kitchen, he mumbled something about the drinks in the fridge finishing so fast all in the name of visitors and then afterwards, he'll be accused by his master of stealing drinks in the fridge.

Minutes later, Doctor Obiora approached the visitors with smiles on his face as he shook hands with Onyeka, but his mood changed to a scoff when Mummy introduced him as Raaluchi's husband. Mummy expected that from him because she did not inform him about Raaluchi's wedding, but she didn't mind if he was angry, all she knew was that she wanted an urgent help from him as a medical doctor. She was now ready to accept the help of arranging a psychiatrist for Raaluchi. Doctor Obiora pretended to be okay with the introduction just to know why they had come to see him and when Mummy and Onyeka narrated Raaluchi's present predicament to him, he was shattered with fury and then told Mummy to see him in privacy. Mummy followed him to the second living room where Obiora blurted out words of anger on Mummy.

"You gave Raaluchi out to marriage knowing the kind of problem she had? Why didn't you tell me about Raaluchi's marriage? You mean that Raaluchi's bride price was paid and nobody told me about it? You gave out my niece to marriage against my will, you gave Raaluchi to marriage in her immaturity and psychological trauma and you've come to tell me that she's in police custody for murder? You are a disgrace to motherhood and you are very selfish! You abandoned a sick girl to marriage to face marital problems at her young age and to aggravate her condition! What kind of mother are you?"

"Obiora please calm down, *biko wetuo obi*" Mummy said in Igbo, with pleading gestures. "I didn't tell you because I knew you would be very much against it. Her bride price was paid to Nnabueze your father. He was the one that represented Raaluchi's father."

"Of course he would take the bride price because all he cares about is money for his snuffs. You are very wicked, and I'm sure that my late brother would be very disappointed in you for what you did to his only daughter. You have come to me to render the help I told you about, now that her situation has aggravated. If anything happens to my niece, I'll tear you into pieces and make sure that you are disowned from the family of Ezechikwelu, now get the hell out of my house, you insensitive woman!"

Mummy wept in the car on their long drive home. Onyeka

understood how Mummy felt because he had overheard their discussion in the second living room. Onyeka felt pity for Mummy. He understood that Mummy did what she did for his own sake, because she really wanted him to marry Raaluchi. But he was also bitter that Mummy did not tell him about Raaluchi's psychological state on time. If she had told him on time, he was sure that this whole mess would not have occurred. If he had known about Raaluchi's condition on time, he would have taken her to India for a sound treatment.

That night in his depressed state of mind, he called Jerry and warned him never to show himself in the company the next day and when Jerry quickly demanded to know the reason, Onyeka hung up and switched off his cell phone. He didn't want to hear his rotten explanation on phone. He wanted to see him face-to face; he wanted to watch him give him concrete reasons why he lied to his mother-in-law on his behalf.

Mummy was restless that night. She had been sending apology text-messages to Doctor Obiora but wasn't getting any reply. She kept calling but he did not answer. She finally felt relieved in the morning when Doctor Obiora sent her a text message telling her to come and collect a doctor's report that will specify that Raaluchi had been mentally deranged. He said he would meet a psychiatrist that will write the report and then, he told her that he was only doing it for his late brother and not for her. The first thing that Mummy did in the morning was to prepare and take the first bus to Asaba, hurrying to Onyeka's house to tell him the good news.

Fifteen minutes after Mummy arrived at Onyeka's house, Jerry entered Onyeka's living room looking like a harassed man, his eyes glazing on a pale face. A mere look at him would send a message that he didn't catch any sleep last night. Onyeka watched his countenance when he greeted Mummy. Jerry's countenance sent a signal to Onyeka that he had actually lied to Mummy. He had greeted Mummy with eyes sharply averted, focusing on Onyeka alone. Jerry began to apologise to Onyeka after he had been told of his offence. He accused the devil of being responsible for it. After some interrogations from Onyeka, Jerry admitted to Onyeka that he did it for Ego. He had an affair with Ego because he gave in to her seduction, and she took a video of their affair without him knowing about it. She blackmailed him with the video.

Ego had told him that she would take the video to his wife if he failed to carry out some functions for her. Ego had wanted Jerry to create a space for the planned action that would hold in the hotel on the second day of September, in the year 2010. She had told Jerry not to cause any distractions by letting visitors visit Onyeka for the rest of his stay in the hotel room, and Jerry had carried out the assignment because he had been blackmailed. Onyeka fired Jerry for lying in his name, for being an accomplice to ruining his marital love, and for being part of his wife's trauma in the cell. If he had allowed Mummy to see him at the hotel, she would have told him about Raaluchi's psychological problems, perhaps, he wouldn't have slept with Ifeoma that night.

* * * *

Onyeka and Mummy brought Barrister Ekpereka and Doctor Julius, the psychiatrist to the police station and Raaluchi was called up to see them. Barrister Ekpereka introduced himself to Raaluchi as her lawyer who was willing to do his best to make sure that she won the case. He also told Raaluchi that he was her husband's childhood friend. Raaluchi recognized him. He had visited them at home some weeks after their wedding to give reasons he didn't make it to their wedding ceremony, although Onyeka knew the main reason he did not come for the wedding: He was mad at Onyeka for marrying a naïve girl who almost crushed his heart.

"Hello," Doctor Julius said, half-smiling. He appeared plumpy and pot-bellied in a tight white shirt and brown trousers. He asked how she was, and immediately held his comment, wishing he hadn't asked, as he absorbed her pains. It was very obvious that she was going through so much pain. Her hair was unkempt, her eyes swollen from profuse tears, the whip marks Ego gave her still showed from her arms and hands, and she was inside a purple maxi gown, because she had lost so much weight.

Barrister Ekpereka began to write down some information as soon as Raaluchi began to talk to Doctor Julius. He was looking at Raaluchi with a keen assesing eyes, as though he was trying to know from her mien, how psychotic she was. Dr. Julius questioned Raaluchi about the voices she was hearing and Raaluchi gave him the graphic detail. She told Doctor Julius that it was as though the voices controlled her actions. They were the voices of her late father, and even her own voice. She heard the voices whenever she was angry, and whenever she thought too much or meditate. The voices were always mean to her, they were always mocking and threatening her and the weird thing about the situation was that they forced her into impulsive actions.

The voices made her see herself as a worthless person in life, as if she was born by mistake, as if she could never be given a chance of happiness in life. The voices had caused her so much pain in life. Doctor Julius made Raaluchi to understand that she was sick in the mind, and that she was probably suffering from schizophrenia- a disease of the mind, that those voices were her own thoughts. She might have overstressed the brain due to her excessive thoughts in her depressive state. She had been very depressed about her father's death, and the fact that she was very close to her father, aggravated the situation. She also suffered serious challenges of waiting for admission into UNN, a university that she had loved so much to attend, and she also underwent the challenges of waiting long for a baby in her marriage. It had all been a very traumatic experience for her.

"You are going to be fine," Doctor Julius assured her with a pat on her shoulder.

Onyeka was given some privacy with his wife and he fed Raaluchi with some fruits, afterwards, he held her hand breathtakingly close to his chest, bent over, and kissed her left hand, and Raaluchi smiled. Her gold wedding ring still glistened on the fourth finger of her left hand. Their eyes met and held and from his stare, she saw love, she felt warm and she wished she would disappear with her husband to a very far place, a place where they would enjoy peace, a place where there wouldn't be more obstacles to their love life, a place of safety.

"I'll never stop loving you, Raalu," Onyeka said softly to her and she smiled and reciprocated, prophesying her undying love for him, and just like a magnet, their faces slowly met and they kissed passionately. Just then, one of the policemen gave a noisy clap and told Onyeka that his time was over. Onyeka joined others outside and they all drove out of the compound. That evening on a telephone conversation, he pleaded with his friend to do all he could to save the life of the woman he loves. He promised himself that if Raaluchi ever won the murder case, he would do all he could to give her a sound treatment, and the happiness that she really deserved. That evening, after they had all left the cell, Father Joe visited Raaluchi and prayed for her, and advised her to have faith in God for He alone is capable of saving her. He assured her that she would conquer all obstacles in her life through the help of God and Raaluchi believed him. Father Joe promised her that he would be there in the court to pray for her. That evening as her loved ones all left her alone in her gloomy cell, Raaluchi sobbed bitterly in her awful loneliness, begging God to save her dispirited soul for she was slowly passing out.

* * * *

Amaechi waited in the living room for his cousin's return after he had eaten the delicious *jollof* rice that Nanny Nene cooked. It was nine o'clock that Thursday night when Onyeka returned, looking very exhausted as he tried to relax on the

236

sofa beside his cousin who had fallen asleep and was snoring heavily. Nanny Nene served him his dinner at the dinning table but he refused to eat, instead, he demanded for a cup of coffee and toasted bread. Nanny Nene frowned when she carried her tray of jollof rice back to the kitchen. She wanted to say something to Onyeka. She wanted to tell him how much time and strength she had spent in cooking that rice, only for him to reject it, just like that. Onyeka's phone beeped and he quickly grabbed his phone from the centre table in the living room, hoping it was a text message from his friend Barrister Ekpereka but it turned out to be Ifeoma. She was demanding Onyeka's presence in a hotel, exactly the same hotel that he had fallen so helplessly into temptation of sleeping with her.

He tried calling her to express his anger and rebuke at her, but withdrew himself to think for a while and suddenly, he came up with a brilliant idea and decided to go and answer Ifeoma's invitation at the hotel. But before he left, he prayed for a brief moment and told God to save him from any temptation.

Amaechi was sitting at the front seat of the car still feeling asleep when Onyeka drove speedily to the hotel. Still inside the car after he had parked in the compound, Onyeka made sure that Amaechi was really awake before he gave him the instructions on how to use the tape camera. He was going to record every conversation he would make with Ifeoma and he was going to take pictures of them. Onyeka walked majestically to the reception and searched for Ifeoma but didn't see her. He called her on phone and Ifeoma told him to come upstairs to room 20. He told Ifeoma that it would be nice if she came downstairs at the reception and take him to the room herself, and then, Ifeoma foolishly obeyed. But before she came downstairs, Onyeka was already taking a bottle of Maltina and Amaechi was sitting at a distance in the reception, drinking a glass of chilled orange juice. Ifeoma appeared looking glamorous in an orange strapless short gown. She stifled a smile and bent over to kiss Onyeka but Onyeka withdrew his mouth from being kissed.

Ifeoma chuckled and sat down opposite Onyeka at the round glass table.

"You don't look like you are mourning your sister, Ego," Onyeka said to Ifeoma, sipping his drink.

"Must I wear a mournful look to show people that I'm mourning?"

"The way you cried your hearts out in the police station, one could not help but feel pity for you for your painful loss, even the DPO."

Ifeoma did not reply to Onyeka anymore, instead she began to give Onyeka a striping look, borrowing his drink and sipping it slowly with dimmed eyes. Onyeka ignored her. If there were any feelings he had left for Ifeoma, it was hatred. He hated her for all the pains that she and her sister had caused his marriage.

"Tell me the reason you asked me to come here. I don't have any time to waste."

"What have you to say to my proposal?" Ifeoma asked Onyeka with a seductive smile as she sipped Onyeka's drink again.

"What proposal are you talking about?" Onyeka asked her searchingly, that was his delaying tactics to get enough evidence that can render her powerless in the law court. Ifeoma chuckled at the question.

"Come on Onyi, don't be a boy. You know exactly what I'm taking about. You know how much I love you. If you agree to get married to me and divorce Raaluchi your barren wife, then I'll withdraw the charges I passed against Raaluchi."

"Mind your words, Ifeoma. Don't insult my wife in my presence. I can't marry someone that took part in making my marital life miserable. I can't marry a whore," Onyeka said sternly and Ifeoma frowned. Onyeka continued: "I was there in the bungalow that I rented for you. I was there on that faithful morning, eavesdropping on you and your sister, Ego. Both of you had a deadly deal to ruin my marriage. Ego, your sister monitored my movements through my naïve wife and then she sent you to seduce me and have an affair with me so that both of you can have my money all to your selves."

Ifeoma began to stutter and tremble in fear and then she reminisced immediately about what Onyeka had just said to her. She now knew the reason Onyeka was cold to her when they were traveling to Abuja for the Singing Award Competition.

"It's true that my sister and I made a fool of you to get your money and attention, but that does not make me a whore." Ifeoma said, shedding tears, wanting to get Onyeka's sympathy. She wanted him to apologise to her like he used to do whenever he told her awful things that made her cry, but Onyeka did not look at her feigned crying face. He continued to tell her the truth: "you are a whore to have seduced me in my hotel room on that September night and I was drunk when I slept with you, until you deceived me with your fake sympathetic stories to attract my friendship. You are a whore to have accepted the deal from your deadly sister. A responsible woman would not stoop so low for seduction. You know, you are really the blood sister of Ego because, men-hunting runs in you people's veins. I'm sure your sister must have told you that she wanted to have an affair with me but I practically refused, that was why she was bent on destroying my happiness. Is that not the truth Ifeoma?"

"It's the truth but you have to understand me Onyeka…"

"I have nothing to understand you for. I will not do what you want me to do. God will fight for me over my love for Raaluchi and not even you can stop it," With that, Onyeka walked out of the hotel reception and Amaechi followed suit after doing his own job. When Barrister Ekpereka watched the tape, he warned Onyeka not to bring the tape into the law court for it was capable of ruining Raaluchi's case. It would only testify that Raaluchi carried out the murder to intensify her anger on Ego for destroying her marital happiness.

CHAPTER TWENTY-SEVEN

A WEEK LATER, Raaluchi and Ifeoma were brought before the magistrate court for the hearing of their case. When the facts of the case were read by the court attendant, Mr George Ubah the Judge, asked Raaluchi whether she accepted the claim against her, Raaluchi said 'yes' and began to sob in the duck. She looked completely deranged.

"Why did you take a life that you cannot give?" The judge asked Raaluchi, looking very serious on his scowled face that revealed his unshaved white beards. He was wearing a big spectacle of which the lens lay below his eyes, just on his cheeks. It made it look as though it was his nose that needed the spectacle, and not his eyes. His eyes looked weak as he bent his face to have a steady gaze at Raaluchi. It frightened Raaluchi to death that she believed in her heart that he was going to sentence her to ten years imprisonment.

"I wasn't in my right state of mind when I did it," Raaluchi replied with tears streaming down her cheeks. Just then, Barrister Ekpereka stood up to defend his client, proving that his client was sick in the mind, and had been diagnosed as a schizophrenic patient. Barrister Ekpereka stated the symptoms of schizophrenia and how dangerous it can be for the sufferer. He stated the auditory hallucinations in schizophrenia and proved Raaluchi to be a sufferer of partial delusion. In this sense, Raaluchi may have the sense of reasoning for only a period of time, and then swings to insanity when attacked by the auditory hallucination. Barrister Ekpereka proved that at that time of murder, Raaluchi was attacked by the voices she was hearing. She was pushed to commit the crime by the voices, of which she didn't even know that she was committing a crime at that moment. Barrister Ekpereka stated the Mc Naughton's rule of insane delusion: code 931 which states that: "To establish a defence on the ground of insanity, it must be clearly proved that, at the time of the committing of the act, the accused was labouring under such a defect of reason from disease of the mind, as not to know the nature and quality of the act he was doing, or if he or she did know it, that the person did not know that he was doing what was wrong." Barrister Ekpereka proved beyond reasonable doubt to the Judge, and to the honourable court, that Raaluchi was insane at the time of the crime.

"Objection! your honour" Barrister Lilian Ojemba stood up to speak for her client and her objection was sustained by the Judge. 'This is not true. We all know that when something serious happens, the accused would look for something sympathetic to gratify her actions. Ego the deceased sister of my client was responsible for the kidnap of the Ibekwe's, and this horrible experience is sure to infuriate the victim because, lots of pains must have been inflicted on her during the kidnap, and this could cause anybody without self control to retaliate in anger. Your honour, this is pre-medicated murder. I'm sure that the accused was in her right state of mind when she committed this devious crime. If you doubt my facts, your honour, give the accused a gun to pull the trigger on her husband, and know if she's really insane. " Barrister Lilian was Ifeoma's lawyer, a tall plump single woman in her artificial light skinned complexion, whose face was full of pimples and wrinkles. A mere look at her would pass a message that she was in her late fourties but she was still single. The judge scribbled some notes in a book, as he listened to Barrister Lilian Ojemba, who was making her clear points authoritatively.

Raaluchi did nothing but to cry in the duck and as her mother watched her, her heart sank in grieve just like that of the Blessed Virgin Mary, as she watched her son go through an excruciating pain in the hands of the executioners. Onyeka patted on Mummy's shoulders in consolation as he fought with his own tears, wishing that it wouldn't begin to tickle. He didn't want to be such a cry baby yet, he wanted to keep faith in God for his wife. He knew that God would never allow his wife to rot in jail.

"Mrs Raaluchi Ibekwe, were you hearing voices before you got married to your husband?" Raaluchi was dumbfounded by the question that the Judge asked. Barrister Ekpereka expected the question from the Judge, and so, he had prepared Raaluchi on how to answer the question assuming the Judge finally threw the question at her. He had told Raaluchi to say the truth to the Judge because it sure would save her. Raaluchi stood in the duck contemplating whether to say the truth or not. All her mind could focus on, in her fatigue, was the consequences of ingenuity in her life. If she must learn another lesson from all her misfortunes, it should be that "Ingenuity" was the cause of her marital problems. She had hidden the real part of herself from her husband by not telling him that she heard voices. She had lived in pretence in her matrimonial home; pretending that she was sound in mind, while she wasn't and hadn't been for a long time. And now, as she stood in the duck, she was willing to give the truth a chance. She was willing to face a new phase in her life.

"Yes Sir, I was hearing the voices before I got married to Mr Onyeka Ibekwe. The Judge nodded and scribbled some notes on his notebook.

"Tell me what prompted the voices...I mean, how and when did you start hearing the voices?" The Judge asked her searchingly, his eyes fixed on Raaluchi's eyes, that it made Raaluchi so uncomfortable. He was reading up Raaluchi's mien.

"Actually, it all started when I was fifteen years old; when I lost my father. I was so depressed that I thought that my entire life had been crushed, because I knew that I could never be as happy again as I use to be with my father. We shared a bond and we were inseparable, but then, death took him away from my life. Six months of mourning wasn't enough for me to mourn my father, I mourned him for so long that I allowed the mouth of depression to swallow me up. My mother and my younger brother did all they could to put back a smile on my face, but all to no avail, until I began to hear strange and tormenting voices.

While hearing on the voices, I was also challenged with another traumatic experience; I waited for admission into the higher institution for three years despite my intelligence..." The voices tormented me especially when I wavered my mind in thoughts; thoughts of depression and envy. I was so depressed that I believed that God hated me because He was blessing other people, instead of me. Raaluchi began to sob all over again, before she mustered some courage to continue. "I got married to Onyeka when I discovered how much love and care he had shown to me in my miserable life...but not even for once did he know that I was hearing voices. My mother warned me not to reveal the truth to him because it would be an obstacle to my marriage to him. My mother loved and respected him to be my husband, considering the fact that she witnessed how much love and support he gave me." Raaluchi said in between sobs, and Father Joe watched her with narrowed eyes, shocked at her last statement, and then, he shook his head.

"Have you for once done something terrible to your husband in your marriage?" The Judge asked Raaluchi, sipping a cup of coffee. The case was becoming very interesting to him. The courtroom was silent. The people were listening attentively to Raaluchi. They couldn't wait to hear the final verdict of the murder case.

"In my marriage, I did so many stupid things like stabbing my husband after believing a stranger who desperately wanted to ruin my marriage and pouring a glass of water on him in any slightest offence, because the voices always controlled my actions." Raaluchi hiccupped between sobs that she couldn't speak any further. The Judge requested for Onyeka's presence and with a little privacy, he confirmed the truth. He saw the old scar on Onyeka's belly and shook his head after he had confirmed the truth.

"I have gone through the medical reports of Mrs. Raaluchi Ibekwe and they clearly notified by the psychiatrist, Doctor Julius Ekwueme that the accused Mrs. Raaluchi Ibekwe is suffering from schizophrenia, and therefore, needs urgent medical treatment. I have also screened the accused with evidences in this honourable court, and I discovered that the accused is really mental. This is my judgement...The accused is herby certified NOT GUILTY of the crime she committed due to insanity." The judge gave his final verdict and rose. The two lawyers gave each other brief hugs and handshakes when the judgement was over, and Ifeoma stood in the witness box looking bemused. She was reflecting on Raaluchi's insanity. She was only fighting for her sister's murder but she was very surprised about Raaluchi's insanity.

* * * *

That evening, Father Joe requested for the presence of the couple and their families in his office, and they honoured the invitation. What Raaluchi heard from Father Joe made her raise her wet face with curiosity and looked at the Reverend Father with mouth agape. If that was the case, then she needed to leave. She needed a space. She needed freedom from all the pains she had experienced in life, all the pains she had caused her husband. Her pathetic life was absolutely unbearable for her. It had been so since Nnanyelugo died, and it had also been so since she accepted to take the life long journey.

"Any marital vow taken by an insane person makes the marriage void. Any marriage founded on deceit, also makes the marriage void. I'm sorry, but you need to know the truth... your marriage is null and void and can be annulled. But, you are free to separate for sometime, until Raaluchi regains her sanity and is sure of her decision of marriage, " These words of Father Joe recited in Raaluchi's mind as she looked at Onyeka and their eyes met and held until she saw tears forcing its narrow way down to his cheeks.

* * * *

"You can't continue with that Marriage! Do you want to die early? No! I can't watch my only son go down to the grave because of some stupid love for an insane woman!" Papa said furiously to his son, pointing his walking stick in Onyeka's face and jerking because of his old age. He was wearing a red chieftancy cap with a dark blue caftan, and in his old age, he had a shriveled dark skin. Onyeka was telling his parents that the stab injury was nothing serious and that his marriage to Raaluchi cannot possibly end because he still loved her. Papa infuriated at his son for being so sturbborn and Mama calmed him down and led him inside the bedroom to take his rest, leaving Onyeka alone in the living room, in his parent's house in Umudioka. Onyeka paced the living room, heaved a deep sigh and sat down forcefully on the couch. He had been calling his wife for the past three days, ever since she was released; ever since they left Father Joe's office on that same evening but it seemed that Doctor Obiora had taken charge of his wife's phone because he had been answering the call, and he had been telling him to stop calling the number.

Doctor Obiora always stressed that Raaluchi needed privacy to get her sanity back. Onyeka in his wavering mind sent a mail to Father Pius and told him everything about his wife and he waited impatiently for his reply. And when he finally did in an hour, he smiled as he read the messages in his phone. He loved reading Father Pius's counseling mails because he always felt as though Christ was talking to him in his use of biblical messages. Father Pius always had the right biblical answer to his problems; as though he was tactical in handling people's marital problems with the use of biblical messages. Onyeka was encouraged at the thought of Father Pius's words to him.

True love stands a test of time. When Christ was accused of casting out demons with the power of Belzebub and not the power of God, he didn't take offence that can stop the work of God from moving on simply because he loves us so much to withstand all challenges and obstacles to our freedom. Devil does not like marriage because he knows that it is a great sacrament of God based on true love which is the most important commandment of Christ to the Christians, and so, he fights to pull it down. Those who let him into their hearts are those who push for divorce in any marital challenge, simply because they cannot endure the true test of love they had confessed in their wedding vows. And that is why there is high rate of divorce in the Christendom. Headaches should be cured by taking medicines that can stop the headache and not by cutting off the head.

Onyeka understood from Father Pius's mail that if he really loved Raaluchi unconditionally, then he would have to wait for her recovery, and not discarding her like garbage. It wasn't her fault that such a thing happened to her. It wasn't her fault that she had such a challenging destiny in life. Patience remains the ultimate key that can unlock the hardened closed door of trials. Father Pius encouraged Onyeka not to loose hope in his love for Raaluchi. But Onyeka's father did not want to understand that. He was insisting that Onyeka must annul his marriage to Raaluchi before she introduced the gene of madness into their family. He was using the fact that Raaluchi didn't have any child for Onyeka to prove God's unfailing favour upon the life of his son and upon their family. Papa had insisted that it wasn't too late to dismiss the insane Raaluchi. Onyeka was in a very tight corner.

* * * *

Doctor Obiora employed a very good make-up and costume artist that would be responsible for making up Raaluchi's face, and providing the suitable dress for her to wear every day and just three days after Raaluchi's release, Raaluchi glistened in her usual beauty. It was a good thing that Obiora's residence was located in a very secluded area, and the tranquility helped in Raaluchi's healing process. Doctor Julius never failed to come over to Doctor Obiora's house and give Raaluchi her medications. Doctor Obiora wanted it that way because he was only trying to deprive Raaluchi the chances of meeting Onyeka if she got admitted in A Psychiatry Ward. He knew that Raaluchi had desperately wanted to speak to Onyeka ever since he brought her to stay in his house; ever since they left Father Joe's office in the evening of Raaluchi's release.

Doctor Obiora had told his niece on the night he brought her to live with him in Enugu that he would have to learn to stop contacting Onyeka, for that was also part of her healing process. He had taken Raaluchi's phone after he had gently spoken with her, and gently forced her to understand that he was doing her a whole lot of good.

* * * *

Nkiruka paid Raaluchi a visit in her uncle's house in Enugu and the two friends hugged each other for a long time, tears of joy coursing down to their cheeks. They were sitting under a coconut tree at the little garden beside the gate. The garden was decorated with green flowers and green carpet grass. It was on a sunny Sunday afternoon, and Raaluchi was resting in a shade under the coconut tree when Uchendu told her that someone wanted to see her. At first, she had thought that the person was Onyeka and she had sat up curiously to see him but her expression changed from curiosity to a gentle happiness at the sight of her friend Nkiruka.

"I'm so sorry about everything you went through, Raaluchi. I couldn't stop crying when your mother told me everything and I've been trying to reach out to you on phone but your phone was switched off. But Raaluchi, we've been friends for ages and you have never told me that you hear voices," Nkiruka said to her friend, with an arm around her friend's shoulders. She was giving Raaluchi a sympathetic look.

"I didn't tell anybody, not even my husband knew about it. I didn't want people to see me as an insane person because my mother and I never believed that I was insane. We believed that I was only possessed with a demon, but the fact about me is that I'm really insane, and my insanity has caused me so much pain and also to people around me," Raaluchi said in soft sob and the voices spoke, reminding her that she was really useless and insane. Just then she remembered what Doctor Julius told her. He had said that she should always try to keep herself happy and stop lamenting over her condition. She should focus her mind on positivism and anything that can make her happy if she really needed a fast recovery. Doctor Obiora emerged at the garden after Uchendu had served drinks to the visitor. Again, he was wearing only red shorts, and was sweating profusely. Doctor Obiora called him back and looked askance at him.

"Is that the only shorts you have?" Doctor Obiora asked him with a smile but he didn't smile back, he remained very serious.

"No sir, but it is the only shorts I love to wear because 'red' is my best colour."

"In that case, I'll give you some money to buy more red shorts with different designs, and you can also buy some deodorants for your arm pit."

"But Sir, you have told me to stop buying food from the 'restaurant' since I can cook better than Ada Ugoye, that 'restaurant' woman. As for my arm pit, I don't need my arm pit to help me swallow the restaurant *foo foo* while I have my mouth to do the job well."

And just then, Raaluchi and Nkiruka laughed raucously, and Uchendu stood looking bemused about the laughter, wondering what he had said to elicit such laughter from the two ladies. They laughed because Uchendu had just mistaken the word 'deodorant' to be 'restaurant'. Doctor Obiora simply dismissed the poor boy with a wave of hand and he left their presence, mumbling some words to himself. Doctor Obiora welcomed Nkiruka, and asked after her family, and she responded that they were all doing fine before she left them.

"*Ehe,* has your daughter started walking?" Raaluchi asked Nkiruka and she answered with a nod. She was drinking her chilled orange juice that she felt was suitable for the sunny afternoon.

"Have you found a perfect Igbo name for her? Raaluchi asked her friend again, and Doctor Obiora came into the discussion by wanting to know the reason why the baby has not been named since birth. But Raaluchi told her uncle that the baby was baptized Anne two months after birth, but her mother had been looking for a perfect Igbo name for her daughter.

"Yes Raaluchi, I finally named her Odichimma last week Sunday, and you know why? Raaluchi shook her head and Nkiruka swirled the glass of juice and continued to speak. "It's a good thing that I have finally decided to stay married to Jekwu, and it is good to God because, it had been His will that we should stay married, by making me fall in love with the mysterious book that actually changed me." Nkiruka beamed. Just then, Doctor Obiora's phone rang. He had an emergency at the hospital and Doctor Paul his assistant who was supposed to be on duty for the day, just rushed his pregnant wife to the hospital, for she was in labour. The two ladies started pacing round the little garden, caressing the green flowers as they talked.

"So, what has surprised you the most about being changed?" Raaluchi asked Nkiruka and she smiled in response before answering the question.

"My lust for materialistic lifestyle, I started wondering if something was wrong with me; if someone had taken the huge part of me and left me light and free."

"It's always like that when we see the light. I mean, look at me, I don't sneer at girls on trousers anymore. A new cell inmate was brought to share my cell with me a day before the hearing of my case. She was wearing trouser, and I didn't shift to the extreme of the wall just to avoid her, and show God that we are different, and that she was a sinner, and me, a saint. I was able to socialize with her, to hear her out somehow and preach to her and with me by her side, she didn't feel rejected, she regained hope. All thanks to my mother, Onyeka and Father Joe. God used them to shed light to my life," Raaluchi said with lowered eyes releasing tickles of tears, and Nkiruka knew that she was being sincere of everything she had just said.

"I didn't know that your mother, who doesn't belong to any pius society in the Catholic Church, except for C. W. O would be responsible for shedding light to you." Nkiruka said.

"I've really discovered the sincerity of Christ when He said that 'the first would be the last, and the last the first.' I mean, it's not about how hard we carry our big bibles for people to see, how authoritavely we preach the word, its about oneness…the power of being one in God, whether black or white…the power of humility is all that matters, and is all that breeds positive results." Raaluchi said, and as soon as she said that, she noticed again, a knot untying itself inside her.

"Yes, you are right. The light that shines in our lives is beautiful and powerful. Ever since I saw the light, I don't let my heart get troubled about how much money I should own, what designer shoes and bags I need to have, the Armada Jeep I need to ride, and the Las Vegas I need to see. I see these material things as things that are waiting for me to have them at the right time, and that the most important thing that must come first is 'Love.' When we love, we are humble, and when we achieve material things with these qualities, we embrace peace. Why should we let our hearts be troubled, when we have Jesus who is the love of our lives?" Nkiruka said with smiles, looking at the green flowers they've been caressing in their discussion, and knowing how green their friendship had been.

Nkiruka arrived home by 7.30 pm in the evening, and met her husband playing in the living room with Odichimma their daughter. Odichimma released herself from her father's lap and ran to give her mother a welcome embrace. Nkiruka squatted and kissed her forehead and she smiled.

"Welcome home Nky," Jekwu said to his wife with a smile. She asked her husband if they ate the rice and fish sauce she prepared in the morning before leaving for Enugu, Jekwu nodded, and commended her for her delicious cook. Jekwu stopped eating outside his matrimonial home, ever since Nkiruka changed. He stopped drinking palmwine to stupor in Madam Caro's bar. He stopped beating her up, ever since she stopped provoking him. He noticed that Nkiruka had stopped insulting him by comparing him with his rich mates whenever he gave her money for food and her toiletries. She accepted any amount given to her, with gratitude but would gently tell him to increase the amount if he still had money, so that she wouldn't be stranded in the market, while buying expensive valuable foodstuffs. If he had no other money to give, she would manage the money and buy only what it can buy in the market, cook the meal, and they would all eat happily. That Sunday night, some hours after the arrival of Nkiruka, after Odichimma slept off, Jekwu sat beside his wife on their matrimonial bed and offered her a gift. Nkiruka smiled as she opened it. It was a necklace in a small case. She knew it wasn't a gold necklace but she accepted it from Jekwu and hugged him tightly in appreciation.

"Thank you Darling. I love the necklace and I'll always wear it."

Jekwu gave her a surprise stare when she gave him the necklace to help her fix it on her neck, to know if it really fitted her. He did as she requested and watched her smile widely, in front of her dressing mirror. Jekwu knew that she liked it, and also knew that she knew it wasn't a gold necklace, but she accepted it wholeheartedly.

"Nkiruka is really a changed person," Jekwu said in his mind, and as though Nkiruka read his thoughts, she walked back to

the bed and sat beside her husband with an arm around his shoulder.

"Do you think I'll fling it on you?" Nkiruka asked Jekwu with a smile and Jekwu nodded sheepishly with mouth agape. Nkiruka's mind focused on the mysterious book. She remembered that the writer discussed about 'showing gratitude'. According to the writer, *"Real gratitude is showing appreciaction over little things. Nobody can boast of riding a car without ever trekking and nobody can boast of going to college without kindergaten. The journey of a thousand miles begins with a step, and one cannot climb a mountain without starting from the cradle. How can one handle big things without learning how to handle small things first?"*

"Nky, you have really changed. What happened to you? Who changed you?"

"I read a book and I was inspired by the grace of God to change for the sake of peace. I've decided to quit being a faultfinder and be concerned more about being good to you. I want to be concerned more about you, than how you make me feel. I want to see the qualities you have by being good to you, and instead of judging you, I examine myself. I try to understand my weaknesses and seek for the grace of God to change them because that is the only way you can change too. I've deciced to love you unconditionally."

Jekwu heaved a sigh of relief and hugged his wife. They were lost in embrace for sometime before they slowly disengaged themselves from the embrace, and Nkiruka asked him a question that she had been saving to ask him in a conducive moment.

"Jekwu, tell me the truth. Why did you marry me?"

"I married you because I love you."

Jekwu looked into his wife's eyes and narrated everything to her. He used to come to U.N.N (University Of Nigeria Nsukka) to supply exercise books and pens in a bookshop. He had been on this business for quite a long time. On one of his visits to the school bookshop, he saw Nkiruka drinking with her friends in a kiosk beside the bookshop. He watched her demonstrate something for her friends, and he fell in love instantaneously with her height and her ebony beauty. He admired her and craved to know her. He decided to stay back at the bookshop just to listen to her discussion with her friends. He heard her telling her friends that before she accepts a man's marriage proposal, the man must show her the key to *Armada jeep* and he must be someone that is conversant with traveling abroad. To Nkiruka, those were her own conditions for accepting a marriage proposal.

Jekwu told Nkiruka that he went home that day and pondered on what she said, and because he was attracted to her, he went back to her school and asked some girls about her. He had heard some of her friends hailing her and calling her *Nky BabyOku,* on his previous visit to her school, the very day he saw her. When he told some girls her nickname and described her to them, they knew her and told him that she was very popular in English department. Jekwu went to her department but did not find her. He made inquiry about her academic performance and the boy he asked, told him that Nkiruka had never failed any of her courses.

To Jekwu, 'beauty and knowledge' were his own prerequisite for marriage. Every other virtue can come afterwards. He believed so much in a woman's knowledge. He wanted someone that can think fast and come up with a brilliant idea in any situation. To Jekwu, if Nkiruka could pass all her courses, it meant that she was a fast learner. Jekwu gave Nkiruka her prerequisites for marriage by borrowing some money from his rich friends just to entice her and even had to borrow Armada Jeep from his friend and Nkiruka fell for his love advances and marriage proposal.

After his narrations, Nkiruka smiled at him and took his hand in hers.

"Didn't it occur to you that you were being selfish?" Nkiruka asked her husband.

"I was selfish for love. I didn't know how I would have married you if not through this way, Nky, I'm really very sorry for everything I've done wrong. I promise to be a better husband to you. Do you accept me now for who I am?" Jekwu caressed her face as he spoke softly to her. Nkiruka nodded. "I accepted you for who you are after I read the mysterious book. I think that God used the book to teach me something that I needed to know. God also used you to make me humble. I wouldn't have encountered humility if I did not face the challenges about you. We need humility in this marriage, because in it, we find love." The couple embraced each other again and even Odichimma smiled in her sleep.

* * * *

When Doctor Obiora came back home in the morning, Raaluchi served him his breakfast: *Moi moi* and white oats. But Doctor Obiora told Raaluchi to leave all cooking of meals for Uchendu because he didn't want her to stress herself in the kitchen yet. He wanted her to observe rest very well. After taking his breakfast, he took Raaluchi to the living room and told her in their discussion that her psychiatrist Doctor Julius felt that it would be a good thing for her to travel to India for a fast treatment.

Doctor Julius had told Doctor Obiora earlier that morning that Raaluchi's blood test result had shown that she had hormonal imbalance due to an anxiety disorder, and lots of brain disorder, due to excessive fluids in the brain. She needed to carry out a pet scan to know how badly the brain was damaged in her psychotic depression. She needed antidepressant psychotherapy, but unfortunately, Enugu Institute of Mental Health (E.I.M.H) – the government psychiatric hospital in Enugu where Doctor Julius worked, was not highly equipped enough to aid faster treatment. Raaluchi gave Doctor Obiora an understanding nod. She suggested contacting Onyeka and discussing with him about her intended departure so that he can assist in the bills, but Doctor Obiora refuted the idea, telling his niece that he can afford the bills, and he should try and observe what Father Joe said.

"Separation is the answer to your problems until you gained back your sanity," Doctor Obiora said, and Raaluchi frowned.

It was no doubt that she had been longing to see or even speak with Onyeka since a month, ever since she was released. She had forced herself to keep the separation but she just couldn't stop longing for him. She was always reminded of good memories with him, especially when they sang at the pool, and what seemed to worry her most times was that Onyeka may decide to end their marriage because she was insane. She had forced herself to prepare to accept that, assuming that was what Onyeka wanted. She had forced herself to give Onyeka a chance of marital happiness by marrying someone else, since she had caused him so much discomfort in their marriage, but although she wanted him to be happy in his marriage to another woman, the jealousy she felt imagining him with some other girl, perhaps Ifeoma, made her to reconsider, praying in her mind that God will keep her husband for her. Raaluchi craved for her husband.

"Uncle, why do you hate Onyeka so much? I know that your constant disagreement about him is not only for the fact that you are protecting my health," Raaluchi said with a growl, and was surprised that her uncle was upset over what she just said. She had expected that Doctor Obiora would respond to her calmly, perhaps with a chuckle, she had expected that her uncle would find it amused.

"Yes, I hate that wicked husband of yours! I hate him for marrying a naïve girl and I hate him for so many reasons that I can't say. Here you are, still habouring hope that you two can wind up together again, and there he is filing papers for divorce." Raaluchi started with puzzled lines on her forehead when she heard her uncle blurt out words in anger, and then she began to cry when Doctor Obiora continued to speak: "You think he loves you so much to tolerate insanity? I'm sorry to let you know that he can't do all that for you, because love has a limit to it. I'm only trying to help you come out of your miserable life, and instead of showing gratitude, you keep bugging me about that foolish husband of yours."

Raaluchi burst into tears, ran to her room and bolted the door. She sat on her bed and wept bitterly. She didn't open her room door when her uncle pleaded for apology and brought her dinner since she didn't come to eat with him at the dinning table. And early the next morning, he left a note for Raaluchi on the dinning table before he left for work.

I'm sorry, my pretty niece. It was just a slip of tongue made in anger. When I come back at 7 this evening, we'll have dinner at a pacific restaurant of your choice. I'm sure this mistake will never happen again.

Raaluchi read the note with a smile and tore it afterwards. Uchendu came to the living room to ask her if she wanted juice and she nodded, engrossed with the small framed photograph of her uncle with a beautiful chocolate skinned lady on a brown sleeveless gown. The lady was wearing a brazillian hair that hung down her shoulders. In the photograph, Doctor Obiora's hands were around her waist and they were smiling warmly in a romantic embrace. The photograph was hung on the wall, just beside the wall clock and Raaluchi wondered why she hadn't seen the photograph since she came, maybe because the photograph was too small to be noticed, or because her eyes didn't want to notice it before. She called Uchendu and questioned him about the lady in the photograph.

"She used to spend the weekend with us. *Oga* told me to call her Aunty Joy. She was the woman that taught me how to cook egusi soup without *mkpulu*" Uchendu said, scratching his head, his eyes focused on the photograph and then he continued to speak: "But *oga* beat her badly one day, her mouth was full of blood and she ran away with her bag. Since then, she never came back again." Uchendu said, with his eyes fixed on the photograph, as though he was talking to the photograph and not Raaluchi. Raaluchi nodded gently in affirmation of what she had suspected to be true about her uncle: his bad temper was obviously the reason why he was still a bachelor.

"What about you? Does your master beat you?" Raaluchi asked him, looking directly into his eyes. But his focus was still on the photograph.

"My master beats me badly too. But I'm used to it, and I cannever run away from my master because he takes good care of me."

Raaluchi smiled at him, and dismissed him from her presence by demanding for a glass of juice, and Uchendu left the living room, mumbling something about Raaluchi, Aunty Joy and his master.

That evening, Doctor Obiora fulfilled his promise to Raaluchi by taking her to BUBBLES RESTAURANT at New Heaven in Enugu. Raaluchi saw New Heaven a very busy place, cars moving up and down and honking noisly, pedestrians walking briskly, hawkers hawking their goods, advertising their goods in the very best way they could, their voices very loud and energetic. The restaurant was a very big one built with marbles, well equipped and enriched with classy decorations. As they settled down in a neat glass table for two, Doctor Obiora beckoned the waitress and they requested for chicken pepper soup. Raaluchi's heartbeat raced, and as her eyes met Onyeka's again, their eyes interlocked and Raaluchi wanted to go to him. Onyeka was talking with his friend Barrister Ekpereka and a fair lady in red beside him in a table for three when Raaluchi and her uncle entered the restaurant. Raaluchi was wearing a peach dinner gown with a very light make up. Her natural long hair hung down her shoulders and Onyeka gazed at her striking beauty as soon as she entered the restaurant and settled down with her uncle. Raaluchi smiled at him, but he did not smile back. And just then, he withdrew his eyes from Raaluchi and tried to focus on the discussion he was having with his friends.

Raaluchi only wished that her uncle would not notice that Onyeka her husband was present in the restaurant. But she was bothered that something had changed with her husband. She couldn't really tell, but she knew that something was actually missing from Onyeka. She couldn't stop staring at him, and when Onyeka's eyes met with hers, he quickly withdrew them, as though he was trying to avoid her. Raaluchi wanted to go to him and talk to him because she was uncomfortable with his emptiness. He looked empty to her because she wasn't able to see any reaction of love from his eyes. He was empty to her because she knew that he was avoiding her, and that made her so uncomfortable.

It was tragic for Raaluchi because she couldn't have who she craved to have especially when he was very close to her. Raaluchi almost choked with the chicken that the waitress had served her when he saw the lady in red peck her husband's right cheek, and just then, she excused herself from her uncle, demanding to powder her nose at the restroom. At the hallway to the ladies restroom, Raaluchi stopped and cried. It was true that Onyeka was filing for a divorce because she was insane. Her uncle was right after all. That lady in red must be his girlfriend, perhaps his fiancée. The lady in red must be the reason he had looked so empty when her eyes met his. She had watched the lady so closely to know if she was Ifeoma, but she wasn't. She had lost the battle for Onyeka. She knew it. She also knew that it was time to let the bird out from the nest to fly with freedom. It was time to leave Onyeka to his life of true happiness, since she had deprived him of such for almost three years. Raaluchi cried bitterly, her tears tickled down to her cheeks, and she was wiping them with her palms, since she had left her handbag where her handkerchief was, in the restaurant.

She stood at the hallway for a long time waiting for Onyeka to come for her, but he didn't, and when she walked back to the restaurant in half an hour, she looked so pale and depressed. She looked at the table where she had seen her husband, but there was no sight of Onyeka and his friends. He had left the restaurant with Barrister Ekpereka and the lady in red. The voices began to torment her again, reminding her that she was nothing but a looser. Her uncle was startled to see her look so different. She had changed from one strikingly pretty lady to a pale depressed woman, and just when he wanted to verify what had gone amiss, Raaluchi fainted, and he rushed to hold her head from landing on the marble floor.

CHAPTER TWENTY-EIGHT

RAALUCHI WOKE UP only to discover that she was in her room, in her uncle's house, and she was taking a drip. Mummy was sitting on an arm chair beside her bed, and she was saying her rosary. Raaluchi coughed a bit and Mummy opened her eyes and went to her daughter, thanking God that she had recovered from the faint. Mummy rushed to bring some food for her daughter in the kitchen and Uchendu handed Mummy a plate of *ukwa* and she took the food to the room to feed Raaluchi. Raaluchi ate just a little of the food because she had lost her appetite.

"I want to see Onyeka, Mummy. I just want to hear him tell me that he doesn't love me anymore," Raaluchi said hoarsely with tears rolling down from her eyes and Mummy wiped her tears and caressed her face.

"Raaluchi, you have to understand that you have no power to control destiny. Let God take control of everything. You have to be strong for yourself, be strong for your health, my dear."

That evening, Doctor Obiora entered the room and removed the drip from Raaluchi's vein when he saw that the drip was almost finished. He announced to Raaluchi and Mummy that he had booked their flight to India and had prepared some necessary documents that would be useful to them in India. They would be leaving for India at 2pm on Sunday afternoon, on the fifteenth day of September 2013. Mummy stood up and thanked Doctor Obiora, shedding tears of joy, assuring him of God's unfailing favour upon his life. Doctor Obiora stifled a smile and advised Raaluchi to relax her mind before he left the room. Mummy switched on the wall TV for Raaluchi and soon, she was engrossed with a Nollywood movie playing on the TV and Mummy was grateful to God that it was a comedy acted by Osuofia and Mr. Ibu. Soon, Raaluchi was smiling widely as she saw the movie.

Nkiruka was there for her friend. She would visit in the morning with Odichimma, they would all crack jokes, and in the evening, they would leave for Nsukka. She visited everyday that she made Raaluchi happy and fit to fly to India, and on Saturday evening, the two friends hugged each other so tight knowing in their hearts that they would miss each other so much. Raaluchi promised to keep in touch with her and advised her to always say her prayers.

* * * *

Doctor Obiora drove Mummy and Raaluchi to Enugu airport on Sunday morning and by 8 am, the plane took off for Lagos airport where they settled down at the lobby and waited for their flight to India. Raaluchi noticed that her mother had been sending and receiving messages because her phone had been beeping and when she did ask her, she told her that the messages were just from her customers who wanted to buy some things. She was only telling them that she had traveled. Raaluchi nodded at her. They had waited for six hours after taking their lunch and having some soft drinks. It was exactly 2.30 pm when the flight broadcaster announced their flight: Emirate Air Line, flying from Lagos to Bangalore airport India. They stood up and joined the cue for their boarding pass to be checked and they settled down in their seats in economy class.

Raaluchi was forced to remember the honeymoon with her husband in America, the flight they had taken back home, how Onyeka assured her that he would be responsible in keeping her happy. Mummy turned to watch her daughter slowly drifting to the roads of depression. She beckoned to a flight stewardess and told her to connect the little TV that was attached to the back of each seat in the plane. The flight stewardess concurred with a smile and in no time, the TV was fixed for Raaluchi to see a movie. The flight stewardess demonstrated the cabin rules, and others made sure that all the passengers were wearing their seat belts. In less than ten minutes, the plane taxied and then took off with a swift leap that Mummy almost shrieked. Raaluchi smiled at her and told her to relax, and to avoid making a scene by showing people that it was her first time of entering a plane. Mummy did make a scene that Raaluchi had been scared of when she fell from a rolling step in Bangalore Airport.

"Nna o! Nna o!" Mummy screamed, calling her heavenly father to save her from the fall. It was a good thing that she had no serious injury. It was a good thing that Raaluchi and a young Nigerian lady behind them helped her up and held her hand for the rest of the movement on the rolling step. Some people were laughing at her as they headed to the check point. It was half past six in the evening when they entered an airport taxi that took them to ZINATA HOTEL beside Yarana Teaching Hospital. They made the necessary hotel payments after changing their dollars to rupees, and they relaxed in their room, trying to recover from their jetlag by drifting to sleep.

* * * * *

In the morning at exactly 9am of India time, they entered YARANA TEACHING HOSPITAL to commence the necessary procedures for Raaluchi's treatment, using Doctor Julius's directions. The hospital was a gigantic buiding and was very elaborate. But the psychiatrist they were directed to see was not on duty that Tuesday morning. They asked around and a white Indian man with black curly hair, who was drinking a cup of coffee, and at the same time, working on a computer, informed them that Dr. Raffi Kubar was still on leave and would resume work by next week.

"Raffi is not in the office, nuh? She's on leave, so, come back next week by *tweluwu* in the noon, *nuh*? She *willu* resume next week *nuh*?" The white Indian said, speaking English with Indian dialect, in a very fast manner, and jerking his head as he spoke. Raaluchi just noticed how dead the words 'twelve' and 'will' have become in the hands of the Indians, because they seem not to use them properly. It was so funny watching them speak.

They left the hospital looking gruesome with scowled faces, angry that they didn't achieve their mission. At the street, they caught a glimpse of some fresh fruits displayed on a table by the sellers. The apples looked very big and reddish, the paw-paw was yellowish and the oranges were orange in colour, not green. Mummy and Raaluchi smiled at the sight of the fresh- looking fruits, the fruits made their mouth produce more salivary gland and they swallowed their spittle in desire as they paced to the table to prize the fruits. They bought lots of them because they were so cheap and walked back to their hotel room to eat them. Raaluchi was becoming very impatient to see her psychiatrist because the voices still tormented her especially when she wavered in her inevitable thoughts of Onyeka, Nnanyelugo and her past. She was tired of staying in the hotel room doing nothing but to see India movies and take short walks around the hotel garden. Ever since they came, they had been afraid of taking long walks in the city of Bangalore because they could miss their way and transportation was expensive. They still had to economize since they had lots of expenses to make in the future.

On Tuesday of the next week after their arrival, at exactly 10 am, they impatiently went back to the hospital to see Doctor Raffi. They settled down at the hospital hallway to wait for her. Mummy's phone beeped and after she had read the message, she left and promised Raaluchi to be back soon. Raaluchi nodded and gave her mother a quizzical look, wondering who she had been chatting with on her phone, wondering if she had a boyfriend. Suddenly, she saw a couple, lost in a sweet embrace, with tears rolling down the face of the lady, and her husband was assuring her in English that she will not die, that their love was too strong to let any of them die and that she had to accept to do the surgery and live for him. Raaluchi looked sympathetically at them, and her mind drifted in reminiscences of her husband and the love he professed for her at the police station. Her eyes filled with tears, knowing that those love words were dead because she knew for sure that her husband was going to divorce her because she was insane. She was convinced because she had seen it in his eyes that evening, at the restaurant in Enugu. She stood up and moved further, sobbing uncontrollably. She wanted to hear those comforting words that came out from the mouth of the man in a sweet embrace with his wife. She wanted to hear those words again from Onyeka her husband. She wanted nothing else but that comfort, before entering to see the doctor.

She was standing at the hallway facing the window. The rays of the morning sunlight shimmered through the glass window and as she watched the sun, she squinted and wished that she could touch the sun; wished that she could get the longing comfort from the sun. She sobbed until she was startled at a gentle touch on her left shoulder. She turned to face her husband Onyeka offering her a white handkerchief to use for her tears. Raaluchi stood motionless staring at his overwhelming handsome face, and wondering how she located her, wondering if he had really known that he was the only person that she wanted to see at that moment. He was looking very handsome in a neat designers white shirt and a black pair of trousers. The fragrance of his perfume magnetized Raaluchi when he moved closer to help her wipe her tears. Raaluchi searched the pages of Onyeka's green album with red designed hearts in her mind and then she focused on the first page:

The most beautiful encounters are those with painful tears waiting for the right person to wipe them off and make them happy.

Mummy smiled at them and gave them a moment of privacy. Onyeka bent over and stole a kiss from his wife and immediately, Raaluchi withdrew her face and gave him a slight push.

"You look beautiful, my queen." Onyeka said softly to her.

"At least I'm not better than the fair lady in red who pecked you at the restaurant."

"I feel an over-exalted excitement whenever you get jealous of a threatening rival, because it makes me secured of your undoubted love for me." Onyeka said softly to her and chuckled afterwards, leaning on the wall, his eyes fixed on Raaluchi.

"So, have you been filing for a divorce?"

"What are you talking about?" Onyeka asked, raising his eyebrow in uttermost surprise.

"Just go straight to the point Onyeka, there's no need pretending. You don't have to pretend over divorcing me and marrying that lady in red just because …"

Onyeka hushed his wife with a finger on her lips and it prevented her from finishing her statement.

"My wife is not insane. The lady that pecked me is a colleague from Italy who had come for the yearly pharmacists' meeting in Enugu. She's biracial, a Nigerian Italian, and the peck is their way of saying good bye."

Raaluchi heaved a sigh of relief and questioned her husband about the emptiness, she had soul-searched her husband at the restaurant and found him empty. Onyeka shrugged off the question and changed the topic by asking her how she's been faring and he confessed to her that he had been keeping touch with Mummy from *Whatsapp messenger*. Raaluchi smiled. She still couldn't believe that her husband Onyeka was with her again. She thanked God that Onyeka still loved her and she got the comforting words she needed from him some minutes later before they all entered the Psychiatrist's office. It looked like a dream and she had been pinching herself in the doctor's office, hoping to wake up from this dream but everything to her greatest surprise was just a reality. She was with her husband in India and he had finally kept his promise of not leaving her. She was so excited, and she smiled to herself, taking the peaceful journey of her recovery from the tormenting schizophrenia.

PART SIX

A LOT MUST DEPART

2013-2014

A lot must depart for a new beginning.

CHAPTER TWENTY NINE

MUMMY LEFT THE couple alone to their sweet world of togetherness and she was grateful to God that her daughter was happy again. The constant dimple on her face whenever she stayed with Onyeka was the evidence that she was happy again. And that was part of the therapy that Doctor Raffi had recommended for Raaluchi's quick recovery: that she must always be happy come what may. Onyeka and Raaluchi visited the hospital every morning for her pet scan, injections and other medications for the hormonal imbalance and schizophrenia.

And later in the evening they visited a sea in Bangalore, and had good times taking walks in the tranquil environment near the sea. And by 8pm at night, they went back to the hotel to feast on Mummy's already prepared rice and delicious fresh tomatoes chicken stew. On one of their romantic nights, they talked about their future. Raaluchi seemed to be responding to treatment. The voices were no more as loud as they used to be on her and Onyeka believed that soon, she would recover completely and they would be going home.

"Dear, I have a surprise for you, guess what it is." Onyeka said almost like a whisper to his wife and Raaluchi chuckled and narrowed her eyes in a guess.

"Fanco Pharmaceutical Company has won another award."

"No"

Raaluchi laughed and told her husband that she wasn't good in guessing and what she heard from her husband came as a shock to her. The fact that her husband was going to buy a house in America was too much for her to believe and the fact that they would be moving to America was the most excitingly shocking news that she had ever heard.

"What about the company?"

"It will still be in existence in Asaba. I'll employ Okwudili, Barrister Ekpereka's younger brother. He's a Pharmacist and I think he can handle the firm well. And I'll have to look for a pharmaceutical company to work with in America for some time. Father Pius had promised to help me get a job after he had told me of a house on lease at Dorchester in Boston Massachusetts. And may be, by the grace of God, I'll open my private pharmaceutical company in America. What do you think?"

"It's okay, but why are you doing this?"

"I think we both need a change of environment after all we have gone through. I think it is high time I practiced the law of leaving father and mother behind and clinging to my lovely wife in a far place." Raaluchi tickled his cheeks and they laughed before Raaluchi finally reminded him about her studies. Onyeka promised to help her get her transcript from Delta State University Asaba Campus. She'll continue her studies in America. And that very night, the couple slept peacefully in each other's arms grateful for the decision they had made.

* * * *

Raaluchi completed her therapy at the second week of October and Doctor Raffi repeated her medical counseling to Raaluchi in the presence of her husband and her mother. She started hearing the strange voices when she was depressed about her father's death and her loss of admission into the university of her choice, and to stop the voices from re-occurring, she must stay happy at all times and cease from thinking too much. They all left India on the 18th day of October 2013 and when they reached Asaba in the night of the 19th day, Bobo recognized Raaluchi. He abandoned his bowl of cornflakes and hurried to hug Raaluchi, shouting: "Mummy! Mummy!" Nanny Nene didn't stop shedding tears of joy, admitting to the couple that she had prayed for a miracle to come and the reconciliation and happiness were indeed the miracle she had prayed for.

The couple continued their chapel visitation. They visited the chapel for prayers every evening. Onyeka prayed that Doctor Obiora would reconsider his perception about him and accept him as his son-in-law. And God really answered him when Doctor Obiora honoured his party invitation. Onyeka invited Raaluchi's family and even his parents for a brief re-union party in his house. The living room was spacious enough to contain every body. They were eating fried rice and chicken and drinking assorted wines. Onyeka told every body that Raaluchi was now free from the voices because she was given a very good treatment in India. They were thrilled to hear that, and they applauded happily.

After some refreshment, Onyeka pleaded openly to Doctor Obiora to reconsider his perception of him, assuring him that he loved Raaluchi to marry her again, and the two men hugged each other in reconciliation, thumping each other on their backs. Mummy openly apologized to Doctor Obiora again for not informing him of Raaluchi's marriage, and he assured her of his forgiveness. Raaluchi hugged Mama, and Papa her father in law, and Papa smiled warmly at her. They all made peace and understood within their hearts that the marriage between Raaluchi and Onyeka was indeed the will of God of which no mortal could separate.

Just when they were toasting in happiness, they heard the news about a young lady that committed murder by poisoning a white man in a hotel room just to make away with his portfolio that contained the sum of twenty thousand dollars. A hotel cleaner had caught her covering the dead man with a white hotel bed sheet and she alerted the hotel manager on phone immediately. The terrible incident happened in Abuja on the twelfth day of the month of October, in the year 2013,

271

exactly three days before the couple came back home. They all looked up at the Plasma TV screen and saw Ifeoma in a state of disarray. Raaluchi and Onyeka glanced at each other and smiled. The newscaster announced that Ifeoma had been arrested by the police and is now at the police custody in Abuja high commands.

"It serves her right. This is the ultimate price she has to pay for being an accomplice in ruining my marital life." Onyeka muttered in an impish grin.

* * * *

The interview between the American interviewer, at the Lagos embassy, on the 20th October 2013, was very hectic and the interviewer was a very haggard looking lady that seemed difficult to please, insisting that they had no concrete reason to live in America. They were denied visa, but they did not give up. As Onyeka looked at the long cues waiting to be interviewed, and the people that had been interviewed; that had actually left with angry faces, he wondered if there would ever be a visa to be issued. Just then, a young man in his late twentiees started demanding for his visa fee to be refunded to him.

"You are all stupid and inconsiderate! You are all thieves! How can you take my visa fee only to tell me that I'm not qualified to go to America? Refund me my money or I'll pull down this buiding!" The man shouted angrily with tears rolling down his eyes, wishing to break the glass counter and fight his interviewer: a brown-haired white man in a brown suit, who was already jerking in fear. Some security men took the frustrated man away. Onyeka saw in the young man a frustrated man that may have used all his income to pay his visa fee.

They rescheduled for another interview, this time they went to Abuja embassy, and the person that interviewed them was a very gentle young man who was absolutely a fan of all young couples who are truly in love. As soon as he heard from Onyeka that he wanted to relocate to America because his wife needed it as part of her therapy to avoid schizophrenia, he told the couple to come back for their visa in five days time which was going to be the last day in the month of October. They left the embassy with joy in their hearts. Outside the embassy, as they were walking hand in hand to their car, someone ran towards Raaluchi, calling the name 'Queen' which looked absurd to Onyeka because he didn't know his wife to bear such name even though she looked like a queen.

Raaluchi turned to see Jess, one of her wayward friends at the computer school. She was looking very unkempt in her long black maternity gown and she was tying a black scarf on her head, looking mournful. And Raaluchi just noticed that she was a recharge card hawker, who hawks at the embassy. Raaluchi introduced her to her husband as 'an old friend' and Onyeka shook hands with her. He told Raaluchi that she was free to have some privacy with her for some time and that he'll be waiting in the car. Raaluchi thanked her husband and then took Jess to a nearest café from the embassy, and they sat down to talk. They sat side by side in the tiny café that smelled of fresh snacks. Raaluchi beckoned the waiter: a fat boy who was practicing a dance step, shaking his waist in a funny way that some people in the café found him entertaining. They couldn't take their eyes off him. The waiter came to them with a smiling face, and Jess ordered for fresh meat-pies, egg-rolls and can juice. Jess began to cry. She told Raaluchi that she was completely different from her because she looked so beautiful and rich, while she had been wallowing in great difficulty ever since she lost her newly married husband.

When Raaluchi asked about Peppy and Abby, she cried harder and told Raaluchi the main story. After they parted ways with Raaluchi when she told them about her accident and her inability of making money from Chiedu, they entered into a covenant of prostituting and stealing from rich men, mostly the Hausa Alhajis. They were on the business for two years, making lots of money before something awful happened. On one of the usual club nights they attended in Abuja, they happened to meet three rich Hausa men: Alhaji Musa Danfodio, Alhaji Sule Omosho and Alhaji Abubaka Talawa. These rich men squandered them with so much money and gifts, slept with them in luxurious hotels, took them to drinking joints where they took lots of alcoholic wines. And one night, after drinking lots of wine in a joint,and were heading to a hotel with the Hausa men, they lost consciousness and regained their consciousness in a shrine, little did they know that the Hausa men wanted to use them for ritual sacrifice. Jess told Raaluchi that she watched a ritualist kill and cut the heads and the private parts of Peppy and Abby.

Raaluchi shook her head and tears rushed down her cheeks. What she was saying in her mind was that she would have ended that way if she had continued her friendship with the "girls on top". She was thanking God for saving her from their company. Jess told Raaluchi that when it got to her turn to be killed, there was confusion between the ritualist and the Hausa men. They heard noices, and it was as though some people were coming into the shrine. The ritualist took the body parts of Abby and Peppy and ran away with the Hausa men. That was how she escaped from her early death. She told Raaluchi that the reason God kept her alive was for her to tell her story to people and repent from her sins, not because she was better than Peppy and Abby. She told Raaluchi that the only punishment she was receiving for all her sins, was that she lost the only man she fell in love with, the only man she had married, just five months after her wedding. Since then, her life had been nothing but a nightmare that she had craved for it to end. All the money she made from her prostitution was spent in her wedding ceremony expenses and when she lost her husband in a serious accident, she realized that she was alone in her miserable world to bring up her unborn child. She apologized to Raaluchi to forgive her for all the insolent text messages she joined Peppy and Abby to send to her. Raaluchi told her that she had long forgiven them and she sympathized with her. She only paid for her snacks and can drink and promised to call her, after taking her phone number.

* * * *

"It was so hard not to pity her, poor Jess, that experience must have been very traumatic for her," Raaluchi said to Onyeka and he immediately took her by the hand and pecked her palm. They were sitting side by side in a small dinning table inside their hotel room in Lagos, and soon, they were holding hands. A yellow light was shinning from the chandelier on the POP ceiling, beside them was a large bed well made with white bedsheet and pillow cases, and outside their hotel room was a dark night with rays of white light that came from the street lights. Cars were still moving on the express roads even at 11:45 pm, at that hour of the night.

"We all had our traumatic experiences. The most important thing is that we learn from our mistakes because they are the lessons of life," Onyeka said softly to her, still holding her hand.

"I know she must have learned from her mistakes. I saw her genuine regrets when we talked," Raaluchi said.

"I understand how sorry you feel for her. Do you want me to do some thing for her?" Onyeka asked her, but she did not say anything, and in her facial expression was the comment: 'I don't want you to feel that I'm telling you this for you to do something for her." Onyeka understood her mien.

"Raalu, you have forgiven Jess, and I think she'll realize your forgiveness if you help her overcome her problems. I'll write a check for her. She needs to start a new business that'll enlarge her income," Onyeka said, and she gave him a slow long smile in return, and in that smile that revealed her dimples, was her gratitude.

* * * *

Jekwu got a job as 'excercise books supplier' to most of the primary and secondary schools in Nsukka, and his first income was awesome. One day, he was in the kitchen peeling *ora* leaves with his wife, and they were talking about his income.

"I suggest that you should enlarge your coast. You should rent a shop for your books. Go back to those schools and find out the text books they are using, buy the books and supply them to the schools. You'll make higher income." Nkiruka said to her husband, who was smiling at her and nodding in agreement. He was thrilled that his wife just came up with a good idea. That was what he had always wanted in a woman he would call his. And that night in their bedroom, they prayed about the idea and God answered them by making the idea fruitful.

The couple hugged themselves in excitement when Jekwu came home with the good news. Jekwu decided to celebrate his success with his family by taking them out for dinner. They dressed up in good outfits. Nkiruka was wearing a dark blue silk dinner gown that had the length end below her knees, with red sandals and handbag. Odichimma was wearing a sleeveless blue gown with a golden pair of sandals, feeling happy to be going out with her parents. Jekwu was wearing a sky blue shirt and a dark blue pair of trousers with black sandals. They were all strolling down the sandy lanes of Ikogu Street in Nsukka, heading to the junction where they could get a taxi. They walked pass Madam Caro's bar and she gazed at Jekwu with mouth agape, wondering if the neat handsome man walking with his family was Jekwu or Jekwu's twin brother. She tapped some men drinking in the bar; men who she knew were familiar with Jekwu, and they gazed at Jekwu as though they had seen a ghost.

"I've lost my regular customer," Madam Caro said in bitterness, her face scowled. She knew that Jekwu would not come back to her bar. She knew that people visited her bar for different reasons, but Jekwu's main reason was to drink his frustrations away. He was always frustrated whenever he visited, but as she looked at how different he looked, she knew she had lost him for good. He had embraced peace and was enclosed in his peaceful family, and they looked happy together. Madam Caro was not pleased with this peace.

Jekwu was happy to be in his bookshop that was located at the University areas. He was making a good sale. Many students from the University and University Secondary School were buying books from him and he was happy. A man entered his book shop to buy books for his son who he had just enrolled in the University Secondary School. He was very hasty and he just handed Jekwu the list of books to place the text books in his son's school bag, without realizing that he brought out from his pocket, a single key with the list of books. The key fell on the red rug that Jekwu had used to cover the floor of his bookshop, and nobody seemed to notice.

"Fine boy, what's your name?" Jekwu asked the man's son after he had placed all the books in his school bag. He liked the boy and he just wanted to be friendly. He was smiling at him.

"My name is Chizaram Okoli. I'm in J.S1B" The boy replied, smiling back at Jekwu. His father smacked his head.

"Don't be a fool. He only asked you your name." His father said hastily to him and told him to go back to his class room at once. Jekwu watched the boy run inside the school with his heavy school bag on his back. The man hastily paid Jekwu his money and drove off immediately. When Jekwu saw the single key on the floor of his book shop, the next morning, he knew that it belonged to the hasty man, because he was the last person that entered his book shop the previous day. The key was golden in colour and long. It was very unique and Jekwu knew that it must be a key to a very important place. He quickly made his way to the University Secondary School and went straight to Chizaram's class.

* * * *

Jekwu stood in front of the hasty man in his office at 3:30

pm that afternoon. Chizaram had given him his father's office address after saying that his father had been looking for the key since yesterday, and that the key was very important to his work in his company. The hasty man expressed his excitement by giving Jekwu a tight hug, taking the key from Jekwu, and gesturing at an office chair opposite him, for Jekwu to make use of. Soon, they engaged in a chat, and the hasty man was beaming as they talked about the key.

"This key is of a great value to this company, and I just handed my General Manager to the police this morning, insisting that he did not hand over the key to me yesterday. I was thinking that he wanted to steal from this company, because this key is the key to the strong room where our recharge cards are kept, and they worth millions of naira. It's a good thing that you found it and returned it to me. You are such a good man," The hasty man said.

"I can't possibly take what does not belong to me, I mean, what can I use the key for? I know it's of great value to you, that's why I'm returning it to you." Jekwu said.

"I'm very grateful to you. What can I do for you to express my gratitude?" The hasty man said hastily, he seemed to have a fast manner of talking. He was already making a phone call, and in his call, he told the police to release his General Manager. Jekwu knelt down, and begged the man to grant him a little favour.

"Sir, if you must repay me for what I've done for you, I beg you to grant me this favour…"

"What is it? What favour do you want me to grant you?"

"Sir please, I want you to grant my wife the opportunity to work in this honourable tele-communication network company. She's a smart woman, and I promise you that she wouldn't do anything to disappoint you."

Jekwu watched the man roll his eyes, hesitantly giving his condition a thought.

"What is her qualification? I need intelligent smart ladies for this company."

"She holds a degree in Bachelor Of Arts, Second Class Upper Division, to be precise," Jekwu said. "And I bet that she has all the qualifications you need." Jekwu added, watching the man roll his eyes again, and he prayed in his mind for God to arrest his decision.

"It's okay. Let her come for the interview first. I'll hire her if she meets up with the demands of the interview." The hasty man said and Jekwu smiled in faith, believing that his wife will get the job. "But just in case, I don't hire her, I can still repay you in another way, for returning my key to me," The hasty man added. He gave Jekwu the date of the interview and he left his office looking happy.

That night, they prayed for the Job, begging God to make it an easy interview; begging God to give Nkiruka the job. Afterwards, they cuddled each other in bed, ready to fall asleep, believing in their hearts that God heard their prayers and would surely answer. And their faith worked on the third day of November, on Wednesday evening, Nkiruka had just returned from the bookshop with her husband when her phone beeped, indicating an unread message. And when she read the message, she discovered that it was from 3Mobile Tele-Communication Network Company. She was hired for the post of Assistant General Manager. She was given an official car, and a bungalow that was situated in Opara Layout, a serene environment in Nsukka. Her monthly salary was awesome. The couple hugged each other so tight, with tears of joy streaming down the cheeks of Nkiruka.

"Thank you darling, God used you to make a way for this job. God has promoted us." Nkiruka said to her husband, and again, they hugged each other with smiles on their faces.

* * * *

It seemed to Nkiruka as though she had looked away for a moment, and looked back to find her life transformed to new phases, just after a year. Her marriage to Jekwu was blooming. They used their fat incomes for the growth of their little family. Odichimma was enrolled in a good private school, and she seemed to be doing well with her speech. Jekwu was erecting a mansion in Nsukka. Their former bungalow was rented, and was yielding income. An unborrowed Armada Jeep was parked in the compound of their new bungalow in Nsukka, and there she was, holding her international passport with a Nevada Visa. She was going to tour Las Vegas with her family, just like she had desired, and she was riding Armada jeep, plus Honda Accord, her official car. But she wasn't mesmerized about them anymore: the Armada Jeep and her tour to Las Vegas, as though they were what she valued more, because he had fallen in love with her husband, and had chosen her husband's love over those material things. She knew that God had given them to her, just for her to know that she could have them at the right time, she could have whatever she needed only with love.

The real time for every expectation comes only when we walk in the light," Nkiruka soliloquized with smiles.

CHAPTER THIRTY

ONYEKA BOUGHT THE cozy apartment in Dorchester from Celine Rock, a young widow who admitted that the only reason why she wanted to sell the house was that the building always reminded her of her husband and the sweet memories of their love life in the house before his death, which always depressed her. She was advised by her doctor to leave the house and relocate to another house with her children. She was advised to fall in love again and not abandon her young life in the hands of depression. Onyeka told his wife that they were going to live in Celine's house and give life to her dead love life with her husband, by continuing with their sweet love.

When they arrived at Boston, they went to the parish house and stayed there. Father Pius told Onyeka that they would have to stay in the parish house for some time until they fixed the apartment to suit their taste. Raaluchi was good in interior decoration and so after she had bought household equipments with the help of Father Pius's parishioner: a kind lady who had taken her to places where she was able to buy beautiful and durable household equipments, she performed a very good job by changing the house to the level that it looked superb, and Onyeka her husband commended her for it.

* * * *

Onyeka went for series of interviews in most of the pharmaceutical companies in Boston that Father Pius had recommended for him, and they had all kept him waiting for their appointment letters. The renewed couple had prayed endlessly in a chapel at Father Pius's parish but it seemed to be taking lots of time to hear from them. Even Father Pius could not understand why his appointment was being delayed. He knew that Onyeka was qualified enough and he had also trusted his friends in the pharmaceutical company to give Onyeka a job. The renewed couple had to depend on the money that Okwudili was sending to them from Nigeria. They used the money for feeding and other necessary things. But Onyeka was being very impatient.

He wanted to earn a good living in America. He wanted to take care of Bobo and Raaluchi. He wanted to give them a comfortable life in America, and not making love all day long to Raaluchi and strolling on the streets of Washington in Dorchester neighbourhood, a town where they had resisded, a town contented with itself; a soporific initiation for lazy people and retired workers. Onyeka strolled to a shimmering blue lake, the blueness so tranquil that even as he sat down at a corner, it motivated his uncontrollable thoughts of positivity. He was going to get a job in a Pharmaceutical Company. He was going to get a job. All he needed was to remain calm just like this lake. He thought. Raaluchi was also worried about her education. She had applied for admission in the University of Boston. She had taken examination, a little screening exam to taste her knowledge and adequacy and they had promised to give her a call but for the past six weeks they lived in America, Raaluchi hadn't heard from the school. She didn't want to apply for another school because she didn't want to stay at a distance from her house.

Just when they relaxed and seemed to forget about their needs, spending most of their free times with God in prayers, Father Pius and other priests in the parish house, Onyeka received a call from one of the pharmaceutical companies which he applied for a job, perhaps somewhere very close to his house: Dilax Pharmaceutical Company Boston, a call to inform him that he had gotten a job as the Accountant of the Company. The pay was awesome and Onyeka did not mind the fact that it seemed like a demotion, from the managing director of his firm in Nigeria to a mere Accountant.

A week after Onyeka started work, Raaluchi got the long-waited call from the University of Boston and the caller told her to enroll and resume school the next day. She was offered admission to study English and Literary Studies for just three years. Raaluchi was overwhelmed with joy and the renewed couple did not stop thanking God for His favours upon their lives. Onyeka celebrated Raaluchi's successful admission at a movie. He had taken Raaluchi and Bobo to a movie gallary. Bobo kept chuckling and pointing at the movie scenes. The movie playing was a dramatic comedy and the lovely family sat together in a mesmerized state, smiling widely and chuckled when they had to, their past sorrows forgotten and it was as though a new chapter of their love life had just begun.

* * * *

On the nineteenth day of December 2014, Onyeka threw a little birthday party for his wife in their house and they also marked their fifth year wedding anniversary. The couple invited Father Pius and his priest friends in the parish house and some of Onyeka's colleagues at the pharmaceutical company. They all celebrated in excitement and Raaluchi made a wish after she had cut her birthday cake.

"God is so awesome and I can't thank him enough. I make a wish this evening that my renewed love for my husband will never be shattered again. I'm going to make him happy for the rest of my life. I'm going to graduate with a very good result. I'm going to be an astute writer that will live to write my story. I'm going to sing more songs for my husband, and for anybody who cares to listen. We shall all live happily forever in thanksgiving to God. I believe that these wishes of mine will be a reality because God is awesome and He grants our heart desires," Raaluchi said in excitement and they all said 'Amen' and popped Champaigne. And that night after the guests left their house, they all had their bath and cuddled under the blanket with Bobo lying in the middle of the couple and within a short time, he drifted to sleep.

"I love you Mummy", Bobo said in his sleep and the couple laughed.

Uncontrollably, Raaluchi remembered her father, Nnanyelugo and wished that he was still alive to witness her happiness. She was an undergraduate in one of the best colleges in America. Her life with her husband in America was impeccably lovely.

"Dad, I know that you are happy with me wherever you are," Raaluchi said to herself, almost like a whisper, and just then, her head ached and she heard the tormenting voices again, but this time, they were no more as loud as they used to be on her. The voices reminded her again of how useless she was, and that she would never be a happy person. She was shaking on the bed, like a seizure attack, when she heard the voices, unaware to Onyeka who was sleeping beside her. Her breath began to cease, and it was as though she was slowly passing out, until she focused her mind on Jesus, and then, she regained her self.

Raaluchi was shattered and confused when she regained her consciousness after the voices spoke to her. She couldn't believe that she was still hearing the voices, after all the treatments she had in India. She couldn't believe that she had almost died few minutes ago, because of this dangerous sickness. She knew that the only problem she had was that she never stopped thinking about her father. She never seemed to forget about him.

"Could it be the inevitable thoughts of my father that brought back this traumatic sickness to me?" She said in her mind.

* * * *

One Saturday afternoon, when Raaluchi was making use

of the dish washer in her kitchen, her cell phone rang and she answered the call. The caller was her mother, and she was sobbing when Raaluchi heard her voice.

"Raaluchi, it's... your father," Mummy said hoarsely. She was still sobbing and it made Raaluchi difficult to understand what she was saying. Raaluchi's mind focused on her father. She wished that Mummy was telling her that her father did not actually die, that her father resurrected or something like that, that there was a miracle somehow that sustained her father's life. What she heard next from her mother got her very confused. What was her mother saying? Her father made a confession in a note? Confessing what actually? Why wasn't the note discovered soon after his death?

"You have to come back to Nigeria Raaluchi. It is very important that you come back."

Raaluchi discussed what Mummy said to her with her husband later that evening and Onyeka admitted that Mummy called him too. They scheduled a flight after Onyeka had taken permission from the company he was working for. They informed Father Pius about their departure. He blessed them as usual, and they left on Monday morning.

* * * *

Mummy and Father Joe were waiting for the couple in his office when they came in, the next morning. From the look on their faces, all was not well at all. Mummy was wearing a tear-filled face with her left hand under her jaw, and Father Joe was shaking his head in disbelief, wearing a face full of wrinkles on his forehead. He was frowning, and he seemed to be lost in thoughts. The couple settled down on the plastic chairs opposite Mummy and Father Joe. Father Joe came close to Raaluchi and patted her shoulder before he spoke.

"According to our lord Jesus Christ, It is good to know the truth, because it is only the truth that can set us free. The truth is the bright light that shines in our lives to eliminate darkness,"

Father Joe said softly and handed her father's note to her and Raaluchi took it with trembling hands. It startled her that the paper was still a sparkling white long note, even after so many years. She recognized her father's writing and she read the words out.

Obiageli, many years before I married you, after my West African Examination in Abatete, I had a relationship with a very pretty girl named Raaluchi. She had a birth mark, like a dot on her forehead just like our daughter. We were very close and so much in love with each other that she compelled me to take a blood convenant with her, just to stabilize our relationship, and I did. We made promises to each other, professing undying love for each other. She lost her virginity to me and I got her pregnant. She wanted us to get married when she discovered that she was pregnant, but my love for her was not strong enough to marry her in my youthful exuberance. I was only twenty years old. I still had a very long way to go with my studies, and marriage was not on my mind.

When she came to my house with her mother and reported about her pregnancy to my parents, I denied my responsibility for it. I was only protecting my studies and I couldn't father a baby at that time. I knew I hurt her, but I believed that she would survive the pains and I would marry her and father our child when i'm financially stable.

When I heard that she died in the process of aborting her pregnancy, my life turned upside down. I wished that I did not hurt her. I wished that I admitted my responsibility for her pregnancy and that I had begged her parents to be patient with me. A lot of wishes came to my mind but then, it was already late. Raaluchi's spirit kept tormenting me and I was so restless, even after I visited so many native doctors. I never knew God because I was always afraid of keeping His commandments and I was a great sinner and I didn't want to repent, yet, I attended Mass every Sunday. I wanted to go to a Catholic Priest for deliverance, but I changed my mind because I felt very guilty of my sins and I believed that God would not forgive me and deliver me, no matter how sorry I was.

I decided to go to Amaekwere river in Abatete and there, I evoked the marine spirit, the goddess of Amaekwere river to help me chain the spirit of Raaluchi so that she would stop tormenting me in my dreams, and causing nightmares for me. The goddess of Amaekwere river was a pretty woman with great height and long dark hair. She promised to help me upon a condition that I give my life to her. I agreed without knowing the consequences of what I did. The goddess gave me wealth and business connections. Raaluchi's spirit stopped tormenting me but I was given an assignment by the goddess to initiate youths that were fourteen years of age to her kingdom every new year, and I've been carrying out the assignment by throwing parties for the youths of Abatete every new year and selecting the ones that have come of age, until I got married to you.

Obiageli, out of jealousy, she tied your womb. That was the reason you did not conceive on time. I was able to make her untie your womb when I told her that I would initiate my first child to her kingdom on his or her fourteenth year on earth.

I initiated our daughter to her kingdom with a bottle of wine. I did not only initiate her to the kingdom of the goddess of Amaekwere, but united her mind with mine with my voodoo, through the help of the goddess. I did that because I wanted to be reading her thoughts, I wanted to know what entered her mind and what didn't. I wanted to be united to her because I saw Raaluchi, my girlfriend in her, because she reminded me of my girlfriend with that birth mark on her forehead. I wanted to make it up to the dead Raaluchi by giving her everything she needed, by showering her with so much love even though I knew that she was my daughter.

For the first time, I disobeyed the goddess of Amaekwere when she told me to kill Raaluchi our daughter. I also knew that she was jealous of my close relationship with Raaluchi my daughter.

I preferred to die to doing what she asked me to do. I couldn't do it because I loved Raaluchi so much. Angrily, she struck me with a terrible sickness—cancer of the liver and I knew that I was going to die in it because she gave me my death date. Please don't mourn my death. None of my children should mourn my death because I really deserve it. Please forgive me from the bottom of your heart. Tell

Raaluchi my daughter that I'm very sorry for what I did to her. Take her to a powerful man of God for deliverance, if not, the goddess would torment her life until she finally kills her.

Raaluchi wept bitterly after she read her father's note. She couldn't believe that her father was actually responsible for all her miseries. Mummy began to weep all over again. The fact that she was only a subtitute for her husband was unbearably painful to her. How could he see his dead girl friend in his own daughter? Mummy wondered if that was also the reason Nnanyelugo insisted that he named their daughter Raaluchi even after she suggested Ngozichukwu. She understood that Nnanyelugo continued from where he stopped in loving his dead girlfriend by showering excessive love on their daughter Raaluchi.

Onyeka consoled Raaluchi and Raaluchi admitted to him that she was still hearing the voices. She was eager to have a deliverance prayer to be performed on her by Father Joe, but he told Raaluchi that he was only gifted in counseling people, and not deliverance prayers. Mummy suggested that Raaluchi should meet Father Gilbert in Enugu, who was very popular for his deliverance prayers that bred miracles of God in people's lives.

Raaluchi agreed to meet Father Gilbert for her deliverance prayers and Father Joe called him on phone to inform him of Raaluchi's problem and her intention to meet him. He spoke with Raaluchi on phone and gave her an appointment to meet him in his Adoration Ministry after she must have carried out a 6 to 6 fasting for seven days, and prayed for God to deliver her from the marine spirit that was tormenting her. When Father Joe hung up, Raaluchi took the razor blade that she had been eyeing on Father Joe's table. She excused herself, and outside the office, she shaved her forehead, shaving off the black dot on her forehead. Her blood oozed out, but she didn't care. To her, she has broken the connection.

"What have you done to your face?" Onyeka asked her

looking terrified. Raaluchi remained silent. Her face was bleeding profusely, and just then, Onyeka carried her and rushed her to the nearest chemist and her face was taken care of.

Onyeka joined her with her fasting and prayers, praying for God's divine mercy in his wife's life and for God to deliver his wife from the tormenting marine goddess of Amaekwere.

On the twenty-ninth day of December in the year 2014, which was exactly the day of Raaluchi's appointment with Father Gilbert, Mummy, Onyeka and Raaluchi climbed in the car at exactly 6 am, and Onyeka drove off, speeding to Enugu. Raaluchi almost screamed when she saw the congregation of people in Father Gilbert's Adoration Ministry. They all joined in the worship songs and intercessory prayers. It was around 3.00 pm in the afternoon, that Father Gilbert called up Raaluchi to the altar and made her face the Blessed Sacrament. Raaluchi looked unto Jesus and spoke to Him as though she was speaking to a friend. She believed that Jesus was right there in the Blessed Sacrament listening to her prayers. She believed that Jesus would deliver her from her problems. She repeated these words after Father Gilbert: "Lord Jesus, you are my God, the author and finisher of my faith. I do not have any other God but you. You know me very well, even more than I know myself. I did not give consent to the evil spirit that had been attacking my happiness. The goddess of Amaekwere is not my God and she had been using me for her evil manifestations without my consent. Lord Jesus, I pray that you deliver me from her kingdom, the kingdom of darkness and keep me in your light. Darkness and Light have nothing in common and so with my faith in you, I have nothing in common with darkness. Sanctify and deliver me Lord Jesus Christ, and let me continue to see the beauty in your bright light. I make this prayer in the name of the Father, Son and the Holy Spirit. Amen."

Father Gilbert told Raaluchi to keep gazing at the Blessed Sacrament and she obeyed. She noticed that there was something going on in her head, like a knot that was untangling from a tight tie. She knelt gazing at Jesus for three hours before Father Gilbert said the last prayer for her, and then, anointed her forehead, and told her to go back to India and repeat her psychotherapy medications, for her nerves to relax. Raaluchi watched him with an air of freedom. His white cassock glistened, and there was a red stone lying on his neck.

"I will, Father," Raaluchi said, and he nodded in response, and watched her leave the altar. Later, during the thanksgiving for the Adoration Minisrty Prayers, Onyeka, Raaluchi and Mummy went to the altar and thanked God for Raaluchi's deliverance with a huge amount of money written on a cheque, and lying inside a white envelope.

In Raaluchi's dream that night, she saw rays of bright light shinning down on her and she was very happy. She woke up with a peace of mind, and even when she thought about her father, she didn't hear his voice again. She didn't hear the evil voices again. She had been delivered and she was a child of God. But she would still obey Father Gilbert by repeating her therapy in India. She rolled over to her husband's side and woke him with a gentle kiss on his cheek. He woke up and smiled at her.

"I want to ask you for a favour."

"What is it?"

"I want you to start calling me Gabriella. I want to activate that name because it is my baptismal name."

"Alright, Gabriella, if that's what you want."

The couple smiled at each other, and was entwined in a tight hug. They were peaceful and safe in this hug, and they would be in this peaceful state when they renew their marital vows in the presence of God and Father Joe the next day.

THE END

Printed in the United States
By Bookmasters